Praise for *Collecting Cooper*, a *Suspense Magazine* Best Book of 2011

"A pulse-pounding serial killer thriller . . . The city of Christchurch becomes a modern equivalent of James Ellroy's Los Angeles of the 1950s, a discordant symphony of violence and human weakness. Cleave tosses in a number of twists that few readers will anticipate, but the book's real power lies in the complexity of its characters, particularly the emotionally tortured Tate."

—*Publishers Weekly* (starred)

"Paul Cleave writes the kind of dark, intense thrillers that I never want to end. Do yourself a favor and check him out."

—Simon Kernick, internationally bestselling author of *The Payback*

"Horrormeister Cleave . . . will scare you to death, or at least to the point of keeping a night light on."

—*Kirkus Review*

Praise for *Blood Men*, a winner of the 2011 Ngaio Marsh Award for Best Crime Novel

"Compelling, dark, and perfectly paced, New Zealand writer Cleave's psychological thriller explores the evil lurking in us all, working relentless magic until the very last page. There's nary a misstep in this riveting thriller about the bad deeds even good men sometimes do."

—*Booklist*

ALSO BY PAUL CLEAVE

PAUL CLEAVE

THE
CLEANER

A THRILLER

ATRIA PAPERBACK

New York London Toronto Sydney New Delhi

ATRIA PAPERBACK
A Division of Simon & Schuster, Inc.
1230 Avenue of the Americas
New York, NY 10020

First Atria Paperback edition December 2012

ATRIA PAPERBACK and colophon are trademarks of
Simon & Schuster, Inc.

For information about special discounts for bulk purchases,
please contact Simon & Schuster Special Sales at 1-866-506-1949
or business@simonandschuster.com.

The Simon & Schuster Speakers Bureau can bring authors to
your live event. For more information or to book an event,
contact the Simon & Schuster Speakers Bureau at 1-866-248-3049
or visit our website at www.simonspeakers.com.

Manufactured in the United States of America

10 9 8 7 6 5 4 3 2 1

Library of Congress Cataloging-in-Publication Data

Cleave, Paul, date.
   The cleaner : a thriller / by Paul Cleave. — 1st Atria Books trade paperback ed.
      p. cm.
1. Serial murders—Fiction. 2. Christchurch (N.Z.)—Fiction. I. Title.
PR9639.4.C54C57 2012
823'.92—dc23   2012030312

ISBN 978-1-4516-7779-9
ISBN 978-1-4516-7780-5 (ebook)

To Quinn
We all still miss you, buddy.

THE
CLEANER

CHAPTER ONE

I pull the car into the driveway. Sit back. Try to relax. The day, I swear to God, has to be at least ninety-five degrees. Christ-church heat. Schizophrenic weather. Sweat is dripping from my body. My fingers are wet-rubber damp. I lean forward and twist the keys in the ignition, grab my briefcase, and climb out of the car. Out here, the air-conditioning actually works. I reach the front door and fumble with the lock. I breathe a sigh of relief when I step inside.

I stroll through to the kitchen. Angela, I can hear, is in the shower upstairs. I'll disturb her later. For now, I need a drink. I walk to the fridge. It has a stainless-steel door in which my reflection looks like a ghost. I open the door and squat down in front of it for close to a minute, making friends with the cool air. The fridge offers me both beer and Coke. I take a beer, twist off the cap, and sit down at the table. I'm no heavy drinker, but I knock this bottle back in maybe twenty seconds. The fridge offers up another bottle. Who am I to say no? I lean back in the chair. Put my feet up on the table. Consider taking off my shoes. You know that feeling? A hot day at work. Stress for eight hours. Then sitting down, feet in the air, beer in hand, and you take your shoes off.

Pure bliss.

Listening to the shower upstairs, I casually sip at my second beer of the year. Takes me five minutes to finish this one, and now I'm hungry. Back at the fridge and to the slice of cold pizza I spied on my first trip. I shrug. Why not? It isn't as though I need to watch my weight.

I sit back at the table. Feet in the air. The same thing works for pizza as it does for beer once you get those shoes off. Right now, though, I don't have the time. I wolf down the pizza, pick up my briefcase, and make my way upstairs. The stereo in the bedroom is pumping out a song I recognize, but can't name. Same goes for the artist. Nevertheless, I find myself humming along as I lay my briefcase on the bed, knowing the tune will be stuck in my mind for hours. I sit down next to the briefcase. Open it. Take the newspaper out. The first page offers up the sort of news that makes newspapers sell. Often I wonder if the media makes half this stuff up, just to inflate sales. There's definitely a market for it.

I hear the shower turn off but ignore it, preferring to read the paper. It's an article about some guy who's been terrorizing the city. Killing women. Torture. Rape. Homicide. The stuff movies are made of. A couple of minutes go by and I'm still sitting here reading when Angela, wiping her hair with a towel, steps out of the bathroom surrounded by white steam and the smell of skin lotion.

I lower the newspaper and smile.

She looks over at me.

"Who the fuck are you?" she asks.

CHAPTER TWO

The sun is heading toward the horizon with only a few hours of life left today, it's blinding her, making beads of sweat run down the inside of her dress and dampening the material. It glints off the polished granite gravestone, making her squint, but she refuses to look away from the letters that have been scripted across it for the last five years. The bright light is making her eyes water—not that it matters; her eyes always water when she comes here.

She should have worn sunglasses. She should have worn a lighter dress. She should have done more to prevent him from dying.

Sally clutches the crucifix hanging around her neck, the four ends of it digging hard into her palm. She can't remember the last time she took it off, and she fears that if she did she would roll up into a small ball and just cry forever, spending the rest of her days unable to function.

She had it when the doctors at the hospital gave her family the news. She held it tightly as they sat her down, and with their somber faces told her what they had told countless other families who knew their loved ones were dying but who still held out hope. It was hanging over her heart when she drove her parents to the funeral home, sat down with the funeral director, and, over tea and coffee that nobody touched, shopped through coffin brochures, turning the glossy pages and trying to pick out something her dead brother would look good in. They had to do the same for the suit. Even death was fashion conscious. The suits in the catalogs were photographed hanging on mannequins; it would have been in bad taste to have had them on happy-go-lucky people smiling and trying to look sexy.

She has had the crucifix every day since, using it for guidance, using it to remind herself that Martin is in a better place now, that life isn't as bad as it seems.

She has been staring at the grave for the last forty minutes, unable to move. Fifty feet away a set of oak trees form a partial barrier between her and a small lake which she guesses must almost be right in the middle of the cemetery. A few months ago some bodies were found in that lake. Every now and then the nor'wester will snap one of the growing acorns from the branches and throw it onto a gravestone, the clicking sound like that of a breaking finger. The cemetery is an expanse of lush lawn broken up with cement markers and, at the moment, mostly deserted, except for a handful of people standing in front of gravestones, all of them with tragedies of their own. She wonders whether more show up during the day, whether the graveyard has peak-hour traffic. She hopes it does. She doesn't like the idea of people dying and other people forgetting. The grass is longer than usual, and messy around the gravestones and trees. Even the gardens are overgrown. There used to be a caretaker out here who would regularly steer his riding lawn mower like a racing car through the rows of graves, but then he retired or died, she can't quite remember which, and in the following months nature has been reclaiming the land.

She doesn't even know why she's thinking such things. Caretakers dying, peak-hour traffic, people forgetting the dead. She's always like this when she comes here. Morbid, all messed up, as if somebody has put her thoughts into a cocktail shaker and shaken the hell out of it. She likes to come here at least once a month, if *likes* is an appropriate word. She always, absolutely always, makes it here on the anniversary of Martin's death, which is what today is. Tomorrow would have been his birthday. Or still is. She isn't sure whether it counts once you're in the ground. For some reason she can't explain, she never comes here on his birthday. She's sure it would induce the same result as if she were to take off her crucifix. Her parents made it out here earlier in the afternoon, she can tell by the fresh flowers next to her own. She never comes here with them. That is something else she can't explain, not even to herself.

She briefly closes her eyes. Whenever she comes here, she always ends up dwelling on what she can't figure out. The moment she leaves, things will be better again. She crouches down, caresses the flowers sitting in front of the gravestone, then runs her fingers over the lettering. Her brother was fifteen when he died. One day away from sixteen. One day's difference between a birthday and a death-day. Probably not even that. Probably only a matter of half a day. How can it make sense that he should die at fifteen, almost sixteen? The other people planted in this location average sixty-two years old. She knows that because she added them all up. She walked from grave to grave, plotting in the numbers on a calculator and then dividing them up. She was curious. Curious as to how many years Martin was cheated of. His fifteen—sixteen years on this earth were special, and the fact he was mentally handicapped actually was a blessing. He enriched her life, and her parents' lives. He knew he was different, he knew he was challenged, but he never understood what the problem was. For him, life was all about having fun. What could possibly be wrong with that?

CHAPTER FOUR

I live in an apartment complex that would be worth more if sold as scrap. Because of its location, it will never be torn down and replaced because a new apartment complex isn't going to fetch any more rent. It isn't exactly the worst part of town, according to those who live here, but it is according to everybody else. It's barely habitable, but it's cheap, so that's the trade-off. The complex is four stories high, covers the best part of a block, and I live on the top, giving me the best part of a very poor view. In total I think there are maybe thirty apartments.

I see none of my neighbors as I make my way upstairs, but this is neither bad nor uncommon. I find myself dwelling on poor Fluffy as I unlock the door and walk inside. My apartment has two rooms. One of these is a bathroom, and the other a combined everything else. The fridge and stove look so old I doubt carbon dating would identify an age. The floors are bare and I have to wear shoes all the time to avoid splinters. The walls have cheap, dark gray wallpaper so dry that it crumbles a little bit more every time I open my door and create a draft. Several edges of it have peeled away and hang like flat tongues. A set of windows runs along one wall where my view consists of power lines and burned-out cars. I have an old washing machine with a noisy spin cycle, and hanging on the wall above it is a dryer that's just as loud. Along the window is a line where I hang my washing during the summer. Currently nothing is hanging on it.

I own a single bed, a small TV, a DVD player, and some basic furniture that's sold in a box with assembly instructions in six different languages. None of it sits straight, but I don't know anybody who would visit to complain. Select romance paperbacks that I've read are dumped on my sofa. The covers are full of strong-looking men and weak-looking women. I throw my briefcase on top of them before checking my answering machine. The light is blinking, so I push play. It's my mother. She's left a message telling me about her powers of deduction. She believes that since I'm not home, and not at her place, it means I have to be on the way to her place.

I said earlier, "God rest her soul." I didn't mean she's dead. She soon will be, though. Don't misunderstand me. I'm not a bad guy or anything, I would never do anything to harm her, and I'm disgusted at anyone who would think otherwise. It's just that she's old. Old people die. Some sooner than others. Thank God.

I glance at my watch. It's already six thirty. It's starting to get dark. I make room on the sofa, stretch my arms out behind me, and try to relax. Think about what's best for me. If I don't go to my mother's for dinner the results will be disastrous. She will ring me every day. Nag me for hours on end. She is unaware I have a life. I have responsibilities, hobbies, places I want to go, people I want to do, but she doesn't see it. She thinks I live just to sit around my apartment waiting for her to call.

I change into some more respectable clothes. Nothing too flashy, but slightly better than casual. Don't want Mom insisting on buying my clothes for me like she used to. She went through a stage, a year ago, of buying my shirts, my underwear, my socks. Sometimes I remind her I'm more than thirty years old and can do this myself, but sometimes she does it anyway.

On the small coffee table in my small living room, in front of the small sofa that looks like it belongs in some hippie recording studio, sits a large goldfish bowl with my two best friends inside: Pickle and Jehovah. My goldfish don't complain. Goldfish have memories of five seconds, so you can really piss them off and they won't remember. You can forget to feed them, and they'll forget they're hungry. You can pull them from the water and throw them on the floor, and they'll flap around and forget they're suffocating. Pickle is my favorite; I got him first—two years ago. He is an albino goldfish from China, with a white body and red fins, and is slightly bigger than the width of my palm. Jehovah is a little smaller, but she's gold. Goldfish can live up to forty years, and I hope to get at least that out of mine. I don't know what they get up to when I'm not watching them, but so far no little goldfish have appeared.

I sprinkle in some food, watch them rise to the surface of the bowl, and watch them eat. I love them dearly, yet at the same time I feel like God. No matter who I am, no matter what I do, my goldfish look up to me. The way they live, the conditions they live in, when they get dinner—these things are all up to me. I like having that responsibility.

I talk to them while they eat. A few minutes go by. I have talked enough. The pain of killing Fluffy is nearly gone now.

I head outside. The sun has completely gone now and the streetlights are on. A few of them on my street are busted. Tomorrow it will get darker earlier by a minute, and the same every day after that until we break through winter. Or perhaps winter won't come this year. I walk to the nearest bus stop. I wait for maybe five minutes in the warm evening air before a bus finally comes along.

Mom lives in South Brighton near the beach. No green lawn out here. Like the plants, it matches the shade of rust that visits every metal surface exposed to the salt air. Grow a rosebush and the entire block goes up in value. Most of the homes are sixty-year-old bungalows that are struggling to hold on to their character as the paint flakes away and the weatherboards slowly rot.

All the windows are clouded over with salt. Wooden joinery is stained with dead pine needles and sand. Patches of sealant and plaster block up holes and keep the insides dry. Even crime out here has its downside—when you weigh in the cost of gas it takes to get here against the value of anything you might find in any of these dumps, it's hardly worth breaking into somebody's house.

It takes thirty minutes for the bus to get to Mom's house. When I get out, I can hear the waves crashing against the shore. The sound is relaxing. This is the only benefit to South Brighton. It is a minute's walk to the beach from here, and if I still lived in this suburb, I would walk that extra minute and just keep on swimming. At the moment it feels like I'm standing in a ghost town. Few houses have their lights on. Every fourth or fifth streetlight is busted. Nobody around.

I suck in a deep breath of salty air while standing at the gate. My clothes already stink of rotten seaweed. Mom's house is in as much disrepair as any other house in this neighborhood. If I came around here and painted it, her neighbors would probably kick her out. If I mowed the dry lawns, I'd have to mow everybody's. Her house is a single-story weatherboard dwelling. White paint, now the color of smog, falls from the warped boards and settles in the yard alongside the dusting of rust from the iron roof. The windows are held in place with both cracking joint compound and luck. A real-estate agent would call Mum's house a great investment for the handyman.

I walk up to the door. Knock. And wait. A minute goes by

before she finally ambles to it. It sticks in the frame and she has to pull it hard. It shudders open and the hinges squeak.

"Joe, do you know what time it is?"

I nod. It's nearly seven thirty. "Yeah, Mom, I know."

She closes the door, I hear the rattle of a chain guard, and then the door swings back open. I step inside.

Mom will be sixty-four this year, but looks a good ten years older. Or a bad five. She's only five feet two, and has curves in all the wrong places. Some of those curves stretch out over others, some are heavy enough to tighten the wrinkles in her neck. Her gray hair, she keeps pulled back into a tight bun, but at the moment she's wearing something over it—one of those old hairnets with curlers tied into it that for some reason makes me think of black-and-white movies and women smoking cigarettes. She has blue eyes so pale they are nearly gray, covered by a pair of thick-rimmed glasses that may, with a lot of luck, one day come into style. On her face are three moles, each of them with a dark hair that she won't cut. Her upper lip is cultivating a soft line of fuzz. She looks like she belongs in a nursing home as the head matron.

"You're late," she says, blocking the doorway while adjusting one of the curlers in her hair. "I got worried. I nearly called the police. Nearly called the hospitals."

"I was busy, Mom, with work and everything," I say, relieved she didn't file a missing person report.

"Too busy to call your mother? Too busy to worry yourself about my breaking heart?"

I'm all she has left. My dad died a few years ago, and I've always considered him to be the lucky one. It seems the only thing Mom has to live for is talking. And complaining. Luckily the two go hand in hand for her.

"I said I'm sorry, Mom."

She clips me around the ear. Not hard, but enough to show me her disappointment. Then she hugs me. "I made meatloaf, Joe. Meatloaf. Your favorite."

I hand her the rose I picked from Angela's garden. It's slightly crushed, but Mom's expression is priceless when I hand over the red flower.

"Oh, you're so thoughtful, Joe," she says, taking it to her nose to smell.

I shrug. "Just wanted to make you happy," I say, and even for an optimist like me that's always been a pretty ambitious goal. Her smile is making me smile.

"Ow," she says, pricking her finger on one of the thorns. "You give me a rose with thorns? What sort of son are you, Joe?"

Obviously a bad one. "I'm sorry. I didn't mean for that to happen."

"You don't think enough, Joe. That's always been your problem. Along with always being late. I'll put it in water," she says, and steps aside. "You might as well come in."

She closes the door behind me and I follow her down the hallway to the kitchen, passing photographs of my dead dad, a cactus that has looked dead from the day she got it, and a seascape painting of a place my mother would maybe like to visit. The Formica-top table has been set for two.

"Do you want a drink?" she asks, putting the rose into a glass.

"I'm fine," I say, tightening my jacket. It's always cold in this house.

"The supermarket has Coke on special."

"I'm fine."

"Three dollars for a six pack," she says. "Here, I'll find you the receipt."

"Don't worry, Mom. I said I'm fine."

"It's no hassle."

She wanders off, leaving me alone. There's no way to say it nicely, but my mother is getting crazier by the day. I believe her that Coke is on special, yet she still feels the need to show me the receipt. A few minutes go by where all I can do is look at the oven and microwave, so I spend the time figuring just how awkward it would be to fit an entire person into either one of them. When she comes back, she has also found the supermarket flyer advertising the Coke.

I nod. "Three dollars, huh? Amazing."

"So you'll have one then?"

"Sure." It's the easiest option.

She serves dinner. We sit down and begin eating. The dining room connects to the kitchen, and the only view I have is either of my mother or the wall behind her, so I watch the wall. Some of these appliances here went out of date when electricity was invented, and the rest not long after. The linoleum floor looks like it was made from Kermit the Frog after he was hunted down and skinned. The dining table is the color of bananas. The legs are cold metal. The chairs are padded and wobble slightly when I move. Mom's has been reinforced.

"How was your day?" she asks. A tiny piece of carrot is stuck on her chin. One of the moles there looks as though it's trying to skewer it.

"Good."

"I haven't heard from you all week."

The meatloaf is a little dry, but I don't dare add any more gravy to it in case my mother thinks I'm unhappy with it. "I've been busy with homework."

"The job?"

"The job."

"Your cousin Gregory is getting married. Did you know?"

I do now. "Really?"

"When are you going to find yourself a wife, Joe?"

I've noticed that old people always chew with their mouths open, so you get to hear the food slopping against the roof of their mouth. It's because they're always about to say something.

"I don't know, Mom."

"You're not gay, are you, son?"

She says this while still chewing. Like it's no big deal. Like she just said, "That shirt looks good on you," or "Nice weather we're having."

"I'm not gay, Mom."

In fact, it isn't that big a deal. I have nothing against gay people. Nothing at all. They are, after all, just people. Like anybody else. Now it's people I have something against.

"Huh," she huffs.

I pause with a forkful of meatloaf inches from my mouth. "What?"

"Nothing."

The meatloaf goes back onto the plate. "What, Mom?"

"I'm just wondering why you don't ever bring a girl around."

I shrug.

"Men shouldn't be gay, Joe. It's not . . ." she searches for the word, "fair."

"I don't follow."

"It doesn't matter."

She seems happy to let the subject go, and I'm happy to let her. We eat in silence for a minute, which is all my mother can handle before talking again. "I started a jigsaw puzzle today."

I'm not brave enough to tell her I'll alert the media. Instead I go with, "Uh huh."

"It was on special. Down from thirty dollars to twelve."

"Bargain."

"Here, I'll find you the receipt."

I add more gravy to my dinner and try to eat quicker while she's gone, knowing that eating quickly doesn't necessarily mean a quick escape, but also knowing it's worth a shot. I watch the clocks on the microwave and the oven, and I race them against the clock hanging on the wall, but they all drag along at the same pace. It doesn't take Mom long to find the receipt so I figure she must have kept it aside to show me. She waddles over with the advertising flyer as well. I do my best to calm my excitement.

"See? Twelve dollars."

"Yeah, I see." The flyer has *Chockablock with Entertainment* written across it. I wonder what the person was thinking when they wrote that. Or what they were on.

"That's eighteen dollars. Well, actually it was twenty-nine ninety-five down to twelve dollars, so that's eighteen dollars and ninety-five cents."

I do the arithmetic as she talks to me, and quickly see she's off by a dollar. Best not to say anything. I'm figuring if she realizes she saved eighteen dollars and not nineteen, she's going to take it back. Even after she's done the puzzle.

"It's of the *Titanic*, Joe," she says, even though the picture in the flyer is of a large boat with the word *Titanic* stenciled across its helm. "You know, the boat?"

"Oh, that *Titanic*."

"A real tragedy."

"The movie?"

"The boat."

"I hear it sank."

"Are you sure you're not gay, Joe?"

"I'd know, wouldn't I?"

After dinner, I offer to clean up, even though I know what she's going to say.

"You think I want you around here to be my maid? Sit down, Joe. I'll clean up. What sort of mother won't take care of her son? I'll tell you what sort—a bad mother, that's who."

"I'll do it."

"I don't want you to do it. Now go and wait in the living room."

I sit down in the living room and stare at the TV. There's a news bulletin on. Something about a dead body. Home invasion. I change channels. Finally Mom comes through to the living room carrying a cup of tea for herself and nothing for me.

"It seems my whole life was spent cleaning up after your

father, and now I'm spending the rest of it cleaning up after you."

"I offered to help, Mom," I say, standing up.

"Well, it's too late now. It's done," she snaps. "You should learn to appreciate your mother, Joe. I'm all you have."

I know this speech, and have apologized as many times as I've heard it. I say I'm sorry once again, and it seems offering apologies to my mother makes up fifty percent of my conversations with her. She sits down and we watch some TV—some English drama about people who say *nuffink* instead of *nothing*, and I don't even know what in the hell *bollocks* really means.

Mom watches it as if she can't already predict that Fay is sleeping with Edgar for his inheritance, and Karen is pregnant from Stewart—the town drunk and her long-lost brother. When the commercials come on, she fills me in on what the characters have been up to, as if they're part of the family. At least she isn't offering to cook them meatloaf. I listen and nod and forget what she says within seconds. Like a goldfish. When it comes back on, I end up watching the carpet, finding more entertainment in the brown, symmetrical patterns that were all the rage back in the fifties—proving that everybody was completely mad back then.

The drama ends and the highly depressing theme music starts to play. As sad as the tune is, I'm feeling in high spirits because that music means it's time for me to go. Before I leave, Mom tells me more about my cousin Gregory. He has a car. A BMW.

"Why don't you have a BMW, Joe?"

I've never stolen a BMW. "Because I'm not gay."

I'm the only person on the bus. The driver is old, and his hands shake as I give him the exact change. As we drive along, I start to wonder what would happen if he sneezed. Would his heart explode? Would we career into other traffic? I feel like giving him a dollar tip when he gets me safely to my stop, but I figure the excitement will finish off what the

Grim Reaper started years ago. He wishes me a good night as I leave the bus, but I don't know if he really means it. I don't wish him anything back. I'm not looking to make any friends. Especially old ones.

When I get home I step into the shower and spend an hour washing away my mother. When I climb out, I spend some time with Pickle and Jehovah. They look happy to see me. A few minutes later and it's lights out. I slip into bed. I don't ever dream, and tonight is going to be no exception.

I think of Angela and Fluffy, and finally I think of nothing.

CHAPTER FIVE

Right on seven thirty, I wake up. I don't need an alarm clock to pull me from sleep. My clock is internal. Never needs winding. Never breaks down. Keeps on ticking.

Another Christchurch morning and I'm already bored. I look at the clothes in my wardrobe, but it's pointless. I get dressed, then start breakfast. Toast. Coffee. Doesn't get more sophisticated than that. I talk to my fish and tell them about Karen and Stewart and the rest of the *nuffink* squad, and they listen intently to what I have to say, and then they forget it. I feed them as a reward for their loyalty.

I head outside. It's another summer day in autumn. There aren't many people around. Unfortunately I don't have a car. Angela's I left parked on the other side of town. I left the keys in the ignition in case somebody else wanted to take it for a spin. Stealing keys is a lot easier than hot-wiring the thing, though I've got plenty of experience when it comes to both.

I am at the bus stop with my ticket in my hand when the bus pulls up. The side of it is covered in advertisements for vi-

tamin pills and contraceptives. The doors open with a swish.
I climb on board.

"Hey ya doin', Joe?"

"Joe's fine, Mr. Stanley."

I hand Mr. Stanley my bus ticket. He takes it from me and,
without clicking it, hands it back. Winks at me like old bus
drivers do. The whole side of his face crushes down like he's
having a stroke. Mr. Stanley is probably in his sixties, and
looks like he gets a kick out of life. On mornings like these,
he always likes to say, "Hot, ain't it?" He wears the uniform all
bus drivers wear: dark blue shorts, a light-blue short-sleeved
shirt, and black shoes.

"This one's on the city this morning, Joe," he says, still
winking, just in case I hadn't noticed. "Sure is a hot one today,
Joe, ain't it?"

I figure if I smile back, I'll get more free bus rides. "Gee. Joe's
thankful, Mr. Stanley."

Mr. Stanley smiles at me and I wonder how he would look if
I opened my briefcase and showed him what's inside. Putting
the bus ticket into my pocket, I walk down the aisle. The bus
is fairly empty—a handful of school kids scattered randomly, a
nun in one of those stiffly starched black-and-white outfits, a
businessman with an umbrella even though it has to be ninety
degrees outside.

Regular people. Like me.

I sit near the back behind two sixteen- or seventeen-year-
old schoolgirls. I prop my briefcase up on the empty seat next
to me. Nobody is sitting behind or opposite me. I thumb the
combination on each side of the case. Slide the latches. Open
the case. I have my knives stored away carefully inside—three
in the lid, and three in the base. They're held in place by
strands of material that loop over them and snap into place
with metal domes. The gun is the only thing that floats around
free, but it's in a black leather pouch to protect it, and the
knives. The gun has three internal safeties, so I'd have to be

three times unlucky—or stupid—to have any sort of accident. Ahead of me, the schoolgirls are giggling.

I take out a knife with a blade only two inches long, which cost twenty-five dollars. It takes a lot of stabbing to kill somebody with a knife that short. Once, about eighteen months ago, it took me a good forty or fifty goes. Small cuts. Lots of blood. I was sweating like a pig afterward. My shirt was pasted to me. He deserved it, though.

Mr. Stanley is a much nicer bus driver.

I'm absentmindedly running the blade up and down the back of the seat of the girl on the left. I'm thinking about women in general when her friend, the blond girl, turns around at the sound. I hide the knife behind my leg. Smile innocently as if I have no idea where I even am, as if all I'm doing is singing mentally to myself: *The wheels on the bus go round and round, round and round.* She glares at me. Watching her, I can feel the beginnings of a relationship.

She looks away without comment, and they return to their giggling. I tuck the knife away in my briefcase. I'm not even sure why I got it out. I stare out the window and watch as the bus approaches the central city. More traffic, more smog, more aggravation as people get caught up at traffic lights. We pass a guy sitting on the side of the road next to a mountain bike, the front wheel all buckled up, both of his knees are bleeding. He catches me staring at him and gives me the finger.

I have the briefcase closed up by the time my stop appears. Mr. Stanley makes a special exception for me, stopping the bus directly outside my work. I give him a smile from the end of the bus. We exchange waves as I step off from the back exit.

Christchurch. City of Angels this isn't. New Zealand is known for its tranquility, its sheep, and its hobbits. Christchurch is known for its parks and violence. Throw a bag of glue in the air and a hundred welfare recipients will knock each other over in an effort to sniff from it. Despite the blue skies, Christchurch City is still mostly gray. Many of the buildings date back a hundred years, some even more, gothic architecture imported from England along with the population back then. Gray buildings, gray roads, lots of office and shop windows reflecting it all. However there is the occasional splash of greenery: trees, shrubs, flowers. You can't take twenty paces without passing something out of nature. Walk ten minutes to the west, and you'll find the Botanic Gardens; more than twenty hectares of land dedicated to showing the rest of the world how clever we are at turning seeds into plants. In these gardens are thousands of flowers and hundreds of trees, but you can't go there at night without getting stabbed or shot, becoming fertilizer.

I take a few paces forward, and my boredom does nothing to let up. It's this city. Nobody can feel excited surrounded by buildings that date back a hundred years. Between the buildings is a warren of alleyways that any self-respecting drug addict can walk with their eyes closed. Christchurch patients live down these alleyways. If a businessman or businesswoman were to venture down one, they would have more of a chance of finding Jesus than getting out of there without being molested or urinated on. As for the shopping, well, shopping here is going out of style, and that's reflected in the empty stores with signs hanging in the windows saying *For Lease* or *For Sale*. Even so, you can never find a damn parking space anywhere.

Christchurch is voted one of the friendliest places in the world. By who, I have no idea. Certainly not anybody I've ever met. But despite all of this, Christchurch is my home.

The air shimmers with heat, and in the distance it makes the roads look wet. Cars have their windows down and drivers' arms are hanging in the breeze, cigarette ash dropping onto the sidewalk. Plenty of traffic is racing by, too much for me to run through, so I push the button for the crossing signal and wait. When it flashes and beeps for me to walk, I wait a few more seconds for the red-light runners to speed by, then cross the road. I roll my sleeves up. The air feels good on my forearms. I can feel beads of sweat running down the sides of my body.

Two minutes later I'm at work.

I walk directly to the fourth floor, taking the stairs since stealing cars doesn't provide any real exercise. The stairwell smells of urine at the bottom, and more like disinfectant the higher I get. On the fourth floor I enter the conference room and place my briefcase, locked, down on the table, and move over to the photographs pinned to the wall.

"Morning, Joe. How are you this morning?"

I look at the man I've positioned myself next to. Schroder is a big guy with more muscle than brain. He has those rugged good looks of an action-movie hero, but I doubt he has any heroism left. He hates this city as much as anybody else. He has buzz-cut graying hair that would look better on a sixty-year-old drill sergeant than on him, an almost forty-year-old homicide detective. His forehead and face are covered in stress lines, which I no doubt put there. He has bags under his eyes, no doubt put there by the new baby he has at home. At the moment he's going for the hard-worked-detective look, and with his cheap shirtsleeves rolled up and his thrift-store tie loosened, he has certainly achieved it. He has a pencil jammed up behind his ear, and another one in his hand, which he was chewing on before he spoke. He is standing with one foot forward, slightly ahead of the other, as if ready to pounce at the wall and start pounding on it.

"Morning, Detective Schroder." I nod slowly toward the photographs like I'm agreeing with what I just said. "Any new leads?"

Detective Inspector Schroder is the lead detective on this case, has been since the second murder. He shakes his head like he's disagreeing with himself, straightens his back and massages out a crick by pushing his palms against it, then gets back to looking at the photographs.

"Nothing yet, Joe. Only new victims."

I let his statement hang in the air. Pretend I'm thinking about what he's saying. Thinking and processing. Has to take me longer when I'm standing in front of a cop.

"Oh? Did this happen last night, Detective Schroder?"

He nods. "Sick bastard broke into her house."

His fists are shaking. The pencil he's holding breaks. He tosses it onto the table, where a small graveyard of other broken pencils lies, and then grabs hold of the one from behind his ear. He must keep a supply just for these occasions. He chews on it for a few seconds before turning toward me and snapping it in half.

"I'm sorry, Joe. You'll have to excuse my language."

"That's okay. You said victims. Does that mean there was more than one?"

"Another woman was found in the trunk of her car, parked up the victim's driveway."

I exhale loudly. "Gosh, Detective Schroder, I guess that's why you're the detective and I'm not. I would never have looked in the trunk. Even now, she'd still be in there, alone and everything." Like the detective, I'm shaking my fists now too, but unlike the detective I don't have a supply of pencils to start breaking. "Gee, I would have let everybody down," I add under my breath but loud enough for him to hear.

"Hey, Joe, don't beat yourself up. Even I didn't look in the car. We didn't even notice the second victim until this morning."

He's lying. His rugged face is looking at me with pity.

"Really?"

He nods. "Sure."

"Can I get you some coffee, Detective Schroder?"

"Well, okay, Joe, but only if it isn't any hassle."

"No hassle. Black, one sugar, right?"

"Two sugars, Joe."

"Right." I make him remind me every time I offer. "Can I leave my briefcase on the table here, Detective Schroder?"

"Go ahead. What do you carry in that thing anyway?"

I shrug and look away. "You know, Detective Schroder, documents and stuff."

"Thought so."

Bullshit. The bastard figures I have lunch in there, and maybe a comic book. Nonetheless, I walk from the room and into the corridor, where I move among dozens of offices and officers and detectives. I head past several cubicles, and straight to the coffee machine. It's easy to use, but I make it look more complicated than it is. I'm thirsty, so I make myself one first and quickly drink it since it's not that hot and because it tastes like dirt. Most of the other cops nod at me. It's that dumb silent greeting that's in fashion at the moment—the one where you nod abruptly and raise your eyebrows—and starts to get uncomfortable when you keep passing the same people. Then you have to make idle chitchat. Mondays are okay, because they ask how your weekend was. Fridays are okay too, because they ask what you have planned for the weekend. But the days in between really are a bastard.

I pour Schroder his coffee. Black. Two sugars.

For the last few months, the police station has been alive with the hustle and bustle of stressed and anxious detectives. The immediate day of a homicide and the day after are when that hustling and bustling are at their greatest. Meetings are held every hour of the day. Statements are pored over by eager eyes, looking for vital clues or discrepancies from anybody who knew one of the victims. Information is gathered only to become forgotten evidence the moment another killing takes place. After all these killings, they still have nothing. I actually feel bad for them in some ways—all this never-ending work that produces nothing. During the day, reporters keep showing up every time they hear a new piece of evidence has been uncovered, a new witness spoken to, or—their personal favorite—when a new victim has been found. The latter ensures them more sales of newspapers and of revenue from ads as the bulletins go to air. Reporters armed with microphones fire questions at anybody who looks like a policeman as they come and go. Cameras are rolling. All this and they ignore the one man who can give them the inside scoop.

I carry the coffee back into the conference room. By now, a few other detectives are milling around inside. I can feel the anguish in the air—the desperation to catch the man doing this to them and their city. The room smells like sweat and cheap aftershave. I hand Schroder his coffee with a smile. He thanks me. I pick up my briefcase to leave and the knives don't jingle.

My office is on the same floor. Unlike the cubicles, mine is actually an office. It's at the end of the corridor, just past the toilets. The door has my name on it. It's one of those little gold plaques with black lettering. *Joe*. No second name. No other initial. Just *Joe*. Like an everyday average Joe. Well, that's me. Everyday and average.

I have my hand on the handle and am about to turn it when she comes up behind me and taps me on the shoulder.

"How are you doing today, Joe?" Her voice is a little loud and a little slow, as if she's trying to break through a language barrier with somebody from Mars.

I force the smile onto my face, the one that Detective Schroder sees every time he shares a pleasantry with me. I give her a big-kid smile, the type with all teeth, spreading my lips as far apart as possible in every direction.

"Good morning, Sally. I'm fine, thank you for asking."

Sally grins back at me. She is dressed in a pair of black overalls that are slightly too big for her, but don't hide the fact that she is slightly too big herself. Not fat, but somewhere between solid and chubby. She has a pretty face when she smiles, but it isn't pretty enough for somebody to ignore the few extra pounds and slip a ring on her finger. At the age of twenty-five, it's her chances that are getting slimmer, not her weight. Smudges of dust on her forehead look like the remnants of a fading bruise. Her blond hair is tied into a ponytail, but it doesn't look like it's been washed in weeks. She doesn't look slow—it isn't until she speaks that you know you're talking to somebody whose parents kept dropping her on her head for fun.

"Can I get you a coffee, Joe? Or an orange juice?"

"I'm fine, Sally. That was nice of you to ask, though."

I open my door and get half a step inside before she taps me on the shoulder again.

"Are you sure? It really wouldn't be a problem. Not really."

"I'm not thirsty right now," I say, and she looks sad. "Maybe later."

"Okay, great, I'll check on you later then. You have a good day, okay?"

Sure, whatever. I slowly nod "Okay," and a moment later I get the rest of the way into my office and close the door.

CHAPTER SIX

Sally says hello to everybody she knows on her way to the elevator, and to those not in earshot she offers a small wave. She pushes the button and waits patiently. She never feels the temptation to keep pushing the button like others do. The elevator is empty, which is a shame, because she would have liked the company on the way to her floor.

She thinks about Joe, and what a nice young man he is. She's always had the ability to see people for what they really are, and she can tell Joe is a wonderful human being. Though most people are, she thinks, since they're all made in God's image. She wishes there were more like Joe, though. Wishes there was more she could do for him.

When the elevator comes to a stop, she steps out, ready to smile, but the corridor is empty. She makes her way to the end of the hallway and walks through the door marked *Maintenance*. Inside, the room is full of neatly kept shelves on which are several varieties of hand and power tools, different types and sizes of wooden beams, metal beams, spare panels of suspended ceiling, spare floor and wall tiles, pottles of adhesive and grease, jars full of screws and nails, clamps, a spirit level, various saws, different types of everything.

She moves over to the window and picks up the glass of orange juice she set there twenty minutes earlier, just before rushing downstairs to say good morning to Joe. She isn't sure why she made the effort. Probably because of Martin. She thinks about Martin more than ever over these two days of the year, and that has somehow led her to start thinking of Joe. People outside her family did very little to help Martin. Some, and she thinks about the kids at school, went out of their way to make life hard for him. It was the same for all the kids who were different. It will always be the same, she thinks, as she sips from her orange juice. It's warmer than she would have liked, but the taste still makes her smile.

She finishes her drink, then moves over to a large box full of cardboard-wrapped fluorescent tubes jammed tightly. She takes two out, one for this floor, the other for the ground floor. While she replaces the first blown tube, she remembers how Martin's disability changed her own life. Growing up with him, she had the idea that she wanted to become a nurse. She wanted to be able to help people.

She had spent the last three years of her life, until six months ago, at nursing school. It was difficult to decide exactly which path she wanted to follow, whether to work in a hospital, in a retirement home, or whether to help those who were mentally challenged like Martin and Joe. There were plenty of options, but she never got the chance. Martin died, and that made wanting to help people harder to do. There were too many diseases out there, too many viruses. You could live life the best you could, do the right things, make the right decisions, and still be struck down by something you were born with that had been biding its time. There were simply too many ways to die, and she didn't want to see that happen to people she knew she would become attached to.

The other factor was her father. Two years ago he was diagnosed with Parkinson's disease, which quickly led to him losing his job. Since then the disease has advanced. He can't work, and his weekly benefit payments aren't enough to cover the medical bills. She didn't have the luxury of completing her studies. Her family needed her, not only to help look after her father, but to help them survive. She had to earn money. She had to help them get through this. She couldn't afford to keep studying.

Her father had a friend who was a full-time maintenance worker at the police station, a friend who was getting older and needed an assistant who would one day replace him. Sally took that job, and now, six months later, she even has his desk and view.

She catches the elevator down to the ground floor; the entire trip down she thinks about Joe, and she thinks about what she can do to make his life better.

CHAPTER SEVEN

The police station is ten stories of nothing-going-on, made from concrete block and bad taste. My office is small, perhaps the smallest in the whole damn building. Still, it's mine, I share it with nobody, and that's the most important thing.

I dump my briefcase on the bench, walk to the window and look out to the city beyond. Hot out there. Warm in here. Warm and stuffy. This is great weather not to be working in. Women walk the streets wearing skirts and tops made from nearly nothing. On a good day, from up here, you can see right down their tops. On a really good day, you can see nipple. By the end of the day, all these women are hidden away. They're scared they might be the next victim plastered across the news. The nighttime air has a charged feeling of fear, and it isn't going to change anytime soon. They do what they can to pretend nothing bad can ever happen to them.

I turn from the window and undo the top button of my overalls. My office consists of a bench that stretches the length of the room—about thirteen feet—along the same wall as the window. The other half of the furniture is a chair. Stacked around the office are paint tins and plenty of rags, brooms, and cleaning solvents, which sometimes give me a headache. There are buckets and mops, tools, cables, spare shelving, spare parts, spare lots of things. The office is well lit because it gets the sun most of the day, which is just as well, because fewer than half of the four fluorescent lights in the ceiling actually work. I keep forgetting to get Sally to replace them, and when I do remember, I'm afraid to ask her. I'm sure she has a crush on me, which is normal for most women, but creepy when it comes to someone like Sally.

Because my office has faulty air-conditioning and a window that doesn't open, I have an electric fan that sits on the desk and whirs noisily when turned on. Next to it is a coffee mug with my name stenciled on it. A well-thought-out gift from my mother. On the end of my bench is a framed photograph of Pickle and Jehovah that I gave to myself last Father's Day.

I grab the bucket from the corner of my room, pick up the mop from next to it, and head for the air-conditioned third floor. Then I walk into the even cooler men's bathroom. The smell of disinfectant forces me to breathe through my mouth for fear of passing out.

"Hi there, Joe."

I turn to see a man who is trying to hide his geekiness with a handful of hair gel and a half-grown mustache. "Morning, Officer Clyde," I say, setting the bucket on the floor.

"Beautiful morning, Joe, ain't it?"

"Sure is, Officer Clyde," I answer, agreeing with his outstanding perception and thinking he'd get on well with Bus Driver Stanley. I stare at the wall, trying not to glimpse his small dick as he finishes taking his long leak. He bends his knees as he zips up, as if he needs all the momentum he can muster to close his fly. He doesn't wash his hands.

"Have a good day, Joe," he says, pitying me with a smile.

I start filling my bucket with water. "I'll try."

He winks at me and at the same time uses his fingers to imitate a gun, and then shoots me while clicking his tongue as he leaves. The bucket full, the cleaner added, I throw the mop back and forth across the toilet floor. The linoleum soon glistens and becomes a health hazard. I set a plastic sign on the floor that has the word *Caution*, states that the floor is wet, and has a picture of a red stick figure slipping, about to crack open his perfectly round stick-figure head.

I've been working here more than four years now. Before that, I was unemployed. I remember killing somebody, I can't remember his name, but he was my first. Well, kind of my first—there was that one kid back in high school, but I don't like to think about that one. This guy I do consider to be my first was Don or Dan or somebody, I think. What's in a name? I killed him when I was twenty-eight years old. It was a time in my life when the fantasy of wondering how it would feel blended with a desire that became a need to know. The fantasy wasn't as good as the reality, and the reality was much messier, but it was an experience, and they say practice makes perfect. Ron or Jim or Don or whoever must have been somebody important because two months after they found his body, a fifty-thousand-dollar reward was posted. I'd only found a few hundred dollars in his wallet when I killed him, so I felt cheated. Like God or fate was mocking me.

I began getting nervous. Agitated. I needed to know if the police were close to catching me. I couldn't help it, the desire to see where the investigation was kept me without sleep for those two months. I could feel myself cracking up. Every morning I would wake up and stare out at my shitty view, wondering if this was the last time I'd get to see it. I started drinking. I ate badly. I became such a desperate wreck that I did the boldest thing I've ever done: I came down to the police station to "confess."

Detective Inspector Schroder dealt with me. It was the first time I met him, and within seconds I wasn't scared because I was too smart to be scared, and much smarter than any cop. I had left no evidence—burning the body had destroyed any DNA I had left behind, and dumping the burned carcass into a river washed away whatever was left. I was pretty confident I knew what I was doing. Would I do it again? Definitely not.

Two of them sat me inside a small interrogation room. The room had four concrete walls and no view and smelled of chewing gum and sweat. In the center were a wooden table and a couple of chairs. There were no potted plants. No paintings. Just a mirror. The legs on the front of my chair were slightly shorter, and I kept sliding forward, which was pretty uncomfortable. A tape recorder sat on top of the table. I clean that room once a week now.

I started off by saying I'd like to confess to the murder of that woman who was killed a few months back.

What woman, sir?

You know. The dead one with the reward.

That was a man, sir.

Yeah, I killed him. Can I have my money now?

It wasn't hard for them to doubt my story, and when I pushed for the reward, saying I had earned it by killing him, and then used the word *outside* to describe where I had stabbed my victim, my Slow Joe act was cemented. As I turned from Hannibal Lecter to Forrest Gump in a matter of seconds, I learned the police had no suspects at all. I didn't get any reward, but I was given coffee and a sandwich. That night when I got home, I slept like a rock. The following day I felt like a new man. I felt fantastic. When I came back to "confess" again, this time to a murder I knew nothing about, they took pity on me. I was a nice guy—they could see that; I was merely looking for attention in the wrong places. When one of their cleaners "happened" to disappear, I applied for and was given this job. Because of government regulations in a world trying to be as politically correct as possible, departments all over the country have a quota to fill when it comes to hiring people who are fucked either physically or mentally. The police seemed happy to hire me since they figured a cleaner didn't need to know much more than how to run a vacuum cleaner and dunk a mop in water. It was either me, or go through the employment lottery where they'd have to choose some other disabled guy.

So now I'm the harmless guy who waltzes up their hallways with brooms and mops, a minimum-wage lackey. But at least the sleepless nights are a thing of the past.

It generally takes me an hour to clean the toilets. Today is no different. When I finish I go through to the women's toilets and do the same, hanging a sign on the door first to say that cleaning is in progress. Women never come in here while I'm cleaning. Maybe they think the red stick figure they see on the sign is a pervert. When I'm done I empty the contents of the bucket, then store it and the mop back in my office. I grab a broom and slide it back and forth down the corridors and around the cubicles, heading toward the conference room. When I get inside I don't need to make myself invisible because I'm the only one in here. The day's work has begun. Leads have been found. Evidence to follow. Prayers go unanswered.

I lean my broom against the door. The conference room is pretty big. To my right, a window the width of the room overlooks the city. To my left, a matching window looks into the fourth floor. At the moment the view is only of thin, gray, venetian blinds, which have been pulled closed. In the center sits a long rectangular table with several seats around it. In the past this room has been used to interview suspects because it looks intimidating. What happens is hundreds of photographs are hung up, stacks of paper are piled against the walls, and officers walk past the window carrying files before popping in to whisper something to the detective doing the interview. The murder weapon is nearby so the killer gets a good look at it, and he soon feels they have more than enough information on him. He cracks under the pressure. In the corner, alongside the window, is a huge potted plant. I take special care when watering it.

I step up to the wall of photographs—pictures of victims and crime scenes have been pinned to a long corkboard. Pictures of the latest victims, Angela Durry and Martha Harris, are up there, making a total of seven bodies over the last thirty weeks. Seven unsolved murders. It only took two for the police to make the connection, even with the different MO. Modus operandi. An MO is what's similar about the way two or more crimes are committed—the same gun, the method of breaking in, the way he confronts his victim. This is different from a signature. A signature is what a killer needs to do for fulfillment—he may need to masturbate over the body, or follow a script, or force his victim to participate. An MO is upgradable. The first time I broke into a house I smashed a window. Then I learned if you put duct tape over the glass, it doesn't shatter and make as much noise. Then I learned how to pick locks.

A signature isn't upgradable. A signature is the whole point of the murder. It's the gratification. I don't have one because I'm not like those sick perverted bastards who go around killing women out of a sexual need. I do it for fun. And that's a big difference.

Of the seven unsolved murders, only six are mine. The seventh has been tacked onto my lot because the police are inept. It's strange how things in this world have a way of balancing themselves out; one woman I killed has never shown up. And where is she?

Long-term parking. I dumped her body inside the trunk of her car, drove into town, grabbed a ticket for a parking building, and left the car on the top floor. It's very rare that the building is so full that cars reach the top floor. I wrapped her body in plastic, figuring it would stop the smell for maybe a day or two. Three, if I was lucky. If I was really lucky, nobody would go up there for maybe a week.

She was the second of my seven, and she's still there now, with the wind gusting through the exposed top floor and dissipating the scent. The chances are high that nobody has even been up there.

I would never have thought to look in the trunk, Detective Schroder.

I still have the ticket as a memento. It's hidden beneath my mattress at home.

When I first started out it seemed to me that dumping the body was the way to go. That quickly evolved, though, because in all the other cases somebody ended up finding them anyway, and the first place the cops went after identifying them was to their houses. All I was doing was putting myself to extra work. Well, live and learn, I guess. I decided to start leaving them in their homes.

The woman in long-term parking isn't among the faces looking at me. Instead a stranger looks out from the lineup. Number four in the allotted seven. I know her name and I know her face, but until her picture was pinned up I'd never seen her before. She has been up there for six weeks now, and every day I pause to look at her features. Daniela Walker. Blond. Pretty. My type of woman—but not this time. Even in death her eyes sparkle out from her corpse like soft emeralds. She has both a pre- and post-death photograph. At first Detective Inspector Schroder didn't want me coming in here because of these pictures. Either he simply forgot after a while, or he just doesn't care.

The picture of Daniela Walker in life shows her as a happy thirtysomething, two or maybe three years before her death. Her hair shimmers over her shoulder as she turns toward the camera. Her lips are parting in a smile. Her picture has been on my mind every day since it has been up here. And why?

Because whoever killed her pinned her murder on me.

Whoever killed her was too scared to take the credit, so rather than try and get away with it in his own clever fashion, he gets away with it by using me. All without my permission!

I keep looking at her picture. One in life. One in death. Green eyes sparkling in each.

For the last six weeks I've thought of little other than finding the man who did this to us. Can it be that difficult? I have the resources. I'm smarter than anybody else in this department, and that's not just my ego talking. I scroll my eyes over the victims. Look at them closely. Fourteen eyes staring at me. Watching. Seven pairs. Familiar faces.

Bar one.

A ring of deep bruises form a necklace around Daniela Walker's throat from strangulation. They aren't consistent—ruling out a scarf or a rope—and look like they were formed by knuckles. More pressure can be applied with knuckles than fingers. It's also harder to defend against. The problem with strangulation is it takes four to six minutes to complete. Sure, they give up struggling within the first, but the pressure needs to be kept on for at least another three to starve the body of oxygen. That's three minutes I could be using for something better. Using knuckles increases the chances of crushing the victim's windpipe.

Beneath the corkboard is a set of shelves, and on top of these are seven piles of folders—one per victim. I head over to them. It's like looking at a menu and already knowing in advance which item to choose. I walk to the fourth pile and pick up one of the folders from the top. Every detective on the case has one of these folders and the spares are here for anybody who becomes assigned.

Like me.

I unzip the front of my overalls, stuff it down my front, then zip them up again. Back to the wall of the dead. I smile at the latest two. This is their first morning here in the assembly. No doubt they were pinned up last night. They don't smile back. Angela Durry. Thirty-nine-year-old legal executive. She suffocated on an egg. Martha Harris. Seventy-two-year-old widow. I'd needed a car. She had caught me taking hers.

I take my spray bottle and rags and move to the window. I spend five minutes cleaning it, staring beyond the streaks and my reflection at the world outside to the little people walking among the little streets. I spend some quality time with the plant. I replace the microcassette tape from the audio recorder I have hidden in there, careful to touch the recorder only with the rags. I tuck the tape into my pocket. I still have a job to do, and I head back to my office to grab the vacuum cleaner, then return and use it to clean up.

Ten minutes later I leave the conference room as I found it—only tidier and without as many files. I wheel the vacuum cleaner into the supply room on the other side of the floor and start vacuuming. Nobody is around so I do the Boy Scout thing and stock up on a few more pairs of gloves—not that I'll be killing anybody tonight. I don't suffer from compulsions to kill all the time. I'm no animal. I don't go running around venting childhood aggressions while looking for excuses to kill. I'm not itching to make a name for myself or gain the notoriety of Ted Bundy or Jeffrey Dahmer. Bundy was a freak who had a following of groupies during and after his trial, and he even got married after he was sentenced to death. He was a loser who killed more than thirty women, but he got caught. I don't want fame. I don't want to be married. If I wanted fame, I would kill somebody famous—like that Chapman chap who loved John Lennon so much he shot him. I'm just a regular guy. An average Joe. With a hobby. I'm not a psychopath. I don't hear voices. I don't kill for God or Satan or the neighbor's dog. I'm not even religious. I kill for me. It's that simple. I like women, and I like to do things to them they won't let me do. There have to be maybe two or three billion women in this world. Killing one every month or two isn't a big deal. It's all about perspective.

I grab some other stuff. Nothing major. Gear officers are always taking. Nothing anybody will notice gone. Nobody notices anything around here. The supply room is good like that. It supplies. No reason for it not to supply me. I look at my watch. Twelve o'clock—lunchtime. I head back to my office. The tools and the cords and the paint—this gear I don't get to use. All I do is clean. Everybody here thinks I have the IQ of a watermelon. But that's okay. In fact, it's perfect.

CHAPTER EIGHT

My chair is uncomfortable and my lunch isn't that great. With several nice sights out the window, I lean over and look at the women out there as prospective lovers. Should I go down there? Find where one works? Where she lives? Then, one night, find her in between those two places?

Men and women are walking back and forth, treating the warm afternoon street like a singles bar. Women dress like whores and take offense when men stare at them. Men dress like pimps and take offense when nobody notices. I use the two-inch knife to cut into my apple, small drops of juice spraying out. I slice it into sections. I'm chewing them while picking a target. My mouth waters before taking each bite.

Of course, I can't go down there. I have other things to do now, a new hobby. What sort of guy would I be if I picked up a new hobby and dumped it after only an hour? I'd be a loser. The sort of guy who can't finish what he starts. And that's not me. I didn't get to where I am by never finishing anything.

My thoughts are interrupted by a knock on my door. No-body ever comes here while I'm eating lunch, and for the briefest of moments I'm sure the police are going to burst in and arrest me. I start to reach for my briefcase. A moment later the door swings open and Sally is standing there, making me think I need to put a lock on that door.

"Hi, Joe."

I lean back. "Hi, Sally."

"How's the apple? Is it nice?"

"It's nice," I say, though I'm quickly losing my appetite now. I jam a slice of it in my mouth so I don't have to make more conversation. What in the hell could she want?

"I made you a tuna sandwich," she says, closing the door behind her and heading over to my bench. My office has only one seat and I'm in it. I don't offer it to her because I don't want her to stay. I take the tuna sandwich from her and smile at her, showing my fake gratitude along with a mouthful of apple. She offers me the kind of smile that suggests she would sleep with me if only, *please God, if only he would ask*. But I'm not going to ask. Her tuna sandwiches are always pretty good, but not that good. I swallow my piece of apple and take a huge bite of tuna and bread.

"Yummy," I say, making an effort to have crumbs spill from my mouth. Just because Sally is an idiot doesn't mean I can drop the Slow Joe act around her. I can never, never let any-body—not even Fat Sally—get an idea just how intelligent I really am.

Sally leans against the bench and looks down at me as she takes a bite out of an identical sandwich. I guess that means she's planning on hanging out here for a bit. She keeps smil-ing at me as she chews. Crumbs don't fall out of her mouth, but if they did it might help her lose a bit of weight. I can't remember ever seeing her without that stupid grin on her face. She talks to me as I eat my lunch. Tells me stuff about her mom and dad, about her brother. She tells me it's his birthday today, but I don't bother asking how old he is. She tells me anyway.

"Twenty-one."

"You doing anything to celebrate?" I ask, since it's expected of me.

She starts to say something, then pauses, and I realize she's going through one of her simple/special people routines where she has to think things through, starting with whether or not she even has a brother, and if he really is twenty-one today. Women may be from Venus, but nobody knows where the hell people like Sally come from.

"We're just having a simple thing at home," she says, sounding sad, and I guess I'd be sounding sad too if I had to have a simple family celebration at home. She reaches for the crucifix hanging from her neck. I've always found it ironic that retarded people can not only believe in God, but think He's a pretty good guy. The crucifix has one of those bulky soldered-on metal figures of Jesus, and this Jesus looks to be in pain—not because he's been crucified, but because his head is permanently cast downward forcing him to look down Sally's top.

I can feel the minutes slipping away. The file is still in my overalls. I want Sally to leave me alone, but I don't know how to say it. I start on the second sandwich she gave me. She tries to include me in her conversation by asking about my own family. I don't have anything to offer on that subject, other than my mother is nuts and my dad is dead, and that neither of those things is ever going to change, so I keep it to myself. Then she asks how my day has been going, how yesterday went, how tomorrow is going to be. It's as bad as talking about the weather—it's all conversational filler I couldn't be any less interested in.

After twenty minutes of chewing really slowly and nodding at the same pace, of having my stomach itch from the edges of the file, Sally finally straightens up and leaves, throwing a

Be seeing you soon at me on the way out the door. As soon as she is gone, I pull the file from my overalls and lay it on the bench. I never used to be nervous with what I brought in here to look through, but now I am. Sally could come back in, but I figure she wouldn't understand what she was looking at, so it's safe for me to carry on. Carefully, like an archaeologist opening a just-uncovered gospel, I open the cover. The first thing I see is Daniela Walker. She looks up at me with eyes open and neck bruised. I pull the photo out and lay it faceup on my bench. It's only one in a series of ten. Not all of them are of her, though most are.

I lay them side by side in a row like I'm playing some freak game of solitaire with creepy playing cards. She looks at me from four of the photographs, and in the progression it seems her skin gets grayer. Time codes on the pictures suggest they were taken over the course of an hour, so she may well have been changing color. In fact, in the last picture, her twinkling green eyes no longer twinkle. They have taken on the texture of spoiled plums. The other six photographs are of the bedroom from varying angles.

According to notes in the file, another one hundred and twenty photographs were taken—quite the portfolio—and these pictures detail many of the items in the house, as well as the rooms. The catalog of those photographs is specific: door, stairs, bed, furniture, smudges on the handles. Anything and everything.

I look hard at the pictures, but see nothing. So I look at them harder. I'm trying to imagine myself inside her house. It's hard, because the pictures I have were all taken in the bedroom. The natural insight I was waiting to experience from my own experience doesn't come along.

I glance through the report. She was found by her husband, her entire body draped by a sheet. Did her killer feel bad at what he'd done? Was covering her an act of decency?

I read the toxicology report. It takes most of my lunch break to decipher that the ten-page report says only that I've just wasted my time, that there were no drugs in her system. Or any alcohol. Or any poisons.

The postmortem is an even longer report, but less complicated. It makes for easy reading, and I know how it's going to end even before I finish it. It reveals in an exceptionally unenthusiastic manner what Daniela went through, probably because the pathologist has seen it all before and has got bored with it. The report comes with pre-illustrated diagrams of the female body and its anatomy, and the pathologist has used these to point to where and what was damaged during her ordeal. There were no traces of semen. A condom was used. Her pubic hair had been combed and washed by the killer, removing any hair and skin cells he would have left behind. This isn't something I've been doing, and I won't do it now—even though it isn't such a bad idea. It indicates her killer is far from crazy, and has an insight into police forensics.

There were extensive bruises in all the places where there ought to be bruises, and she suffered two cracked ribs. She was punched once in the eye and once in the mouth. There were other, older injuries there—some as recent as two months before she died. Injuries that had not been reported. Injuries, in the opinion of the pathologist, consistent with being beaten. So Daniela was used to what she was getting. Cause of death: strangulation.

The rest of the postmortem is both standard and uninteresting. It's like reading a mechanic's report about fixing a car. The body was fully dismantled and tested. The weight of the organs. The size of her brain. Detailed references to photographs taken during the autopsy take up two pages—photos of her hands, of her neck, of her feet. I don't bother with any of this.

DNA was found at the scene. No fingerprints. The killer used latex gloves, like the type I wear. A residue from the gloves was left on the door handles from the tips of his fingers.

Also there was plenty of residue all over the victim. The only prints found were latent smears on her eyelids, but these were only partial and too badly damaged to be of any use. That's the beauty about human skin—it's one thing fingerprints struggle to stick to. They did find hair, though, in other places. And carpet fibers. And shoe prints. So far they have narrowed them down only to the husband who found the body, and the officers and detectives who worked the scene. It's impossible to keep a crime scene free of any contamination. In order to do that, the room would need to be inside a large plastic bubble that nobody would ever be allowed to go inside to collect the pristine evidence.

The police have their own DNA databases of their people who go to scenes. This way they eliminate evidence left by their own men and women. Next, they take blood from the victim's family, friends, and neighbors, until they narrow the field right down. Last night, I left plenty of evidence behind: saliva on the two bottles of beer, carpet fibers, hair. But I have no criminal record. Nothing to match my name to these samples. So I'm a free man.

Whoever killed Daniela may have a criminal record. The evidence I leave behind ties my killings together. I don't know whose decision it was to include Walker among those women, but it was a bad one. Lunchtime is nearly over. I'm still hungry. No eggs today. I keep studying the autopsy report. Her fingernails were clipped after death, so it seems she scratched her killer. I've been scratched several times, never in the face, though, and I don't mind because that would be like a chef complaining about getting burned or a crash-test dummy complaining about being dumb—it comes with the job. I just never roll my sleeves up until those scratches are gone. I've never even thought about clipping their nails afterward to hide the evidence. Why would I cut the nails from this victim and wash her pubic hair, and not any of the others? How can the police really toss this death into the same mix?

I put the photographs and files into my briefcase, along with the microcassette tapes from the conference room, lock it, and leave it on the bench. I head up a floor, where there are more rooms and fewer people and no conference room. I repeat the same procedure up here with my mop and my vacuum cleaner. Say hello to everybody. Everyone smiles at me as if I'm their best friend.

I do my job and I do it well, and I finish it at four thirty, earlier than anybody else. This enables me to catch an earlier bus home. I say hello to those I pass on my way out, and they tell me to have a nice night. I tell them I intend to. Sally calls out a good-bye, but I pretend I can't hear her.

Christchurch is buzzing with life. Traffic blocks the roads. Pedestrians block the sidewalks. I walk among them and none of them knows who I am. They look at me and all they see is a man in overalls with a happy-go-lucky look about him. Their lives are in my hands, but I'm the only one who knows it. It's both a lonely and a powerful feeling. A little bit of the day's heat has ebbed away, but not much. There's still going to be sun for a couple of more hours. I start to think about what I might want to do tonight. I reach the bus stop. I wait for only a few seconds with a bunch of nondescript people I could kill right now if I wanted to before the bus shows up. As usual, my briefcase is in my right hand, my ticket in my left. I hand it over.

"Hi there, Joe." She gives me a big smile.

"Hi, Miss Selena. How are you?"

"Very well, Joe," she answers, punching my ticket. "Missed you yesterday, Joe."

I couldn't exactly catch the bus to Angela's house. "I was late, Miss Selena."

She hands back my ticket. I study how she moves, how she sounds, the way her eyes look me up and down. She smells like soap and perfume and makes me think of other women I've been with. Her shoulder-length black hair is slightly damp, and I can only assume she has showered with seeing me in mind, and since I'm in the process of assuming that, I like to assume she was in pretty good spirits as she soaped herself down. All that assuming makes the front of my overalls go a little tight. Her olive skin gives her a slightly exotic look, and she talks with an accent that's erotic. She has a nice tight body and firm skin. Her dark blue eyes look into mine, and they see me differently from how Mr. Stanley sees me. He sees a defunct personality caught inside a healthy body. Miss Selena sees me as a man who can satisfy her. Her fingers deliberately brush against my hand. She wants me. Unfortunately, I like her too much as a bus driver to indulge her. Perhaps I'll wait until she changes jobs.

I walk down the aisle. The bus isn't packed, but I'm forced to sit next to some young guy dressed as a punk. He looks like he couldn't make conversation about the weather unless it included beating the shit out of a weatherman. He's dressed entirely in black, with a black studded collar around his neck. He has red hair, spikes in his nose, and faucet washers stretching his earlobes. Another regular citizen of this fine city. A chain runs from his lower lip to his throat. I consider pulling on it to see if I can flush his mind. His T-shirt says *Don't worry, I know the hymen maneuver.*

It's five thirty when I get home, by which time the front of my building is in complete shade. Somebody has tipped over some trash bins, so the sidewalk right outside is covered in old food and lawn clippings, and the old food and lawn clippings are themselves covered in flies. I climb the steps to the top floor and the first thing I do when I get into my apartment is open the window, then the second thing I do is close it because something out there smells bad.

I turn on an electric fan that looks just like the one at work and, I must confess, actually came from work. I open my briefcase on the sofa, take out the microcassette tape, and listen to it while I change out of my overalls. The tape contains nothing interesting. Inside the conference room they admit to themselves they have nothing. Outside to the media, they have several leads.

I stifle a laugh and toss the tape back into the briefcase. I'll swap them again tomorrow.

I sit on the sofa and watch my goldfish. I give them some food and they swim up and start eating. Five-second memories or not, they always recognize food. They also recognize me. When I put my finger on the edge of the bowl, they follow it. I sometimes think that society would be great if we all had five-second memories. I could kill as many people as I wanted. Of course, maybe I wouldn't remember that I liked killing people, so maybe it wouldn't be that great after all. I could be right in the middle of tying somebody up when I'd forget why I was there. A five-second-memory society would just be full of awkward moments like that.

When Pickle and Jehovah have eaten and are back into their happy routine of swimming around and around, I lock up and head downstairs, keeping a tight grip on my briefcase.

I walk a few blocks, studying all the cars parked along the side of the road. Fifteen minutes later I'm driving to the address on page two of the folder I picked up earlier. I'm in a Honda that's ten years old and has the aroma of cigarette smoke stained into the seats and carpet, but despite that it's a pretty nice ride. I find them easier to steer without the weight of a body in the trunk. I drive slowly past Daniela Walker's house. It is a two-story town house that looks like it was built only yesterday—bright red brick, dark brown steel roof, aluminum window framing. I'm surprised there's no price tag hanging off one of the corners. The garden is looking scruffy, not that it's very extensive: a few shrubs, a couple of baby trees, clumps of flowers that have wilted in the sun. No price tags on those either. The driveway is paved with paving stones. A pathway to the front door is cobbled with cobblestones. The lawn is dry and long. The mailbox is full of circulars. A garden gnome with painted red pants and a painted blue shirt is lying on its side in the garden. It looks like it's been shot.

I circle the block and come back, then, satisfied nobody is watching, I pull up outside. I hop out of the car, straighten my tie, adjust my jacket, then realize the back of my pants have been tucked into my socks on the left side. I flick it out. I take my briefcase to the front door with me. I seldom leave it behind.

Knock.

Wait.

Knock again.

Wait. Again.

Nobody home. Just as the report confirmed. Since the murder, the husband—who I have already chalked up as suspect number one—hasn't been back in the house. His mail has been redirected to his parents' house, where he's now staying with the kids.

The police tape crisscrossing the front door was taken down two days after the murder. That's the sort of thing that invites trouble. Invites vandalism. It's like putting up a large button with a sign saying *Don't Push*. I figure it'll be a miracle if I walk inside and don't find giant penises painted all over the walls and the furniture not nailed down missing. I fish into my pocket and find my keys hiding beneath my handkerchief. Fumble with the lock for maybe ten seconds. I'm good at this.

I take a quick glance over my shoulder into the street. I'm all alone.

I open the door and walk inside.

CHAPTER NINE

Sally leaves work the same time Joe does, and though she tries to catch up to him, even calls out to him more than once, he doesn't hear her. He reaches the bus stop, and a moment later the bus pulls away, spitting out a cloud of diesel fumes, some of which stick to the back of the bus, the rest disappearing into the air. She's curious about where Joe goes. Sometimes he walks, sometimes he catches the bus. Does he live with his parents? Does he live with others like him? One of the things she likes the most about Joe is that he appears independent, and it wouldn't surprise her if he lived in a flat or an apartment somewhere, fending for himself. Does he even have family? He's never spoken of them. She hopes he does. The idea of Joe being all alone in this world is unsettling. She must make more of an effort to involve herself in his life, the same way she would want people to involve themselves in Martin's life. If he were still alive.

He would be twenty-one today. What would they have been doing to celebrate? They would have thrown a party, invited family and friends, strung up a bunch of balloons and stabbed twenty-one candles into a chocolate cake shaped like a racing car.

She walks toward the parking building where she keeps her car. She ought to offer Joe rides home—he might like that. And she'd get to know him better too. Tomorrow she'll ask him.

Christchurch is beautiful, she thinks, and she especially loves walking alongside the Avon River with its dark waters and lush, green banks—a strip of nature running through the city. Though the banks aren't quite as lush as normal because of the lasting summer, but they're still pretty green close to the waterline. Sometimes she eats her lunch out here, sitting on the grass, watching the ducks, throwing them pieces of bread as they play and feed in the water. She ought to ask Joe to join her. She's sure he would like it. More and more he reminds her of her brother, and since she can no longer help Martin, perhaps she can help Joe. Is that such a crazy idea?

There is a homeless man sitting a few yards from the doorway into the parking building. He's wearing a dark-blue tracksuit jacket that you only see in TV shows that came out of the '80s. He's got on a pair of plastic sunglasses with green arms, and a baseball cap with so much paint splashed on it she can't read the team. He has a few days worth of stubble, which means somehow he's still finding a way to shave. It makes Sally happy to know he still thinks appearances are important. She smiles at him and he smiles back, and she hands him a small plastic bag jammed full with sandwiches.

"How are you feeling today, Henry?"

"Better now, Sally," he says, standing up and tucking his T-shirt into too large, too worn jeans. "Better now. How's your dad doing?"

"He's doing okay," she answers, but of course he isn't. He's doing badly. That's what happens with Parkinson's disease. You never get any better. It gets into your body and sets up a home and has no intention of ever leaving. Doing okay is the best anybody can hope for. "It's his birthday this week. We're going to take him out to dinner," she says, but it won't be fun. His birthday never is, not since Martin died. Maybe it would be if it had been a month before or a month after, but having it the same week . . .

"Well, you have a good time," Henry says, interrupting her thoughts. "And say hi to him for me. And remember, Sally, that Jesus loves you."

She smiles at Henry. She knows that Jesus loves her, and that Jesus loves Henry too, and at the end of the day that makes everything okay. When she first started to make Henry sandwiches (she would never give him money, which would surely go toward substances that would make him sin) she used to be the one telling him that Jesus loved him, and his reply was never positive. He used to tell her that God and Jesus hated him. God had made him unemployed. God had made him homeless. She pointed out it was more likely that Henry himself had been the cause of that. He had replied by telling her that God had given him his gambling habit—or at the very least hadn't taken it away. She asked if Henry still gambled now, to which Henry said no, to which Sally pointed out that God had indeed helped him.

"Then God has a bad sense of timing," Henry had said, and even though Sally didn't like it, she certainly recognized there was an element of truth to that. Henry then went on to point out that if man was made in God's image and man was doing nothing to help him, then God would be doing nothing too. If God came down to walk about the earth, Henry said, and saw him sitting there outside the parking building, begging for change and food, then God would look right through him and just walk on by. The same way everybody else did.

Sally could almost see his point, but at the same time found it easy to dismiss, mainly because Sally never walked past Henry without helping him. After months of bringing him sandwiches, he finally allowed her to teach him more about God's will. She knows it's possible he only says these things to her so she will continue to bring him food, but she likes hearing it.

"I'll see you tomorrow, Henry. Take care now."

Henry sits back down and goes about taking care of himself the way she suggested, starting by reaching into the plastic bag. She walks inside and takes the elevator up to her car.

A moment later her car is mingling with the town traffic. It really is a beautiful city, she thinks. Voted friendliest in the world. It's obvious why. So many good people. Caring people. She just wishes that sometimes they could show it a little more.

By the time she climbs three flights of stairs, she's puffing. She could take the elevator, but she's been taking the elevator all day at work and this is her best chance for exercise. Lord knows she would be thankful to lose a pound or two. She reaches her car—a twenty-year-old sedan that doesn't have much in the way of features but has plenty in the way of rust, but every day the engine keeps on ticking over and Lord knows she's thankful for that too.

The building exits on a different street from which she came in. Traffic is thickening, and in an hour, some of these streets will almost grind to a halt. She smiles as she strikes a string of green traffic lights. The sun is still out, there's a warm breeze, and everywhere around her people are happy. She winds down the passenger window, but the one on her side doesn't work, but that's okay because enough of a breeze still makes it inside. She keeps smiling as she drives. There are so many flower beds, so many trees, a river flowing through the center of town—who would want to live anywhere else?

CHAPTER TEN

The first thing I notice is how stuffy the house is. It's like the inside of a dryer. The summer heat has built up. I wish I could leave the door open. The second thing is that miracles do sometimes happen—no genitalia have been painted on the walls, there are no indications anything has been stolen. A quick flick of a light switch shows even the power is still on.

Time for a casual stroll. I find a few bottles of beer in the fridge. I also find several foods that have gone past their expiration date, chunks of furry mold growing from wet-looking surfaces. It's almost enough to put me off the beer—but only almost. It doesn't have a twist-top cap, but there's a bottle opener in one of the drawers. The beer is refreshing as I sit down and glance back through Daniela's file. When I finish, I put the bottle in my briefcase, along with the cap and the bottle opener, and head upstairs.

Up here it's even hotter. It's as if the heat from last summer and the one before that is being stored up here too. I take off my jacket and lay it on a small upstairs table, knocking the vase onto the floor to make room for it. It breaks. Oh well. The body was found in the master bedroom. Rather than wasting any more time, I head directly there.

The windows face west, and the lowering sun is coming right in. The bedroom is around the same size as any other I've broken into. The dark carpet looks both blue and green, but probably looks gray to anybody colorblind. Spread across the floor are more than a dozen plastic markers, each of them numbered. They're bigger versions of ones some restaurants and cafés hand out to keep track of who ordered the salmon or the latte. In the file, the numbers represent things that were found on those points, things like hair, blood, and underwear. Spare evidence bags are littered here and there. No wonder the police can't stick to a budget. Each time I kill somebody, that's more money they have to come up with. Hopefully this doesn't end up affecting my wages.

The walls are covered in red textured wallpaper that's slightly too bright for this room, making it feel, if you can believe it, even hotter. The smell of death hasn't left. It's soaked into the carpet pile and will probably always be there. The windows take up most of the opposite wall, and beside me is a walk-in closet. A print of some foreign landscape that could be African or Australian hangs above the bed, and I think about taking it home for Mom. A bedside table has the usual ensemble of crap resting on it: a packet of painkillers; a small, smooth jar of night cream, whatever that is; an alarm clock; and a box of tissues. The alarm clock is still keeping accurate time. There's a similar table on the other side of the bed. Scattered across the room, as it's been scattered everywhere else in the house, is white fingerprinting powder. It looks like Detective Schroder and his pals had a cocaine party.

I take a look at the sketch map of the bedroom that was in the file. There's also one of the entire floor. Can't get lost in here. The purpose of the map is to show in an even perspective where everything was found. It tells me that on the far side of the bed is a door leading to a bathroom. I follow the map and see it speaks the truth.

The body was found on the bed. There's no tape or chalk outline of where her body was, because that's only a TV thing. It's a shame, because that would be a pretty sweet job to have. I can imagine the interview: *Well, if you can trace an outline around this orange, the job is yours.*

I pick my way across the floor, stepping over the plastic numbers and evidence bags. I sit on the corner of the bed. The duvet sags and moves a little. So far, my effort has consisted of knocking over a vase and sitting on a comfortable bed, yet already I'm sweating. When I wipe my shirtsleeve across my forehead, it comes away wet. I roll up my sleeves and rest the briefcase on the bed. I open it so the gun is easily accessible. I see the empty bottle of beer and fight the temptation to go back downstairs for a fresh one.

I don't know exactly what I'm looking for, so I decide to break my evening up into goals. Baby steps. My short-term goal has to be simple: find something to work with, work with it, then turn it into a long-term goal. Set this guy up for the entire seven killings, and the eighth one too, if she ever gets found. I still have the ticket from the parking garage as evidence that I can plant. I close my eyes and imagine it all unfolding, then open them because I'm jumping ahead. I need to reach the short-term goal first.

I begin looking around. Nice place. I could live here. A nice twenty-inch flatscreen TV in the corner that would look good in my place. It's been turned off, though in the photographs it's on. Maybe the killer watched TV while he was attacking her. Or maybe she watched. I wonder what was on at the time, if Walker was being raped to boring British theme music. The generic photographs of her family where they all fake smiles for the camera fill the room. There are some on the bedside tables; others hang on the walls. If their eyes are looking at me, I don't feel it here.

A crossword-puzzle magazine sits on the second bedside table, along with a telephone. The phone is no good, though. It's been torn from the wall. On the floor by the bedside table is the remote to the TV. It has white fingerprinting powder on all the buttons. I put the crossword magazine in my briefcase, then check out the closet. Nice clothes. Hers aren't my type. The husband's are the wrong size. I rummage through a chest of drawers and find nothing. Her underwear smells like fabric softener and feels soft against my face. I drop a pair of panties inside my briefcase.

There is nothing of interest in the bathroom. The husband's electric razor, sitting above the sink, looks nicer than mine. It's one of many things the husband has left behind. Back in the bedroom, I sit down on the same corner of the bed and put the razor into my briefcase, first wrapping it in the underwear to protect my knives. Red walls. Blue-green carpet. I've never known what fashion is in or out, so I'm not sure whether these colors are on their way in for the first time or are already too old, or if they're coming back in fashion. I'm not sure whether I should like them.

Concentrate.

I think back to the autopsy report. Daniela was able to scratch her killer, and since there were marks on her wrists from being bound, she must have scratched him before he started to strangle her. Once my chest was scratched so badly I needed stitches, but because I couldn't go to the doctor, I went to the supermarket and bought those Band-Aid stitches. Used half a dozen to close the wound. Healed up nicely. Except for the infection.

The only blood found at the scene was hers. He didn't stab her—just punched her in the face a few times. The drops of blood on the pillow from having her face pressed into it look like tears, as if a sad clown wept into it. More droplets have been sprinkled over the floor. On the handle to the front door, accompanying one of the latex smudges, is a smudge of her blood.

I read through the reports once more, then check the statements. Putting my money on the husband isn't looking like a safe bet—he has an exceptionally good alibi. Her body was found with her arms folded across her chest, and a sheet was pulled up over her. Her eyes were open, but the smears on her eyelids suggest the killer closed them before he put his gloves on to clean up. If so, they opened by themselves. Again I think maybe he felt bad at what he had done. I spend a few seconds wondering what that would feel like—about feeling bad—but can't get a feel for it. That doesn't mean others don't understand it. Maybe the guy who did this was deluded enough to think giving her some dignity in death made up for killing her. It looks like a classic domestic homicide, except for the alibi. Plus I saw the husband at the station the morning after the murder, and he looked genuinely messed up, as if he couldn't believe anybody could do this to his wife.

I look back down at the report. It's getting harder to read as it gets darker outside. Nothing has been reported stolen: no pieces of missing jewelry, no missing cash. In most cases the guilty husband would have tried to make it look like a burglary gone wrong. I never take anything when I kill, and since this person was trying to copy me, he never took anything either. How did he know that? Not through the media, that's for sure. Is it just a coincidence?

I don't know. All I do know is that I've been here for nearly forty minutes and still don't have any answers. I'm starting to think more and more of the beers downstairs. I should have opened a window. The air's still stuffy, but the sun is no longer as strong. I loosen my grip on the thick file and the contents spill onto the bed. My ideas are starting to dissolve. Time keeps passing and I realize my mind has stagnated. I start running my eyes over the scene, imagining what happened here, putting myself in the killer's mind. Getting inside is easy for a guy like me. So that's what I do—I get inside his mind, I imagine her dying, and for a few minutes I can almost feel her beneath me.

Still—no great insights, no flashing sirens or ringing bells to signify a great breakthrough in the case. There are no breakthroughs, just one sloppy coincidence and a sweat-soaked shirt. I thought it would be easier. Hell, it should be easier. Only things never are. Not when it's something you really want. I want to help this dead woman as much as I want to help myself, but does that matter? Does that make the answers any easier to find? Of course not. The only thing I feel like doing is taking my free electric shaver and crossword puzzles out of here and never coming back. Go home, feed my fish, and take a nap. Put this episode behind me, like I have other episodes in my life, like I have with all of them. Move on. To what, I'm not sure.

I start stretching and yawning, ready to leave, ready to give up. The warm air is only helping to maintain this feeling of despondency. The yawning leads to blinking, quick, rapid-fire blinking, and this in turn increases the blood flow to my eyes. They begin to sharpen, the room taking focus again, the objects standing out like 3-D images. . . .

And there it is!

In an instant I'm overcome with several different thoughts and emotions. First of all I feel disgust. I'm ashamed with myself for being here so long and not seeing it until now. I'm excited that I'm suddenly looking at something—or not looking at something, to be exact—that may be crucial. And most of all, I'm relieved. I'm thankful I can move forward again, thankful I don't have to give up the investigation—at least not yet, and relieved that Daniela may get the justice she deserves.

I start grinning. I almost can't believe my luck. But of course it isn't luck. Well, some of it is, I guess—because in another ten minutes it would have been too dark to see anything unless I turned on the light. So sure, it's luck, but it's brilliance too. And insight. Yeah, it's especially about insight.

I grab the photographs and begin flicking through them until I find one that shows the wall and the doorway to the hallway. I hold up the picture. Study it. Hold it away. Study the scene. The doorway is in each of them. Same walls. Same carpet. Same décor. A potted plant that looks lushly green in the picture is brown and disheveled in real life. In the photograph—lying against the base of the wall, next to the live plant—there is a fountain pen. In reality, lying next to the plant is a ballpoint pen. Sure, it's only a pen, minor in the scheme of things, but what makes it interesting is the fact that it hasn't been cataloged and taken away, meaning it was considered irrelevant.

Well, it's pretty relevant all right. Was the original pen a weapon? Was it mightier than the sword? I move over to the plant, crouch down, and peer at the wall. It's hard to see the small mark embedded in it, but not impossible. I lean in closer. I can see a tiny dot of ink in the center. Was the original pen thrown against the wall? Where's that pen now? Why the swap? Did Daniela cut him with it? Is that why it was thrown over here? If so, it has her attacker's DNA on it. It's a map to her killer. The pen is the sort of thing that would have its own individual photograph. Probably two or three. It would even have had its own individual report.

I pick up the ballpoint pen in my gloved hand. It's coated in a thin film of white dust. It has been printed and put back down, but nothing of interest came from it. I line it up with the small indent in the wall but can't find anyway for it to fit. The pens were switched at some point after the photograph was taken, and before the fingerprinting took place. So who switched the pens?

The answer is obvious. The killer. That's who. And the only people in this room during that time frame were people who worked the scene. Her killer has to be a cop. That's obvious too. Even more obvious, now that I think about what I've read, about their knowledge in police procedures. For a few seconds I close my eyes and visualize what happened. He came here. Attacked her. Hit her in the face. Then she stabbed him with the pen. Not seriously, but enough to anger him into throwing it against the wall. The nib chewed into it. He threw her onto the bed. He hadn't planned on killing her, but he had to prevent her from identifying him. It was spontaneous. Unplanned. He had to use items in this house to bind her. He used her nail clippers to cut away any skin evidence from beneath her fingernails. He used her comb to rake through her pubic hair. He didn't bring any of this with him because it wasn't part of the plan. When she was dead, he felt immediate guilt. He did what he could to hide any evidence he left behind, then he covered her body, closing her eyes first. But he had to get out of here. Fast. Maybe he said a prayer for her. Maybe he didn't. But what he did do was forget about the pen—until he came back to investigate her death. Then he saw the pen on the floor and remembered. The photographs had already been taken. He couldn't just pick it up. But he didn't have another fountain pen to switch it with. So he took the gamble that nobody would notice the difference and, for a while, nobody did. I'm nobody, and nobody's perfect. It's just a pen, a pen in the corner of the room next to a potted plant. In the center of the room was a dead body. The corpse ended up being a classic case of misdirection. Look at one thing and miss another.

I open my eyes. That's how I see it, but of course that may not be what happened. It feels right, though, and I'm sure some, if not most of it, will be. It doesn't really matter how it happened, what matters is who made it happen. I've been here for an hour and already I know her killer is a policeman. What's more, I know for sure I'm right. In all the books I've read, the serial killer is always the policeman. Or the coroner, or some forensic officer. So why not now? Why should this be any different? Perhaps clichés in fiction come from clichés in real life? In some weird way it's disappointing to find that police work in the end is pretty simple. If the killer isn't a husband or boyfriend, just get a witness to view a lineup of cops and pick one.

I leave the pen where it is since it can't offer me any more help. I turn away and pack up my briefcase. I have an urge to shout, to sing, to dance, to hunt for those sirens and bells and whistles that ought to accompany a moment like this. By the time I reach the front door, via the kitchen and the fridge, it's dark outside. I face the hallway and rooms as if to say good-bye to this house. I have no reason to return.

No reason at all.

Unless . . .

Grinning, I put the beers and the bottle opener back and rush upstairs.

CHAPTER ELEVEN

When she gets home from work, Sally finds her mother upstairs, crying. At first she pauses at the door, unsure whether to enter her parents' bedroom. Her mother cried a lot after Martin died, and these days she's crying a lot too.

"Sally?"

"Hi, Mom. Are you okay?" Sally asks, thinking that for her mom, *okay* ended a long time ago.

"I'm fine," her mother says, offering a smile that she doesn't quite get right, and of course Sally hasn't seen one that has fitted right and she knows it's because her parents blame her for what happened to Martin. "I don't really know why I'm like this."

When Sally puts an arm around her mother's shoulders, she flinches at first, then relaxes. The room smells of incense and the warm air is slightly stale. She knows exactly why her mother gets like this, and her mother knows too. Martin's birthday. She bought her dead brother a birthday card, filled it out, then buried it deep in her drawer beneath a pile of clothing. She isn't sure if her parents do the same or similar things, and suspects it may not actually be that healthy if they do. Of course they never dare talk about it. To talk about it would allow their grief to take on more life, to continue to rise above them and push them down. In some ways she envies Joe. She wants to be as simple as him, not having to worry about the pain in the world, just moving along from A to B, keeping people happy, staying out of their way, making a life for herself that is good.

"It's okay, Mom," she says, and there's that word again. "I think Dad's looking forward to his birthday."

Her mother nods, and they begin talking about how nice it's going to be to go out for dinner. Her father's birthday will be a challenge too. In the last year he has stepped outside the house for doctors' appointments and graveyard visits and nothing else. Whether they make it to dinner on Thursday night is still something of a gamble.

Sally opens the window. The air outside has cooled off. The warm air from the bedroom starts to waft out as fresh stuff replaces it. She wishes her dad's disease could be swapped just as easily. She would happily take it into her own body to relieve him of it if she could. It would be the least she could do after what happened to Martin.

"I'm sorry," her mother says, looking up and releasing her grip on a damp handful of tissues. "I used to be stronger than this." She starts rubbing the silver crucifix hanging at her neck between her thumb and forefinger.

"It will be okay, Mom," Sally answers, staring at the crucifix coming in and out of view, the *okay* word hanging in the room in the thick air. "You'll see."

Of course her mother has said those same words many times since the day when Martin's doctor gave them the news that led them to start thinking about where they wanted to bury their son. Strangely, it was Martin who suffered the least, because he didn't understand he was dying. Even at the end he thought he was going to be getting better. Didn't they all think that?

Yes. Life was always going to get better.

All they have to do is remember that. All they have to do is have faith.

Her mind slowly turns toward Joe. She wonders if he believes in God, and assumes that he does—he's too good-natured not to. Still, she decides to find out, because God may be the one thing they have in common.

CHAPTER TWELVE

I'm not actually sure where ideas come from, whether they're just floating around out there in some dimension close to but not quite of this world, where our minds can reach out and pluck them, whether a series of firing synapses in our mind weigh up cold data into cold possibilities, or whether it comes down to a simple train of thought riding through Lucksville. Ideas come at any time, often when you're not expecting them. I've had them in the bathroom, cleaning floors. I've had them when dreading the walk from the sidewalk to my mother's front door. The spontaneous ideas are often the best. Sometimes they shock you into making a decision. Only hindsight tells you whether it was good or not.

The only light coming into the room now is from the streetlights outside. I turn the duvet over to hide the splashes of blood. I pick up the plastic markers and throw them into the closet along with the evidence bags, next to a shoe rack and a pile of old clothes. The room no longer looks like a crime scene, but something out of *Poor Housekeeping*. I wipe away the fingerprint dust with the husband's shirt, then I close the curtains knowing that when I come back I'm going to have to turn on the lights. I make my way downstairs in the dark and do the same thing. By the time I finish up and get outside it's after nine o'clock.

I walk down the sidewalk to the Honda and climb inside, tossing my briefcase onto the passenger seat. From the moment I first saw this car, I've been wearing latex gloves. My fingers are sweating beneath them, but it's better than leaving fingerprints. I pull them away from my hands. They're like an extra layer of skin. I don't put on a replacement pair and make a mental note to remember to wipe down every surface I touch. I drive toward town. I have a job to do, but I don't want a particularly late night. Rather than looking for an innocent victim, I decide to look for somebody who will gladly be one for a price.

I find her standing on a Manchester Street corner in town. A skirt so short it's more of a thick belt than anything else. Low-cut top. Fishnet stockings. Costume jewelry on her fingers. A small tattoo on her neck and another at the top of her left breast. Other hookers are hanging around trying to attract business, women who look like they've been dragged out of a trailer park by their teased hair. If her pimp is nearby he may or may not note down the registration plate of my stolen car, but in this city I can't imagine pimps caring enough. It doesn't matter either way.

Before the car comes to a complete stop, she opens the passenger door and offers up today's specials as if reading from a menu. I accommodate her by clearing the seat. She tells me what I can get for twenty dollars, sixty dollars, and even a hundred. I ask her if there's a cash discount and she gives me a confused look until I tell her I'm just joking. She doesn't laugh. Then I ask her what I can get for five hundred.

"Is that you still being funny?" she asks.

I reach into my pocket and pull out my wallet. I show her what five hundred dollars looks like.

"You can have whatever you want, baby," she says, and I'll certainly hold her to that.

She closes the door and the interior light blinks out, but not before I end up taking a longer look at her than I would like. She's in her late twenties, though that's really just a guess. She's underweight, which isn't a guess, and looks like an ad for starving children in Third World countries. She has blond hair with black roots and so much hair spray the strong nor'westers we've been getting wouldn't budge it. Her brown eyes reveal nothing, as though her mind is somewhere else, maybe in a world where she doesn't have to wrap her thighs or lips around men for money. When she smiles at me, her swollen lips glisten with either moisture, or her last client.

I head back to Daniela's house. We make small talk on the way, mostly about the weather. I'm sure she's heard the news and knows what's been happening to all sorts of women in the city, but she doesn't look nervous sitting in a car with a man she's known all of two minutes. She can't afford to be nervous. I have no interest in what she does outside working hours. She doesn't care who I am. Then we start setting the mood. She tells me I have a nice car. I tell her she has a great body. She tells me she'll be an awesome fuck. I tell her for five hundred dollars she ought to be. We reach the house and I don't bother driving around the block, but opt to park up the driveway. If anybody is around they won't be able to get a good look at me. Even if they do take a peek, they'll think it's the husband returning home to quench his sexual thirst.

"Can you grab my briefcase from behind you?"

"Sure thing, sugar."

The evening has dropped a few degrees since I left the house. We reach the front door, my guest walking a little slower than me, and not in the same straight line. I left the door unlocked earlier, but I lock it behind us once we're inside.

"Would you like a drink?"

"Sure is hot in here."

"So that'd be a yes?"

"Sure."

She follows me through to the kitchen. I don't need the map of the house to know where I'm going. I turn on the light knowing it can't be seen from the front of the house, but it can be from the back if the neighbor over the fence is a practicing Peeping Tom. I open the fridge and grab a couple of beers. She is halfway through hers before I even manage to pry the top off mine. I leave the bottle opener and the caps on the bench. I'll pick them up on my way out. I keep making a list of surfaces I've been touching. Fridge. Door handle. Drawer handle. What else?

She finishes her beer and I start mine. The more light we have the worse she looks. She looks drugged up. Maybe if she hadn't spent too long focusing on sleeping with her step-father, dropping out of school early, getting pregnant, having an abortion, and getting pregnant again, then she could be living a more respectable life. I'm not saying prostitutes aren't respectable—they fulfill a societal need. Where else can you get somebody to kill on such short notice and have nobody care? They'll willingly go with you wherever you want to go. It's crazy. They take their lives in their hands every night, and offer them up to their johns to take away. The only other easy victim, but not as readily available, is the hitchhiker. The trick is to pull up alongside her and glance at your watch, giving the impression that you're due somewhere, perhaps at a meeting, and mumble that you only just have time to drop her off close to where she wants to be. It lulls her into a wonderful sense of false security, then lulls her into your car. Only I didn't pass any hitchhikers on the way into town. I looked, but didn't see any.

I lean against the kitchen bench, pulling at my beer, and the hooker in front of me is available and so used looking that instead of her looking better with every sip I take, she just keeps on looking worse. Her makeup has been caked on thickly. I have an idea why her lips are swollen, and know it costs sixty bucks.

"What's your name?" I ask.

"Candy."

Candy. Sure. Why not. "Call me Joe."

"I will be," she says, stepping closer to me. "So what's it to be, Joe?"

I shrug, pretty sure if I told her what it was exactly I was after, she'd make a run for the door. "Let's go upstairs." She's still carrying my briefcase for me as I lead her upstairs. I sip at my beer. It's nice and cool. Refreshing. I'll take the rest with me.

"So how long you been doing this, Candy?" I ask, always willing to expand my knowledge of how things work.

"Six months. I'm just trying to earn enough so I can afford to go through university."

I take a slight pause on the landing, her answer throwing me a little, until I realize she's just saying something she thinks I want to hear. Telling her clients she was trying to raise enough money to bail her boyfriend out of jail for selling drugs is no doubt a real turnoff.

I decide to play along with the game. "What do you want to study?"

"I want to be a lawyer. Or an actor."

"Same thing, isn't it?"

When we reach the bedroom she tosses my briefcase onto the bed. The contents jingle.

"What you got in there? Whips and stuff?"

I'm smiling, because she really has no idea. "Something like that."

She smiles, and small cracks appear in the makeup around her eyes and mouth. "I like whips and stuff, only it'll cost extra if you wanna use them."

I doubt she'll like my definition of whips and stuff. She starts loosening my tie. She unbuttons my shirt. "You've got a great chest."

She leans forward and starts kissing it. This is great. I've never done anything like this before. I reach forward and start pushing at her breasts. She starts moaning. Sounds like a shampoo commercial. Can she really be enjoying it that much?

She starts fumbling with my belt, like she wants to get this over with and say *next please* to the next guy driving along. This makes me realize she's faking her moans, that she's not enjoying this at all. I'm just another customer. Well, for me, she's just another tool. Like Fluffy the Floppy Cat.

"So what's it gonna be?"

I swallow. Hard. "Go back to the bed."

She starts walking backward, at the same time pulling her top up over her head. Her breasts are small. I'm looking at them and thinking that padded bras have a lot to answer for. The tattoo she has there is of a small dragon. It could symbolize something, or maybe it's her only friend. I walk with her. She sits on the edge of the bed and continues undoing my pants. It doesn't take her long. The buckle on my belt rattles.

I've had sex before, but never with somebody consenting, and this makes me nervous. What if she doesn't enjoy it? What if she thinks I'm no good? Will she laugh? None of the others laughed. Why would they? The enjoyment quickly fades.

I can think of only one way to bring it back.

I slam my fist into the side of her head. She jerks backward and tries to stand, but hits the edge of the bed and ends up falling onto her ass, her hands going behind her to break her fall. She looks up at me and I can't tell behind all her makeup if she's frightened or annoyed, but know it has to be at least one of them. There are tears in her eyes and for the first time she looks at least a little attractive.

"That'll cost you extra."

"I thought I could do what I wanted."

"If you want to beat me up, it'll cost you a grand."

I shrug. Lean forward. Pull her back up by her arm. "Then I better get my money's worth."

I try to drag her onto the bed, but it ends up getting difficult because my pants fall around my ankles. I grab her arm, roll her over, and twist it up her back, trying my best not to break it—but these things happen. She begins screaming, so I push her face into the bed to muffle her, and it works pretty well. I let go of her arm. It doesn't move. Just juts out at an angle I've never seen on an arm before. Her other arm is pinned beneath her. When I try to move the broken one, it grates where the bone has snapped. The pain is too much for her to struggle, so she stops fighting back.

I kick my pants off. The romance is quick and fulfilling, only it seems I keep too much pressure on the back of her head, because when I finish and pull away, I've suffocated her. It seems I can't get anything right these days. At least I've saved five hundred dollars. Or was it a thousand?

I start to get dressed. It's been a big night for me, and the effects of the combined excitement are starting to wear off, and by the time I've got my shirt buttoned up I'm starting to feel tired. The plan to kill Candy where Daniela Walker died has worked without a hitch. It will leave a message to the original killer. I can study the policemen at the station, watch them closely. One of them will become nervous. One of them will know that somebody else knows. He'll wonder what they want. He'll react. He'll be an absolute nervous wreck. He'll be easy to spot. I decide to grab the pen after all to highlight the message.

Of course it could be a matter of days, maybe weeks, before she's found, and this is a problem. If I let it go that long, then bringing Candy back here would have been for nothing. Wrinkling my shirt and getting blood on it would have been for nothing. I grab my briefcase and head downstairs first to the fridge, then to the front door, using Candy's bra to wipe down any surfaces I've touched. Tomorrow I'll phone in an anonymous tip from a pay phone, telling the police there's a body here.

It hasn't gotten any darker or any colder since spending quality time with Candy. A million stars shine down on me, making my pale skin look even paler. I park the Honda just outside of town and wipe it down. The breeze blows against my face as I turn toward home. I dump Candy's bra in a trash can outside a corner store. I pass other women on the way, most of them streetwalkers, but I don't give them a second look. I'm not an animal. I'm not going to kill somebody just because they are there. I hate guys like that. That's what makes me different from anybody else. That's my humanity.

CHAPTER THIRTEEN

My apartment is the size of a closet compared to the house I've just visited. Sometimes it's all I need. Other times it's not enough. Can't complain. Who'd listen? Well, who'd listen and still remember five seconds later?

The first thing I do when I get inside is open my briefcase and dump the folder on the table with the others I've taken over the last few months. These others are souvenirs, but I hadn't taken Daniela's folder before because there was never any point. Why keep a memento of another man's crime? I have yet to get a copy of the two victims' folders from yesterday. And one for tonight's murder won't be available for a few more days.

I watch Pickle and Jehovah for a few minutes, wondering what they are thinking, before heading to bed. I set my internal alarm clock to seven thirty and am just in the process of climbing beneath the sheets when I notice it—the answering machine. The message light is flashing. Great. I'm in my pajama shorts and not really in the mood to hear what anybody has to say to me, but I figure it's probably Mom. If I don't see what she wants, she'll only keep calling me back.

Six messages. All from her. If I don't show up, my life is going to be hell. Last time I didn't show up for dinner when it was planned, she spent all week on the phone to me, crying her heart out and forcing me to admit I'm a poor excuse for a son. I decide to take my punishment and head over there tonight.

I climb off the bus a couple of blocks before her house, go into a twenty-four-hour supermarket, and do some quick shopping. The guy behind the counter is so tired he short-changes me, but I'm having such a good day I don't point it out. Heart racing, I walk to Mom's house. Standing on the sidewalk I suck in a deep breath. The air tastes like salt. I look up at the dark sky. Is there any way of avoiding this? Short of hospitalization, the answer is no. I knock on the front door. Two minutes go by, but I know she's not in bed because the lights are on. I don't knock again. She'll open it when she's ready.

After a few minutes I hear footsteps approaching. I straighten up, not wanting her to correct my slouch, and start smiling. The door shudders, the hinges squeak, and a small gap appears.

"Do you know what time it is, Joe? I got worried. I nearly called the police. Nearly called the hospital. Do you not care about my broken heart?"

"I'm sorry, Mom."

The safety chain stops the door from opening any further. My mom, God bless her, put the safety chain on her door four years ago when the "neighborhood kids" stole her money. But she put the chain going up and down, not side to side, so all any intruder needs to do to unhook it is put his finger inside and lift. She closes the door, removes the chain, and opens it back up. I take a step inside, bracing myself, because I know it's coming.

She clips me around the ear. "Let that be a lesson to you, Joe."

"I'm sorry, Mom."

"You never come and see me anymore. It's been a week since you were last here."

"I was here last night, Mom," I say, and I've had conversations like this with her before, and will have more of them until the day she dies.

"You were here last Monday."

"And it's Tuesday now."

"No, it's Monday. You were here last Monday."

I know better than to argue, but I do point out once more that today is Tuesday.

She clips me around the ear. "Don't talk back to your mother."

"I'm not talking back, Mom, I'm just telling you what day it is."

She raises her hand and I quickly apologize, and she finally seems appeased by the gesture. "I cooked meatloaf, Joe," she tells me, lowering her hand. "Meatloaf. That's your favorite."

"You don't need to remind me."

"What do you mean?"

"Nothing." I open up the supplies I brought with me, and pull out a bunch of flowers. I hand them to her. No thorns this time.

"They're beautiful, Joe," she says, her face beaming with excitement.

She leads me through to the kitchen. I set my briefcase down on the table, open it up, and look at the knives inside. Look at the gun too. My hand rests on the handle of the Glock, and I try to take some strength from it. Mom puts the flowers into a vase, but doesn't put in any water. The rose from yesterday is gone. Perhaps she thought it was a week old. She reaches up into a cupboard and grabs hold of a packet of aspirin, and drops one into the vase.

"It keeps them alive longer," she says, turning and winking at me, as if she's letting me in on a family secret. "I saw it today on a TV show."

"You still have to add water," I point out.

"I don't think so," she says, frowning.

"I'm sure of it," I tell her.

She looks uncertain. "I'll try it my way this time," she says, "and your way next time if it doesn't work. How does that sound?"

I tell her it sounds fine. I don't tell her that adding aspirin to flowers in water doesn't make a lick of difference anyway.

"I brought something else for you, Mom."

She looks over at me. "Oh?"

I pull out a box of chocolates and hand it to her.

"You trying to poison me, Joe? Are you trying to put sugar into my cholesterol?"

Oh, Christ. "I'm just trying to be nice, Mom."

"Well, be nice by not buying me chocolates," she says, looking really annoyed at me.

"But Coke has sugar in it, Mom."

"Are you being smart?"

"Of course not."

She throws the box at me and the corner bounces off my forehead. I see stars for a few seconds. I rub my head where it hit. The box has left a small impression, but no blood.

"Your dinner's cold, Joe. I've had mine."

I put the chocolates back into my briefcase as she dishes my dinner. She doesn't offer to heat it for me, and I'm too frightened to ask. I head over to the microwave to do it myself.

"Your dinner's cold, Joe, because you let it get cold. Don't think you're going to use my electricity to warm it up."

We walk into the living room and we use her electricity to get the TV working and we sit in front of it. There's some show on—I've seen it before, but don't know what it's called. They're all the same. Bunch of white guys and girls living in an inner-city complex, laughing at everything that goes wrong for them, and there's a lot that goes wrong. I wouldn't be laughing if those things happened to me. I wonder if there's a complex like that in this city, or even in real life. If so, I wouldn't mind finding it. According to the TV the women in those complexes are damn sexy. I seem to recognize this episode but can't be sure it's a repeat since they do the same thing every week.

Mom doesn't talk to me while I eat. This is a surprise, because I generally can't shut her up. She always has something to complain about. Normally it's the price of something. I'm grateful for the silence, so much so that I consider maybe I should be late more often. The downside is her disappointment hangs over the room. I'm so used to it it's almost part of the furniture. As soon as I throw the last cold scoop of meatloaf into my mouth she uses the remote to kill the TV, then turns toward me. Her mouth sags open, she bares her teeth, and I can see the start of a sentence forming.

"If your father knew you treated me like this, Joe, he'd be rolling in his grave."

"He was cremated, Mom."

She stands up and I shrink back, expecting her to tell me off, but instead she puts her hand out for my plate. "I may as well clean up for you."

"I'll do it."

"Don't bother." She grabs my plate and I follow her into the kitchen.

"Do you want me to make you a drink, Mom?"

"What, so I'll be up all night running back and forth to the toilet?"

I open up the fridge. "Anything in here you want?"

"I've had dinner, Joe."

I need to cheer her up, so I turn the subject toward something in her element. "I was at the supermarket, Mom, and I saw they have orange juice on sale."

She turns toward me, still scrubbing at my plate, the flesh around her mouth moving aside for her beaming smile. "Really? What brand?"

"The brand you drink."

"Are you sure?"

"Positive."

"In the half gallon?"

"Yeah."

"How much?"

I can't just say three dollars. I have to be accurate. "Two ninety-nine."

I can see her thinking about it, but I don't interrupt with the answer. "That's two forty-four off. Quite a savings. Have you seen my latest jigsaw puzzle?"

It's actually two forty-six off, but I say nothing. "Not yet."

"Go and take a look. It's by the TV."

I look at the jigsaw puzzle. I mean, really look at it because I know she'll quiz me on it. A cottage. Trees. Flowers. Sky. Jigsaw puzzles are like sitcoms, I guess—they're all the fucking same. I head back into the kitchen. She's drying my plate.

"What did you think?" she asks, using a tone that suggests my answer is important to her, but only as long as it's the right answer.

"Nice."

"Did you like the cottage?"

"Yeah."

"What about the flowers?"

"Colorful."

"Which ones did you like the best?"

"The red ones. In the corner."

"The left or right corner?"

"You've only done the left corner, Mom."

Satisfied I'm telling the truth, she puts the dishes away.

Back in the lounge we sit down and continue talking.

About what, I have no idea. All I can think about is what it would be like if she lost her voice.

"I'm just going to get myself a drink, Mom. Are you sure you don't want one?"

"If it will shut you up, I will. Make it a coffee, and make it strong."

I head into the kitchen. Put the kettle on. Scoop some coffee into two cups. I grab the bag of rat poison that was also on sale at the supermarket, but not quite as good a savings as the orange juice I didn't buy, but Mom would still be proud of the savings nonetheless. I scoop a generous amount into her coffee. Mom needs her coffee strong because her taste buds are failing her. When the kettle has boiled, I stir the stuff for two minutes until it dissolves.

Back in the living room she has the TV going again but starts talking to me anyway. I hand over her drink. She adjusts the volume on the TV so she can still hear the voices while talking to me. The white guys are doing something oddly funny. I wonder how funny they would be if they lived in an apartment complex like mine. Mom hunches over and slowly drinks her drink, holding the cup defensively as if she's expecting somebody to make a grab for it. When she finishes, I offer to wash her cup. She refuses, does it herself, then complains. Since she is complaining anyway, I make a deliberate show of looking at my watch, scrunch my face up in surprise at how late it is, and tell her I really need to be going.

I have to go through the whole scenario of kissing her good-bye on the doorstep. She thanks me for the flowers and makes me promise to stay in touch, as if I'm heading to another country rather than the other side of the city. I promise I will, and she looks at me as though I'm going to ignore her for the rest of her life. It's her guilt look, and I'm familiar with it. Nonetheless, it makes me feel bad. I was already feeling bad. Bad that she is alone. Bad that I am a bad son. Sad that one day something may happen to her, God forbid.

I wave from the sidewalk but she is already gone. Where would I be without Mom? I don't know and I never want to find out.

The bus comes along and it's not the same old guy from last night, and I'm pretty sure I know why that is. This is some young guy in his midtwenties. He calls me *man*, grins at me, and because I'm the only person on the bus, he feels obliged to make conversation. I stare out the window and nod and say *yeah* when he expects it, which is far more often than I'd like. There isn't much in the way of life beyond the bus windows; the occasional taxi, the occasional person out late walking a dog, those occasions become more regular the closer we get to town, then less regular once we pass through it. I am more than three-quarters of the way home when I see it. It's just lying there on the side of the road, still moving. Kind of.

"Stop the bus," I say, standing up.

"You said . . ."

"Just stop it, okay?"

"You're the boss, buddy."

He stops the bus, and if I really was his buddy he would give me a quarter of my fare back. The swish of the doors as they close behind me, the purring of the motor, the shuddering of heavy metal, and the bus leaves me behind. We're about halfway between town and my apartment. It's a suburb where people who have made poor choices in life live. I rush over the road and crouch next to it. It's mostly white, with a few streaks of ginger through it. Its mouth is slightly open. It's not moving: maybe I made a mistake when I first saw it. When I put my hand on its side, it's still warm. Its eyes open and look at me. It tries to meow but can't. One of its legs sticks out in that same awkward way as Candy's arm.

Funny what fate does to us. Two nights ago it wasn't my place in this crazy, mixed-up world to question the fact that animals are used as tools. They're used every single day.

Chemicals are tested on them so we can have higher-quality health care, higher-quality shampoos, matching eyeliners, warmer clothes. Others are killed for food. And here's my opportunity to balance the scales for what I did to poor Fluffy.

I pick the cat up, careful to keep my hands away from its broken leg. It meows loudly and tries to struggle, but doesn't have the energy to struggle hard. The long graze down the side of its body looks bloody and raw. Its fur is matted. Strange sounds are coming from it. Rather than holding it against my body, I remove the plastic bag that the groceries came in from my briefcase and rest the cat inside. I begin to walk home.

After less than half a mile I come across a phone booth. I find the number for an all-night vet and tell them I'm on my way. Then I call a taxi. It takes five minutes to arrive. The driver is foreign and speaks the same amount of English as the cat. I've torn the page from the phone book and I hand it to him. He reads the address and starts driving. The cat is no longer meowing, but it's still alive. I let it out of the bag before stepping through the vet doors.

Inside a woman about my age waits behind a counter. She has long red hair tied in a ponytail. She wears little makeup and doesn't need it—she's a natural beauty with soft brown eyes and full lips. She's wearing a white medical jacket unbuttoned halfway down, as if she's about to step onto the set of a porn movie. Beneath it is a blue T-shirt. A great set of breasts pushes its way forward. She smiles at me for less than a second before her concern turns to the cat.

"You're the man who just called?"

"Yeah."

"You ran the cat over?" she asks in a soft voice, without managing to sound accusing.

"I found him," I say. "I don't have a car, that's why I had to catch a taxi here," I say, and for some reason it's important to me that she believes that.

She takes the cat from me without comment then disappears. I'm left standing by myself. I take a quick look around the clinic. Not much to see. Two walls are dedicated to products like leashes, collars, flea powder, bowls, cages, and food. Another wall has a thousand brochures and pamphlets that don't concern me since none of them is about getting away with murder. I take a seat. I should have been in bed by now. Should have been asleep. I stare at a display of bags of cat litter. I know from experience it's twice the price here than at the supermarket.

I sit patiently. Five minutes turn into ten, then into twenty. I pick up a pamphlet on flea control. On the cover is an artist's impression of what a magnified flea would look like if it were wearing sunglasses and a leather jacket and hosting a party in the fur of a cat. On the next page is an actual photograph of a flea, magnified several hundred times. It seems the artist had it completely wrong. I'm halfway through the brochure, thinking about how scary the world would be if fleas were actually several hundred times bigger, when the redhead comes back out. I put the pamphlet down and hold my breath and stand up.

"The cat's going to be okay," she says, breaking into a smile.

"What a relief," I say, almost too tired to mean it.

"Do you know who he belongs to?"

"No."

"We're going to need to keep him here for a few days."

"Sure, sure, that sounds good," I say, thankful for her help. I realize I'm nodding like an idiot. "Umm, what happens if you can't find the owner? I mean, it won't get put down, will it?"

She shrugs, like she doesn't know, but I think she does. I give her my name and phone number, then pay for the medical attention the cat will need using the money Candy no longer needs. She doesn't try to stop my generosity, but she does point it out. She says I'm an incredibly nice man. I see no need to argue. She tells me she will call to let me know of the cat's progress.

I ask her if she can call me a taxi, but she says she's about to leave, and offers me a lift home.

I glance at my watch. It would be fun to get a ride with her, but where would I dump her body? "I don't want to put you out. A taxi's fine."

She seems disappointed, but doesn't strengthen her offer. The taxi driver is a large man whose stomach rests on the steering wheel and toots the horn every time we go over a bump. He drops me off outside my apartment, the potholes in my street making him wake up the neighbors in the process. The trash outside my apartment has been added to by more trash, and I have to bat away a few flies as I make my way inside. I'm struggling to stay awake as I climb my way up to my door. Inside I ignore my fish, making me not quite the nice guy the vet receptionist thought I was, opting to spend some quality time with my bed instead. I lie down and close my eyes and pretty much fall right asleep.

CHAPTER FOURTEEN

Seven thirty my eyes open. Right on time. I don't have to worry about shaking away any dregs of a dream, because I never dream. I guess I don't because half the shit people dream about I actually do. If I did, I suppose it would be of being married to some plumpish woman with poor taste in everything from fashion to sexual positions. I'd be living inside a house with a mortgage that would take a lifetime to pay off, getting nagged by two unfit kids every single day. I'd be taking out trash and mowing lawns. Each Sunday morning as I pulled out of the driveway in my station wagon on my way to church, I'd have to avoid running over the dog. A Goddamn nightmare.

I share my morning routing with a feeling I can't quite shake, like there's bad news I haven't been given yet. It becomes so strong that I have to take a few minutes to sit down on the sofa and take some deep breaths. My eyes blur with tears, and even playing with Pickle and Jehovah can't cheer me up. I think of the cat I saved last night. That can't cheer me up either. Something bad has happened. I think of Mom and hope she's okay.

I make myself a quick breakfast before going to work. No need to walk around hungry just because of bad premonitions. I'm running late so have to run for the bus. Mr. Stanley sees me coming and waits. "Almost missed you this morning, Joe," he says, and this time he punches my ticket—perhaps as punishment for putting him thirty seconds off schedule. Despite that, I still like him. He's an okay guy.

Now, Mr. Stanley lives my nightmare. He's married with two kids, one of them in a wheelchair. I know all this because I followed him home one day. Not as a potential victim (though everybody has potential, so I learned in school), but just out of curiosity. It's amazing that a guy with a useless kid and an ugly wife and a crappy job can be so friendly every day. Perhaps more suspicious than amazing. I want to ask him what his secret is.

I walk down the aisle. Find a seat behind a couple of businessmen. The two of them are talking loudly about money, mergers, and acquisitions. I wonder who they are trying to impress on this bus. Maybe each other.

Mr. Stanley stops the bus directly outside work for me. The doors open. I climb out. It's another hot summer day. It will get somewhere around eighty-five or ninety degrees, I'm guessing. I lower the zip on my overalls from my neck down to my waist, revealing my white T-shirt, and I roll up my sleeves. There haven't been any scratches on my arms for nearly two months.

The air shimmers. The day is still. It's classic global warming weather. I wait for two cars to run the red light before I cross the road. Outside the police station the drunks from the night's holding tanks are being let out, their faces scrunched up in the bright autumn sun.

The air in the police station is cool. Sally is waiting outside the elevator. She spots me before I can make a dash for the stairs, so I have to head over. I push the button, then keep pushing it because it's what's expected of somebody with no clue how things in this world work.

"Morning, Joe," she says in the carefully structured, drawn-out way of a woman struggling with the concept of speech. I have to offer my own version of it, because retarded or not, everybody around here expects me to talk like an imbecile.

"Hi morning, Sally," I say, and then I smile the big-kid smile with all the teeth, the one that suggests I'm proud to have strung three words together to make a sentence, even if I did fuck it up.

"What a beautiful day. Do you like this weather, Joe?"

Actually it's a bit hot for my taste. "I like the warm sun. I like summer." I'm talking like an idiot so Slow Sally can understand me. "I like Christmas even more."

"You should join me for lunch by the river," she says, hitting on me and almost making me gag. I can just imagine how much fun that'd be. How much fun I'd have as the other people walk by looking at one person pretending to be retarded while the other pretends to be normal. We could throw bread at the ducks and tell each other which clouds look like pirate ships and which look like the bloated corpses of drowning victims. Damn, does Sally even know she isn't normal? Do their kind know that about themselves?

The elevator arrives. I'm confused as to whether I should do the gentlemanly thing and let her step in first, or do the retarded thing and push ahead of her? I do the gentlemanly thing, because the retarded thing means I'd have to scream as the elevator goes up a few stories and then pretend to be in awe at how the scenery has changed when the doors open.

"Fourth floor, Joe?"

"Sure."

The doors close.

"So . . ." she says, then doesn't finish.

"So?"

"So what'll it be? You want to join me for lunch?"

"I like my office, Sally. I like sitting there and looking out the window."

"I know you do, Joe. But outside is good for you."

"Not always."

She seems to think about this, then slowly nods, but her gaze is distant and it looks like she's agreeing to something I haven't said. Then her eyes snap back into focus and she smiles at me. "Well, I made you some lunch again. I'll drop it by."

"Thanks."

"Do you enjoy catching the bus home?"

"Huh? Sure," I say, and the rate the elevator is moving at makes me think the fourth floor has been raised a few levels. "I guess so."

"I can give you a lift sometimes, if you'd like."

"I like the bus."

She shrugs, gives up on our conversation. "I'll drop off those sandwiches for you soon."

"Thanks, Sally. That'll be nice."

And it would be nice. Sally may be a dimwit, she may have a crush on me, but she's always been good to me. Always friendly. Nobody else has ever offered me food, or offered me a lift home (though surely she can't drive—she must mean a lift with her mom or something), and I could do a lot worse. Even though I don't like her, I don't not like her as much as I don't like everybody else. In a way that makes her the closest thing I have to a friend. Outside of my goldfish.

The doors close, and the smile I offer Sally as they do isn't forced, it's natural, and I realize this too late to change it to my big-boy grin. She stares at me with a blank look on her face, then the doors close and Sally is gone, and a moment later she is gone from my thoughts. I head straight to the conference room.

"Hi there, Joe."

"Morning, Detective Schroder."

I start looking at him as a suspect, trying to picture him killing Walker. It's easy to do. Of course it's easy to picture any of these people killing her, from the photographer to the pathologist. The first thing I need to do is get a list of these people, then begin eliminating them. As suspects, that is.

"How's the in . . . inv . . . invest . . ." I stop. Just long enough for him to think I'm in that small percentile of the population with an extra chromosome. "How's the case going, Detective Schroder? Found the killer yet?"

He shakes his head slowly, as if he's trying to line up a few thoughts in there, but not too hard in case some of them get broken.

"Not yet, Joe. Getting there."

"Any suspects, Detective Schroder?"

"A few. And Joe, you can call me Carl."

I'm not going to call him Carl. He's asked me before. Anyway, I've already shortened *detective inspector* to just *detective*. And as for there being a few suspects—he's lying.

He stares at the photographs, grimacing, like he does every morning now. Almost as though he's expecting to come in and find one of the victims has reached out from her portrait and written an answer up there for him. In reality he has nothing. He knows it. I know it. Everybody knows it. Especially the media.

"Are you sure they've all been killed by the same person, Detective Schroder?"

He turns and stares at me, and I regret my question. "Why's that, Joe? Have you been listening in on our conversations?"

I shake my head. "No, never," I say. "I would never do that."

He doesn't look convinced.

"I just thought that maybe seven different people killed them because nobody can be that mean, can they?" I ask.

His expression softens, and slowly he shakes his head. "People can be that mean, Joe, and it's probably best you stop trying to think like Sherlock Holmes."

I look down. "Umm . . . I was just, you know, curious."

"Life is curious, Joe, and to answer your question, all of these murders all related."

I lift my head up fast and look over at him, widening my eyes in what hopefully looks like surprise. "They're all sisters, Detective Schroder?"

I ought to get a Goddamn Emmy for this performance.

"Not related that way, Joe," he sighs, and after a pause of a few seconds he carries on. "I mean they were all killed by the same person."

"Oh. But that's good, right? Better to have one killer out there than seven?"

He nods. "It doesn't make any difference to them," he says, pointing at the photographs. "But in this case," he says, then pauses, "you're not going to repeat any of this to anybody, are you, Joe? You don't have friends in the media?"

I shake my head, trying to keep a similar pace to Schroder's shake a few minutes ago. He thinks I have no friends. He doesn't know about Pickle and Jehovah. "You guys are the only friends I have, Detective Schroder."

"Have you ever heard of a copycat killer, Joe?"

I stop shaking my head before whiplash sets in. "Why would somebody kill cats?" There's another long sigh from Schroder, and I realize I might be laying it on a bit thick.

"Not quite, Joe. A copycat killer is somebody who kills to imitate a serial killer."

"Why would they do that?"

"Because they can. Because they want to. Because they're insane."

"Oh. Then why are these people out there, Detective Schroder? Why don't they get put in jail?"

"That's a good question," he says, and I smile at his praise. "And it comes with a simple answer. The world is screwed up. You know when you turn on the news and some bastard has gone and shot his family and a few of his neighbors?"

I start nodding. Stab thy neighbor. I'm familiar with it.

"The family, the other neighbors, they all say what a quiet guy he was. He had a collection of gun magazines and problems. Then we use hindsight as a preventative, even though it's too late by then. There's nothing to prevent, because everybody's already dead. . . . I'm sorry, Joe," he says, sighing. "I'm rambling on a bit. And venting. I shouldn't be burdening you with any of this."

"I don't mind."

"I just wish we could do more. I mean, we see these guys every day, but can we do anything about it? No. Because they have rights. Just like the rest of us. And until they finally kill somebody—and they often try to—those rights make them untouchable. Do you know what I mean, Joe?"

"Kind of, Detective Schroder."

He waves his hand at the wall. "A hundred to one we've spoken to this guy at some point in the past. We know he's got either a drug or a mental problem, but we could never do anything about it. Right now he's watching us, mocking us, laughing at us. I guarantee we've wanted to lock this guy up before, but weren't allowed. I guarantee we've had this guy in this building before."

He's right and wrong, but I can't point this out to him. Can't take a bet on his odds. With all his sermonizing I quickly lose faith in Schroder as an appropriate suspect.

"I understand, Detective Schroder."

"You'd be one of the few if you do, Joe. You want to know something funny?"

"Sure."

"Serial killers like to stay ahead of the game, and you know how they do that?"

Fact is, I do know. They hang around the edges of the investigation. They might come into the station and say they saw something going on. They come in and try to get a feel for the investigation. Some even hang around in cop bars, listening to idle chitchat, even participating in conversation. Or hang out with reporters looking for an inside scoop.

"No. How?"

He shrugs again. "Sorry, Joe, I shouldn't be chewing your ear off like this."

"So what about the cat killer?" I ask.

"Some other time," he sighs, and he says it in a way to indicate the conversation is over. I leave him staring silently at the wall of the dead.

I reach up and run my finger across the nameplate on my office door. To the sides of it are four small screw holes. There never used to be anything on it until Sally showed up one day with a small sign with my name on it. Inside I swap my thoughts for a mop and bucket, and then go about cleaning the toilets. Before lunch I carry the vacuum cleaner into Detective Superintendent Stevens's office just as he is leaving. Stevens is the guy everybody answers to, even though he doesn't do any of the footwork, groundwork, or thought work that goes into solving this case. Stevens has been flown down from Wellington, and is one of the highest-ranking detectives in the country, though I can't see why. All he does is sit in his appointed office, ordering people about while demanding answers. Occasionally he walks back and forth, grabbing a pile of papers or a folder, just trying to look as though he has something to do or someplace to be. Most of the time he's a pretty pissed-off guy. I don't like him, but can't do anything about it. Murdering a police superintendent would be like playing with fire.

Stevens is in his late fifties, has thinning black hair, and looks like the sort of policeman you wouldn't approach for help. He is just over six feet and solidly built, but has these black eyes that any author would associate with crazed serial killers. He has a long face with wrinkles that run its entire length, like shallow knife wounds. His tanned skin is pitted with old acne scars around his neck. When he talks, he has a deep voice and an accent that sounds Caribbean, but that's probably because of the cigars he's always smoking. He's one of those useless bastards who wear sports jackets with elbow patches sewn into them.

I wonder if the ballpoint pen that was left behind was his. I look into his black eyes, searching for the evil that fiction suggests should be there, but I can't see any of it.

He tells me to do a good job, says he'll be back after lunch. That gives me plenty of time. So it's just me in his office, me and Mr. Vacuum Cleaner. I sweep it around the carpet like it makes a difference, looking left and right for any information that will help. Like the conference room, Stevens's office looks out onto the fourth floor, meaning people can look in if the blinds are open, as they are. Ten minutes of sucking the same piece of carpet go by, and it's not getting any cleaner. I drop a rag behind his desk, bend down, and use the chance to peek into his desk drawers. I rummage through them, finding a roster of everybody involved in the case in the third drawer I check. I slip it into my overalls. Then I start coughing. Yep, Joe the retard needs a drink. I head to the water cooler. On the way back I pass the photocopying room. It's empty, so I step inside and photocopy the roster. Walk back to the office. Place the document back into the folder. Finish vacuuming in time for lunch.

The sun is shining through my office window, so I sit in front of it and pretend I'm getting a tan. I'd have to pretend really hard for other people to see it. Sally knocks on my door, then steps in and hands me a small parcel of food. I give her a small *thank you* in return. She asks me again if I want to join her outside, and I make the mistake of saying maybe next time. She positively beams at this before she leaves. I stare out the window on the chance I might see her out there, but my view doesn't overlook the river so the only people I see are strangers. On the horizon I see something I haven't seen in weeks—rain clouds. They're too far away to tell which direction they're moving.

I eat my sandwiches while looking at the list. With over ninety names on it, ninety-four to be exact, it's pretty big. I don't know what I expected—maybe half a dozen or so—but ninety-four suggests a lot of people running around not knowing what's going on. Dozens more officers took statements, but it's only the detectives who work the scene. Only the detectives who see the body.

I begin to panic: this could take me forever. The feeling that this is going to be a big waste of time is creeping deep into my thoughts. But not all of the people on this list would have been to each of the crime scenes, right? Maybe half of them at each one, maybe not even that. The trick is to figure out which of these ninety-four people went to Daniela Walker's house.

Call sheets.

Daniela was discovered late on a Friday night. Therefore, several phone calls had to have been made to the people who are on this list. None of the detectives would have been working that late. They were off eating with their wives or girlfriends and were interrupted with the news that dinner was over. Only one of them already knew, because one of them had built up an appetite by strangling Daniela and throwing her pen across the wall. Lunch isn't over yet, but I'm too excited to keep eating. I head into the records room and give it a good spring cleaning. I take extra time near the hard copy of the phone records, giving the area around it an extremely thorough polishing.

On the night Daniela Walker was killed, fifteen phone calls out of twenty were successfully made. These are the people who showed up. Fifteen people, plus however many officers showed up on the scene to report it.

The original phone call made from the victim's husband to police dispatch is here too. I start reading, but find it has little interest.

Dispatch sent the nearest car to the scene to begin con-

trolling things before the cavalry arrived. Two officers. Their
names are on my list. I circle them. I also circle the fifteen
called that night—including the pathologist, the photographer, and Detective Superintendent Stevens with the jet-
black eyes.

This means I've just cut nearly eighty people off my suspect
list. The fear I have of this being a waste of time creeps away.
I'm down to seventeen people. I doubt the two officers who
first responded to the husband's call have anything to do with
her death. First of all, they were together for the previous six
hours on their shift, and the body was discovered only an hour
after she was killed. Second, what are the chances that the
person who killed her was the very officer called to the scene?
Pretty low, that's what. I cross their names off the list.

Fifteen people.

I think about the pathologist. He found several differences
between this body and the others. Because he works alone, he
could have easily manufactured evidence to make the residues
and fibers on this victim identical to the others, but he didn't.
Who was going to check his work? Nobody. That's who. If he
had killed her, the results would be identical to the others.
But they're not.

So it isn't him.

Fourteen people.

Could this be any easier?

I glance at my watch. It is nearly four o'clock. I have been
in here all afternoon, cleaning the room for most of that.
The smell of furniture polish is close to making me gag, and
I'm getting concerned about how my lungs are looking after
breathing in a couple of cans. I head back to my office, grabbing a coffee on the way and pausing in the conference room
to switch audiotapes.

Back in my office the sun is no longer streaming in, instead
one of the rain clouds is covering it, but the cloud is still holding onto its payload. I can't remember the last time I saw rain.

When I sit and look at the list again, I see something obvious I missed while in the records room. Of the fourteen left, four are women. I cross them off the list. I could have narrowed down the original ninety-four the same way, but it doesn't matter now. Ten people. I write their names onto a fresh piece of paper, then sit there staring at them until four thirty comes along and says hello. I say good-bye to everybody who crosses my path on the way out of the building. Sally isn't among them. On the way to the bus stop I remember the feeling I had this morning that something was wrong with my mother, and I chide myself for being foolish. If something had happened I would have got the bad news by now.

I catch the bus home. The trash outside my house has been collected. I lie down on my bed. Stare at the ceiling. I've narrowed down the suspects to ten people. The police have narrowed theirs down to about ten phone directories. I glance at my watch. I can't lie down on the bed forever. Ceiling isn't interesting enough for that. I get to my feet and grab my briefcase. There's still plenty of work to do.

CHAPTER FIFTEEN

The smile has been with her all day. From the moment the elevator doors closed on Joe's smile, she's been able to think of little else. She's always thought his big, expressionistic smiles were so natural, so pure, because they were the same as Martin's. But this morning's smile was something different. Pure? She thinks so. Joe has a pure soul, but there is something about it, something she is struggling to recognize. In those few seconds Joe was more of a man than a boy, more sophisticated than clumsy. There was a spark there that suggested Joe is more of everything else than she had thought.

But what, exactly?

She likes to think that it means Joe likes her, that their friendship is moving along the way she wants. Of course, it might have been a fluke. Joe might have been staring off into space as he is apt to do when she is around him.

Yet there is no denying that it didn't only make him look grown-up, it made him more . . . more . . . attractive?

Sadly, the answer is yes. Joe is attractive, and she had never noticed it before. She doesn't want to think about it now, either, because she finds it confusing.

She spends the day at work fixing a section of faulty air-conditioning. It's a job that has taken the last few weeks of her time. It breaks down every year or two, and the government isn't prepared to budget more money for police, let alone make their surroundings slightly more comfortable. So she does what she can—stopgap measures that will keep it working until the day those measures fall short.

Yet her mind keeps returning to Joe. She's sure he doesn't know that he's not the only cleaner employed here. After six o'clock every night, well after Joe has gone home, a team of cleaners come through and do their thing. They vacuum, wipe, dust, sanitize the bathrooms, refill the paper towel dispensers, clean and put away the dishes in the coffee rooms, replace dirty towels with clean ones, and empty the trash cans. Some of these things Joe will do once a week, or once every few weeks, but he doesn't know other people are taking care of them every single day. Joe is here during the day to keep things tidy and, she suspects, to keep people happy. Special people like Joe can struggle to find work, and in a world where they must contribute, where they must fend for themselves, sometimes the government must step in and create positions for them. She knows nobody has told Joe he's not alone in his profession here because it might shatter the image he has of his importance. Sweet, sweet Joe.

She doesn't see Joe when she leaves work. Only a few people finish at four thirty, and because of her father's illness, she's one of them. She heads down Cashel Mall, a shopping street that runs through the center of town that's a few blocks from the Christchurch Cathedral, the city's most iconic church that's made of stone and was built well over a hundred years ago. She tried once to go inside and sit in the silence, only there wasn't any—too many tourists for that. She doesn't make it as far as the church today, instead she pauses outside shop windows and occasionally goes inside, searching, hunting, trying to find a gift for her dad that he will appreciate. She needs a card too. Something funny. Something that for the briefest of moments will take his mind off his failing body and her late brother. Just what do you buy for the parent who's losing everything?

The answer is a DVD player. With the salesman's advice, she finds the simplest-to-use player in her price range, and she chooses four classic westerns she's confident her father will love. All have Clint Eastwood in them. Could there be anything better?

She carries her purchases back to her car, pausing only to give Henry another small bag of sandwiches. She wonders if a guy like Henry ever tries to save for anything. How hard it must be to have goals in life when you have nothing. It's not like the poor guy can buy a suit and go to a job interview. It's not like he can show up to one dressed the way he is. She thinks she ought to try and help him out there.

"Jesus loves you," he reminds her, opening the bag. "Remember that, Sally, and everything will be okay."

By the time she reaches her car, she feels like crying. Not even thinking about Joe's smile can cheer her back up.

CHAPTER SIXTEEN

I pull out the latest cassette tape from the conference room and listen to the private words falling from the small speaker of my recorder as I pace back and forth. Not just hear, but really listen. I've heard all of the other tapes over the months, but I was only ever listening to see how the investigation was going. Now I have something new to listen for.

Detective Taylor is for the theory that they're looking for more than one killer.

So is Detective McCoy, who suspects the killers are working together.

Detective Hutton is still of the opinion that it's one person. Other theories. Mixed theories. Confused theories.

A confused investigation is a messy investigation. Nobody can agree. Nothing gets done. This makes people hard to catch. Makes things good for me.

I make some dinner. Nothing exciting. Instant pasta that cooks quickly in the microwave, and some coffee. Then I change into something more casual—jeans and a shirt. I'm looking pretty good, better than good. I put on a dark jacket. Even better.

I'm just about to go out when the phone rings. My first thought is that it's Mom, and then I remember the bad feeling I had this morning, so my next thought is it may not *be* Mom, but somebody calling *about* Mom. I have no idea where it comes from, but an image of making funeral arrangements and sausage rolls for the after-funeral party flashes through my mind. I sit to prepare for the shock that will put both my investigation and my life on hold. My heart races as I put my hand out to the receiver. Please, God, don't let it be so. Don't let anything bad happen to my mother.

I pick it up and do my best to sound calm. "Hello?"

"Joe? Is that you?"

"Mom, boy, am I glad to hear from you," I say, the words coming out in one long clump.

"It's your mother. I've been trying to ring you all day."

I look at my answering machine. The little light isn't flashing. "You didn't leave any messages."

"You know I don't like talking to a machine." This, of course, is a fallacy. Mom will talk to anything if the opportunity is there. "Are you coming to see me tonight, Joe?"

"It's Wednesday."

"I know what day it is, Joe. You don't need to tell me what day it is. I just thought you might want to come around and visit your mother."

"I can't. I've got plans."

"A girlfriend?"

"No."

"Oh. I see. Well, I wish you weren't—"

"I'm not gay, Mom."

"You're not? I thought that maybe—"

"What do you want, Mom?"

"I thought you might want to come and see me after I was sick all night."

"Sick?"

"More than sick, Joe. I've been up all night sitting on the toilet," she says, and already that's more information than I needed. Before I can stop her or shoot myself she carries on. "I had stomach pains. I've never experienced anything like it. I was squirting water." I look around my room for a security blanket, something to keep me in reality, to stop me from fainting. To kill the imagery. Luckily I'm sitting down. Luckily I was expecting a shock. "The diarrhea was so bad, Joe, I spent an hour running back and forth soiling my nightgown before deciding to spend the whole night in there. I ended up taking a blanket because it was cold, and I took my jigsaw puzzle in with me to stop the boredom. I actually got the other corner done. It's looking good. You should come around and see it."

"Good thinking," I hear myself say.

"I didn't even need to push, Joe. It was just falling out of me like, well, like water out of a garden hose."

"Uh huh. Uh huh." To me my words sound like they're coming from a mile away.

"I felt so sick."

"I'm sorry, Mom, I'll come over one night soon and help, okay?"

"Okay, Joe, but—"

"I've really got to go, Mom. Taxi's waiting. Love you."

"Well, okay, Joe, I love—"

"Bye, Mom." I hang up.

I go to the sink. Gulp down a glass of water. Rinse out my mouth and pour a second glass thinking I need something stronger, then remembering the beers I transferred from the Walker fridge. I grab one and pop it open with the Walker bottle opener. Pictures of my mother sitting on the toilet with a thousand-piece jigsaw puzzle on a board on a stool in front of her and soiled underwear around her ankles are hard to shake. Cottage . . . blue sky . . . flowers . . . trees. I walk over to the sofa and sit down with my fish. I feed them, and a second later, the phone rings. What does she want now? To tell me how many sheets of toilet paper she used? I let the machine get it.

It's the woman from the veterinary clinic. She identifies herself as Jennifer, and tells me the cat is doing fine. She tells me they've had no luck in finding the cat's owner. She asks me to call her, and adds that she'll be at work until two in the morning.

I finish the beer and say good-bye to my fish and am just heading out the door when I suddenly remember I have done nothing about Candy—haven't made the anonymous call I was supposed to make. I'll wait now until I narrow down my list. It will be easier to watch for Daniela's killer when there are only a few names left.

Because the police have no leads, I have no time limit for solving my own case. I can take days or weeks. However, I have this competitive streak inside me. Right now it's ordering me around, telling me to keep focused and sort out this investigation. I want to prove to myself I can do this, and do it well. I want to prove I'm better than the police, not just at eluding them, but at solving their own case. What sort of man doesn't try to better himself? What sort of man doesn't test himself?

Another part of me, the more recreational side, is suggesting why not make it harder for the police? Throw in another victim to investigate? When investigations deal with only one victim, the police can take statements from two or three hundred people, even a thousand. They cross-reference these statements in an attempt to draw a map of the person's activities that day. Toss in another victim, and the number of statements doubles, and so does the workload. They spend less time with the people from the previous killing, and close to none with the people before that. One trail is fresh while the others get cold. Soon they stop focusing on the evidence, and wait for the next victim, hoping that will be where they catch a break in their case. They become increasingly understaffed and overworked. A stressed detective is a sloppy detective. Kill two people in a row, and all previous statements are tossed into a pile beneath a conference room table in a large box.

I vacuum around them every couple of days or so.

I catch the bus into town. Getting into a police station is easy when you work there and have a swipe card to open one of the side doors. I do just that, and step into a rear stairwell. I know a record is taken each time an ID card is swiped, but there is no reason for the records to ever be checked. If they are, and I get asked, I'll simply say I got confused about the time, or that I came to get my lunchbox. I make my way to the fourth floor, taking the stairs. Less risky this way. I encounter nobody. Detectives, unlike beat patrol officers, work gentlemen's hours. Unless a homicide is reported, or one is in the process of being solved, the detectives work from nine o'clock until five thirty. After that they go home, and the cubicles, the conference room, and the offices are close to empty.

I take another look at the conference room wall. The prostitute I killed last night is still to be discovered. Same with the woman I stuffed into the trunk at the long-term parking garage. Not wanting to hang around, I quickly swap the cassette tapes and leave. The microcassette recorder I use has a voice-activated system. This allows the unit to be left on standby mode, where it won't actually start recording until it hears sound. When the sound stops, it stops, so I can leave it on and there will be no wasted tape. I also replace the batteries.

Of the ten names on my list, only a few work on this floor. Some of the others don't even work in this building, but have come here from other cities to help with the investigation. The chances are high that it's going to be one of these men—taking the opportunity of killing while away from the wife and family is pretty hard to turn down.

I decide to begin with the first name on my list.

Detective Wilson Hutton has been a detective far, far longer than I've been cleaning, and he has been overeating far,

far longer than he's been a detective. He, like the others, likes me. I move down the aisle, glancing at the cubicles to my left and right, double-checking that I'm alone. Most of the ceiling lights have been turned off. Only every fifth one is going, so it's pretty dim, like being outside under a quarter moon. This gives the place a slight look of life, while also saving power. It also enables staff to come here and not knock themselves out on furniture. I can hear the slight humming of the lights. The ticking of the air-conditioning. But I can't hear a single person. The floor has the feeling of an empty house. Like a tomb. No glowing desk lamps, no squeaking office chairs, no shifting of weight, or a cough, or a yawn. Things look tidier in this light. Cleaner. That's because an hour and a half after I leave, a team of cleaners comes in and spends two hours doing all the things they think I'm too stupid to manage. Nobody has ever mentioned it to me. Maybe they think I think a team of magic trash fairies comes in and makes things sparkly and clean.

I find Hutton's cubicle and sit down. He's a big guy, and the ass groove in his reinforced office chair reflects this as I try to get comfortable. At forty-eight years old, he's a candidate for a heart attack, and it wouldn't surprise me if he has already had several minor ones. The only exercise I've ever seen him do is chew junk food. I feel nauseous just sitting in his chair. I also feel like I'm putting on weight.

I turn on his lamp. Staring at me is a name plaque sitting on his desk, probably a gift from his wife. It says *Detective Inspector Wilson Q. Hutton*. I don't know what the Q stands for. Probably *queer*. I look at the photographs of his family that he's pinned to the inside wall. His wife has similar weight issues, but her problems don't end there. The hair on her arms and legs, and the small splashes on her face, look like wool. The couple looks happy together. I cross his name off the list and flick off the lamp. Mr. Doughnut didn't do this. It isn't possible. He would have come close to dying just chasing the victim up those stairs, and I doubt his ability to gain an erection—something the killer repeatedly used. Though he must have used one at least twice: there are two overweight children in the photographs.

Nine people left.

I push the chair back into the position it had been in, which isn't hard to find. The carpet is nearly worn through where the casters normally sit. So is the floor beneath it. I move into the opposite cubicle.

Detective Anthony Watts has been with the police department for twenty-five years, a detective for the last twelve. I'm considering him as my next suspect as I sit down and flick on his lamp. There's a photograph here. Watts and his wife sharing a happy moment together. Jesus, these people get happy and some prick has to take a picture as proof.

Once again I begin to see things for what they are. Watts has that wrinkled look that comes with being sixty. He has gray hair, but not a lot of it left. I'm trying to imagine him having the strength to fight Daniela, let alone strangle her, but I can't do it. So I try to imagine him raping her in the way she'd been raped. Can't see him doing that either. Watts just doesn't have it in him. Daniela didn't have him in her.

I cross him off the list. Turn off his lamp. Push his chair back into place.

Eight suspects. I'm beginning to enjoy myself.

The center aisle, once it reaches the end of this floor, branches into a T formation. I go left, directly to Detective Shane O'Connell's cubicle.

Here I don't even bother sitting down. O'Connell, a forty-one-year-old detective with the ability to solve cases that involve signed confessions and not much more, broke his arm three weeks before the murder. His arm had been in a cast when Walker was killed. Even if he did have the strength to do this, there were no suggestions of plaster fibers found on the body or on the bed.

Seven suspects.

The next stop and two cubicles along for me is Detective Brian Travers. I slip in and flick on his desk lamp. No photographs of family here—all I'm seeing are swimsuit calendars. This year's, last year's, and the year's before that. I can well understand his hesitancy in throwing away the old calendars.

I flick back through last year's calendar. Look at the date Walker was murdered. He hasn't marked anything on it. I flick through an old desk calendar and see the same thing. There isn't any note saying "Kill bitch tonight. Buy milk."

I open the desk drawers and rummage around. Look through files, folders, any scrap piece of paper, but there is nothing here relevant to the case. I find nothing to suggest his guilt. Or his innocence. I listen to his phone messages with the volume turned down low. I tip back the trash can under his desk, but it's empty.

Travers is in his midthirties. He has a lean and strong body. Just under six feet, he has the type of casual good looks that easily attract women and could get him off on a rape charge with the *He's so clean cut he could have any woman he wanted* defense, which juries still fall for. He doesn't have a wife, and if he has a girlfriend, unless she's Miss January, he hasn't put up any pictures of her.

I put a question mark next to his name.

Still seven suspects.

I continue on my merry way and sit down behind the desk of Detective Lance McCoy. I start out with the same procedure I used in Travers's cubicle. McCoy is in his early forties, married, with two kids. The photograph telling me all this sits in a small frame on his desk, center stage. Other pictures hang on the walls of his cubicle. His wife looks ten years younger than him. His daughter is quite attractive, but his son looks like a moron. McCoy is a dedicated family man, I can tell just by sitting here in his extremely tidy cubicle. Small mottoes are pasted around the place, on coffee cups and notepads and plaques: *Work to live not live to work*, and *Sloppiness leads to a path of depression*. I look for but can't find one that says *The only good bitch is a dead bitch*, so I can't have him as my lead suspect. I can't find any notes that he's made on the case. I put a small question mark next to his name.

Seven suspects. Isn't this supposed to be getting easier? I check my watch. It's nine thirty-five, but my internal clock tells me it is only eight thirty, so something must be out of whack. When I enter Detective Bill Landry's office—yes, an office, not a cubicle—I confirm that my watch spoke the truth. Like Schroder and many of the other detectives, Landry is involved with trying to solve other crimes and finding other killers. A few months ago bodies were found in a lake in a cemetery, making me not the only serial killer in town—which, I have to say, is actually pretty annoying. It would have been great to have been the only one, just as it would have been great to have been the first. Before recently, the country had only ever seen one serial killer, and that was a guy who had a thing for killing prostitutes, and that was twenty years ago, a guy by the name of Jack Hunter who the media called "Jack the Hunter," a cute allusion to Jack the Ripper.

Of course being the optimist, I can also see the positive side of there being another serial killer on the loose. It keeps the police busy.

Landry has been helpful by making a list of notes that point out how different the Walker scene is from the others. He wouldn't do that if he were the killer. In fact his notes have the word *copycat* at the top of the first page, with a ring around it and a question mark next to it.

I cross Landry off my list. Then I head back up the center aisle and directly to Detective Superintendent Dominic Stevens's office. Fumble with the lock. Eight seconds.

I close the blinds and use the small flashlight I've brought along with me. Sneaking around in Stevens's office is far more obvious than sneaking around the cubicles. There's a copy of a report he has written for his superiors on his desk. It explains in detail where the investigation is, which, in simple terms, is nowhere. It explains the running theories, while adding his theory that Daniela Walker was killed by somebody different. He recommends a separate investigation into her death. If Stevens is the killer, he sure as hell wouldn't do that. I cross him off the list.

Five suspects left, and I'm starting to get the bad feeling I could end up crossing all of them off over the next few days, that I'm overlooking something.

When eleven o'clock rolls around I decide it's time to go. I catch the bus toward home, but get off a half mile or so before my street hoping a walk in the fresh air will help clear my mind. It's a beautiful night. There's a nor'wester blowing like a cure for anybody feeling down. Same nor'wester that irritates everybody else. Weather's great like that.

But I'm not interested in making a forecast.

Ahead of me are more long days and plenty of late nights, so I hit the sack the moment I get inside. I realize I didn't call Jennifer about the cat, but that can wait. Right now I'm just too busy falling asleep.

CHAPTER SEVENTEEN

At two minutes past eight I'm sitting on the edge of my bed covered in sweat. For the first time in years, I've dreamed. Though the sensation wasn't entirely unpleasant, the dream certainly was. I was a policeman, investigating myself for murder. Attempting to coerce a confession, I played good cop, bad cop. Yet I wouldn't give in. Instead I suggested and then mimed a rather lewd act to myself, which was followed by a demand for a lawyer. When a lawyer did arrive, it was Daniela Walker. She looked exactly as she had in her photograph. The bruises around her neck were like a string of black, deformed pearls. She never blinked, not once, her glazed-over eyes staring at me the entire time. Her only words were to tell me to confess to her murder. She repeated them over and over like a mantra. I was confused and confessed to a whole bunch of murders. Then the walls of the interrogation cell slid away as if I were in a game show, revealing a court of law. There was a judge and a jury and a lawyer. I recognized none of them. There was even a band. One of those old swing-time bands with guys dressed in suits. They were holding up freshly polished brass instruments but none of them were playing. Even with a guilty plea on offer, there was still a jury, and the jury found me guilty. So did the judge. The judge sentenced me to death. The band started playing the same song I'd heard on Angela's stereo, and as they played, the two businessmen I saw on the bus yesterday rolled in an electric chair. I woke just after the clamps of the electric chair locked my arms and legs into place.

I can smell burning flesh even now as I sit on the edge of my bed. This is the first time my internal alarm clock has ever let me down. I close my eyes and try to push the big buttons inside to reset it. Why did I dream? How is it I've slept in? Because I'm trying to do something good? Could be. I'm trying to give Daniela Walker's family closure, and that doesn't feel right. I must suffer for my humanity.

I don't want to miss my bus, so I skip breakfast. Can't make myself lunch either, so I toss some fruit into my briefcase, then race out the door. I don't even have time to feed my fish. The day is overcast and muggy. Warm and lethargic. This is worse than a sun-shining-hot day. I'm already sweating by the time Mr. Stanley refuses to punch my ticket.

I walk down the aisle and sit behind the same businessmen who were in my dream, making me suspect for a moment that I'm still in it, and I watch the walls of the bus to see if they give way to another court of law and another swing-time band. They don't. The businessmen are already talking loudly. Business this. Money that. I begin to imagine what they do in their spare time. If they're not sleeping with each other, they're probably married to women who are having affairs. I doubt they would have the courage to dump their bitches if they found out they were being cheated on. And I don't mean divorce.

Sally is waiting for me outside the police station. No shimmering heat today. Just wet heat, helped by the thick clouds above that are light gray over the city, but black out to sea.

Still no signs of rain, though. Sally looks as though she's trying to figure something out, as if she knows me, but can't place exactly who I am. Then her face brightens and she reaches out and touches me on the shoulder. I don't feel the need to pull away.

"How are you, Joe? Feeling up to another hard day at work?"

"Sure. I like working here. I like the people."

She seems about to say something, then closes her mouth and opens it again. She's fighting with something, and ends up losing the battle. Her arm falls back to her side.

"I'm sorry, Joe, but I didn't get to make you lunch today."

I'm not sure whether she makes the lunch, whether she buys it, or whether her mom makes it for her not knowing it's for me, but when my face sags a little at the news, it's genuine. "Oh. Okay, then," I say, not knowing what I'm going to do. No breakfast. No made lunch. Just some crappy fruit in my briefcase to last me all day. Why the hell did I think two days of her bringing me food was the start of a pattern?

"It's my dad's birthday today."

"Happy birthday."

She smiles. "I'll pass that along."

The air-conditioning is working in the foyer. One day it does, the next it won't. The old maintenance worker who used to work here must have died: I haven't seen him for a while. Sally used to work for him, doing things like grabbing rags and washing tools. The sort of thing that warms people's hearts, seeing the trolley-pushers of this world given a low-paying, shit-eating job that gives them a place in society.

"What did you do before you came to clean here, Joe?" she asks.

"Ate breakfast."

"No, I mean a few years ago, before you started this job."

"Oh. I don't know. Not much. Nobody wanted to give somebody like me a job."

"Somebody like you?"

"You know."

"You're special, Joe. Remember that."

I remember that the whole way up to my floor in the elevator, and I keep remembering it as I say good-bye to the woman who didn't bring me any lunch today. Even when I ignore the conference room and go straight to my office I keep thinking about how special I really am. I have to be, right? That's why I'm down to five suspects and the rest of the department is throwing darts at a phone book.

Five suspects. Travers, McCoy, and Schroder are the local three. Then there are the two that have come from out of town—Calhoun and Taylor. These two are going to be the harder ones to figure out. Calhoun has come from Auckland, and Taylor from Wellington. I'm still doubting Schroder is the guy after the speech from yesterday morning, but I can't be hasty. And I think I have a way to cross Travers off my list. But until then all five of them will have to remain suspects.

The day drags on, the daily routine cometh. I spend it learning nothing I don't already know and not eating the sandwiches Sally didn't make. I clean and mop and vacuum. Live to work. Work to live. McCoy's coffee cup had it wrong.

When four thirty comes around, rather than going home, I wait for Travers. He's out in the field interviewing witnesses and doing what he can to find a killer. He's due back around six o'clock, so rather than sitting outside the station, I head off to a nearby food court. I'm absolutely starving, since I've only eaten fruit today. I have Chinese. *Flied lice*. The guy who serves me is Asian, and must figure I am too, since he speaks to me in his language. I feel a little silly still wearing my overalls as I sit eating my chicken fried rice, the food court full of moms with strollers and school students eating the kind of food that will have many of them fifty pounds overweight by the time they hit their twenties.

When I'm done I head into the nearest parking building and I steal a car. I consider a late-model Mercedes, but you can't steal expensive European cars and sit around in them outside a police station. I go for a nondescript and hopefully reliable Honda that takes me less than a minute to break into and hotwire. I adjust the seat and open my briefcase and pull out a baseball cap and put it on. When exiting the building I hand over the ticket that was on the dashboard along with some loose change to the guy at the booth on the way out. He hardly notices me.

The car I've selected is one of the dirtiest I could find. I drive to a supermarket and use one of the knives in my briefcase to remove the license plates. I switch them with a Mitsubishi, then drive to a nearby service station and take it through the car wash. When the car is clean, I drive back to the police station, satisfied I have taken most—if not all—of the risk out of being caught. No risk means no excitement, but I'm not looking for excitement right now.

It is six sixteen when Travers arrives back. It is another thirty-five minutes before he leaves. I follow him home thinking about the list, the all-important list. He lives in a nice neighborhood. The houses aren't rusting and the gardens are alive. Shiny homes with clean windows and nice cars parked up paved driveways. His house is a single-story place that's probably around thirty years old, aluminum windows, well looked after. I wait outside for an hour before he leaves again. He has changed into red jeans and a yellow polo shirt that looks like casualwear for Ronald McDonald. He tosses a sports bag into the passenger seat and pulls out onto the street. Over the last twenty minutes or so the last of the daylight has gone, and it's almost dark now.

I knew Travers was going out tonight—I'd heard the message on his answering machine. I follow him through a couple of suburbs until he finally arrives outside an attractive two-story house in Redwood, where the houses are shinier and the cars slightly more expensive. He parks in the driveway, drags out his sports bag, and locks the car.

A guy, also in his midthirties, answers the door. When Travers is in, his friend—a fellow with dark brown hair and a small, trimmed mustache—scans the street, like he's looking for something or somebody. If it's me, he doesn't find it. Playing with the collar of his lime silk shirt, he turns and whisks the door closed behind him.

They're having dinner in tonight.

I'll have to wait a few hours. I have brought Daniela's crossword magazine to fill the time and to keep my mind ticking over, using a nearby streetlight so I can see. Four down. An omniscient being. Three letters. Middle letter, O.

Joe.

Time dribbles. I look for, but can't find, any active life in this well-kept suburb, and I wonder where everybody is. Maybe they're all dead. I polish off a few crosswords before the lights finally come on upstairs in the house and the ones downstairs disappear. I wait another ten minutes until the upstairs lights twinkle off. A smaller and dimmer version replaces them. A bedside lamp is my guess. Travers is still inside.

I open my briefcase. Take out the Glock. I stuff the gun into the pocket of my overalls. Ideally I would like to scale a nearby tree to see, unfortunately, what needs seeing. I've seen some pretty strange things in my time, but never this. I suck in a deep breath. Focus on the job at hand. I only have to see it.

You don't need to do it. It's my mother's voice, coming from nowhere.

Fumble with the lock. My hands are shaking. Fifteen seconds.

The house is so neat it looks like a show home. I walk softly through the downstairs living area, pausing at the big-screen TV, wishing there was a way I could take it home. I'd like to take the lounge suite too, if I could fit the damn thing in my apartment. The large rug in the middle of the room ties everything together and would tie everything together back at my place too. Everything in here is colorful: the sofas are bright red, the carpet tan brown, the walls a sunburst orange. I realize I'm stalling for time.

Gun pointing ahead, I make my way to the stairs and slowly start climbing. I keep my feet near the carpeted edges to minimize any sound and it works well. When I get to the top the grunting I hear means any sound I would have made would have gone unnoticed. I stand still and think of the list. Five names. A simple peek into the bedroom will make it four. The grunting gets louder.

The hallway branches into maybe four rooms up here, but it's the closest one I'm concerned with. I reach the master bedroom where the sounds are coming from. It sounds like somebody is having a pillow stuffed down their throat. The door is slightly ajar. Doesn't matter. If it had been closed I could have opened it undetected. If not, I still have my gun. I poke my head forward and try to see through the small gap. All I need to do is take a glimpse, and then I'm out of here. Downstairs and into the night, and my list will be smaller. But I can't see much. The bed isn't in sight. I lean further around until things come into view.

Suddenly I feel sick. Nauseous. I pull away, nearly dropping to my knees. I suck in a deep breath and try to control the urge to vomit, but I'm not sure I can. My legs become jelly, and my mind is spinning. I saw what I expected to see, but I didn't count on feeling this way. My stomach is trying to escape up through my throat. I push a hand against it and lean against the wall. More deep breaths, then I hold it for half a minute. The urge to throw up on the carpet slowly fades.

I'm down to four suspects, but it doesn't make me feel any better.

I hobble to the stairs and grab hold of the banister to keep myself from tumbling to the ground floor. I pause to think about what I've just seen. I think of my mother and how she keeps asking me if I'm gay. Is this why I feel sick? Because she thinks that what I just saw is the sort of thing I do?

Something else is banging around in my thoughts too. Something I can't quite get a firm grip on. I can see the edges of it floating back there, but when I try to haul the damn thing in, I lose my grip on it and it falls completely away. Will it come back if I take another peek? No way in hell am I going to find out.

I raise my hand to my mouth and bite my knuckle. I can hardly feel a damn thing. My hand tastes of sweat. I wonder if Dad ever thought I was gay.

Should I go back and shoot these two men for making me feel this way? I look up at the ceiling and nearly lose balance. My knuckle is still in my mouth. What would Jesus do? It would be rather Christian of me to go in there and shoot them. Abnormal acts like that only mock Him.

What would Dad want me to do?

I have no idea why I even consider his outlook on this. So now I'm standing here with another dilemma. I'm sure God won't mind if I shoot them, but Dad will. In fact, God's probably urging me to. I'll be doing both Him and humanity a favor. But do I feel like doing God a favor? I try to think of one favor He's done me, but all He's ever done is take away my father and give me my mother. No, I owe Him nothing.

I turn back toward the bedroom. I can hear Dad telling me that they're just people doing what people do, and I should leave them be. People are allowed to be happy. Nobody has the right to judge people who fall in love with the same gender. That's what he'd say. Only I'm not listening to him, because he's dead, and dead people's opinions don't really account for much, and even so Dad is wrong because this isn't what people do.

That's enough for the night. It's time to focus on the positives. It's time to be Optimistic Joe. When I call in Candy's body tomorrow there will only be four people to watch closely. It's getting late. If I don't get home soon, I might sleep in again tomorrow. I should have been out the damn door by now.

But this is an opportunity. I'm already inside the house. I

already have a gun. And neither of them is aware of my presence. They're both too wrapped up in each other. Does that mean they deserve to die? The only thing I know for sure is they've brought this confusion over me, this nausea, and for that I should get even. Nobody does this to me. Nobody.

Yet is it really their fault?

My God! How can I even question this? What sort of person am I becoming?

I'm Joe. *J* is for *Joe*. *J* is for *judge*. I'm strong and I'm in control, and what I decide is my decision—not God's. Not Dad's. I don't care what either of them thinks.

I make my way to the bedroom. Stop at the door. Point my gun directly ahead. But I'm not pulling the trigger. Instead I'm thinking about the technical side. The ballistics of the bullets will match against one of the victims I shot. The serial killer strikes again, and this will confuse them. It will blind them to any real motive. Why has the killer targeted a gay policeman? But how ideal is it if the other detectives become conscious that somebody is after them? How easily could I go through their houses if I needed to? Or their motel rooms?

I take a step back just as the grunting from the bedroom gets louder, as if I've given the sound waves more room to travel and amplify. The creaking bedsprings sound like they're screaming in fear. I push my hands against the sides of my head, but it isn't working. I jam the barrel of my Glock into my right ear, and stuff my middle finger into my left, but it doesn't help me think. The sound is still there. And the only way to get rid of it is to either shoot myself, or to shoot them. But I don't have to shoot them. I'm not an animal. I have the ability to think this out. I know right from wrong. I'm not insane. An insane person would jump in there and start firing because they wouldn't be able to control themselves. The interesting thing about insanity is that *Insanity* is strictly a legal term, not a medical one. Patients like me are not insane—we just plead it if we're caught. The reality is if we really were insane, we wouldn't be trying to evade conviction—we'd be caught at the scene smeared in blood and peanut butter and singing Barry Manilow tunes.

I lower my gun. I could kill them just for the hell of it, just because I'm here. In life you take what comes along in this crazy mixed-up world. Other times you need to let it pass you by in case something better comes your way. Life is like a highway with many dirt roads veering off it.

I'm at a junction right now, standing in the hallway of some guy I have never met. A memory in my mind that I can't reach. A headache coming on. Pounding. Sweat running down the sides of my body. Trickling. Grunting filling my ears. Pounding. Do I kill them? Throw a few of those red herrings into the investigation? Or does it only make things worse?

I make my way downstairs. The kitchen is full of stainless-steel appliances that cost more than I make in a year. I sit at the breakfast bar on a bar stool and rest the Glock in front of me. Tagging Travers for gay was simple—it was the calendars. *Overcompensation* was the key word there. Knowing I'll think better on a stomach that isn't so empty, I open up the fridge and rummage around inside for some food. I end up making myself a corned beef sandwich—Travers's boyfriend is an excellent cook. I grab a can of Coke—it's on special after all—to wash it down. The fizz burns away any fantasy I hold that what I am listening to could be anything other than two men having the time of their lives.

Upstairs, the bed is slamming the bedroom wall, like it too wants to have bolted out the front door half an hour ago. I sit down at the bar and start tracing my finger along the edge of it, flicking some of the crumbs from the sandwich while doing my best to dismiss the thought that because I ate from the same food these people ate from that I'm gay now, but of course that's silly, it's silly, but the thought stays with me as I consider what to do next.

CHAPTER EIGHTEEN

The restaurant is full of conversation, nice smells, good people, decent music, and a warm atmosphere. The waitresses all have perfect hair and trim bodies, shown off by tight clothing. Everybody else has gone to a lot of effort to look casual—jeans, tidy T-shirts, smart shoes.

Sally's father is working away at a chicken dish, her mother tackling a salad, while Sally pushes a fork back and forth in her tortellini. The day has gone well. For the first time in ages, her father, fifty-five now, looks close to his age rather than several years beyond it. The DVD player went down well; it was no problem for her to install it, and her father spent ten minutes playing with the remote, learning how to drive it. The buttons were difficult to push with his shuddery hands, yet his frustration stayed at a minimum. Whether that will still be the case in another year, or even another few weeks, is anybody's guess.

She stabs a few pieces of pasta and puts them into her

mouth. She loves pasta. She could live on it quite happily, yet tonight her appetite isn't allowing her to enjoy it. Her mother and father are laughing. She is happy for them, happy that for an hour or two they don't look so empty.

When she finishes her meal, the friendly waitress who has been helping them all night comes over and sweeps away their plates, then just as quickly replaces them with dessert menus. She scans through the choices. She doesn't really feel like any of them, and looking at the waitresses, she doubts any of them have touched any type of dessert in their entire lives. She looks up at her dad and identifies the strain in his features as he tries to keep his body under control. He won't be able to hold on much longer, she thinks.

Sally is a few bites into a chocolate sundae when she starts to feel guilty about Joe. She hopes he wasn't relying on her for his lunch today. Of course what makes her feel really bad is what he said this morning. *Somebody like me.* She hadn't been aware till then that Joe knew people were treating him differently, and she was doing so too. Nobody else was making him lunch. Nobody else was pestering him to sit outside on the banks of the Avon River and throw stale bread at the ducks.

Two things occur to her then. The first is there's a reason why Joe always has turned down her offer to have lunch together, or to be given a lift home. She has been treating him differently.

The second thing is that this sundae isn't going to help her waistline. Anyway, it's starting to taste plain. Just chilled soggy cream. She pushes her spoon around it, making it even more runny. What she needs to do, she realizes, is to make an effort to get to know Joe while pretending she isn't making an effort. She smiles at her parents, glad they are having a good time. Her mother's metal crucifix is hanging outside her blouse, the light from the candles glinting off it. Through everything, her parents still have their faith. Again she thinks that she can use faith to bring herself closer to Joe.

She looks back down at her sundae. Today is day one to become a better person, a more caring person, a thinner person. She pushes her dessert aside and promises herself never to touch one again.

CHAPTER NINETEEN

The bed is no longer banging. It could be broken. The mattress might have worn out. Maybe they've moved to the floor. Maybe they're spent. Thinking about it makes the corned beef sandwich threaten to come back up, and I'm threatening to let it. Problem is, it won't just be the sandwich. It'll be everything I've eaten for the week.

I've made my decision. I'm going to let God down by allowing them to live. Hey, I don't owe Him any favors.

I leave the empty can on the table and the leftover makings of my sandwich on the bench. I've never been that domesticated. I'm wearing gloves. When Travers finds the can in the morning, I wonder if he will have it tested for a link with the bottles found at Angela's house. It's a big parallel to draw—too big for a policeman, anyway.

I don't bother locking the front door behind me. If somebody else happens to break in and kill them, then who am I to interfere with God? I start to laugh at the thought of their faces in the morning when they see they've had a visitor.

Laughter is the best medicine for what I've just been through. What will they do? Report it? No. Travers wants his secret kept. I can't imagine him going to work tomorrow and telling everybody what happened. For a while he's going to live in fear. As will his buddy. And so they should—mocking the Bible and humanity with their actions.

Mocking me with them.

I part company with the car a half mile from home and build up a sweat while walking the rest of the way. My briefcase feels heavy in the wet heat. Maybe one day I'll buy a car.

When I get inside, I see two messages waiting for me, both from my mother. I erase them without listening to them, wondering two things at the same time. First, why I love my mom so much, and second, why she can't be deleted just as easily.

I sit in front of Pickle and Jehovah and watch them as they swim in their endless cycle of memory loss. They see me, suspect I am about to feed them, so they race over. I haven't fed them all day, so I don't waste any time. I glance at my answering machine. Maybe Mom will call tomorrow. Ask me around for meatloaf. Show me her newest jigsaw puzzle. Give me some Coke. I look forward to it. I feel bad for not having listened to her messages.

Before going to bed I dig out an old alarm clock from the bottom of my small closet. Set it to seven thirty-five. This way I give myself a chance to wake up at seven thirty. It's like a test. A test with a backup.

I wish my fish good night before going to bed. I close my eyes and try not to think about my mother as I wait for sleep to come and take me away from the pain of what I've seen tonight.

CHAPTER TWENTY

"Late night, Detective Schroder?"

"We found another body."

What? I start scanning the corkboard. "Was she dead, Detective Schroder?"

Christchurch is overcast and gray. No sun. Lots of heat. Wet heat like yesterday. My sleeves are already rolled up. Schroder gives me a look as though I never cease to amaze him with my well of knowledge. I look back at him as if the characters from a Doctor Seuss story are dancing back and forth in my mind, singing songs and holding hands and doing what they can to keep me permanently entertained.

"Yeah. She is, Joe."

I look up at the wall and it takes all my control to keep in the role of Slow Joe when I see her photograph. I point to it. The picture of Candy. "Is that her?"

He nods. "Name's Lisa Houston. She was a prostitute."

"Dangerous job, Detective Schroder. Being a cleaner is better."

The photograph of Candy is one of those after shots that make people's passport pictures look good in comparison, especially in this case because it was taken after two days spent in an upstairs bedroom in sweltering heat. Decomposition has not been kind to her. The skin slippage around her hair and face is extensive. Her skin is blotchy purple. Another day or so, it would be blotchy black. Her eyes are milky. Her arm is crooked and bruised. The skin on her hands looks like wet gloves.

"Did she die last night, Detective Schroder?"

"Longer than that, Joe. We'll know exactly when later on this morning."

The pathologist will figure out the day by examining the insect larvae growing around her battered face and torn vagina, and from the compound fracture in her broken arm, where the bone peeped through and said hello.

"You know, Joe, you really shouldn't be seeing these sorts of pictures."

"They're okay," I tell him. "I just pretend they're not real people."

"I guess that must be a luxury."

"Coffee, Detective Schroder?"

"Not this morning, Joe. Thanks."

I wander off to my office. I'm desperately curious about how the body was found, who found it, and who showed up at the scene. Detective Travers certainly hadn't. He was tied up.

It was probably the husband, coming home to get his life back on track. Wondered what the smell was coming from upstairs. Déjà vu. Whether you breathe through your nose or your mouth, or even if you don't breathe at all, the smell of decaying death will always get to you. It takes on a life in the same way fire does, looking for oxygen to burn to keep it alive, and, like fire, it has a hunger to be fed. A purpose for its survival. I wonder if the husband will ever walk up those stairs again.

I've heard of cases where old people have lived with their dead spouse for months because they didn't want to part with their loved one. They lay them down in bed or set them in front of the TV watching game shows with their favorite cushion in their lap. Hold conversations with them. Hold their hand, even though the skin is slipping from it in rotted abrasions. For a while after Dad died, I kept checking on Mom to make sure she was home alone—I thought she might break out the superglue to try and piece Dad's ashes together so she could nag the poor bastard to death one last time.

I remember a story I once read in a newspaper. Some guy in Germany had died, and although his rotting body stank, none of the neighbors wanted to disturb him. He was there for a couple of months and wasn't found until the landlord wanted his rent. He'd been eaten by his flock of cats, and was mostly bone by that point. Guy probably got more pussy in death than he did in life.

I mop floors. Wipe windows. Get talked to like I'm a moron. Throughout the course of the morning, I eavesdrop enough to learn the footprints at the scene are identical to those at the other scenes. Residue from my gloves. Carpet fibers. Hair. Daniela Walker's husband had come home to get his electric shaver—my electric shaver now—and had found her.

Because of the several differences between Lisa the Hooker's death and Daniela the Battered Housewife's death, more detectives have changed over to the theory that they are hunting two killers and not one. Each victim has been killed differently (though I'm repetitious in my day job, I don't like to be with after-hours activities), but at each scene I'm leaving behind similar evidence, be it clothes, fibers, or saliva.

Two killers. It is the general assumption. Nobody who thinks otherwise has any theories as to why the killer returned to the scene with a hooker.

Just before lunch I run into the local gay cop and say hello to him. He isn't in a talkative mood and dismisses me with a quick greeting. He looks distracted. He also looks tired.

I'm left with four men to study. Lunch comes and goes without a visit from Sally, and more importantly, without any of her sandwiches. I make do with the food I have. After lunch, using the computer and personnel files in one of the records rooms upstairs, I reproduce department records for each of the remaining four men for later reading. I'm getting excited at how my list keeps narrowing itself down. What I can't figure out is why I have to eliminate all but one name until I find the killer. Why can't the next person I investigate be the man I want?

Why must luck be against me? I decide to start with the two I don't know as well, the two out-of-towners.

I'm in the records room running the vacuum over a toner-stained piece of carpet when Sally opens the door and steps in. She doesn't look surprised to find me here, which means she must have been keeping an eye on me. Maybe I ought to be keeping more of an eye on her. I turn off the vacuum cleaner.

"How's your day going, Joe?" she asks, always asking me the same thing, as if one day I'm going to have an answer different from *Fine* or *Okay*.

I decide to liven up her day and mix up the conversation.

"It's going real good, Sally. Just like all the other yesterdays. I like my job."

"I like my job too," she says, and then she lowers her voice even though there is nobody else here to overhear her, "but I must admit I find it a little boring. Don't you ever feel like you want to do something else?" She walks over to the photocopier and leans against it. The records I printed off are safely in my overalls, and the originals back where they belong. "I mean, don't you think there ought to be more to life?"

"Like what?" I ask, genuinely curious. I can learn from this woman. If she has low-end goals in this world, I can say I have those same goals if it will help my act. This is what Method actors do.

"Anything. Everything," she says, and maybe it's the smell of the vacuum cleaner, or the window-cleaner fumes getting to me, but for the first time Sally sounds as though she's thinking outside the box, beyond her limitations.

"I don't understand," I tell her, and I really don't.

"I'm sorry," she says. "I'm not making any sense. Don't you have dreams, Joe? If you could be anything in the world, what would you want to be?"

The answer is simple. "Joe."

"No, I mean a job. Any job in the world."

"A cleaner."

"Besides that?"

"I'm not quer . . . qual . . . fied for anything else."

"Do you like the idea of being a fireman? Or a policeman? Or an artist?"

"I drew a house, once. It had no windows."

She sighs, and for a moment I think about documentaries on TV where some retarded guy will marry his female equal. Surely these are the conversations they must have during foreplay before trying to make mentally disabled babies. I decide to put an end to it and help her out.

"I would like to be an astronaut."

Her face beams at my answer. "Really?"

"Yeah. Ever since I was a boy," I say, winging it now because even though it isn't my fantasy, it sounds like the kind of thing any man—regardless of IQ—would like to do. "I looked up at the moon and wanted to walk there. I know you can't live there, but I could at least fly there and make snow angels in the moon dirt."

"That sounds nice, Joe."

I'm sure it does. I decide to go another step further into this romantic notion. "I'd be alone up there. I'd not worry about what people think about me. It would be peaceful."

Her smile starts to waver. "You worry about what other people think about you?"

"Sometimes," I say, though that isn't necessarily true. I only worry about what other people think I'm *capable* of. "It's not easy being retarted," I say, putting emphasis on the second *t*.

"Retarded."

"What?"

"It doesn't matter," she says. "What about God?"

"God?" I ask, as if I've never heard of the guy. "Do you think he's retarted?"

"Of course not. But do you ever worry about what He thinks?"

It's a good question. And if I really believed in all those God-loves-you and God-will-smite-you fairy tales, then sure, I'd be worried. I look at the crucifix hanging from her neck. It's an icon that introduces her to the world as somebody who believes in Heaven and Hell and all the good and bad things in between.

"I always worry, because God is always watching," I say, and her face lights up again and I realize that if Sally doubled her IQ and halved her weight, she could be the kind of person I'd find myself following home.

"Do you ever go to church, Joe?"

"Church? No. Never."

"You should."

"I get confused," I say, looking down while I say it, as if I'm admitting something that makes me feel ashamed of being a God-loving, God-fearing Christian. "I wish I could, but I can never make it all the way through the . . ." The what? The lesson? The sermon? The boredom? I'm not sure of the answer. "You know. The three hours of sitting still and listening. Plus I find some of the things hard to understand. It seems to me that the Bible doesn't really make a whole lot of sense." Which I'm sure is true. I look back up and I smile away the ashamed look I had put on my face. The big-boy grin gives her smile a new lease on life.

"I go to church every Sunday," she says, reaching up and touching the crucifix.

"That's good."

"You're welcome to come along. I promise it won't be boring."

I have no idea how she can promise something like that unless the priest is planning on breaking at least half the commandments. "I'll think about it."

"Do your parents go to church?"

"No."

"It's good that you have faith, Joe."

"The world needs faith," I say, and then Sally prattles on for five minutes, telling me things she has been able to learn from the Bible. I figure that to absorb all that Christian bullshit she must have forgotten other things along the way, which is why she's so incredibly dim.

At the end of it all she asks me what I have planned for my weekend. I tell her I have lots of plans, like watching TV and sleeping. I'm worried she might suddenly suggest we do either one of those things together at her place.

But she lets me off the hook. "Have I ever told you about my brother?" she asks.

"No."

"You remind me of him."

Her brother must have been awesome, but I find it a little sick that she must have wanted to fuck him, too. "That's nice," I guess.

"Anyway, I wanted to let you know that if you ever wanted help with anything, or wanted to just do something, like talk or have coffee or something, well, I'm always available."

I'm sure she is. "Thanks."

She reaches into a pocket and pulls out a business card. Her phone number is written on it—she has that same cute, happy handwriting that normal women have. Seeing it there makes me realize she had this whole speech planned out. She hands it over. I turn the card over and see it's one of Detective Schroder's cards. There's also a coffee-colored ring stain on it—she's recycled the card rather than stealing a new one.

"You ever need anything, Joe, I'm only a phone call away."

"A phone call away," I say, giving her my big-boy grin and tucking the number into my pocket while the back of my neck breaks out in goose bumps.

"Well, I guess I'd better get back to work," she says.

"Me too," I say, looking down at the vacuum cleaner.

She heads out of the room, closing the door behind her. I take her phone number out of my pocket and am about to tear it up, but she might come back through the door. Best to dispose of it after work. Maybe at home.

Four thirty rolls around. Time to stop working. It's also Friday, so time to stop thinking. Putting in too many extra hours will only stress me out. A stressed cleaner is a sloppy cleaner. Therefore, when I climb off the bus near home, I decide not to continue investigating into the weekend. A stressed detective is a sloppy detective.

I will use this weekend to unwind. Try to enjoy myself. Spend some quality time with Joe. Perhaps watch my fish for a while. Perhaps visit Mom. Maybe read another romance novel. I walk up the stairs to my apartment, unlock the door, and push my way inside. A moment later I pull the folders from my briefcase. I'm telling myself not to open them up, not to start reading, but perhaps I'll have a quick browse. . . .

No. Must. Not. Work.

I sit down on the sofa. Put down the files. Feed Pickle and Jehovah. While they're eating, I check my answering machine. Mom hasn't called. Odd.

I move back to the sofa and look at the files I don't want to read. This must be how some cops become dedicated to solving a crime. Unfortunately, you only let yourself down, not for working so hard, but for working so hard and getting nowhere. You can't stop working, because suddenly nothing else really matters anymore. You become obsessed.

I am at that point now. It's like a need, I guess, or a craving. I've opened this investigation. I'm experiencing the exact reason for so many divorces in the police department. Unless I put the folder down right now, I'm going to end up spending my entire weekend sitting on my bed and reading. Working. Stressing. But it is a challenge. . . .

I walk over to the sink and splash cold water on my face. Do I want to be this dedicated? Who am I to spend my weekend solving a crime I've no real interest in?

Ah, and that's the problem. I *am* interested. Have been for the entire week. How can I not be? Is this a product of my lack of a life? Must I solve a murder to enjoy myself?

And here's the killer blow—I actually *am* enjoying myself. Sure, all along I've been enjoying narrowing down my suspects, but I've also enjoyed everything about the entire investigation. I like the espionage—the way I feel like James Bond, sneaking into Mr. and Mr. Gay's house, darting into the cubicles and offices at the station. The long hours. The continuous mind drain. The logic and the reality. It's all been a buzz.

The problems are the late nights. The dreams. Not waking on time in the mornings. The disrupted routine. But I don't want my life to be a routine. After this, I might take on another case. The satisfaction of knowing I am better than anybody else at the police department satisfies my ego, but is that enough of a reason to keep doing this?

I think it just might be. Sometimes killing is all about ego, especially for other people, but I remain comfortable with the knowledge that I'm not like other killers. I know what I do is wrong, but I won't attempt to justify it. I won't say God or Satan made me do it. I won't say they had it coming. Nor will I pretend an abusive childhood sent me spiraling onto this dirt road from the main highway of life. My childhood was normal, at least as normal as it could have been with my crazy mother. She never abused me, never neglected me—though it would have been easier growing up if she had. The abuse would have given me a reason to hate her. The neglect would have given me a reason to love her.

If I could point to my childhood and choose one thing that made me the man I am today, it would be the exact opposite of neglect. It would be the constant talking, the constant explaining, the *always being there*. So no deep-seated reason why I grew up to enjoy killing people, no inner turmoil or conflicts or resentment at the world or at my parents. Neither of them was an alcoholic. Neither of them molested me. I never burned down the school, never set fire to the dog. I was a normal kid.

I turn away from the sink and look out my small window onto the city. It's still gray out there. I run some more water over my face, then towel myself down.

Just how dedicated do I want to be?

Dedication is willpower. I squeeze my eyes shut. To work or not to work? That is the question.

The phone rings. It startles me and I look at it expecting to see it rattling on the hook. My first thought is Mom. Has something happened to her? I'm not sure what the statute of limitations on premonitions is, but the one I had yesterday morning must have expired by now. Mom's okay. Mom's always going to be okay. I snatch it up before the answering machine kicks in.

"Joe? Is that you?" she asks before I even get the chance to say anything.

"Mom?"

"Hello, Joe. This is your mother."

"Mom . . . why . . . why are you ringing me?"

"What's this? Do I need an excuse to ring my only child who I thought loved me?"

"I do love you, Mom."

"You have an odd way of showing it," she says.

"You know I love you, Mom," I say, wanting to add that I

wish that for once she could say something positive toward or about me, because if she could it'd make loving her a whole lot easier to do.

"That's great, Joe."

"Thanks."

"You misunderstand," she says. "I'm being sarcastical."

"Sarcastic."

"What, Joe?"

"What?"

"What did you say?" she asks.

"Nothing."

"It sounded like something."

"I think I have a bad line," I tell her. "What were you saying?"

"I said I was being sarcastical. I'm saying that it's great that you now think I'm only imagining you love me. Are you saying I'm supposed to assume that you love your mother? I don't see how I can assume such a thing. You never visit me, and when I call, you complain! Sometimes I just don't know what to do. Your father would be ashamed to see how you treat me, Joe. Ashamed!"

Part of me wants to cry. Another part wants to scream. I do neither. I sit down and let my head and chest sag down slightly. I wonder what life would be like if Mom had died instead of Dad. "I'm sorry," I say, knowing I can only apologize rather than try to correct her way of thinking. "I promise to be better, Mom. I really do."

"Really? That's the Joe I know. The loving, caring son who I knew I could only have had. You truly can be an angel at times, Joe. You make me so proud."

"Really?" I start to smile. "Thanks," I say, praying she isn't being *sarcastical*.

"I went to the doctor today," she says, changing the subject—or more accurately, getting around to the reason she actually called.

The doctor? Oh Jesus. "What's wrong?"

"I must have been sleepwalking last night, Joe. I woke up this morning with my bedroom door open, and I was lying on the floor."

"The floor? Oh my God. Are you okay?"

"What do you think?"

"What did the doctor say?"

"He said I had an episode. Do you know what an episode is, Joe?"

I feel closer to crying than screaming. I think about Fay, Edgar, Karen, and Stewart from Mom's favorite program. Yeah, I know what an episode is.

"What kind of episode?"

"Doctor Costello says it's nothing to be worried about. He has given me some tablets."

"What sort of tablets?"

"I'm not sure. I'll tell you more when you come over. I'll cook meatloaf. It's your favorite, Joe."

"Are you sure you're okay?"

"Doctor Costello seems to think so. So what time will you be coming over?"

Suddenly I'm not so sure there was an episode. In fact I'm almost positive Mom is making all of this up to make me feel guilty. "Do you have to go for more tests?"

"No. Around six? Six thirty?"

"No tests? Why? What more are they going to do?"

"I have my pills."

"I'm just worried, that's all."

"I'll be better when you get here."

I suck in a deep breath. Here we go. "I can't come over, Mom. I'm kind of busy."

"You're always busy, no time to spend with your mother. I'm all you have, you know. All you have since your father died. Where will you be when I'm gone?"

In paradise. "I'll come by on Monday, like normal."

"I guess we'll find out on Monday." The line suddenly goes dead.

I stand back up and hang up the phone. Hearing it ring reminds me that I never called the vet back, but being reminded doesn't make me want to do it now. I walk over to my battered sofa. I sit down and throw my feet up onto the scarred coffee table. In the silence of my room I can hear the pump circulating the water around in the fishbowl. I wonder what kind of peace I could find if I was a goldfish with a memory that spanned only the last five seconds of my mother's conversation.

I look over at the folders containing the printouts of the four men left on my suspect list. If I start looking through them, I'll at least stop thinking about my mother. Meatloaf on Monday. It's a prelude to having her nagging me for not living there, for not having a life, for not owning a BMW. Will reading the files put her out of my mind?

I figure it's worth a shot.

I pick them up and begin looking through them.

CHAPTER TWENTY-ONE

Detective Harvey Taylor. Forty-three years old. Married. Four kids. Been on the police force for eighteen years. Became a detective in the burglary squad at the age of twenty-eight. Promoted to homicide at the age of thirty-four. Has been assigned to some of the biggest homicide cases New Zealand has ever seen. He's a part of the team tracking the guy who left all the bodies in the cemetery lake—a guy the media are calling the Burial Killer. He's a part of the team trying to track me too.

I'm reading through Taylor's history, seeing he was a straight-A student at school. Several outstanding sporting achievements. High IQ. The type of guy I hated when I was at school. The type of guy I wanted to be.

Listed in the folder are results from his school days. Results from the Royal New Zealand Police College. Results from psychological tests. I look through the questions for *Have you ever strangled a woman to death after raping her?* but it's not there. I figure he would have ticked *No*. Most of the questions are pretty lame. *What is your favorite color? What is your favorite number? Would you steal if you were desperate? Have you ever smoked drugs? Ever killed a pet? Ever beaten anybody up at school? Ever been beaten up? Do you like setting fires?*

The yes-or-no questions take up five pages before the tests move on to questions that require written answers instead of ticks in boxes. *What should we do with murderers? How did it feel being beaten up at school? What did you do about it?* Why this and why that. Big fucking deal this and big fucking deal that. They're designed to make up a psychological profile. Something like "I was beaten up at school, but my favorite color is blue, which means I can't be gay. Right?" Yeah, right.

I stop looking at the questions and go to the results. Taylor was basically rubber-stamped sane. No further explanation than that. The "insane" graduates become parking attendants.

I continue reading through his record from officer to detective: the arrests he's made, the cases he's solved. The guy has put in several of his own hours into these cases. You don't get compensated for those hours, but you do gain some respect. They help you get promoted, so you can do even more work that you won't get compensated for. The report indicates the man is dedicated, to his work and to his family. I don't know what the balance is, but so far he still has both.

This doesn't eliminate him as a suspect. For all I know he's missing his wife so much his imagination and right hand can't accommodate him any longer. Maybe he seeks sexual release with a stranger. I have no way of knowing. All I do know is that besides the burglary cases, which have such an extremely low solution rate it's appalling, Taylor has solved nearly every one of his investigations. That's why he's here. Not that his being here has helped either investigation.

The photograph supplied with the file is probably ten years old, taken when he was in his early thirties. Even then Taylor looked ten years older than he was. Now, he looks twenty years older. These days his hair is ash gray with peaks at the corners of his forehead that threaten to see him bald within a few years. He doesn't have the black eyes of a killer. Instead his friendly blue eyes mask an intelligence I don't associate with many detectives. His face is lined with wrinkles from age and from the sun. His skin is weathered and tanned, and it's easy to imagine him on a surfboard in the middle of the ocean.

The picture in the folder is in color and shows the sort of fashions we were all wearing back then. I can only hope no photographs exist of me anywhere wearing similar clothes.

I put his folder down. Yawn. Stretch. And glance at my watch. It's already eight o'clock. Somehow I've already been home for nearly three hours. Where does the time go?

If only I knew. My internal alarm sure isn't telling me.

It's Friday night. Party night. Yet here I am, stuck inside my cramped home, my mind elsewhere and my eyes gliding over information that isn't helping. I knock back my coffee. I can't even remember making it, but it's still warm. Reading all this information must have put me into a fugue. I figure it'd put anybody into one. As I take off my overalls, I pull Sally's phone number from the pocket. I'm about to crunch it up into a tiny little ball when I decide to hang on to it. It's nice having somebody's phone number here other than my mother's and work. I use a magnet that looks like a miniature banana to stick it onto the front of the fridge. It makes me feel as though I have friends, and it isn't such a bad feeling.

I take a break. I finally get around to ringing Jennifer at the vet's and I can tell that just hearing my voice has made her day. I ask about the cat. The cat is doing about as well as it can, but is still in bad condition. I ask about the cat's owners. She says there's been no joy there. I ask what they're going to do with the cat if he lives. She says it will go to a shelter. I don't ask what will happen at the shelter. I ask her to keep me updated, and she tells me she will.

I head back to the couch to grab a towel hanging over the arm, but end up picking up another folder. I'm naked, my armpits smell like homeless people, yet I sit back on the couch and continue reading.

Detective Inspector Robert Calhoun. Fifty-four years old. Married. The photograph was taken a year or so before his son visited the big suicide house in the sky. The report is all here. Timothy Calhoun. Little Timmy. I can't imagine having a cop as a parent. That's probably why he hanged himself in their garage. Or maybe his old man was playing doctor and nurse with him.

Want to see a magic trick, little Timmy?

Calhoun entered the police force at twenty-two and was on the beat ten years before becoming a detective. Originally from Dunedin, he was based in Wellington, spent a few years there, and was then transferred to Auckland. The police force is like that. They'll give you a job, train you up, then separate you from your family and friends by giving you a home anywhere in the country where you don't know anybody.

Calhoun worked serious assaults, including rape, for twelve years. After that he was given the opportunity to work homicide. There are no dedicated homicide departments in this country. Not yet. When somebody gets killed, they pull experienced detectives from other areas—generally from sexual assaults, sometimes burglary—to investigate. So when these guys have been working homicide for five years or whatever, they're still first and foremost burglary or fraud cops until opportunity knocks. I figure working rape cases and other assaults for twelve years would surely give anybody a few ideas. It could easily be here that Calhoun learned a thing or two about what women really want.

I look at his photograph. In the passing years, he has aged three years for every one that's passed. His black hair, full and in the shape of a God-fearing mullet, is gray now and receding. His face is long and he looks tired, his eyes and mouth surrounded by tiny wrinkles. No black eyes here either. Instead his are dark brown. They're sad looking, like the eyes of a lost puppy. He has a narrow jawline that's still the same, except for the gray stubble he always has now.

What do we have? A dead son. A wife who probably hasn't touched her husband since then. Assaults. A man who sported a mullet. All these rape cases. The reason the tally of rape cases in this country is so high and only getting higher is that the justice system has never placed a big enough deterrent not to commit them.

I study Calhoun's psychological profile. Nothing too different from Taylor's. I take a look at his college records. Not brilliant, but pretty good. Top twenty percent of his class, but that also makes him in the bottom eighty percent. He hasn't solved all his cases, but not many people do. There are a large number of unsolved sexual assaults that I'd like to believe Calhoun committed, but know he couldn't have—too risky. If a cop does something like that he needs to ensure that his victim can't identify him afterward, for which only one method is truly guaranteed.

Time is flying. My head is spinning. I look down at my lap and see the reason for the blood loss to my brain. All this reading about sexual assault has perked me up. I stand up and grab the towel, but suddenly the idea of a cold shower isn't enough to get me through till tomorrow, not when the night has so much to offer. My body is wound tight and my mind even tighter, and as much fun as it's been being a detective, I deserve a reward for all that hard work—and what better reward is there than letting me be myself again?

I skip the shower. Thoughts of seizing the night pull me away from the files. I get dressed. I have a closet full of nice clothes that belong to men who now have dead wives. I tuck my Glock into the waistband of my jeans and make sure my leather jacket will cover it. I slip one of my blades into the inside pocket.

Dressed to kill. Essential items only.

CHAPTER TWENTY-TWO

Christchurch at night. My city. My playground. Where people who hate you will still call you "buddy." The air is warm, alive with activity, a light breeze coming from the northwest. Not too hot, but muggy. Full of sound as much as moisture. Full of fluorescent light as much as hormones. To the south of the city, on the Port Hills, a million lights twinkle in the distance. In the other directions, just flat landscape with buildings dotted across it. The town itself is full of neon lights—pinks, purples, reds, and greens. All possible colors dazzle the eyes from all possible angles.

The red-light district of Christchurch straddles Manchester and Colombo streets, which run parallel through the heart of the city. On any of these corners you can buy a personal party for twenty, sixty, or a hundred bucks. Circling these streets are two types of people. The first are the boys in their teens and twenties, driving with no destination in mind except to be somewhere else, always on the move like a shark. Modified engines that make more noise than a jumbo jet. Mag wheels shiny and fat. Exhaust pipes wide enough to put your fist into. These are the boy-racers. I couldn't really say how they came into being, but they just did, one day thousands of teenagers driving expensive-looking Japanese imported cars, some of the cars have subwoofers installed in the backs with bass as loud as cannon fire, some cars have neon strips stuck along the base of them, some cars are painted so bright they could cause an onlooker to suffer a brain embolism, all of the cars are a burden on society. Windows in the nearby shops vibrate with the sound of them passing by. Some peel rubber at every set of lights as their tweaked motors lurch into action. Kids trying their hardest to be cool in an uncool world, they're winding down their busy week of cashing welfare checks by impressing everybody with their taste in music.

At the other end of the spectrum is the second type of people. There are the guys who used to do the same thing ten years ago, only back then they'd only cruise up and down the same street. Now these guys are still driving the same cars; older bigger cars that don't get as much mileage. These are guys who wear tight black jeans and black T-shirts with holes in them and the names of heavy metal bands or whisky brands printed across them. They have long hair or shaved heads, nothing in between. Cigarettes or joints hang from their mouths. Their windows are tinted, the side ones wound down so we can all enjoy their presence. They think women who see them will instantly fall in love, and the crazy part is that some of them do. The sluts who wear the tie-dyed dresses and jars of face paint covering their skin—they wear their hearts on their arms along with colorful but cheap tattoos.

The Oxford Terrace line of bars and cafés is known as The Strip. It's a meat market where skanky girls tease a few dozen men for every one they end up sleeping with. Seven or eight of these bars are packed tightly within this block, all of them with a riverside view. On the other side of the river and on a slight diagonal, a few hundred feet away from the closest bar, is the police station. On a Friday night the urine-water mix in the Avon is about fifty-fifty. Eels float along belly up. Ducks pick at used condoms left on the banks. Small fish flop from the water figuring they have a better chance in the air than they do breathing in the same stuff they're swimming in. Every ten meters or so somebody has passed out drunk. As I get closer to The Strip, I take the gun from my waistband and zip it inside my jacket pocket, then take off my jacket and carry it. The night isn't as hot as it'd been over the last week, but sweat still trickles down the sides of my body. I've applied enough aftershave and deodorant to hide any smell my body can come up with, though there's more than enough after-shave and perfume already hanging in the air. Walking down this street has me scented for free within seconds.

It's after midnight and The Strip is getting livelier. All week long women are heading straight home from work and locking their doors, afraid that what has been happening to their counterparts in the news might happen to them. Any other day of the week, there is a general awareness that things are not as safe as they ought to be. Yet come Friday and Saturday nights, all those fears are pushed aside so that the good times can roll. Here, most of the women are young and underdressed. They try to cram their way into clubs they think must be popular because of the lines of people waiting outside. Bouncers stand with their arms crossed and their muscles bulging. They have attitude problems they like everyone to know about.

The Strip is the highlight of town for most locals. Already the drum 'n' bass, the techno, and the hip-hop deafen me. The only thing I know about hip-hop is that I hate it, and I figure that's all anybody knows about it. We may have evolved from something that crawled out of a swamp and continued to evolve as monkeys became men, but boy-racers and hip-hop music are proof we've hit our peak and are now heading backward.

It could take at least thirty minutes to get inside any of these places, so I head deeper into the city, walking down Cashel Mall passing shoe shops and clothing stores in search of another club or bar. Perhaps one that's quieter. I find it eventually—a club with an open front where the music isn't quite so loud and a lot more bearable and there's room to sit. The crowd seems to be made up of people from their mid-twenties through to their late thirties. Guess that makes me average.

I make my way inside, sidestepping the bouncer with a smile and without a comment from either of us. There's a sea of people to greet me, but not an ocean. I push my way through, keeping a tight grip on my jacket. At the bar I'm served by a delicious blonde—tight white top, short black skirt, great tits. I order myself a gin and tonic. Expensive, but you can't go into town on a Friday or Saturday night and not expect to spend a small fortune. I could have stayed at home and had the same drink for a quarter of the price, but there would be nobody to watch. I sit at the bar, nurse my drink, and watch the crowd around me. Mostly men wearing expensive clothing they can't afford, attempting to look richer and more impressive than they really are. Caretakers, laborers, plumbers, shop assistants—all dressed to look like lawyers. Whereas the lawyers are at other bars, dressed to look like casual guys. The women, even the fat chicks, dress to look like sluts. Not that I'm complaining. It's here where men flock to get a glance at potential bedtime stories to tell their friends on Monday morning. Women come here to be easy. To be free.

From all corners of the club, lights flicker and dance and throb and pulse at my eyes. I finish my drink, order another. I look up at the roof and check for any surveillance cameras covering the bar. Nothing. The music is getting louder. My ears are humming.

In a place like this, women only speak to you for one of three reasons: you're either extremely good-looking, you look extremely rich, or they're telling you to get lost and stop bothering them. Tonight I'm wearing expensive clothing. Money's no object when it comes to clothes, because a few of my victims have had husbands my size. I'm also wearing a rather expensive wristwatch—a Tag Heuer that cost victim number three's husband three thousand dollars. It has a sapphire crystal face that can't be scratched and a metal bracelet strap. Not as costly as a Rolex, but Rolexes don't retain a high market value; they're ugly, worn only by old men and Asians.

It takes thirty minutes and three drinks for a woman to come up to me. Out of the overalls, I don't look like the simple guy the guys at the station think I am. Clothes make all the difference. She forces her way to the bar and stands next to me. She turns and smiles. Acknowledges my existence. A good start. She orders a drink. Just one.

"Hi there." I have to shout to be heard over the music.

"Hi."

I peg her to be around twenty-seven, maybe twenty-eight years old. Five feet six, slim. Like the chick behind the bar, she has a nice pair. In this light she looks like she has purple skin. Maybe she does. Her hair looks purple too. I can't tell what color her eyes are.

"How's it going?" I shout.

"Good," she says, nodding. "Good. And you?"

"Yeah. Good," I say, then suddenly realize I don't know what to say next. That's always been my problem. Social skills don't come easy to me. If they did, I wouldn't have to break into women's homes; I'd be able to talk my way in. *So . . . Come here often?* No, I'm not going to ask that. "Boy, I wish I could come up with something that made me sound impressive."

She laughs, and maybe that's because she's heard the line before, or knows how quickly our conversation became awkward. "I was hoping you'd be impressive."

This is a good sign. Funny. Good sense of humor. Great smile. And she's still here, hasn't told me to get lost. I study her outfit. A short black skirt. A dark red top that shows the tops of her firm breasts. The back of the top shows most of her back, except where the material strings across to hold it in place. She isn't wearing a bra. Black leather shoes that have finger-width strands of leather crisscrossing over them. She's wearing a thin gold necklace, and a gold watch that looks like an expensive Omega.

I shrug. "I was kind of hoping for the same thing."

The other thing I keep in mind is that even though women who frequent these places may look like sluts, and may in fact be easy, going home with one takes a mighty amount of skill, charm, persuasion, or dumb luck—none of which I have in spades. It's all about salesmanship. Here you have a good-looking woman, wanting to make a purchase, just looking for the right guy, and knowing that if you're not it, there's another one a few feet away.

She smiles at me. The biggest tool you can have in your armory, besides being good-looking and rich, is humor. If you can make her laugh right away, then you have a chance. If she really laughs—not one of those stupid, polite laughs because you think you're funny—then you're definitely in. At some point in the evening you're assured of at least a friendly grope in the bathroom out back.

I'm hoping for a friendly something else.

"You look familiar," she says.

I smile at her, not really sure how to respond.

"You work at the police station, right?"

I nod. "Something like that."

Now her smile gets a little bigger. "I thought so. I've seen you there."

"You work there?" I ask, hoping she may know something useful, but knowing it's more likely I need to move on.

She shakes her head. "No. So you're a cop?"

"Something like that."

"Name's Melissa," she says, sipping at her drink.

The lighting changes from purple to white, and I get to take a fast look at her. Dark brown hair. Nice complexion. Stunning blue eyes. Sharp cheekbones. Defined nose. No blemishes. Her hair hangs down past her shoulders, both behind and in front. She tilts her head and tucks a few strands behind her right ear. When she pulls the glass away from her mouth I get a good look at her lips. Bright red, full.

The light changes to orange. So does she.

"Joe," I say.

"So what are you working on at the moment?" She knocks back the rest of her drink, sets the glass on the bar next to mine, and continues to give me the sweetest smile. My drink is empty aside from the ice cubes, which are melting in the heat as I keep my hand gripped around the glass.

"Get you another drink?" I ask.

"A Red Bull and vodka," she says.

Great. So I order a gin and tonic for me and the most expensive drink in the bar for her.

I sip at my drink and look at her one, thinking it does look pretty good, but I don't want to mix drinks: headache material for the following morning, memory loss for the night before. It doesn't happen to me often, but there have been a few times over the last ten years.

"You were about to tell me what you're working on," she says.

"You've been reading about the serial killer?"

"You're working on the Burial Killer case?"

I shake my head. "The other one."

"Oh my God, you're working on *that*? The Christchurch Carver case?"

The Christchurch Carver. That's what they call me. I want to tell her she can call me *Carve* for short. Look at a paper and read all about me. It's amazing how quickly the media can come up with a name for a guy committing a string of crimes. It doesn't have to be accurate. Just catchy.

"That's the one," I tell her.

"That's amazing!" she says, and she really sounds like she means it.

"Well, I do what I can," I say.

"It's pretty noisy here," she says.

I agree. Yes. Damn noisy.

We move away from the bar to a table near the front of the club, but not in view of the street. It's less noisy, though only just. Darker, though. Fine by me. At least we no longer need to shout. To the right on the dance floor men and women are trying to lose themselves in an attempt at rhythm. They look like marionettes being controlled by puppeteers with a sense of humor.

"So, what can you tell me about the case? You close to catching him?" she asks, leaning forward. She is running her finger around the rim of her glass, playing with the salt.

I start nodding. "Soon."

"How can you be so sure?"

"I'm not allowed to say."

"You know who the guy is?" She licks at the salt, then goes back for more.

"I'm getting a pretty good idea," I tell her.

"But you can't tell me," she says.

"That's right."

"So you've seen the women he killed, huh?"

"Yeah, I've seen them." I take a sip at my drink. This one has been mixed stronger than the other one.

"What did they look like?"

I'm not prepared for her question, and not so sure she'll like hearing the answer. "Um, well, it wasn't pretty, that's for sure."

"He really made a mess of them, huh?"

I shrug, but it's obvious I'm indicating the mess was bad. We talk about the case and I give her a few of my insights. She seems impressed, but doesn't offer any opinions of her own, though she does tell me she's been following the case closely.

"So what do you do?" I ask, finally changing the subject. She seems disappointed.

"I'm an architect."

Wow. I've never killed an architect. "How long you been doing that for?"

"Eight years."

"You're kidding."

"No. Why's that?"

"I could have sworn you were only twenty-two."

She gives me a laugh, that clichéd laugh reserved for when you totally fuck their age up in the right direction.

"I'm a bit older than that, Joe."

I shrug like I can't believe it. "You come here to wind down?"

"This is about my third time here."

"This is my first time anywhere."

"Oh?"

Another shrug. "Couldn't sleep. Decided to see what fun people do."

Again the laugh. "What do you think so far?"

I put my glass down on the ring of moisture it had left behind. "So far it isn't as scary as I'd thought."

"It may get scarier."

She's got that part right.

"You live in Christchurch, Joe?"

"Yeah. All my life. What about you?"

"I was born and raised here," she says. "Even started going to university here, but moved away a couple of years ago. I just got back and not sure how long I'll stay. It's a cliché, but I'm just trying to decide what to do with life. You know what I mean? In the two years I've gone, everybody has moved on. I don't know anybody here anymore."

Perfect. It also means she isn't a regular at this bar, so not too many people will be keeping an eye on her to see where she goes. I don't normally pick up women at bars. Only once before have I done it. It's all about the challenge. Picking up a woman at a bar is difficult enough, but breaking her afterward is reward enough for the effort. Getting killed is the last thing they expect—though it's always at the front of their mind as their biggest fear. It's one of life's biggest ironies, and they probably see that just before they die.

Like Angela—I could have just broken into her house. Like Candy—I could have simply hired her out. But work is a routine. Life is a routine. Taking the time to enjoy what we love in life isn't a routine, it's a commandment. If you have little to live for, then you need to enjoy it. You need to savor it.

"So you here with friends?" I ask.

She shakes her head. "Sitting at home alone on a Friday night was killing me."

I don't say anything about her choice of words. Don't mention that coming out is what will end up killing her.

"Can I get you another drink?"

"Sure. Another one of these," she says, holding up her empty glass.

"You want me to order you an empty glass?"

She laughs. "You really are funny," she says.

I shrug on my jacket casually as if I'm cold, even though it's at least eighty-five degrees in here with all these people around. I'm hoping Melissa isn't thinking I'm taking it because I don't trust her or not coming back.

I bounce between a hundred other people. My mind is relaxed. It has this weird soft feeling. I order tonic water. No vodka. I can't risk my mind growing any fuzzier. I buy her another Red Bull and vodka, not sure what the weird mix will do to her senses.

Back at the table she turns the conversation toward the case. Toward crime and punishment. We pause to buy new drinks when we need them. Every glance at my watch informs me time is slipping away quite nicely. The atmosphere is loud yet relaxed. I actually feel as though I could stay here all night, just drinking tonic water and making conversation with this beautiful woman.

Until four o'clock rolls around, that is, because then I decide that although I could stay all night, I won't. It's time to wrap things up. Other than confessing what my hobbies are, I can't think of a single thing I could say right now to stop her wanting to come home with me.

"I'd better be going. Way past my bedtime." I push away from the table. So does she.

The music is a little quieter now and the bar has turned more lights on. They want us to leave too.

"You want to share a taxi?" she suggests.

I was about to suggest a similar thing. "Sure."

The night is still warm on account of the breeze. The night-clubbing population has dropped by around half. Others are floating up and down the streets, looking stoned and drunk. Several of them are coagulating in fast-food stores that make thousands at this time of night. A few are looking for fights. Some are just looking for something to do. The taxi stands have long lines.

"Shall we walk?" I ask.

She takes my arm to steady herself. She's drunk far more than me, and that was the plan. "I don't see why not, Joe."

I carry my jacket over my arm so she isn't leaning against the gun or knife. Then I ask the all-important question. "Which way?" I ask.

"Where do you live, Joe?" she says, giving the all-important answer.

"Not too far away. An hour or so if we walk."

"Let's start walking."

I keep my arm around Melissa, and we're walking, but the distance to my house doesn't seem to be closing. I'm thinking about where I'm going to dump her body. Maybe at the faggot's house. I can imagine his face. One morning he wakes up to crumbs and an empty Coke can, the next he wakes up to a corpse. We keep moving at an even pace, but for every step we take, our destination takes another pace away. After a while Melissa takes off her shoes and starts carrying them. She must be one of those women who chooses style over comfort. I'm nowhere near drunk, but there's still a small amount of gin floating around my brain because things aren't as sharp as they ought to be. Melissa is way beyond it. I feel like we've been walking forever, but she's probably thinking five minutes have gone by.

We stumble west. Follow the roads. The ratio of hookers per corner slowly decreases until there are no hookers at all. We make clever conversation on the way, but it's mostly me telling her about the case. An occasional taxi passes us, but we don't bother trying to wave it down. The scenery starts to change, from new town houses painted funky colors to run-down homes with broken windows and doors covered in some kind of funky mold. Unkempt lawns and pieces of abandoned cars killing off patches of grass. Newspapers and advertising circulars litter the front yards.

After half an hour Melissa starts to complain that she's getting cold, so I give her my jacket. It's like getting Candy to carry my briefcase. It's exciting to watch them carrying the weapon about to kill them. I imagine it'd be like getting somebody to dig their own grave.

"There's a gun in there," I say. The alcohol has dulled my mind, but it hasn't taken the edge off the excitement.

"You're kidding me."

I shake my head. "It's a Glock nine-millimeter automatic."

"You carry a gun?"

"Standard law enforcement issue."

"Wow."

Nothing about my automatic is standard. The Glock 17 was issued to the New Zealand police, but isn't carried by many officers. It fires seventeen rounds and weighs over a pound and a half. It's made from a synthetic that's stronger than steel and nearly ninety percent lighter. The gun itself contains a mere thirty-three parts.

"Can I see it?"

Mine, however, is the Glock 26. The basics are the same, but it's lighter and far more compact. Much easier to conceal.

"I shouldn't take it out."

"I would really like to see it, Joe. And touch it."

I'd like her to see it and touch it.

"Plus there's nobody else around," she says.

She's right. We're all alone out here. Well, if she wants to see it, who am I to object?

As I reach around her waist, she nuzzles her face into the side of my neck. Her breath is hot on my skin. Her lips flick against me. I unzip the pocket, take hold of Mr. Glock, and bring him out.

She leans away, looks at it, and repeats a previous sentiment. "Wow."

I hand it to her. She studies the handle, the stainless-steel slide, the dark blue steel frame. It's a nice gun. Some would say a ladies' gun.

Well, sure. I've only ever used it on ladies.

"You ever shot anybody?"

I shrug. Look at the uncocking safety lever on the side. "A couple of times."

"My God. I bet you killed them, huh?"

She's looking the most excited she's been all night. Some women love the element of danger. Some live for it. Some die. "It's part of the job," I tell her.

She puts her small hand around the handle, points it ahead, into the street. "Pow!"

"Pow indeed."

It's time to get the pistol back.

"Is it loaded?"

"Uh huh."

The Glock, as I said, cost me a lot of money. That makes

it difficult for me to be parted from it. I'm sober enough to identify that.

"German made, huh? Germans have the highest quality."

I shake my head and lean my hand out to grab it. They do have the highest quality.

"Austrian," I say. "Made guns for the Austrian army. They first started supplying them to Norway and Sweden, until the United States came into the picture. Then things really took off. Law enforcement agencies all over the world use Glocks."

"You know your stuff."

Sure, I know something about guns. I know if you use jacketed hollow-point bullets, you can make a real mess. The bullet has an opening in the jacket and, on impact, the bullet expands. Small penetration. Huge exit. Yep. I sure know that. Bonded hollow-point bullets can go through the person and carry on, sometimes hitting the next person down the line. The bullets in my Glock are fairly standard. They don't do a lot of damage, and many law enforcement places don't use them for that reason. They have a low stopping power.

I take the gun from her. Fold my fingers around the handle. Feels good.

"Feel safer now?" I ask.

"It feels so good holding the gun. Like there's so much power in my hands. I like holding on to powerful things, Joe. I like touching things that go bang."

I don't know what to say.

"How much further, Joe? I'm anxious to start doing other things instead of walking."

I'm anxious too. "Not far."

I tuck the gun into the waistband of my jeans and pull my shirttail out to cover it. A few minutes later we come across a park only a half mile or so from home.

"It's quicker if we go through here," I say, indicating the park with a sweeping gesture of my arm.

"You sure?"

I nod. Of course I'm sure. Nothing here except us and a whole lot of grass and a few dozen trees. Dawn is on its way. There won't be any traffic for a few hours yet. Saturday is sleep-in morning for most. Only a few poor bastards have to work.

I'm not one of them.

CHAPTER TWENTY-THREE

The sky above becomes crazy with purple light as the dawn begins to intersect with the night. In the park everything is hazy gray, but not black. The breeze has cooled down since we started walking and become refreshing; the air no longer feels like the inside of an indoor swimming complex. Away from town, away from the drunken lights and insulting music, there's just fresh air and this green park that is damp beneath my feet. This is the Garden City. My city. It feels invigorating to be away from the stench of cigarette smoke, alcohol, and vomit, though a faint odor of it all is trapped in the fibers of my clothes. My ears are still ringing from the loud music.

I take Melissa deeper into the park. She's still carrying her shoes. The grass is slightly slippery. It licks at the top of my shoes and wets the leather. Thick patches of trees and bushes break up the landscape, dividing the park into separate areas and hiding us from the street. At this time of the night it no longer feels like summer, but the autumn it's supposed to be. Melissa has her arm around my waist. I sense she is beginning to sober up. Within a few more minutes she'll be scared sober.

"Where are we?" she asks as we come to a stop.

"A park."

"Why are we stopping?"

"Seemed like a good idea."

She smiles. "Oh?"

I smile. "Yeah."

"I like the park. Don't you, Joe?"

Actually I don't really care for it. It's just a big field with a load of grass planted in it that could be ripped up tomorrow and I wouldn't give a damn. "I guess so," I say, mustering up some enthusiasm.

"I like coming out at night. When there's nobody around and nobody to see what you're doing. I'm a night person, Joe. I like being out when people are asleep. They're in their world and I'm in this world. Their world has people with jobs and mortgages who can't afford to take the time to do what they really want to do in life."

She sounds soberer than I thought.

"Do you know what I mean, Joe?"

I've got no idea. Maybe if I listen to her rather than picturing her naked body on the cold grass I'd have a clue. "Sure. I know."

"You ever been inside somebody's house at night when they're sleeping, and you're just walking around taking a look at their stuff?"

Odd. "Um, can't really say I have."

"No?"

"No."

She leans up and kisses me. Hard. Drops one hand down to the front of my pants, the other down the back. She thrusts her tongue into my mouth and for a second I wonder what she would say if I bit it off. Probably nothing, though not by choice.

The hand at the front of my pants starts moving around. It has a lot of area to cover, especially now. While she's kissing me, she can't be talking, but I'm curious as to what she was just talking about. This is fun. Immense fun. And it will be even more fun when I show her my knife.

She stops kissing me and pulls away. Her hand disappears from my crotch.

Her other hand appears as she takes another step back, and in her hand is my gun. It's pointing at me.

My mind's registering what's happening, but failing to process it into the proper information to make me scared. In seconds, I've been reduced to a victim. Of all things!

No, wait. Surely there's something I'm missing. . . .

I'm being looked at by my gun. I'm seeing why people don't like it from this angle. Is this for real? How could control have slipped away so easily? I take a small step back, and my arms rise up to my chest with my palms facing her.

Melissa says nothing. We both stay silent, the gun the noisiest thing between us even though it's offering no sound. I try telling myself this is a joke. Her hands are steady, any traces of drunkenness gone. Was she ever drunk? When she carried her drink with her into the ladies', was she really drinking it? When I used the toilet, was she pouring hers out? Why would she do that?

I could be only seconds away from dying. Then it will be a matter of hours till I'm found, and then not long till I'm linked to the killings. I try to imagine the look on Mom's face when she finds out. I try to imagine the look on Detective Inspector Schroder's face when he discovers my IQ was actually higher than that of the potted plant in the corner of the conference room. I think about how hurt Sally will be. Imagining their reactions gives me some pleasure. It is all I have.

Melissa seems to be waiting for me to say something, but I don't want to be the first one to talk. I know she'll break the silence because women can't stay quiet for long, and I'm sure she'll feel the need to point something out before she shoots me.

"Aren't you going to say anything?" she asks.

I shrug. "What's to say?"

"I thought there would be plenty for a man in your position."

She's right. I have plenty of things I want to get off my chest. "Like what?"

She smiles. "Like 'Why are you pointing the gun at me?'"

"Okay. That then."

"What then?"

"What you said. About pointing the gun at me."

"You don't like it?" she asks.

"Not really."

"What's this little baby loaded with?" she asks, taking a quick glance at the gun.

"Bullets."

"That's very clever."

"Thank you."

"What sort of bullets?" she asks.

"Nine-millimeter Luger."

"Yes, but which type?"

"Jacketed pre-fragmented."

She takes a few steps back so she can throw a longer look at the gun and not be too close for me to jump her. "Ah. Metal jacket, separate projectiles compressed inside. Reliable feeding, and fast too."

How could she know that? I try to add up the distance between us. I'm guessing it's about fifteen feet. Too much ground for me to cover. Way too much ground when the person holding the gun knows how jacketed pre-fragmented bullets are made. I'm sure she wants me to compliment her on her gun knowledge. Well, she's going to have to wait.

"Take your pants off," she orders.

"What?"

"You heard me."

My heart's beating hard. It's really slamming away, both from fear and excitement. I feel woozy, as though all the blood in my body is draining down to my feet. A good amount of it is pooling up in my crotch. I lower my hands to my waist and undo my belt. I keep my eyes on her face. Her blue eyes, even in this purple light, are sparkling. She looks excited.

The gun stays rock steady. She's calm and collected. She knows what she is doing. I have no idea. Has she ever done this before? I keep looking into her eyes, and though I may be wrong, they appear to be getting bluer. They look stronger now that she has all this power. She's getting off on it. Her breathing's becoming louder.

I unzip my fly. Lower my jeans. Then I straighten up and stare at her.

"Take 'em off."

"You gonna shoot me if I don't?"

"I'm going to shoot you either way."

She's being honest. Nothing wrong with that. Guess her mother taught her not to lie too. I bend down and untie my shoes, flicking them off with my feet. I pull my left leg out, then I manage to remove my jeans without falling over.

"Toss them toward me."

They land in a heap at her feet. The belt jingles and my keys fall out. I'm hoping she'll get distracted and look down at them, but she doesn't. I'm left standing in my shirt, boxers, and socks. Oh, and an erection. I'm standing here with a huge one of those.

"Shirt."

"What about it?"

"Send it over."

I pull the polo over my head, screw it into a ball, and toss it over to her. The morning gray is no longer gray, and the purple is fading to blue. She doesn't look down at the clothes.

"How did you get those scars?"

I look down at my chest, my stomach, my shoulders and arms. Scars from women who disagreed with dying.

"Can't remember."

"Catching criminals, was it?"

"Something like that."

"Socks."

I pull them off, wind them into a ball, and flick them over to her. They land on my shirt. The grass is cold and I'm shivering like crazy.

"Boxers."

I don't even hesitate.

She looks at my erection. It's bouncing slightly. She keeps looking down there, and slowly she takes a wider stance. She keeps one hand on the gun, but uses the other to flip her hair back over her shoulder. Then she touches the tip of her finger against her lips. Runs it back and forth slowly as if she is thinking deeply about something.

"Is that all you have to offer?" she finally asks.

"I've had no complaints so far."

"How could you? You probably gag them first."

"What is it you want?"

"See that tree to your left?"

It's a skinny tree, but the only one there. "You want the tree?"

"Head over there."

When I get there I lean against it. She fishes into her handbag and pulls something out, which she tosses over to me. I make no attempt to catch.

"Pick them up."

A pair of handcuffs. Great. "Why?"

She points the gun at my dick. I pick the handcuffs up.

"Snap one of them on your left wrist."

"What are you going to do?" I ask.

"What am I going to do?" she repeats, in case I hadn't heard my own question. "I'm going to shoot your balls off if you don't do what I ask."

THE CLEANER

I quickly snap one of the cold metal bracelets around my wrist. The ratchet in the mechanism clicks as it locks into place.

"Lie down on your back, stretch your arms around the tree, and handcuff yourself on the other side."

"You sure?"

"Positive."

"Still time to change your mind."

"Do it before I get annoyed with your charm."

I follow her orders. The grass itches at my back as I lie on it. I can't get comfortable, but I doubt that would worry her. Nice view from here, though. The stars are still out but fading. It's as though they're leaving this universe, dying in this purple light. I reach around the tree and lock my other wrist into place.

She keeps the gun pointed at me, walks around the tree, and checks. Bending down she tightens the cuffs where I failed. They squeeze against the bones in my wrist. It hurts, but I don't groan, don't show any signs of pain. Yep, I'm a real man. A real man with no idea what's going on.

She comes back around to face me and pulls out another set of handcuffs. She seems to have come prepared.

I consider kicking up at her as she locks them into place around my ankles. Won't do me any good, though. She has the gun. She has the keys. I've nothing but an erection that can't reach her from here. I pull at the handcuffs, then pull at the tree, but it's no use.

"Comfortable, Joe?"

"Not really."

She grabs the sides of my jacket and pulls them outward. "What else do you have in here?"

I'm not answering. Whether I lie or not, she's still going to check. She rummages through the pockets and finds the knife.

"You carry some interesting items, Joe."

I shrug, though she doesn't see it. It's a smaller motion

when you're lying down with your arms stretched over your head. She tosses the knife in the air—end over handle, handle over end—and catches it by the hilt, blade pointing ahead. She handles it better than I do. Maybe she's a chef. She hunts through my jeans and finds my wallet.

"No identification, huh?"

"I'm old enough to drink, if that's your point."

"How long you been a cop, Joe?"

She knows I'm not a cop. Probably has known from the moment we met.

"About as long as you've been an architect."

She laughs. "I bet the police would love to get a look at this knife. They could probably connect it to a few bad things that have happened lately."

"You're talking about my salads?"

She ignores my quip and carries on. "I bet the gun has quite a history too."

"Everything has a history," I say. "What's yours?"

She walks up to me and tosses my wallet—now empty—onto the ground. She stuffs my money into my jacket pocket, telling me I can say good-bye to my jacket too. "I told you my history," she says. "I used to live here, I moved away, and now I'm back."

Melissa, if that's her name, crouches next to me, the gun in her left hand, the knife in her right. I remember thinking of them as the essential weapons before I left home, which starts me reflecting on the previous ten minutes that have brought me here, but my chance of stopping whatever is about to happen ended when I snapped those handcuffs on my wrists. Maybe this was meant to happen all along. In this crazy, mixed-up world. I spend another moment wondering why handcuffs aren't called *wristcuffs*, then I start considering my options. Once again God is doing nothing to help me out, so there's no point in even praying to the guy. I'll leave the toga-wearing hippie alone and keep my prayers to myself.

"Do you really want me to tell you more?"

She holds the knife above me, not in the dagger-plunge style of a virgin sacrifice, more in the way of slicing the top layer off a roast chicken. She rests the side of the blade against my stomach. It's colder than the rest of my shivering body. My erection is lying on the bottom of my stomach. The tip of the knife is only a couple of inches away. Now I do start praying to God, the same God Sally prays to, the same God she wants me to come along and visit on Sunday mornings—and I'll go too, I promise, if He gets me out of this in one piece.

"No," I answer, shakily. No, I don't want to know her history. It will only scare the shit out of me. I don't need to know why she left Christchurch or why she came back. I don't want to know how she has treated some of the men in her past. I show the same respect to the women I mess with. It's my good nature.

It's my humanity.

She tilts the knife so the tip of the blade touches my stomach just above my belly button. Then she pushes down. My stomach offers the same resistance as the skin of a less-than-ripe tomato, then surrenders. The knife cuts into me, but only enough to draw blood. A warm stinging rather than hurting. As I watch, straining my neck to look, she starts running it up my body. I've been cut before. I know what to expect.

CHAPTER TWENTY-FOUR

I'm getting the view thousands of homeless people across the country are getting: a cloudless sky, with fading stars barely twinkling like holes in a purple curtain covering Heaven. If God is up there looking through one of those holes with His large knowing eyes, I wonder what He's thinking. Can He see me? If He can, does He care?

"Are you scared, Joe?" Melissa asks, playing the knife along my body.

I am scared, but I try not to show it. "Do you want me to be scared?"

"It's up to you."

"Should I be scared?" I ask, trying to control my voice.

When the knife reaches my chest, it has formed a reasonably straight line up to the center of my body, spotted only where the skin hasn't broken. The line is red.

"I know I'm not," she says.

"No? What are you then?"

"I'm the one with the knife and the gun."

"Want to swap?"

"No, thank you."

"I'll let you have the knife after we've finished. As a keepsake."

"You're so generous, Joe, but I already have the knife. And the gun. What more could I want?"

I'm not sure, and that's the problem. She traces a finger down the cut on my body, moving it at the same slow pace she was running it over her lips. It tickles and feels kind of nice, yet my skin is crawling. The blood smears into the width of her fingertip.

"How's that feel, Joe?"

"I can show you."

She gets to the end of the line and takes her finger to her mouth, then sucks on the end. She closes her eyes and starts to moan. Then she pulls her finger out, opens her eyes, and smiles. Her blue eyes are locked on mine. I wonder what she sees behind them. In a quick movement, she folds her body so her face is above my chest. Slowly she angles her tongue to touch the cut. Just as slowly, she runs the length of the cut as though she were licking the inside flap of an envelope. Her face moves down to my crotch, but stops right where she really should keep going.

She looks up at me and shudders. "Tastes good."

"I try to eat well."

I'm aroused again. The evidence is plain.

She stands up and looks down at me.

"I know who you are, Joe."

"Oh?"

"The gun. The knife. The scars. I'd have to be stupid not to know. You're him."

"Who?"

"The Christchurch Carver."

I shake my head. "No," I say. Mom's advice about lying hasn't been forgotten, it's just been relegated to the bottom of my priorities.

She gives a small giggle, the type a schoolgirl would give when confronting her rock idol. She points the gun at me. "Pow!"

I flinch and the handcuffs dig into my wrists and ankles. She laughs. "You're him all right. I know it. I was going to be your next victim."

"Don't flatter yourself."

"I'm not flattering myself, Joe. I'm nobody special. Just a girl who likes the night. Just a girl who knows the police don't use Glock twenty-sixes. They use the seventeen."

"You're basing it on that?"

She smiles. "You're just too smart, Joe, aren't you? Would you like to know more?"

"Not really."

"It wasn't pure luck I stood next to you, Joe. I recognized you. I've seen you come and go from the police department because sometimes I like to follow cops home. I've seen you coming and going in your overalls. What are you, a janitor? I still thought you might be interesting to talk to, that maybe you could amuse me for a few moments. Then you said you were a cop and I was curious as to where you were going with it. Then we talked about the case. Your case. You had too many insights, knew too much about the murders, way too much for a guy who shows up and leaves work in a pair of overalls and catches the bus. I hadn't even finished my second drink when I started to suspect who you were. I'm good at reading people, Joe, really good. I didn't used to be, and it's gotten me into trouble in the past, but people learn faster when the mistakes and consequences are bigger, which makes me an expert these days. I just needed to test you. And that was easy. All I had to do was tell you I wasn't from around here, and right away you saw me as a perfect victim. Someone nobody would miss right away. And this," she says, shaking the gun a little, "this just confirms everything I thought about you."

"You're wrong."

"I'm not wrong, Joe."

"You don't know enough about police work to make these assumptions. You don't know enough about serial killers."

"Don't I? You know, Joe, I love cops. I love things that cops do. I also like going through houses. Call it a fetish, call it whatever you want, but I like being inside a place when people are sleeping. Especially a cop's place. Like I said, that's why I recognize you."

"So?"

She raises one leg at a time and pulls off her shoes. I try to get a glimpse of her panties but can't see anything.

"I think it's the control. You know all about control, don't you, Joe? That's part of who you are. Don't you love the way cops can order you around? When they tell you to jump, you jump. The police are the ultimate in control, Joe, the ultimate. We know it. They know it. I like to collect police things. I've got all these books at home on cops, both New Zealand police and overseas. I've got posters, documentaries, movies. I've even got one of these," she shakes the Glock, "but mine's made from plastic. Different model too, but this will replace it nicely. I even have a Ford Falcon. Same model as the police use. I've got the uniforms, the badges, the batons, and the handcuffs, but you already know about the handcuffs."

"So you're a buff. Fine. Some people collect shells. You collect police stuff. Big deal. You want recognition? Write in to the *Woman's Weekly*."

She puts the gun and the knife down and uses both hands to pull her underwear from beneath her skirt. She lifts one leg up at a time. A G-string, I note, with definite approval. She turns her back, bends down to pick up the knife and gun, then walks over to me.

"I'm more than a buff, Joe. I know everything about police

procedure and law. I even had a German shepherd for a few months. Named her Tracy. She's this big dog that loved me and hated everybody else."

Loved? Hated? Did she handcuff the dog and kill it too? "Dogs will do that."

"At night I like to walk around in my house wearing the uniform, but with no underwear. I like the way the shirt feels against my skin, Joe." She rubs her hands slightly over herself. "You have no idea how good it makes me feel."

Oh God. I swallow. Hard. What's she doing to me? Now she laughs again. I mean, really laughs. She steps over me, one leg on each side, then slowly lowers herself down to straddle my waist.

"Open your mouth."

"Why?"

She puts the barrel of the gun into my eye, pushing it hard enough to make both of them water. I open my mouth. A second later the barrel of the gun is in there. It's like sucking on a metal lollipop that can destroy the back of your skull.

She lifts her body up, then, with her other hand, slips my erection inside her. She slides down onto it, tight at first, and painful, but only for a second. She takes me as far into her as I can get. I don't know whether to be my usual optimistic self, afraid, or thankful, and if I'm thankful, I can't be sure what for. I try to move my pelvis upward.

She leans forward and whispers. "You know what else I like about the police, Joe?"

"Ugh," I say softly, whispering the word around the gun.

She slowly begins rocking back and forth, moaning. I keep my eyes on the gun, and it hurts them to focus on something so close. Her finger is locked around the trigger. If she becomes too excited, she may squeeze it. Maybe she's planning to anyway. This has to be the most surreal moment of my life. Am I really here? It seems so.

What's that Latin saying? *Carpe diem? Seize the day?* That's what I need to do now: seize the day—or, more specifically, the moment. Why miss the enjoyment of now, if this is going to be my last moment? I'm no martyr. I'm the condemned man. Melissa is my last meal. As she rocks back and forth, I'm getting hungrier.

"I like sneaking into their houses, Joe. I like to walk around inside, while they're asleep with their families, and sometimes I like to take things away from their homes as mementos."

I do what I can to join her momentum. She speeds up. Her moaning gets louder. The gun rattles against my teeth. Her lack of a condom is both arousing and scary. For all she knows I could have syphilis. Or she could.

Have to concentrate. *Carpe diem.* It's my new motto.

"I have a lot of books about serial killers too," she says, keeping her eyes locked on mine. "About what they do. About what makes them tick. Tell me, Joe, do you have a dominating mother, or an aunt? Are your victims surrogates for her?"

I shake my head. An image of my aunt flashes into my mind but just as quickly I push it aside, a memory showing up that I don't want to think about.

"Enjoying it so far?" she pants, looking down at me.

The gun is restricting my freedom of speech.

Suddenly she stops, and stands up, as if she's suddenly become bored with me. My penis slaps against my stomach.

"You're a killer, Joe, and I really wanted you to be a cop. I really wanted to have sex inside your house, in your yard, in your car. I wanted you to take me every way you could imagine. Not here, though. Not in a park. And now I'm not going to fuck you at all."

The gun is no longer in my mouth, but I can only think of one thing to say. "Huh?"

She screws her face up into a ball and spits on my chest.

"You're just a murderer, and now I've wasted my time." She bends down and strokes the knife where knives shouldn't be stroked.

This can't be good.

She puts her hand around me where hands should be put, but grips me in a way I shouldn't be gripped. She places the edge of the blade against my shaft. I feel like crying when I'm hit with the thought she might be getting ready to take a memento. I go completely still.

"Do you know what I think we should do with rapists?" she asks.

I shake my head. I stop when she jams the gun barrel back into my mouth. It grates against my teeth and is cold on my tongue.

I try to ask her not to do anything, but the gun gags me.

I instantly break into a sweat as I feel the blade run a tight circle around the base of my penis. Oh God. Oh Jesus Christ. I look up at the sky, but neither of them are coming to help me.

I tighten my fists and pull at the handcuffs, but they won't break, and the damn tree won't fall over. I tilt my head up and I don't know whether to be relieved that I can't see what she's doing. I want to buck my hips and start kicking at her, but at the moment it's one hell of a bad idea.

I try to scream, but the damn gun is pushing at the back of my throat and I want to be sick. My scream is a gurgling, gagging sound, accompanied by the sound of my teeth chattering against the barrel. The skin all over my body is shriveling away from her, and I feel so damn cold even though I'm sweating. Tears are springing from my eyes and they tickle the side of my face. The pressure on the knife becomes harder, but I can't do anything about it. This is crazy. I'm the one who decides who lives and dies. I try to push my ass further into the ground but it won't go.

Images of having my penis torn away flick through my mind in split-second images like those on an old movie projector. I squeeze my eyes shut and try to get those images to move backward, bringing my penis back, having the knife taken away, the handcuffs released. I can feel a load of vomit rising from my stomach and pushing at the back of my heart. My entire body is shaking and my feet are beginning to cramp. I can't figure out how anybody could be so cruel.

The temperature keeps dropping and I don't know whether I wish I was dead. The problem is I don't want to die. I have so much to offer. I don't want to be dead and I don't want her to do this to me, but dying will be easier to live with than having my penis hacked from my body.

I sob as more tears blur my vision. I try to plead with whimpering sounds, with my wet eyes, but she ignores me.

Then suddenly she pulls the knife away.

I blink away my tears. Tears of pain are now tears of relief. She'll let me go and then she'll die for this. She'll die slowly and painfully, though I can't even begin to consider how. I try to thank her, try to thank God, but she still has the damn gun stuffed into my mouth.

She reaches into her handbag and pulls something out. Suddenly I realize things are about to get worse.

CHAPTER TWENTY-FIVE

I remember once, when I was a teenager, I'd been playing cricket at school. I was never good at sports, but if you didn't play them, you got thrust into classes like basic art or sewing for faggots. Cricket wasn't fun, but it still beat baking and knitting. One day—and this day haunts my memory—a cricket ball was thumped hard in my direction. I was unable to coordinate my hands in time so my crotch fielded the ball, saving four runs. I fell into a blubbering pile of agony and play stopped for more than twenty minutes until they could roll me onto a stretcher and carry me from the field to the jeers and laughter of my schoolmates. My testicles bruised and swelled up. Had it been a cartoon, they would have been glowing as if they had been smashed by Wile E. Coyote's Acme hammer. I had to take four days off school, and though I couldn't speak, I could certainly vomit. The laughter directed at me over the following months was constant. The boys were bad, but the girls were worse. They teased me constantly and called me Numb Nuts. The girls never forgot about it. Five more years of school, and they never forgot.

I dealt with it, though. I learned that you can put up with anything. Right now, nearly twenty years later, I would give anything for that pain, because I'm sure it would be less than what I'm about to go through. Every pore in my body has a drop of sweat being pushed through it.

In this little park in the early dawn, all time has stopped. I can hear voices whispering to me what is about to come. Pain is the loudest; the voice of anger is a close second. Trailing those two is the voice of regret. They aren't the only ones. There's even the small voice telling me that this is what happens with you not *living to work*, and that I should have stayed at home and continued reading the files.

Melissa's toy is a pair of pliers, which force even more tears from my eyes as she positions them around my left testicle. The gun in my mouth means there can be no conversation, no negotiation. I beg with my eyes, but she doesn't care. I try to sway my body left and right, up and down, but she increases the grip enough to kill that urge. It feels like she's just strapped a block of ice onto it. I'm paralyzed, as if my spinal cord has just been severed.

She smiles at me.

And closes the pliers.

A guttural scream makes it halfway up my throat and then expands, lodging itself there so I can't breathe. Don't want to. She's just crushed my testicle as easily as someone crushes a grape between their thumb and finger—and, like the grape, the insides spill out. My stomach and thighs cramp up. My lungs swell and refuse to offer me air. My scream forces its way north, escaping into the air. Above me, birds are flying from trees, too damn scared to land. From my groin a throbbing heat replaces the ice-cold feeling of a moment ago, a heat that surely cannot be found in any other place than the very core of hell. It boils up through my body, radiating from the epicenter between the pair of pliers.

I still have my erection.

The explosion of heat uses fingers with claws to reach into my soul and tear it open. It shreds every cell in my body and sucks them dry. I can do nothing but scream and cry and curse every living soul as the claws dig deeper. I try to get away from it, try to separate myself from this entity, but it has me in its grip and won't let go. All the pain in this crazy, motherfucking universe has bonded with me and it likes what it finds.

I stop screaming because I'm no longer able. I can hear dogs in the distance, howling and barking and crying. My jaw locks up. My throat is sore and I feel like I've swallowed a soldering iron. I start to black out, but I can't make it there, instead coming back on the waves of pain as they crash against my consciousness. My body is paralyzed except for my head, which moves side to side, the silent screaming still burning my throat and eyes.

Then I see her. She kneels there, this devil who calls herself Melissa, this creature from Hades who has done this to me. She readjusts the pliers, not on the opposite testicle, but on the same one. Every movement she makes down there vibrates up my nerves and right into my mind. She grips it across the width and squeezes, as if trying to push it back into shape.

I scream and scream and scream as if my life depends on it, whereas the only thing I want to do is die. I try to clear my head, try to make it go blank. This is hell and I have been brought here. Fire crawls over my lap, my skin sizzles from this heat: it's blistering, but I can't see any flames. Melissa pushes the gun further into my mouth. The trigger guard etches my front tooth, but I hardly feel it. I beg her silently to pull the trigger.

She doesn't.

My testicle is only a fraction away from becoming two-dimensional. I can feel fluid dripping down my thighs, can almost hear it turning to steam. The aching is so intense, the pain so deep, that I can't believe I'm still alive. Melissa is asking me something, but I can't understand her words. All I can hear is this constant ringing, a ringing louder and deeper in my skull than that from the music at the club.

Carpe diem.

I still can't breathe. My blood is cold and my body temperature high. I close my mouth, bite onto the gun, and pray for Melissa to pull the trigger.

I orgasm.

I'm nearly blind now. Dark shapes shift in the edges of the softening morning. The pain surely must fade, because that's the nature of pain, but at the moment it's defying nature. I can barely make her out standing above me, the pliers now well away from my genitals, the gun away from my mouth. I can talk, but I have nothing to say. Nothing to plead for.

I close my eyes, hoping for death, but when I open them I only find freedom. Melissa has gone and she has taken her handcuffs with her. I'm a free man who has just been fooled by time, but I can't move. I suck in a deep breath. My stomach is hot, my chest warm, my legs cold. I close my eyes again, and the world around me starts to fade away.

I don't know how much time passes before I slowly lift my head and look down my naked body. My penis and thighs are caked in dried blood. My stomach is covered in a mixture of red and white fluids—a cocktail of blood and semen. Vomit has pooled on my neck and chest, and I can feel it crusted over my face and chin. It smells putrid. I can't even remember throwing up. I guess I'm lucky not to have choked to death—then decide I'm unlucky not to have. I gently lower my hand down to examine the damage. Something that feels like spaghetti is pushing out of something that feels like cardboard.

Oh God, no. Please, please let this be a dream!

My arms are stiff, the muscles tender and sore. I put them behind me and lever myself up. Pieces of sick roll down my body. I nearly black out. The pain is nothing compared with earlier and, judging from the sun, I'm guessing earlier was about three hours ago. It's somewhere around nine o'clock, and Sunday morning means people are either still in bed having a lazy morning of bondage, or are at church. Either way, they're being fucked over.

There won't be anybody coming down to the park for a while yet.

I roll onto my side. A scream rises in my fragile throat. I fight it back, but not hard enough.

I look for my clothes and see them about thirty feet away. As I try to crawl toward them, my testicle sways back and forth, jamming between my legs. It feels like the pliers are still clamped on. I keep thinking that if I can make it home I can survive this. I just don't know if I can make it home.

It takes two minutes to cover the thirty feet. I feel like I've just run a marathon. Sweat drips from my forehead. Blood rolls down my thighs. I shrug into my shirt. My jacket is nowhere to be seen. Same with my gun. And my knife.

My keys are sitting on top of my jeans. Rocking as gently as I can onto my back, I try jamming my legs into the denim. Much harder than it sounds. I stop halfway during the movement to take a small time-out, during which my world grays away. My strength drains with it and the pain seems happy to come back. I have to fight to keep from passing out. I wish I had been wearing jockeys rather than boxers, because then the weight of my swinging mess would get braced. Instead it's hanging like a rotten tomato, seeping as if infected from too much sun. I pull up a handful of wet grass and wipe my face. Two more handfuls of grass clean most of the vomit off my neck and chest.

I glance at my wrist and am surprised to see my watch still there. It's only eight o'clock. The last few days I've been running late. This morning I'm thinking it's later than it is. Okay. Time to do this. I make my way to my knees, then onto my feet. All I have to do is get home. Not far. Just one foot in front of the other. Repeat the procedure. Ignore the pain until I collapse onto my bed. One foot forward. This is the first step. I push away from the tree.

The plan is to walk evenly at a slow pace, and I don't appreciate the irony as I try to step slowly but end up running forward in an attempt to maintain balance. Not only do I move fast, but my legs land heavily, jarring me and sending pulsating blasts of heat up my legs into my groin. A combination of staggering and falling takes me sixty feet before I land on my knees in a crying ball of bloody agony. I want to close my eyes and just lie here for a few more hours, but I know I can't. Sooner or later others will arrive in the park. From beneath the benches on the fringes and from the cubbyholes in the children's playground, glue-sniffers will be waking to the morning of another chemical-induced day. They'll eventually find me, but they won't help me—only help themselves to what possessions I have left.

I get back onto my knees. Onto my feet. Start forward.

It's easier this time. I hold my arms out to my sides, balancing myself as I zigzag forward. I keep my eyes focused on the edge of the park. Don't look down. Don't look around. Just keep walking. Just keep walking and I'll be fine. . . . Twenty yards go by, thirty. Then, in a few minutes, I've covered a hundred yards. A few minutes after that and I'm back on my knees fighting to contain a scream. This time I win.

I watch the sun as it crawls up into the sky. I wonder what the weather will be like today. Sunny, warm, with lots of pain scheduled for brief but strong periods over the day. And for the remaining week. Perhaps the whole Goddamn year.

I manage to get back onto my feet. I walk slowly, with my legs spread. I cup my balls in one hand: it hurts like hell, but the walking becomes easier. I stumble a few hundred yards, pause to vomit, then stumble a few hundred more. I even pause to urinate; the sensation is painful yet simple since I just keep my dick in my pants and go. Urine drips down my legs and onto my leather shoes. It is warm, uncomfortable, and it stings.

The journey home takes me more than an hour, by which time the front of my jeans are soaked in piss and blood. Not once do I pass out, but on several occasions the world sways and darkens. I pass a few people on the way; some see me, some don't. Those who do stare at me and say nothing. Nobody offers to help. It's not the kind of neighborhood where people care. I consider it a miracle just to get home still in possession of my empty wallet and watch. When I reach my building, it no longer looks like it was meshed together by a junk sculptor. Instead it looks like a palace. I wish the architect had designed an elevator for it.

I make my way up the stairs by sitting backward and slowly lifting my ass stair by stair, taking most of the weight on my arms. I only have to make three flights, but it becomes an epic journey, like scaling the outside of the Empire State Building—only naked with my balls rasping against the walls and getting caught beneath all the window frames. I keep telling myself I'm almost there, but I know when I reach the top I'm still looking down the road of a thousand problems.

When I get to my door, I dig into my pocket. My jeans tighten across my crotch. I wince as I take hold of my keys. Fumble with the lock. Thirty seconds. And I'm not picking this one.

I close the door behind me, drop my keys on the floor, and stagger toward bed. My entire body is shaking. Is this the next step? Lie down forever?

No. Although I want to do nothing more than rest, I know I need to take care of the injury. Best to do it while I still have the balls . . .

Huh!

. . . to go ahead with such an operation.

I find a towel and toss it onto the floor, then make my way out of my jeans. Don't know if I'll ever be able to wear them again. From my experience blood, unfortunately, stains. I spend fifteen minutes undressing myself, then another five finding a bucket and filling it with warm water. My fish watch me with odd looks on their small faces. I say nothing to reassure them. I want to feed them, but can't.

I grab more supplies, then lie down on the towel on the floor with my ass on a cushion, elevating my hips. The following hour is spent in three ways. The first involves drinking enough wine to have the room spinning. The second has me biting down extremely hard on a broom handle, stifling screams. The third has a disinfectant-soaked rag in my hand, dabbing at what should never be dabbed with disinfectant. I don't know if it will become infected. Thoughts of my testicle becoming gangrenous are so horrifying that the mere possibility keeps me dabbing. When I'm done, I wash down my stomach and see that the long cut Melissa gave me is shallow enough to ignore—not that it matters. I mean, Jesus, my stomach lining could be poking through and it would be nothing in comparison with my testicle.

I don't know if I will ever have sex again. Ever walk properly. Ever talk. All I know is that I need this day to end. This Sunday . . . No, hang on a moment. Saturday?

Jesus, this is Saturday! This means my internal clock is far more damaged than I thought, but also means I have another day before the weekend's over. A whole day to heal.

I am starting to slip into a total-body shutdown. I head over to my bed and lie down. My mind is setting the pain aside and storing it in my memory bank on the chance I can fall asleep, and on the slimmer chance I might manage to wake up again. I wish a blurred good night to my fish. It could be night. Could still be morning.

My head swirling with thoughts of revenge, sluggish from the alcohol, I close my eyes and look for an escape.

CHAPTER TWENTY-SIX

She's watching one of the DVDs with her father when the phone rings. On the TV somebody is trying to put Clint Eastwood into a grave. If you took that out of a Clint Eastwood movie, there wouldn't be a lot else going on. This particular time they're starting by putting his head through a noose. Her father hits the pause button while she gets up and moves into the dining room. On the screen, time has stopped, giving Clint longer to think about what he has done to make these men want to hang him.

Sally is sure the call will be for one of her parents because nobody ever calls for her. For a moment she thinks it could be Joe, but the moment is brief. He probably threw her number out as soon as she left the records room yesterday. Just what had she been thinking? That she could somehow replace her brother?

She reaches out and picks up the receiver. "Hello?"

"Sally?"

"That's right," she says, not recognizing the voice.

"Sally?"

"Who is this?"

"It's Joe."

"Joe?"

"Sally? Sally, you said if I ever needed anything . . ." His voice fades away.

"Joe?"

Still nothing. Is it really Joe? It doesn't sound like him.

"Joe?"

"Please. Sally. Something has happened. I'm sick. Really, really sick. I don't know what to do. I'm in pain. A lot of it. Can you help me? Is there anything you can do?"

"I can call you an ambulance."

"No. No ambulance. Please, I need you to understand this," he asks, talking as if she's the one mentally challenged and not him. "I need painkillers. And first aid. Please, I need you to pick some up and come to my house. It hurts so bad. Please. Do you understand?"

"Where do you live?"

"Live? I . . . I don't remember."

"Joe?"

"Wait, wait. Hang on. Pen? Do you have one?"

"I've got one."

He gives her his address, and then he's gone. She stares out the window at the vegetable garden in the backyard her father has been at war with for the last few years (he is slowly accepting defeat). All the plants and weeds also seem to be at war with each other. The phone call already feels like it just didn't happen. It was short and confusing and so unlike Joe. She realizes she's still holding the phone. That's proof he just rang. She didn't at all like the way he sounded. She punches two of the three required numbers to call an ambulance, then hangs up. She'll hold off calling for help till she's seen Joe. For all she knows, it could be something as simple as a splinter. Sometimes her brother would be the same way for something equally as small.

Up in her bedroom she pulls out a first-aid kit from beneath her bed, unzips the top, and checks to make sure it's fully stocked, even though she knew it would be. She tells her parents she'll be back later, then heads out to her car. It's gray outside, there are a few patches of blue sky out to the east, but not many.

Joe's neighborhood is on the decline, she thinks, as she follows the streets on her map. Many of the buildings and houses need work. Some more than others. A coat of paint and a lawn mower would solve some problems, but nothing short of demolition would fix others. This area wouldn't need to be this way, she thinks, if more people cared.

Joe's apartment building is only a few stories high. It's made of brick, which in places has been tagged by teenagers' spray paint. None of the windows are clean, mildew and mold have discolored the bottom third of the building, and cracks have been patched with mortar and paint. The pathway out front has some weird stains on it and smells like rotten food.

The staircase is dimly lit and smells a little like urine, but it's not dim enough to miss seeing patches of blood every few steps or so. By the time she reaches the top floor she's extremely worried. She looks at the different doors and finds Joe's apartment. As she reaches out and knocks she notices her hands are shaking.

A minute goes by and Joe doesn't answer. Was it him who actually called? It didn't sound like him, but who else could it have been? A second and far worse thought comes to her. What if Joe was so badly hurt, he's died? That's the thought that makes her try the handle. She reaches out and twists it, and when she opens the door the stench of decay and disinfectant pushes out at her, and she has to stifle the compulsion to start gagging.

The apartment is small by any standards. Daylight is flooding through the single window on the far side and it hits every particle of floating dust along the way, making it look as though she's walking into a sandstorm. She's been wondering what Joe's place would look like, but she hadn't pictured this: wallpaper hanging from the walls, filthy and damaged floorboards, old furniture full of cracks and splits, not that she ever pictured she would see it under these circumstances. She hadn't imagined such a mess either, but when she spots Joe lying on the bed she realizes it must only be because of the state he's in. His clothes are heaped on the floor, covered in blood and grass stains and vomit. Bandages and tissues are piled in the middle of the floor. Next to them lies an empty bottle of wine, cotton swabs, rags, even a bottle of disinfectant. A bucket that reeks of bad things stands next to the couch.

Her immediate thought upon seeing all of that is that he's been stabbed. Stabbed and killed.

She closes the door behind her, then quickly makes her way over to him. He's naked, except for a sheet that covers his waist. His entire body is covered in a film of sweat, and has taken on a grayish tinge. His eyes are barely open, and she isn't sure he can even see her. She can see the rise and fall of his chest. She smooths away his damp hair and rests a hand on his forehead. He's burning up.

"Joe? Joe, can you hear me?"

His eyes open slightly further. "Mom? What's happening?"

"Joe, it's Sally."

"Mom?"

His eyes close. The sheet covering his waist has patches of blood on it. More has dried on his stomach. His body is covered in scars, and a recent cut runs down his stomach. The blood on his hands and caked under his fingernails is mixed with dirt. There are smears of vomit on his upper body, along with streaks of grass and dirt.

"Joe, can you tell me how this happened?"

"Attacked. I was attacked."

"I'm going to call the police, then I'm going to call an ambulance."

"No. No. No ambulance. No police. Please."

"Where's the phone?" she asks, and only then do his words start to sink in.

Before she can ask him why, he reaches out and wraps his hand around her wrist. He tightens his grip, manages to keep a hold for a few seconds before it falls away. "I'm Joe Victim," he says, "but Joe doesn't want to be a victim. No police. Just medicine."

Gently she reaches out and picks up the corner of the sheet. Joe starts to shiver. She slowly lifts it aside not sure what to expect, but certainly not this, and what she sees makes her gasp and tears well up and spill down her cheeks.

"Oh, my poor sweet Joe," she says. "Who did this to you?"

"Nobody," he answers, only managing a whisper.

"We need more help."

"People can't know. People laugh at Joe. Laugh more if they find out."

"I have to call the police." She reaches out and grabs hold of the phone.

"No!" Joe screams, sitting up and grabbing hold of her hand again, his hand wrapping around her wrist with so much force she's worried he's going to break it. "They'll kill me!"

Then, the pain of sitting up hits him, he flops down, his eyes roll back in his head, and he passes out.

Sally stares at the phone. What are her obligations here? To help Joe, that's a certainty. Does she do what's best for her patient, or does she follow the patient's wishes? If she makes the call, what happens if Joe is right and people come back to hurt him? The police can only do so much. She puts the phone down. She has made up her mind. God has brought her here to help Joe, not to risk putting him in the path of more violence.

She balls up the sheet and puts it on the floor, out of the way. Standing by the side of the bed, peering at the wound, she can't help but think she's invading Joe's privacy, but of course she's a nurse now, a professional. This is what she trained for. This is what she wanted to be.

Yes, but a professional would know when she was out of her depth. She would know when to call for an ambulance.

That's exactly right. This isn't what she trained for. But a professional making that decision could get Joe killed, if what he said is true. At the very least she'll see what she can do to help him, then reassess the decision. She reaches up to bring the crucifix up to her chin. She holds it there for a few seconds before taking it off and wrapping the chain around Joe's hand so Jesus rests in his palm. Moving back she crouches down to look at the wound from another direction. Joe's penis is lying on an angle, upward across the base of his stomach and pointing at his shoulder. He's placed a piece of duct tape across it, to hold it away from the wound.

"Poor Joe," she says, almost in tears. The way to continue is with the basics. She tells herself this over and over as she pulls on a pair of latex gloves, and as she does, she notices other pairs lying around the apartment. What does Joe use them for? Cleaning, most likely. She reaches over and pushes down on the side of Joe's thigh, trying to get a better look at the wound without touching it. His testicle has been squeezed, mashed, and destroyed by a tool. Her guess is a pair of pliers, or vise grips.

"Mugged," Joe murmurs. His eyes are open again.

"Who mugged you?"

He doesn't answer. Just keeps looking straight ahead.

She continues to assess the wound. The testicle has to be removed. She wishes there were a way around that, but can't see one. There's no doubt it has to go, just as there's no doubt she lacks the qualifications—or even the confidence—to do the procedure.

"We have to get you to a hospital, Joe."

"Can't. They'll come back. Hurt me. Please, can you make it better?"

She smiles down at him. "Of course," she says.

The first thing she does is open the window. It has to be close to a hundred degrees in here, and already she's sweating. Fresh air starts to roll in. While she waits for some water to boil, she soaks a cloth in cold water and rests it on Joe's forehead. He hardly seems to notice.

Her first-aid kit is more advanced than most, as it contains items she has owned since nursing school. One thing she's missing is any form of local anesthetic, but if she's lucky Joe will stay unconscious through most of this. Actually, Joe needs to be the one who is lucky.

She pulls out the handle of her scalpel and drops it in the boiling water. The blade is wrapped in foil, already sterile. She unfolds a plastic sheet and tries to roll Joe on his side and slip it beneath him, but he's too heavy. She does know how to move patients, but not a patient with a testicle that has been ripped into shreds. She rocks him slightly to the side and does the best she can. She leaves the tape over his penis. It's a crude job, but effective enough. She soaks a few small pads in iodine, then begins to wipe the area around the wound. The risk of infection is high, but this is the best she can do.

"Are you sure you don't want to go to a hospital? Joe?"

Joe is staring at her as if he wasn't expecting her to be here. His eyes move to the goldfish bowl on the table. She hadn't noticed it until now.

"Joe?"

"Please . . ." He points to the empty bottle of wine. She takes a closer look and realizes it's still about a third full. She reaches out and hands it to him. It will help, she thinks. She also pulls the belt out of his discarded and bloody jeans. The belt will help too.

She looks down at her hands. They're no longer shaking. She rips open the foil packaging of the scalpel blade and prepares to go to work.

CHAPTER TWENTY-SEVEN

I dream of death and wish I was there. I dream of pain and this is where I live.

My teeth bite down on the end of the wine bottle and I start swallowing what I can. I'm lucky I even own wine. I bought it six months ago when it was my mother's birthday. I thought we might celebrate. She accused me of trying to poison her, and I ended up bringing it back home. Normally the smell of wine is enough to make me gag. Now I cling to the feeling it's giving me, a feeling of hope that I might just slip away from all of this. I try to hold my tongue aside so I don't have to taste it, but it doesn't work. I feel like vomiting after a few seconds, but the more I get through, the less concerned I become about the taste, and the more I begin to enjoy the sensation it's giving me. I let my head rest against the pillow, and look at the person crouching in front of my crotch. The person is wearing a surgeon's mask, but I can tell it's a woman. I pray it isn't Melissa. I don't know why she's here. I can't remember calling for help, and I realize I must be hallucinating. Or just lucky. My face is growing numb, and my vision becomes slow. When I turn my head it takes my eyes a second to catch up.

The pain starts to flare up again. I look around the room, but the surroundings are familiar, not like they ought to be if I were in a hospital. I try to bite down on the bottle, but find I am already biting down on something else. It's my belt. Not the sort of thing a doctor would use.

My hands are shaking, and my entire body feels warm. I don't know how the doctor does it, but she moves so quickly that one moment she'll be holding something sharp in the air, and the next she'll be dabbing something on me. I blink once, she changes position; I blink again, she's somewhere else—I'm slipping in and out of consciousness. Mostly her words are disjointed, but she's trying to reassure me. I watch as she removes pieces of skin and flesh, then I can watch no more.

I stare up at the ceiling. It is sagging slightly in the middle. I try talking to my doctor, but I'm not really sure what I'm saying. Is this all a dream? Am I operating on myself?

I don't know how much time passes, but when I look up again, the doctor is gone. I am all alone, just as my testicle is now all alone. I start to reach down my body, but then think better of it. I'm too scared to see what the damage could be. I close my eyes. Open them again. The doctor is in. I close them. The doctor is out.

What is happening to me?

Am I dying?

I stare at the ceiling and hope that I am.

CHAPTER TWENTY-EIGHT

Sally sits on the couch and stares at the goldfish bowl. When she reaches out and sprinkles in some food, the two fish inside quickly head toward the surface and begin eating.

The surgery, if she can call it that, has gone well. She suspects the chances of infection are slim. She has neatly removed the damage done by the pliers, and used dissolvable stitches internally and normal stitches externally. Of course only time will tell. Now that she's finished, she's hung the crucifix back around her neck.

She had figured Joe needed it more during that time.

She's decided that as much as she wants to call the police, she won't do it. She wants Joe to be healed professionally, and she wants the people who did this to be caught and convicted, but she'll wait until she can discuss it with him. There isn't room out on the streets for people who can commit such an evil act. She thinks about the Christchurch Carver, about the hell he's been putting women through. It's true that the devil can walk among us.

Joe's life is different enough, and she doesn't blame him for not wanting to be the mentally challenged man who was deprived of his money and his dignity. She respects Joe's right to not be known as the man who has lost a testicle. When he is capable, when he is fully aware, she will help him understand that the right path will be to involve others who can help him.

She thinks about the scars on his chest. What sort of life has he had? Who abused him? Is this why he never speaks of his parents?

Joe is unconscious, so she rolls him onto one side, then the other, maneuvering the bloody sheets from beneath him. She wraps the pieces of flesh she has cut away in the plastic sheet and places it in a plastic bag, then throws the bedsheets, jeans, underwear, and shirt into the washing machine and sets the cycle going. She finds a second plastic shopping bag and begins filling it with all the rubbish from the surgery. She wraps the scalpel blade securely to ensure it can never hurt anybody. She takes off her latex gloves and drops them in the bag too.

She puts on another pair, then starts tidying and cleaning the apartment. The dishes piled up in the sink haven't even been rinsed. The food stains on the countertop match the food stains on the table. When she finds a vacuum cleaner, she decides to run it briefly over the floors. None of the noises wake Joe. When the washing machine is finished, she bundles the items into the dryer and sets it going. The paperbacks on the couch are all romance novels. Martin never read anything like this; he only ever read comic books. She finds it odd at first, but encouraging that Joe would read something with more of a story. As she picks up the folders next to the books, the contents of one spill.

"What are you doing, Joe?" she whispers to herself. She recognizes the photograph of one of the dead women. She scoops them up, flicks through them, then puts them back into the folder before moving on to the next. Joe has the complete set—the Christchurch Carver's victims. He also has information on the detectives investigating the case. She looks through them, trying to figure out why Joe would have these here. Does he know the women in these pictures are dead?

Joe wouldn't bring these things home unless there was a good reason, and she's sure he wouldn't be doing it for money. Either somebody's threatening him, or he's got them for himself. But why? Does it have something to do with his attack?

When she looks over at Joe, she sees another folder, this one on the small bedside table. It's a psychological profile of the Christchurch Carver. No way in the world could Joe possibly understand any of this. So why have it? And why have it next to his bed, as if he had recently been reading it? Outside, the streetlights have come on. The road is empty except for a few parked cars and for the first time it's starting to feel like autumn. She closes the window.

She empties the bucket in the sink and rinses it out, then fills it a quarter of the way with water and sets it next to Joe's bed. She imagines he'll use it to urinate into—he won't be able to walk for a few days. She checks the dressing on his wound. No signs of blood. When the dryer stops its cycle, she pulls out the sheets, rolls Joe to one side, then the other, tugging one sheet beneath him. She tucks the second sheet over him, but it's still too warm in here for a blanket. His briefcase, which is heavier than she thought, she puts within reach of his bed in case he needs it. She spends a few seconds thinking that she should open it, that perhaps there are answers in there, then decides against it. Joe trusted she would come and help him, not to go through his belongings.

She checks that everything is tidied away, picks up his keys, her first-aid kit, and heads back out to her car.

CHAPTER TWENTY-NINE

Sunday. Not in the morning, or even in the afternoon, but late in the evening. I have slept for over a day. My internal clock tells me nothing. I am somewhere between hell and the torment of life. I pass in and out of consciousness, hardly aware of the fact that I am even alive. I look at my alarm clock. It's nine forty.

When I toss aside the blankets I'm relieved to see little in the way of blood. A white dressing around my crotch has been methodically applied. It is mostly dry. I try to focus on what happened after I managed to get home yesterday morning, but come up with nothing except a headache.

I have nothing to get up for. My fish need feeding. But my fish can wait. I don't know how long they can survive without food, but we all might be finding out. The bucket, which looks relatively clean considering I've filled it with water and antiseptic, I now piss into. My urine stings and comes in short spurts. When I finish, my room smells worse than normal.

I close my eyes. I can see a woman standing over me with a

mask over her face and a scalpel in her hand. She shimmers, the mask disappears, the scalpel becomes a pair of pliers, my bedroom ceiling becomes a purple sky with dying stars, and the stranger becomes Melissa. Melissa did this to me. Melissa ripped away my testicle.

And it was Melissa who came to help me. Had to have been.

"Goddamn her," I say, opening my eyes. I pull the covers over my body and lean back into the pillow. I need rest, but I'm not tired. I need to think about something other than Melissa, if only for a few minutes. I reach out to my bedside table and grab the folder.

> A loner. Caucasian, as crimes like these seldom cross racial lines and all the women are white. Early thirties. Killings are all at night, suggesting he has a job, but it will be something menial. He feels the job is beneath him, that he is far too good for what he is doing. He lives with a woman who is domineering, perhaps a mother or an aunt.

I remember Melissa asking me about the domineering mother figure. She believes the same bullshit as whoever wrote this.

> He does not have the ability to stand up to this woman and, through transference, he gets back at her by killing different women. It is not the sex he wants, but the domineering power. He uses sex as a weapon. It is highly probable he has a previous police record. Peeping and peering—voyeurism—would be a good guess. Burglary just as likely.

The report goes on to say that I don't have a multiple personality, and that I'm not insane, which means they got at least something right.

If there are constant compulsions for him to rape and kill, then these are not consistent with the times he has committed the acts. Mostly there have been gaps of a month between the deaths. This could be because he has been picked up on other, unrelated charges. Other times there is a gap of only a week. The fact that his victims cooperate suggests he threatens them with a weapon, and since none of the victims has been killed while her husband or partner was home, it is reasonable to assume he is unwilling to risk an encounter with another male.

He shows a lack of organization, using items from the scene to bind the woman rather than bringing items of his own. His sexual nature is becoming more perverse as he continues his attacks. He plans his attacks perhaps weeks before committing them. The covering of victims' faces and the turning down of photographs show he likes to depersonalize them. He covers their faces before he kills them to fantasize that he is killing somebody else, the dominant woman in his life, rather than covering them afterward out of any feelings of guilt. He keeps items as trophies, underwear and jewelry from the scenes, perhaps to relive the moments. He has sociopathic tendencies, he has no conscience, and he does not see his victims as real people.

Grave sites should be kept under surveillance as he may show up, not out of remorse, but to relive the crime. He may call the police to offer help, to offer a witness statement, all to learn where the investigation is at. He may try to hang around police bars, may try talking about the case with them to learn what he can. . . .

The report goes on. It mentions that rape is a violent crime where sex is the weapon. Mentions that sex is used for power and control, that it's used to dominate. Are they right about why I covered their faces? Was I depersonalizing them, or pretending they were somebody else? I'm not sure. They're right about the graves, though. I did consider going there, but luckily I found out that they were under surveillance before I ever tried.

When I was in my late teens, I used to lie in bed at night and think about my neighbors. I used to wonder what they were doing at that exact moment. Were they thinking of me? I used to imagine moving from house to house under the darkness of night, taking what I wanted from them, doing what I wanted to anybody. Back then the fantasy was in getting away with it—not the killing, but the succeeding. Back then I always believed that I could commit the perfect crime. These days the fantasy has become reality. And that's what the profile is missing.

I turn off the light and close my eyes. I'm tired, but the soreness keeps me awake. I get up to four before deciding that counting sheep is one stupid idea.

I don't know how it happens, but the next thing I know I'm waking up in the morning, my alarm clock helping me to escape from another nightmare. I dreamed of Melissa and her pliers. Each time I screamed for her to stop, but nothing would stop her.

I call work. No, I'm not sick, but my mother is. Yes, it's sad. Yes, I'll give her their best. Yes, I'll let them know how she is. Yes, I'll take as long as needed to make sure she is going to be okay. Yes, yes, fucking yes. It hurts to talk, and I feel like my nuts have been run over by a train. I use my bucket to urinate.

I'm tempted to get up for a glass of water, but the temptation loses out to my reluctance to produce more pain than I can handle. Instead I remain thirsty until I finally fall back to sleep. When I awake I'm covered in sweat. My sheets are wet, my face sticky. I'm so thirsty I ball up the sheets and try sucking the sweat out of them. When I can't find enough moisture, I glance at my bucket of urine, but it isn't something I can resort to.

I stagger to my feet and hobble away from the bed to grace the sink with my presence. I throw up into it before filling a glass of water and knocking it back. Fill it back up. Wash out the sink. Then I throw up again. The kitchen counter is tidy. I can't remember doing it. In fact the entire apartment looks like I've cleaned it. Just what in the hell have I been doing while I've been passed out?

In the process of half shuffling and half dragging my feet toward the sofa, I trip and pain explodes through my groin as I hit the floor. The world disappears, and when I come to, I'm in bed. A glass of water with flecks of ice in it rests on my bedside table, alongside a bottle of pills without a label. Several hours have passed. Maybe even an entire day.

I take out one of the pills. It has to be some sort of anti-biotic. I swallow it down with some water. I close my eyes. I don't even know what's real anymore.

I get out of bed, lean against the sofa, and sprinkle some fish food into the bowl. I don't hang around to watch them eat. I look around. My clothes have been washed and folded. The sheets have very little blood on them. I look down at the dressing around my wound. There seems to be less blood there than yesterday. Did Melissa change the dressing when she helped me back into bed? Or did I change the dressing when I helped myself back there? Jesus, what's wrong with me? I pass out the moment I touch the bed.

When I wake up, I pick up the phone and dial the number.

"Joe? Is that you?"

"Yeah, Mom. Listen, I can't come over for dinner tonight."

It's an effort to talk, but I do my best to sound as normal as a guy who only has one functioning testicle can.

"I have meatloaf, Joe. You love meatloaf."

"Right."

"I don't mind cooking you meatloaf. You enjoy it, don't you?"

"Sure, Mom, but—"

"Your father never enjoyed my meatloaf. Said it tasted like rubber-soled shoes."

"Mom—"

"Because if you don't like it, all you have to do is say."

What in the hell is she going on about? Christ. "Listen, Mom, I can't come around. I'm tied up with work."

"How can you be tied up with work? You sell cars. Listen, Joe, I can make something else if you like. How about I make spaghetti Bolognese?"

At first I'm not sure what she's getting at, that she must be talking about my cousin, but then I remember that for the last few years I've been telling her that I sell cars. I find I'm gripping the phone. Hard. "I can't come around, Mom."

"Seven o'clock then?"

"I can't come around."

"Supermarket has chicken on special. Do you think I should buy some?"

I'm shaking my head, gritting my teeth. My remaining ball is throbbing. "Whatever."

"Number eight chickens are cheap."

"Buy some, then."

"You think I should?" she asks.

"Sure."

"Do you want me to buy some for you?"

"No."

"I don't mind."

"I'm fine, Mom."

"Are you okay, Joe? You sound sick."

"I'm tired. That's all."

"You need more sleep," she says. "I have just the thing. You want me to come over?"

"No."

"You don't want me to see your house? Do you have gay things there, Joe? Do you have one of those homosexuals living with you?"

"I'm not gay, Mom."

"So what am I supposed to do with this meatloaf? Throw it out, I suppose?"

"Freeze it."

"I can't freeze it," she says, using a tone that suggests she's wondering how I cope in life if I think freezing meat is the way to go.

"I'll come around next Monday, Mom. I promise."

"I guess we'll wait and see. Bye, Joe."

"Bye, Mom."

I'm sweating. I'm also amazed she said good-bye first. I look down at the bucket. The smell of urine has gone. The water looks clear. I piss into it, my crotch throbbing.

Hanging up the telephone gets me remembering. When I came home from the park, I'm pretty sure I made a phone call. But to who?

Sally?

I get up and walk to the fridge. Her number is still there, but smudged across the paper are patches of blood. I came home. I was in pain. I made a phone call. I think I made a phone call.

I go back to bed. My testicle is gone and when I try to remember cutting it away, I picture first Melissa behind a doctor's mask, and then Sally behind one. I wonder where I put it. Or they put it. Light and dark, sleep and consciousness, awareness of everything and then of nothing. I glide through this existence as best as I can, not bothering to count the hours in case they're not passing by. Other times I am standing in front of Pickle and Jehovah—not even aware of having stood up and moved over to them—watching them swim and wondering if a goldfish had its testicle removed, would it remember?

My testicle is gone and so is my sanity. The former will never come back. I'm holding out hope for the latter.

My internal alarm wakes me at seven thirty on Monday morning. An entire week has passed. Just like that. I climb from bed and find myself walking better than I have all week. At the window I stare out my shitty view, which today is even shittier than normal. It looks cold outside.

I follow my normal weekday routine. I shower and shave, though it takes slightly longer. I make some toast. I feed my fish. My apartment doesn't smell as bad as I would have thought. The bucket I've been pissing into looks like I've only used it a few times. When I go to make lunch, I find most of the food in my apartment has gone off. Still, I feel like I've gone through the week from hell and come out in pretty good shape considering. The stairs are awkward and I struggle to walk down them, but I make it without any blood appearing on the front of my overalls. The temperature has dropped by half since the last time I was outside. Gray skies above and black clouds far in the distance, none of it looks like it's moving. I have to explain to Mr. Stanley why I haven't seen him for a week. *Yeah, Mom's been sick.* On the bumpy bus, what remains of my ball sac threatens to tear open. What I need is a man tampon. Or a time machine.

Mr. Stanley lets me off the bus. I hobble across the road and prepare to start another working week.

CHAPTER THIRTY

"I heard you were back at work," Sally says, and her face seems to be torn between trying to look both happy and concerned.

I am downstairs in the holding cells, throwing a mop back and forth, trying to wipe up all the vomit and piss the weekend drunks have sprayed all over the place. Out of all the things I do here, this has to be the worst. Every month contracted cleaners come in to really give the cells an overhaul, but it's amazing how painted cinder-block walls and cement floors can really soak up the smell, it smells like a zoo, if the zookeepers boxed the animals into smaller cages and never cleared away the shit. I've just spent ten minutes on one particular bad stain that I couldn't say what its ingredients were, and know it will take another ten minutes to finish the job.

I take off the face mask that protects me from the God-awful smell. The cells, with their metal front doors and concrete construction, are damn cold to be in even in the middle of summer, and it's not summer anymore, and the frigid air at the moment is making my ball throb.

"My mother's okay," I say, knowing she must have heard why I was gone.

"Sorry?"

"My mother. She was sick all week. That's why I wasn't here."

"Your mother was sick?"

"Yeah. I thought you must have heard. That's why I wasn't here. Everybody probably knows about it."

"Oh, sure, I get it," she says in hush-hush tones, dragging out the *oh* and the *I*, making it sound like a conspiracy. As if we're having an affair. "Your mother was sick. That's why you had to take the week off."

"Yeah. That's what I said," I say, and something in the way she sounds is wrong, oh so wrong.

"And she's better now?"

"Sure," I answer, dragging out the word and nodding slowly, trying to figure it out. Does she know what happened? Did this woman with an IQ of seventy show up at my house and operate on me?

"And how are you, Joe? Are you better now too?"

"I'm coping. Time heals all wounds—that's what my mom says," I say, wondering if my mom had a ripped-off-testicle kind of wound in mind when she said it.

"That's right. Look, Joe, remember that if you need any-thing, if you want me to help with . . . your mother . . . then just let me know."

Of course the kind of help I really need with my mother isn't the type she would actually be able to offer. Still, if more people were like Sally, maybe the world would be a better place. The problem though is that she sounds like we're both in on the big secret, the one where Joe woke up one morning in a park after having his testicle flattened in a pair of pliers and had to make his own way home.

"Joe?"

However, I can't imagine there ever being a secret both

Sally and myself were in on. This is just Sally being Sally. Just trying to help me out with my mother the same way she helps me out by making me lunch. She's just trying to get on the inside track to getting me into bed.

"Joe? Are you okay?"

"Always," I tell her.

"Okay, Joe, but we need to talk about . . . about your mother being sick. Do you understand what I'm saying? I'm worried about you. I'm worried that your mother . . . she may get sick again."

"My mother is as healthy as an ox," I tell her. "I wouldn't worry. I have to get back to work, Sally."

"Okay," she answers, but doesn't move. She stares at me and I end up staring at the floor, not wanting to make eye contact with her in case she takes it as a sign to start undressing.

"Can I ask you something personal, Joe?"

No. "Yes."

"Do you find murder fascinating?"

Yes. "No."

"What about the ongoing investigation?"

"Which one?"

"The Christchurch Carver."

"He must be intelligent."

"Why do you say that?" she asks.

"Because he hasn't been caught," I say. "Because he keeps getting away. He must be really smart."

"I guess he must be. Does that interest you?"

I act as if I have to think about it, then slowly shake my head. "Not really."

"Have you . . . looked at any of the folders? The photographs of the dead women? Anything like that?"

"I've seen pictures on the wall in the conference room. That's all. The pictures are horrible."

"If somebody forces you to steal because they're hurting

you, then it isn't really stealing. And the best thing to do would be to go to the police."

I don't know what leap she's just made, but it makes no sense at all. She's rehashing the sort of Christian morality bullshit that somebody has force-fed her. She's no idea what we're even talking about now. She could be saying that killing is bad, that vengeance belongs to God, that using his name in vain is bad, that selling your daughter into slavery isn't frowned upon. All these things are in the Bible and for some reason she thinks we're debating it. She could easily have just told me that drowning the elderly is bad.

"You're right, Sally. If somebody was forcing you to do something you didn't want to, that would be bad. The police help people when things happen to them," but of course they don't. I can vouch for that. I can even show pictures.

Then I start to wonder—is somebody doing something mean to Sally?

She seems to take that as some sort of answer to some half-formed dilemma going on inside her head, because she smiles, tells me she should get back to work, and leaves.

Sally disappears, but my paranoia remains, my earlier thought that she could have come to my house is enough to make me nauseous. If Sally did come to my house, then I might have to repay the favor. There are things she might have seen, things I might have told her that would mean a visit to her house in the middle of the night would be in order.

I sit on the bunk in the cell I'm cleaning and lean my forehead against the broom handle. Over the following minutes, I slowly convince myself that I'm going crazy. No way could Sally have come around to my apartment. If she had, she wouldn't be able to shut up about it. She would be asking me how my testicle was. She would think that the very fact that she saw me naked meant we were engaged to be married. Sally is too dim-witted to have helped me, too innocent not to have

called the police, too in love with me not to have stayed by
my side every minute of the week I was laid up in bed. She's
too many lots of things. And I can't imagine Sally getting hold
of any antibiotics. No, it had to have been Melissa. Which
means she is still up to something.

Before lunch I spend twenty minutes in the conference
room studying the information and swapping my tapes while
I clean the windows and wipe down the blinds. I'm reading
statements, studying photographs, making sure nobody is
watching me. The sky outside the conference room window
is getting darker, and as it does it feels like it's getting closer,
like the world is closing in on me.

I discover several local prostitutes have been approached in
connection with the deaths. Hmm . . . interesting. Questions
have been asked about their clients. Is there anybody who has
a bizarre fetish? Somebody who enjoys perverse sexual acts?
Somebody abusive with unusual requests? It's a feeble and
wasted effort. They're hoping that at some point in my life I've
vented my sexual aspirations on a whore. I'd never do that. I
mean, I'd never do that and keep one alive.

The prostitutes have provided a list to the police. An extremely short list. Not many names and, so far, not many leads.

Before my workday ends, I successfully get four color photographs, one each of the four men on my list. Schroder and
McCoy each have recent photographs in their files, but it's a
struggle to get current pictures for the other two—until I realize they've most likely been photographed by journalists and
cameramen over the last few weeks. While I vacuum a room
upstairs, I use the Internet and search through newspaper sites
until I find pictures of a high enough standard I can print out.

When I leave work Sally offers me a lift home along with
the chance to talk about my mother, and I decline. I forgo
my usual bus, and stop at a bank and draw out some cash,
figuring I'm going to need it over the next few nights. Melissa
took all the cash I was using a few weeks ago, along with my

ATM card. Stepping into the bank is like stepping into a small nature reserve. With a few floor-to-ceiling potted plants brightly lit under the glare of halogen lights, and several small ones crammed into most available spaces, it wouldn't be a surprise if there were wild animals living in here. Standing in a line from the counter to the wall is a line of people I don't want to join, but I have no choice. We stand waiting together without daring to make conversation because if any of us did, we'd look like freaks. Eventually the line shuffles forward a few times, and I make it to the teller. She is a tall, masculine woman with large hands who smiles at me a lot, but no amount of smiling would ever get me to sneak through her front door late at night.

From the bank I walk over the road to a supermarket, since most of the food in my house has expired. I walk around, allowing myself to limp slightly now that I'm away from work. It seems strange being here, as if I've slipped into a slice of life that I shouldn't be allowed in, as if the supermarket for serial killers and men who have been assaulted with pliers is the supermarket down the road next to the deli. I stare at beautiful women as I shop, and I begin to feel ill. These women would laugh at me if I attacked them. They would call me Numb Nuts, or maybe even One Nut.

The girl working the checkout smiles at me and asks how my day is going. I want to unzip my fly and show her just how okay it's going. I'm angry as hell. The left one was my favorite.

I climb on the bus and the bumpy bus ride threatens to tear my testicle open. When I reach home it takes me five minutes to climb the stairs. Much harder than climbing down them. I enter my apartment. The light on the answering machine is flashing. A sliver of sunlight arcs through the window as part of the sky clears up. At least the place doesn't smell of disinfectant and stale piss. I can smell the food that has started to go off, though. I open a window before throwing out the old food and replacing it with the new. I sit down on the sofa and try to relax, to regain some energy. Pickle and Jehovah swim for me after they swallow every grain of fish food in sight.

I push play on the answering machine, fearful of what Mom will have to say, but it's the woman from the vet. Jennifer. And she has good news, and good news is something I haven't had in a while. She tells me the cat has made a full recovery. The owners haven't contacted them. She wants to know exactly where I found poor little puss, wants to know if I know anybody who wants a cat. Tells me to call her when I get in tonight. She'll be at work until two o'clock.

Do I want a damn cat? Not really, but I've become somewhat responsible for it. I wonder if I could give the thing to Mom. It would keep her company. Might mean she won't feel the need to call me every two minutes to ask why I don't love her. Hell, she can even cook the fluffy bastard meatloaf every day.

Only she would think I was somehow trying to kill her—the cat would give her allergies, or would suffocate her during the night, or pour rat poison into her coffee.

After four rings, Jennifer answers, and her voice suddenly takes on an excitable tone when I identify myself. She explains in her seductive voice everything she already explained on the answering machine. She makes cat surgery sound sexy. She wants to know if I want to keep the cat, the whole time sounding as though she is only a step away from asking me if I'll sleep with her. I tell her I'll think about the cat and contact her tomorrow night. We wish each other a good night and hang up. I'm expecting her to say *No, you hang up first,* and when she doesn't it makes me a little sad.

At six o'clock, I arrive at Mom's. We make the sort of conversation that makes me wonder how the hell she really could be my mother. We eat dinner, and then I have to watch her do some of her jigsaw puzzle for thirty minutes before we catch up with her soap-opera friends. I feel violently ill and manage to excuse myself from Mom and her Monday night and, amid the complaints of how I never treat her right, I make my way outside.

It's starting to rain. I catch a bus back into town, keeping my hand on my briefcase the entire journey, staring out the window as fat drops of rain smash against it, the attack lasting only five minutes. I take a detour past Daniela Walker's house and she doesn't seem to mind. Two blocks away I steal a car. It's nearly ten o'clock when I reach Manchester Street, armed with photographs and cash. Hookers are walking the streets, some starting work, others back from ten- or fifteen-minute gigs sitting in parked cars in dark alleyways. In the back of my mind I keep asking myself whether this is a valid line of investigation. It didn't work for the police. Why would it work for me? For a start, I have photographs to show them. The detectives didn't. Prostitutes probably need visual stimulation to jog their memories. I watch as two of them get into a shoving match, which is broken up by a third, then a moment later it's hugs all around. Within a minute all three have been picked up by three different cars, making me think their fight was a show for the kind of people who like picking up hair-pulling, palm-slapping girls.

I forgo the massage parlors where the women are monitored by violent men with dirty money and bad reputations. The men who frequent them, if not regulars, are caught on surveillance or, at the very least, remembered. This isn't the kind of place a policeman visits unless he's swapping sex for leniency. The other factor I have to consider is the availability of women prepared to be paid to live out the perverted fantasy of the killer. That sort of thing doesn't happen in parlors without a lot of people knowing about it. A policeman doesn't want a lot of people knowing about it. He doesn't want repercussions such as blackmail and extortion.

The first hooker I talk to has a deep voice that's almost scary. I don't get a name from her and don't want one. Even after I've identified myself as a policeman, she still asks me if

I want to fuck her. I say no. She shows me some nipple, and I still say no. Even if my testicles were intact I wouldn't put them near her. She doesn't recognize any of the photos.

The second hooker doesn't either. At this point I'm deciding not to say I'm a policeman, but a concerned citizen, and she asks me anyway if I'm a cop. She wears a red wig large enough to conceal a small handbag.

I go from slut to whore, hooker to skank, showing them the pictures and getting no helpful response from any of them. My ball starts throbbing as I walk from corner to corner. Of the prostitutes I talk to, none definitely recognizes any of the four men. Some of them find it hard to remember. I give them money, and it doesn't help. I'm having a bad run. The handgun. The knife. Now I'm paying for information that I'm not even getting, and getting wet in the process.

Monday night is less than an hour from Tuesday when my luck starts to change.

I encounter two prostitutes who I believe actually do recognize one of the four photographs, silencing the small voice in the back of my mind telling me this was a waste of time. It speaks again, though, when each of the two women recognizes a different picture.

The first woman, Candy (that's right—sixty hookers, maybe seven names), points to the photo of Detective Inspector Schroder. Carl. I can't be sure she isn't just recognizing him from being interviewed last week for the same reasons. For only four hundred dollars, Candy will show me what she let Schroder do to her.

The second woman, Becky, points to one of the out-of-town cops. Detective Calhoun. From Auckland. Robert. I ask what he'd wanted. She says for two grand, I can find out. Two thousand dollars compared with four hundred. I figure for a street hooker to claim two grand for a performance it has to be one hell of a repertoire.

Two grand. Sure. Why not. I have the money.

I walk Becky to my car and drive her to the Walker residence. I was here earlier in the evening, just after I stole the car. I removed the police tape from inside and hid away any evidence markers. I checked at work today to see if the house was still under surveillance. The answer was no. I open the door and the smell hits me again. The place needs some fresh air.

Becky doesn't mention the smell. Perhaps she doesn't notice.

We walk into the kitchen and make small conversation as I offer her a drink, then I remember I've taken all the beer already. I open the fridge and it's been cleaned out, all the expired food has gone, just empty shelves now.

"Just water," Becky says, and I feel relief.

Becky looks like she's in her early twenties, but I imagine her life has given her the maturity of somebody twice her age. She has black hair that is completely straight and hangs over her shoulders. Her eyes are slightly bloodshot, but in them flicker the signs of a sad intelligence. They're pale green and look like they'd make a nice set of marbles. She's wearing a tight, black, short leather miniskirt. Knee-high leather boots. No bra, and a dark red camisole does little to hide her firm breasts. She wears a thin, black leather jacket that rides up her back and has about a million tassels hanging from it. I like the touch of irony in the small silver crucifix hanging around her neck. The selection of cheap jewelry across her fingers looks plastic. Her diamond studs are cubic zirconia or possibly even glass. She has a small handbag that's probably full of condoms, money, and tissues.

My legs are sore from walking around and, more importantly, my crotch is killing me. I sit down at the kitchen table opposite her and slowly start drinking from a glass of water. As requested earlier, I open my wallet and produce two thousand dollars in cash. I'd withdrawn three grand from the bank. Right now, I hand two-thirds of it over to Becky.

I figure I'll be getting it back.

She sits opposite me and, while drinking her water, she

counts through the money twice, as if she thinks she's being ripped off. I watch her face as she studies each of the notes. Her lips are moving as she counts. A smile flickers across her mouth. I've already paid her, and she hasn't done a thing yet. I can see her thinking she'll shorten her version of the erotica she possibly shared with Detective Robert Calhoun. I can also see her already spending it. She's thinking about taking the week off, or buying a trip to Fiji.

"Shall we?" I ask.

She takes her jacket off. "You want to do it here?"

"Upstairs."

I pick up my briefcase and walk upstairs. At the top I head for the master bedroom then stop, turn back, and head for the kids' bedroom instead.

"Hot up here," she says.

"I hadn't noticed."

I walk into the children's bedroom.

"In here?" she asks, tossing her handbag onto the first of two single beds.

"You need more room?"

She shakes her head. "Kind of kinky."

"Kind of," I agree.

Here will be good for two reasons. First, I want some variety with this house. Life is a routine and all that stuff. Second, the smell of death isn't embedded in the sheets.

We sit down on opposite beds. She begins by leaning back so I can see up her skirt. She's wearing no underwear for quick access.

"What can you tell me about him?" I ask.

"Who?"

"The man in the photograph."

"What do you want to know?"

"Everything."

She shrugs. Looks disappointed, though I don't know why. Wouldn't she rather be paid for talking than acting?

"Well, he paid me two thousand dollars to let him do pretty much what he wanted."

"Two grand buys that?"

"Two grand will buy a lot, honey."

I guess it does. "How often have you seen him?"

"Just the once."

"When?"

"I don't know."

"Well, think."

"Could have been a month ago. Maybe two."

For a woman like this, time doesn't have too big a meaning. She probably has a baby back at home, being looked after by some drug-infested friend who has got off the game but is too damn lazy to make the effort to get her friend off too. Becky will be spending her money on cigarettes and weed, and she'll be sitting back in one of her tie-dyed dresses, smoking in front of the baby. She'll be girlfriended to three or four guys—each with criminal convictions for burglary, drug possession, and assault. There'll be bruises on her thighs that will never heal, but the pain is masked by the drugs. She'll have no long-term goals other than to stay alive and stay inside a drug-afflicted world. To wake from the nightmare she lives in would be to wake to a reality that as a little girl she never believed could exist. Life wasn't supposed to be like this.

She was her daddy's little princess.

I know these people. They're of no use to the community other than to take up space. They spit out babies, not because they can't afford contraception when their welfare checks go toward getting high, but because with every baby that comes along they receive another one of those government subsidies that's never enough to raise a kid properly. This is Becky's world. Some just can't escape, or don't know what to escape to. I wonder if she even knows she's trapped there.

Tonight I'm going to offer her an escape from the pain of life. That's my humanity.

CHAPTER THIRTY-ONE

The children's bedroom has all that happy jolly stuff I never had as a kid. Posters of cartoon characters are stapled to the walls; they chase each other with stupid smiles and homosexual gestures. Even the bedspreads can't just be normal. They too have characters running across them, frozen in a moment of excitement. The clock radio on the small blue desk is in the shape of a clown. The eyes move back and forth, counting the minutes that have passed since the occupants of this room lost their mother. But the clown doesn't know it. He's still smiling, his bright red lips almost the same shade as Becky's, his eyes looking back and forth, back and forth, searching for something he'll never find. Colorful toys are scattered across the floor. Stuffed teddy bears look like they have been massacred by toy soldiers, their bodies dumped in this battlefield of chaos. Piles of plastic board games are stacked in one corner. One is open on the floor and the pieces inside are strewn over the carpet. A bookcase containing more toys than books is pushed against the wall.

The main colors of the room are blue and light pink. Relaxing colors, or so they believe. They've spent thousands of dollars on case studies to prove this. Happy colors mean happy kids. As a kid, I had gray walls in my room. Put a poster up, and I got grounded. Yet look how happy I am. I could have saved those researchers all that money if they'd come to me first.

"You think you last saw him two months ago?" I ask, confirming her guess.

"Yeah. I suppose so."

"Thought you'd remember a client who was paying two thousand dollars."

She shrugs. "Go figure. I remember the money more than anything else."

"What was his name?"

"His name? What's in a name?"

"Everything," I say, wondering if she's trying to quote Shakespeare. I decide I can't credit her with that intelligence, and chalk it up as a fluke. Still, I find it unsettling.

Could a whore actually be that clever?

She shrugs. "He didn't tell me."

"What did he tell you?"

"Just what he wanted."

"And what was that?"

She tells me. It's so graphic I nearly blush. "And you gave him *that* for two grand?"

"Yeah."

Can't quite discern if that had been a bargain or not. What I do understand is the similarity between this encounter and the death of Daniela Walker. Same signature.

"Where did he take you?"

"I thought I just explained all that."

I shake my head. "I mean did he take you back to his house, or to your house, or to a motel room, or what?"

"Oh, that. Well, it was a motel room. We don't usually go to the john's house."

"Can you remember the motel?"

"Some seedy joint across town. The Everblue. Heard of it?"

I nod. Never been there, but driven by it a few times.

"He booked a room while you were there?"

"No. He already had one. We drove straight there and went directly to his room."

"Was he living there?"

"Huh?"

"Did you see any suitcases? Any extra clothes?"

"No, but I wasn't looking for any."

I figure he wasn't staying there. The Everblue is a dive that charges for rooms by the hour, not overnight, just for people like Becky and her colleagues. Becky seems eager to tell me more now. Before she was defensive, guarded about everything. Now she senses she's going to make two grand for talking, and after her candid explanation of the perverse sex Calhoun ordered, she has no reason to hold back.

"Where did he pick you up?"

"Same place you did."

"Anybody else around?"

"Nobody."

"Pimp?"

"Are you a cop or something?"

It is a question I can see she was tempted to ask immediately. Her greed stopped her then, but now that she has the money, and perhaps a switchblade in her purse to protect it, she can ask whatever she wants.

"Or something."

"If you're a cop, this is entrapment."

Great. A Goddamn scholar. "I'm not a cop."

She doesn't look disappointed or relieved at this confession. "Are you going to have sex with me or what?"

"Not sure yet."

"'Cause I should be charging you extra for these questions."

"Fine. Two grand for the answers. If I want sex, I'll pay normal rates."

She seems happy with this.

"So, did your pimp see him?" I ask.

"I don't have a pimp."

"You serious?"

"Yeah. Used to, but he was pretty violent."

"I thought girls without pimps got hassled by the girls that do have them," I say, but to be honest I don't really have any understanding of the pimp-whore world, only what I've seen on TV.

"This guy was worse than the girls."

"So nobody knows you went with him?"

"Just him, me, and God."

God. Huh. I find it interesting she mentions Him. Like He would take the time to look over a piece of trash like her. Like anybody would take the time. Yet she wears the crucifix around her neck because she is a God-luvin' Christian. It doesn't make sense. The good news is she's just told me that only God and I know she's here.

"So you got no name at all from him."

"Listen, honey, nobody gives me names, and those who do are lying. Apart from that, names and faces I forget. It's the sex I remember, and only then if it's something out of the ordinary. Which this was."

"Is there anything you can tell me about him? Type of car? Where he dropped you off? Anything at all that might help?"

"Help what? Why are you looking for this guy?"

"I'd think for two grand, only I should be asking the questions."

"Whatever."

"So, can you remember the car?"

"Sort of. It was nice. Late model."

"That's pretty detailed."

"Don't be a smart-ass."

"You think it was a sports car?"

"No. A sedan. I remember thinking he was going to want me to blow him in the backseat."

"Did you?"

"No."

"What about the front seat?"

"Does it really matter to you?"

It really doesn't. "What color car?"

"Can't remember. It was dark. What I remember most is how the sex was so violent and strange, and afterward he was real nice to me."

I can imagine. "Did you let him drop you back off at home?"

"Shit, no. I didn't want a sicko like that knowing where I lived. I got him to drop me off at an apartment complex and waited for him to go before finally going home."

"How much did he hurt you?"

She shrugs. "I've been hurt before."

"How much?"

"I couldn't walk home, had to get a taxi. Could hardly walk for three days."

I know what that's like. "How bad was it?"

"God, it wasn't as though he raped me, if that's what you're getting at."

Prostitution and rape. Two things that closed-minded people think go hand in hand. Some people think prostitutes even deserve it. Some people think a lot of stupid things. Some even think that raping a prostitute isn't rape at all, that the only difference is whether you fork out your fifty bucks.

"You've experienced the difference, huh?"

She doesn't answer. Instead just looks at me and uses her hands to fish a cigarette packet from her purse so fluidly that one second her fingers are empty, the next they're holding on to it.

"You mind?" she asks.

I shrug. Think about how the smoke is only going to help mask the smell that's coming from a few rooms down. "Go to it."

I notice her hands are shaking slightly. "He told me if any cops wanted to know about him, I was to keep my mouth shut. Said he'd kill me if I didn't."

I can't figure why he just didn't kill her anyway. It's the best way to keep somebody quiet. Maybe he hadn't reached that point in his life.

"So why are you talking to me?" I ask.

"I've got bills to pay."

Sure, that and the fact that money will always win out over fear, loyalty, truth, or whatever other bullshit shoves its way into a prostitute's life. She pulls the cigarette from her pack, bites on the end of it, and pulls out a lighter. She's still silent, just giving her cigarette head. She lets three smoke rings fall from her dry lips.

"Have you got an ashtray anywhere around here?"

"Below your feet. The maid will get it."

She taps the ash onto the red carpet.

"I keep thinking I'm going to give up one day," she says, looking at the cigarette, but I bet she's thinking about the hooking.

"It'll kill you," I say.

"Everything will kill you these days."

She's so right. "So do you think he was a cop?" I ask.

She shrugs. "Acted like a cop."

"Acted how?"

"You know. Kind of reserved. Always looking around to see who was watching. Stiff body action. Knew what he was doing. Decisive like."

"You can tell he's a cop from that?"

"In my line of work, you get a gut feeling for that kind of thing. When he first pulled up I wasn't going to go with him. Thought I was going to be arrested for something, though I don't know what—it's not like what I'm doing is illegal."

"It is if you're not paying your taxes," I tell her, which is true.

"Yeah, well, anyway, my point is he was a cop. I could tell."

"You asked him if he was a cop?"

"Does it matter? He would have lied. Anyway, so we drive directly to the Everblue and I'm starting to freak out a little because I'm thinking maybe he wants more than he's told me, but he's paid me up front and no matter what you think, I'm a professional and it felt too late to back out. I figured a motel was still safer than the bush, and I figured it'd be better than telling him I'd changed my mind. Some people don't like that."

"Where do you normally go, if not back to a motel?"

"Not far from where you picked me up. I generally just sort them out down a nearby alleyway."

From what she said a few minutes ago about Calhoun's preferences, an alleyway would have been far from sufficient. With the type of noise they needed to make, I'm surprised the motel room had been adequate. Then again nobody's going to complain about the noise because people in twenty other adjoining rooms are also making it. There's even a chance Calhoun booked the two adjoining rooms, just to make sure not as many people heard him having the time of his life.

I take the photograph out of my jacket pocket. "Are you sure it was the same guy as the photograph?" I ask her this without showing her the picture.

"Positive."

"What does he look like?" I ask. I hold the picture facing away from her. I'm basically testing her memory, even though she saw it half an hour earlier.

"Like that," she says, nodding toward the photo.

"Describe him."

"Huh?"

"Describe him. Tell me what he looks like."

"Well, he was wearing a white shirt. Light-brown sports jacket. Black trousers."

"Not what he was wearing, bitch . . ."

"Hey."

"Tell me what he looked like."

"Don't call me *bitch*," she says.

"Just answer the fucking question."

"Fuck you."

Where is all this coming from? Why the sudden hostility?

I open the briefcase. Take out a knife.

"Hey, what are you doing?"

"Listen very carefully, bitch, because I don't have time to mess around. If you don't tell me what I want to know, I'm going to start cutting you up. By the end of the night nobody is going to pay shit to screw you. The only way you'll ever score another client is if you're wearing a paper bag over your head."

I study her face, waiting for a reaction. I'm expecting surprise, right? Or for her to even be stunned. Scared maybe. But she starts yawning. When she finishes she puts the cigarette back into her mouth and sucks in another mouthful of cancerous smoke, like she doesn't even care. Becky has obviously been threatened before.

"You think you scare me?"

Yes. Yes, I do think I scare her. I tell her this.

"You like that?" she asks.

"Huh?"

"Scaring people."

"It's what I do."

"Oh."

I'm holding the knife so the blade is pointing toward her. For the first time, I'm beginning to doubt that I'll use it. There's something about her I'm starting to like. No, I'm not going soft, and I'm certainly not going to propose to her, but I'm starting to wonder if it's really necessary to cut her open.

I'm not sure how to carry on, which is probably what she wants.

"So what are you going to do with this information?" she asks, ignoring the knife.

"What's it to you?"

"I'd think a man in your position would be a bit friendlier."

A man in my position. What position? I'm the one with the knife. She's going nowhere unless I allow her to. What she doesn't understand is that my threat is no empty one, unlike those made by the losers she's screwed.

I consider apologizing, but don't want to.

"I think he killed somebody," I confess.

"Jesus, you sure?" she asks, no doubt thinking he could have just as easily killed her.

"Pretty sure."

"You think he killed Lisa Houston?"

"Who?"

"Lisa Houston."

I have to think about it for a few seconds, and then it comes to me. "You mean the pro from a week or so ago?"

"Yeah."

I glance back at the door into the hall, remembering Lisa carrying my briefcase for me on the way, then I imagine Lisa being carried on her way out. "I think so."

"You're saying a cop killed her?"

Sure. Why not? There's nothing she can do with the information. "That's the way it's looking."

"Unbelievable."

"You knew her?"

"We all know each other, honey."

"You liked her?"

"Couldn't stand her. Didn't mean I wanted her dead, but since she is, I guess I'm happy about it."

"Happier than Lisa, anyway."

"Huh. I guess you're right."

I *am* right. I'm in the ideal position to make a solid comparison. "So what can you tell me about him?"

She gives me a detailed description. Nails him to a T.

I show her the photograph for the second time. She confirms it's him. In a matter of maybe an hour, I've narrowed my list down to one suspect. Detective Robert Calhoun. Father to a dead boy. Husband to a disappointed wife. Partner to his morbid desires.

We talk for a bit more. I put the knife back into the briefcase and close down the lid. She doesn't look relieved to see it gone. It's like she never even cared. Just sits there, sucking on her cigarette and talking. And thinking about her money. I'm picturing my two grand in her purse. I don't want her to have it anymore. I glance at my watch.

"Getting late, honey?"

I look up at her. "Yeah."

I still have plenty to do tonight, including picking up the cat.

"So now what?"

I shrug. If I'm not going to get my money back, I may as well get my money's worth.

"Is there anything you would like to do?" she asks.

I nod. I have aspirations. My life is full of things I'd like to do.

"Yeah? What?" she asks.

"Well, I suppose we could make use of the bedroom."

But I don't feel like making use of her, let alone the bedroom. The clown clock with the big moving eyes keeps looking at her, then at me, then at her again. All I feel like doing is going home and hitting the sack. I yawn. Wipe my fingertips at my watering eyes.

"Maybe I'll take a rain check."

"You sure?" she asks.

"Positive." I stand up and grab my briefcase.

"Sure thing, sugar. You ever want to do this again sometime, feel free to call me."

I turn off the lights on the way out. I don't lock the front door behind me. It's stopped drizzling and the wind is cool. Easily the coldest it has been all year. People are all inside, wrapped up in sheets and blankets. In their dreams, people like me are chasing them. Drops of water reflect the street-lights off leaves and fences and my car for the evening.

We head for town. I can't be bothered making conversation and she doesn't seem that eager either, so I turn on the radio. There's some crappy song on, but I don't care enough to change stations. "Where do you want me to drop you off?"

"Wherever."

Should I or shouldn't I? I still don't know. Killing her will get me my two thousand dollars; letting her live still offers her up as help should I need any more information. It's nothing like the dilemma I had at the gay guy's house, but it's still a dilemma. What would God want me to do? He'd probably want me to smite the whore, but she's too likable for that.

I pull into an alleyway between a couple of shops, the headlights picking out dozens of cardboard boxes, chunks of white Styrofoam, and bags of trash. There are small puddles that have rainbows in them caused by exhaust fumes. I smile at her, lean over, and open the door like a gentleman. This woman has narrowed my list down to one suspect, and for that I'm truly grateful. She smiles back at me, and thanks me for a pleasant evening.

"You're welcome," I say, and thirty seconds later, after her body lands on the cold concrete with a slight thump, I tuck the two thousand dollars into my jacket pocket. I wipe the knife clean on her short skirt, then lean back into the car.

Always the gentleman till the end.

CHAPTER THIRTY-TWO

The money feels good inside my pocket. It makes me feel like I'm worth something, that I'm somebody important. The only thing I'm carrying that doesn't feel so good is the guilt I feel about killing Becky. I can't believe how quickly it's hit me. It's like snapping Fluffy's neck. The only way I can balance the scales is if I'm driving home tonight and I come across a hooker that's been hit by a car.

As I back away from the alleyway, my headlights washing across her crumpled body, the pain starts to fade. By the time I get stuck at my first red light, I don't feel bad at all.

I try to figure out why Calhoun did what he did, and the answer is actually pretty simple. His problem was that sex with Becky the prostitute couldn't live up to the fantasy he'd imagined. He thought he could quash his desire for rough sex by having it with Becky, but because he was paying her, and she was only pretending to be afraid, it took away the realism. Becky didn't fear for her life, and Calhoun knew that. It may not have sunk in for a few days, or maybe longer, but in the end he was left needing far, far more. Daniela Walker gave him his fantasy. In the process he knew the differences between right and wrong, gambled with the consequences, and decided the risk was worth it.

I don't bother questioning why he would kill an innocent woman and pass up on the opportunity to kill the hooker, especially when the innocent woman was a harder target. It's all part of the game, part of the fantasy. It's a pure rush to be completely superior, so powerful, so unbelievably dominant. Following Daniela home, confronting her, breaking her, would have been one hell of an ego rush.

The car has a weighty feel, but that's because Candy version two, the four-hundred-dollar hooker, is lying in the trunk where I put her not long ago. I pull over outside the park where Melissa changed my life with a pair of pliers, and walk around to the back of the car.

Candy's short blouse is covered in blood. Her puffy eyes are open and staring at me, through me, and I wonder exactly what it is she's trying to focus on. Her skin is so pale she looks as though she could have been locked in the trunk for the last six months. In contrast, her painted lips are a vivid red, the color of blood. I close the trunk.

There are no lights on in any of the houses, and just under half of the streetlamps are busted. I can see the dark outlines of the trees in the park, but none of the details. No traffic. No pedestrians. No signs of life.

I open the trunk and look down at the dead girl. With my hands gloved, I roll her body over. The pool of blood beneath her looks like oil. Again I look around. When I slammed the trunk on Candy earlier, she was alive. I slam it on her again, only this time she's dead.

I did not kill her.

I walk back to the side of the car knowing there can only be one person who's done this to me: Melissa. I'm not sure exactly when, or why. The same reason she came to my apartment and helped me with the injury. She's playing with me. Toying with me. She's setting something up of which I have no idea at all.

I'm inside and just shutting my door when a movement to my right stops me. I twist my head to see an old man stepping out of the dark toward me.

"My God, is that you, Joe?" He gets a few steps closer, and I give him a casual look up and down, as if I'm out shopping for victims. He looks in his late sixties—his gray hair is combed back at the front, but standing up at the back. His face is a collage of wrinkles that are long and deep. He wears glasses that are broken in the middle, and look to be held together with Velcro dots. They're covered in a thin layer of dust, and I can't pick the color of his magnified eyes. He's holding a hand toward me, not quite pointing, but in a gesture that makes me aware he's about to put his hand on my arm. The sad part is I'm about to let him. He's wearing a flannel shirt and brown corduroy pants. He looks vaguely familiar. I say nothing. I'm in no mood for conversation.

"Little Joe? It is you, isn't it?"

I strain my memory, and in that same moment his face seems to shimmer into focus, along with a name. "Mr. Chadwick?"

"That's right, son. My God, I can hardly believe it." He starts shaking his head. "If it isn't little Joe. Evelyn's boy."

He offers me his right hand. For a second I imagine it sitting in my briefcase along with a small chunk of his wrist. I step out of the car and shake his hand, hoping he doesn't pull me into an embrace.

"How's your mother, Joe?"

I shrug. Mr. Chadwick has always been a nice enough guy, I suppose, once you get past the liver spots and wrinkles, and he certainly seems pleasant enough at the moment. At his age, he must contemplate death quite a lot. I ought to ask him.

"She's fine, Mr. Chadwick."

"Call me Walt."

"Sure, Walt. Mom's just Mom, if you know what I mean."

"She still doing those jigsaw puzzles?"

"Yep." Standing outside of my car, I begin to shiver. A quick glance upward at the covered stars suggests there may be more rain on the way. If so, it's going to ruin my plans.

"She's been doing those as long as I remember."

"Yeah, she really likes her puzzles."

"I bet she's good at them too. Damn good."

"So, um, Walt, what brings you out so late?"

"I'm walking my dog," he says, showing me the leash.

I look around. "Where is he? In the park?"

"Who?"

"Your dog, Walt."

He shakes his head. "No, no. Sparky died two years ago."

I have no answer for that. I do my best to think that he's joking, but I'm pretty sure he isn't. I start nodding slowly, as if I completely understand. He starts nodding slowly too, mirroring me. A few more seconds go by before he speaks.

"What about you, Joe?"

"I'm just driving. You know how it is."

"Not really. I don't drive anymore. Haven't since the stroke. Doctors tell me I'll never drive again. You know, Joe, I must catch up with your mother. Boy, she's some woman. They don't make them like that anymore."

Don't make them insane? Yeah, they do, Walt. I shrug and say nothing.

"What are you doing with yourself these days, Joe?"

"I sell cars."

"Really? I'm in the market for a car," he says, confusing me since he just said he can't drive anymore, and perhaps he's confusing himself too. I'm desperate to know whether he saw the corpse in the trunk. "Where do you work?"

"Umm . . ." I struggle for a name, "Everblue Cars. Heard of it?"

Slowly he nods. "Fine establishment, that one, Joe. You must be proud."

"Thanks, Walt."

"That one of yours there?" He nods toward the car.

"Yeah." Walt is a witness. Nice old Mr. Chadwick. "Want to take a ride?"

"For sale, is it?"

"Yep." I take a stab at the price. "Eight grand."

He whistles. Like people do after you've quoted them a price. The whistling is one step away from tire kicking.

"Gee, that's cheap," he says, and tries to kick the nearest tire, but misses.

We climb into the car. I do up my seat belt and Walt works on his. He starts whistling again, all the time he's looking at the dashboard, air-conditioning, and radio controls.

"You know, Joe, I haven't seen your mother since your dad died."

I envy him.

"That was a real tragedy," he adds, sounding upset.

I find myself nodding. I want to tell him that I thought it was a tragedy too. I want to tell him how it hurt when Dad was no longer with us, how I just wanted him to be alive, but I say nothing. "Yeah," I manage, keeping my voice under control.

"Did I ever tell you how sorry I was?"

I have no idea what in the hell he told me back then. What anybody told me. "You did. Thanks."

He opens his mouth, but says nothing. He seems to be thinking. "How are you coping these days?"

"I'm over it," I say, not bothering to mention how empty life became without him.

Now it's his turn to start nodding. "That's good, Joe. When a man takes his own life, his family can be a mess for years. Thank God you've come out of it as a nice young man."

I'm still nodding. When Dad killed himself, the only thing

I felt like doing at first was joining him. There were hundreds of questions, but the biggest one was *Why?* Mom knows, I'm sure of it. Just as I'm sure she'll never tell me. The second *why* is just as important: why did he leave me alone with Mom?

"She still got the place in South Brighton?"

I stop nodding. I'm thinking of Dad and feeling depressed. I know Melissa is watching me, but for the moment I don't really care.

"Yeah." I start the car. "Shall we take her for a spin?" I ask, needing to change the subject.

"Sure, Joe."

We watch the city go by. Life has wound down in this part of the world. We spot only a few other cars on the road. We pass a service station with a police car parked outside and two officers standing over a man they have handcuffed laying facedown. Walt makes conversation about the car and the weather, and tells me that his dead dog keeps running away.

"My God, who would have thought I'd run into Evelyn's son? You know, Joe, I've known your mother more than forty years."

"Really."

"We're both single now. Single and old. Isn't life sad?"

"Sad," I agree.

I stop north of the city, turning into a long stretch of road just before the highway where a thousand trees block our view in every direction. Out here, we're all alone. Out here, I can do what I want.

"Maybe I'll give your mother a call tomorrow, invite myself around for dinner."

Keeping one hand on the wheel, I reach behind the passenger seat and open my briefcase.

"Something I can get for you, Joe?"

"No. I'm fine."

"Your mother and I knew each other quite well before she met your father. Did you know that, Joe?"

"No, I didn't know that, Walt."

"Would you mind if I called her? I wouldn't mind getting to know her again."

The opportunity knocks so loud I actually drop the knife. Candy's in the trunk of the car, but Walt doesn't know she's there. He couldn't. He's too damn old to make sense of anything even if he had seen her, and he'd be blabbing on about her, asking me a whole bunch of questions. I close my briefcase. If I let Walt live, he's going to spend time with my mother, and that's time she won't be able to devote to me.

"What are you smiling about, Joe?"

"Nothing. You want to drive back, Walt?"

"No, son, I'll let you do the driving."

I drive back toward town. We pass the same trees. Same service station with the same police car parked outside only now the handcuffed guy is in the back of that car. Walt talks the entire way, touching on subjects that I'm still too young to care about. Things about diets and diseases and loneliness. He tells me about my mother, delves into a past that existed before she met my father. Walt speaks so much that I can see why he got on so well with my mother, having the ability to turn nothing into something even less interesting. His sentences flow from one to the next, and mixed in there in those same breaths are directions to his house. The house is small and well kept. It's obvious Walt's dead dog doesn't crap all over the lawn.

"I'll call your mother tomorrow morning," he says, leaning back into the car and smiling at me.

"I think she might like that. Give her somebody to talk to. I think she has issues more in her age group that I can't relate to, like pensions and cancer."

He gives me a knowing nod, his eyes twinkling a little. "Evelyn," he says, more to himself than to me, then he turns and heads up the pathway to his door.

I pull away and head south. I turn on the stereo and sing

loudly. After ten minutes, I pull the car off to the side of the road beneath a bank of trees. The grass, burned dry from the last few months of hot sun, has been sheltered enough by the trees to keep most of the day's rain off. I study the body again, hoping that I might be able to learn something from it, or more likely, that Melissa has left me a message. I shift the corpse slightly. Deep cuts smile at me. Dark red flesh gleams from beneath thick flaps of skin. I have a good idea what caused the wounds. I wrestle Candy from the car, careful not to get blood on myself, and dump her on the ground, which reveals the murder weapon in the bottom of the trunk.

My knife.

Or, to be more accurate, a photograph of my knife.

Seeing this leads me to a couple of conclusions: one, Melissa is definitely stalking me, and two, I'm in serious trouble. The knife has my fingerprints on it, as does my gun.

I remove a red plastic container full of gas and set it on the ground.

Just what game is Melissa playing? If she were going to give the weapons to the police, she would have done so by now. That means she wants something else. And I'm sure she'll let me know soon enough.

I dump Candy back into the trunk. Her hands are still tied, her mouth gagged. Both those are my doing. I wonder what she thought when she was desperate for help and a woman came along and opened the trunk. It was the end of things going badly for Candy. It was the end of everything.

I roll her onto her side in an attempt to fit her back in nicely, but finish with one of her legs sticking out. When I slam the trunk down I break her ankle. She doesn't mind.

I decide to leave the trunk open. I shake the container back and forth, listening as the gas inside sloshes around. It's about a quarter full. I use what's there to soak Candy's clothes, then toss the container in there with her. I reach into the car for my briefcase and use a knife to cut away Candy's blouse. Once I pop the gas cap on the side of the car, I stuff the blouse inside, leaving a tongue hanging out.

The car's cigarette lighter does the job.

I am most of the way back into town when I remember the cat. There is nobody to see me as I steal my second car for the evening.

Jennifer smiles at me when I walk through the door. She looks at me as if we're long-lost friends. "Hi there, Joe," she says, her voice sounding seductive.

"Hi."

She waits for a few seconds, checking to see if that's all I'm going to say. "I'll just get him for you."

"Thanks."

I'm picturing how Melissa would look in a studded dog collar when Jennifer brings the cat out in a small cage.

"I didn't think you wanted to take him," Jennifer says, "after last week."

"Last week?"

"When I rang to give you an update, you said you didn't want any more cats. How many have you got?"

"Last week?" I repeat.

Her smile disappears and is replaced with one of caution. "I called you last week."

"Oh. I was sick last week, really sick. To be honest, I don't even remember you calling. I was in bed all week. I don't know what the hell it was I had, but I was pretty delirious. If you called and I was a bastard or something, I'm really sorry." Though she's the one who ought to be feeling sorry—I'm the one with a missing testicle. Her caution turns to sympathy. "Are you okay now?"

"Getting better. The strange part is that I don't even have any cats."

She smiles, and I wonder why I must keep being nice to people. Why can't I just take her somewhere and do to her what I've been doing to everybody else?

"Well, you've got one now. What are you going to call him?"

"I haven't really given it any thought. Any suggestions?"

"Maybe we could figure one out over coffee?" she offers.

"I didn't know cats drink coffee," I tell her.

She smiles, then stops smiling, and looks a little confused.

"What do I owe you for the cage?" I ask, figuring it wouldn't look good if I pulled a plastic bag out of my pocket and stuffed the cat inside. I bet the cage is going to add a good chunk to what is already an expensive mammal.

"Can I trust you to bring it back?"

"I'm a trustworthy guy."

"Then it costs nothing." She smiles. "You want a lift home, or have you got a car?"

A lift home would be good, since it would give me a chance to test a few things out that haven't been used since my half castration. But my name's on record here, and it wouldn't take long for the police to come.

I thank her for her offer, promise to bring the cage back before the week is out, and ask her to call me a taxi.

The cage moves around beneath my grip. The taxi driver makes some comment on the cat, figuring he can strike up a conversation with me. He figures wrong. When I get home I put the cat in the bathroom and shut the door. When I go to bed, I can hear it crying. Tomorrow I'll buy it some food and myself some earplugs. Then I'll show it around my apartment.

CHAPTER THIRTY-THREE

The following morning my internal alarm clock doesn't let me down. Things are getting back to as normal as they can be for a guy missing his left testicle. I'm still dreaming, though, which is a concern. Last night I was talking to Dad. The dream was disjointed, but I can remember fragments where he was asking me what I was doing. I guess he was asking me because I was stuffing him into the front of the car he was found in. I'd wrapped foam around his wrists, foam and padding, so the rope wouldn't leave bruises. He couldn't wind down the windows or open the doors. He couldn't adjust the air-conditioning or turn off the engine as the carbon monoxide flooded in. He turned blue as he asked me over and over to stop. Mom wasn't there. She was playing bridge down at the local bingo hall. In fact, that was the last time she ever played. He stopped asking me to stop, then told me that he loved me. Then he died. One moment he was my dad. The next moment he was nothing.

I'm not growing at all accustomed to dreams and I've

woken from this one feeling shaky and ill. Of course I didn't kill my father. I loved him dearly and, like my mother, I'd never have done anything to harm him. Walt mentioning my father's suicide must have given me the imagery. Nobody knows why Dad did what he did. Why he sat himself inside the car parked in the garage and pumped carbon monoxide through the side window with a hose. He didn't even leave a note.

I give the cat explicit instructions not to claw the furniture or walls. He doesn't. He looks around for a few seconds before deciding the best way to take a break from being locked inside the bathroom is to hide beneath my bed. I feed my fish, make a mental note to buy some food for the cat, go through the usual routines, then fight the cat back into the bathroom with the aid of a broom.

I turn the radio on, listen to the news.

The fire from the car spread, as I predicted, but the rain over the last day stopped it from spreading far. They say this as if anybody could care about trees and crops, as if the country's running low on them. The news guy makes no mention of the dead hookers. Instead he moves on to a report about sheep. Tells us that we're now outnumbered by them ten to one. He doesn't mention anything about a revolt, doesn't explain why we need to increase their numbers by cloning them.

The walk downstairs is easier than yesterday. The bus ride is also easier. The weather a little worse. It's raining steadily. I learn nothing at work except that the people I work with have no Goddamn idea what they're doing.

"I've made you some sandwiches," Sally says, when she meets me outside my office just before lunch.

"Thanks."

I eat her sandwiches and take another of the pills. It feels like it goes down my throat sideways, and I don't feel any better for it. I think about my dream, and wonder why I'm having so many these days. I put it down to the fact that at the moment I'm not getting to do all the things other people only fantasize about.

A few hours after lunch I'm carrying my bucket and mop when I see her: Melissa, sitting at a desk. For a second, perhaps even two, the world comes to a complete standstill. I can hear blood pulsing in my head, which is a neat trick because I can swear my heart stops beating. She turns to me and winks. I start toward her, then begin to back away, so I end up motionless. I want to look around at the police who are going to start jumping on me, but I can't look away from her. After all she's done to me, there's something about her I can't help but admire.

Today she's wearing an expensive light gray suit that makes her look like an overpaid lawyer. Her hair is pulled back neatly, and she is wearing little makeup. She looks like a woman any man would desperately want to believe.

She flashes a smile at me before turning her attention back to Detective Calhoun. Are they working together?

"Afternoon, Joe. How's it going there?"

I jump and turn and see Schroder standing next to me, sipping from a cup of coffee that I haven't made. He's smiling at me. "Fine, Detective Schroder."

"You know her?"

"Huh?"

He nods his head toward Melissa. "Looked like you recognized her."

I shake my head. "No."

He grins. "Just staring, huh? Don't blame you, and don't feel bad for being caught out."

"Caught out?" I say. Oh, Jesus, it's come to this, it's finally come to this and my gun is in my office. I can't believe it. Weirdly, I feel like crying.

"You're not the only one," Schroder says.

"What?"

"Half the men in here are staring at her."

He's right. Half the men in here are staring at her.

"Just don't let her catch you," he says, and it's good advice—better advice than he really knows.

He disappears back in the direction he came from, as if he'd only shown up to make chitchat. I'm still standing in the same place I was when I saw Melissa, only now I'm feeling more obvious about it. I need to leave. Do I go for my briefcase in case I need to shoot my way out of here, or do I just head for the door now?

I carry the bucket and mop back to my office, close my door behind me, and grab my briefcase and at the same time I'm opening it, I remember I don't have my gun anymore. I slump into my chair. I don't know what to do, with a little more distance between Melissa and my remaining testicle, I can think a little clearer.

Melissa didn't point me out. That's not why she's here. She's here because, just like my gun, she owns me too. This is her game. She's come here today to make sure I know who's in control.

I get out of my chair. I stare down at the city for a few seconds, the people out there moving quickly through the cold. I take one of the knives out of my briefcase. It's small and easy to conceal, but I figure if I'm going down I can take one, maybe two people with me. I slip it into my pocket. When I head into the hallway with the vacuum cleaner, Melissa and Calhoun have gone. They'll be in the smaller of the two conference rooms up here. It's similar to an interrogation room, but with nicer décor, designed to get information from nice people in a comfortable way. There will be tea and coffee and a light lunch, nice music. It's foreplay where the goal is catching a killer. I wish I could be in there listening, and at the same time, I wish I could be a thousand miles away. When I open the door of the main conference room, I see a gaggle of detectives standing around, staring at the board. I expect them to all turn in unison toward me, like I'm a gunslinger entering the local saloon, but only Detective Landry comes over. He's somewhere in his forties. Has those rugged good looks of a movie actor playing a policeman. His clothes are wrinkled, his sleeves are up, and he looks like the sort of guy about to make a breakthrough. He smells of cigarette smoke.

"This probably isn't a good time, Joe."

"Oh?"

"The room's pretty clean. Probably won't need going over for a few more days."

"Okay, then."

He pats me on the shoulder. Does he leave his hand there for a second too long? Is he looking at me differently?

"Thanks, Joe."

I turn toward the door, fighting the temptation to run. I remind myself that I'm the one in control, that I'm the one running this show, but if that were true, I wouldn't have this God-awful sick feeling in my stomach. Throwing one last glance at the board before I step into the hallway, I see a photograph of a burned car. Christ. I'm learning nothing. I'm out of the loop.

Then suddenly a chance appears to learn at least something: Detective Wilson Q. Hutton is blubbering toward me, a chocolate bar clutched in his sweaty hand like it's a tube of insulin. It's obvious the Q doesn't stand for *quitting*. He's wearing a black turtleneck sweater. Fact is I've never seen him wearing anything else. I don't get the look he's going for, and I figure he doesn't know either. Maybe it makes him feel as though he looks important. Or less fat.

"Afternoon, Joe."

"Hi there, Detective Hutton. Looks pretty busy. There something going on?"

He smiles at me with the same pity in his eyes he always has. "You haven't heard?"

"Heard what?"

"We've got a description of the guy."

I feel as though I've just been punched in the stomach, but I force myself to play Slow Joe. Are these people just playing with me? Is this an elaborate trap to call me out? I reach into my pocket and feel for the knife. A guy like Hutton, I just don't think the blade is long enough.

"How?" I ask, trying to keep my voice under control.

"There was another victim last night, Joe. Another prostitute. This time a witness saw him driving away from the alleyway where she was dumped."

Jesus, I wonder how Calhoun is feeling now that the woman he paid for sex two months ago has been killed. Is he feeling worse than me? He'll make the connection with the dead hooker, but will he believe it?

"Have you caught the bad man yet?"

Hutton shakes his head. "Not yet. The car used was stolen."

"You know that already? Wow, you're smart."

"The car was used to dump another body later in the evening."

"Another prostitute?"

"I can't say too much, Joe." He pauses to take a bite from his chocolate bar, like he needs the energy to come up with the words that he can't tell me. Chocolate-stained teeth begin mincing the confectionery. A few tiny pieces flake onto the collar of his turtleneck. I'm not sure why he doesn't just swallow the whole damn thing in one go.

"Any suspects?"

He shakes his head and keeps chewing. "Better carry on, Joe."

"Sure thing."

I head back to my office. My hands are trembling slightly. *Calm down. Calm down.*

It's easy to think, but hard to do. I need to create order from this Goddamn confusion that Melissa has dropped me into. The only problem is I'm coming up with nothing, only more excuses to hurt her. In the end I sneak open my office door and glance into the hallway. It's empty. Could I just leave and follow her? Is it that simple? Will the police let me leave?

I wait for thirty minutes, peering out from my office every few minutes or so, watching for Melissa, watching for the police escort to take me away. It doesn't happen, and I start holding out hope that it isn't going to. I grab the vacuum cleaner and let myself be seen. I mooch around the hallway, sucking dust mites and food crumbs from the carpet, biding my time. Occasionally one or two detectives will come from the conference room and head either to their cubicle, or out to the street, but they don't glance at me. Other times they simply come to get coffee. They nod and smile at me without really seeing me.

The day starts to drag. I keep looking at my watch, almost accusing it of lying. I don't feel so good, and every time I clean a bathroom, I sit in one of the stalls for a few minutes with my face resting in my hands and my fate resting in the hands of those who have sat here before.

I keep an eye out for Melissa, but can't find her. I don't see Calhoun either. Or Schroder.

All the regulars are gone, or maybe they aren't—maybe they're just waiting around the corner, watching and waiting. Except for Sally. She's always there. Just milling around, asking me how I am, how my mother is, asking me if I would like a lift home.

I don't know how, but four thirty eventually arrives. The relief is almost nonexistent, because I have no idea how far I'll get before somebody calls my name and tells me to stop walking, to get the hell down on the ground, to put my arms behind my back. Back in the hallway, with my briefcase, my hands still trembling, I am barely in time to see that Melissa is only just leaving, being escorted by Detective Calhoun, and I wonder if she has waited around for me to finish. Nearly three hours she's been here, talking to detectives. What in the hell has she been saying?

I quickly duck back into my office and watch from the corner of the door. As she stands there, Detective Landry walks from the elevator. In his hand, sitting across the bottom of a clear plastic bag, is a knife. Not any knife, but my knife. One of my favorites. He's carrying it as though he's just found the Holy Grail. Nobody could mistake the look of pride on his face. Melissa and Calhoun head toward him and the elevator, and they pause to talk. I'd love to know what they are saying, and if things go as planned, soon I will. Then Calhoun steps with her into the elevator and the doors slide shut. I rush for the stairwell and race my way to the ground floor, ignoring the throbbing from my groin. And it's worth it, because I'm quick enough to see Melissa as she leaves the building. She's alone now. I head to the door. Nobody puts their hand on my shoulder.

I turn right. Melissa is heading toward the Avon River, so I take the same route, cross the same road, avoid the same people. The sun has come out overhead, but it doesn't look like it will be for long, and it's not helping me feel any warmer. When Melissa reaches the grassy bank, she turns right and keeps moving, staying parallel to the dark water. I do the same, but keep a good fifty yards behind her. I have to be careful, because if she runs from me, I'm in no condition to chase her.

A few moments later she swerves toward a nearby park bench, takes a position sitting at the far end, and looks directly toward me. I stop walking, study the ground like there's something interesting there. I can feel her still looking at me. When I look up again, she smiles.

CHAPTER THIRTY-FOUR

The long summer is finally coming to an end, but that's okay, because she loves autumn. She can't think of anything better than being outside in a nice nor'west breeze as the leaves are changing color, but as much as she loves it, she dreads the months that are to follow. Winter brings with it a grimy film of depression that settles down over the city and soaks into the buildings and the plants and the people, everything touched by rain and the cold wind and the smog.

Sally is confused. About Joe. About his lies.

She understands why he lied about his mother being sick. That was a lie she was happy to go along with, because it protected him. Joe didn't want to be known as the man who had a testicle pulped by a pair of pliers. If something like that had ever happened to Martin, well, she would have wanted somebody like her to have looked out for him. All she can do now is hope the penicillin she gave Joe will help the healing process and fight off any infection. It should. If not he'll have to go to a hospital. He won't have a choice.

She had shown up the day he had been attacked, and each of the following three days—on one of those occasions she had found him passed out on the floor. She wanted to go back the next day too, but her father had had a bad fall and she'd been forced to weigh up her priorities. Family had to come first. She'd still gone to work—she had no more sick days—but from there she'd gone straight home and helped with her father. He'd dislocated a hip and broken a collarbone, but he was mending.

She was going to go back and see Joe on Monday—he still had stitches that needed removing—but he'd shown up at work. They didn't speak directly of the attack. She wants to talk him into going to the police for help, but not at work.

She doesn't like the fact that he lied to her about only seeing the crime-scene photographs in the conference room. He knows it's stealing, but he's obviously reluctant to open up to her about it. The man with the big smile looks so innocent that she can't imagine him deliberately lying, but the man who smiled at her between the elevator doors two weeks ago, well, that was a different Joe, wasn't it? That was a Joe that looked capable of . . .

Of what? Of anything? No. Not anything. But he looked capable of lying. He looked smooth, he looked calculating, as if he knew exactly what was going on. She reminds herself it was a fluke smile, that Joe isn't like that at all.

But why the lies?

Every time she stirs around the possibilities in her head, one keeps on coming up to the surface: Joe is being forced to do something he doesn't want to do. Therefore somebody needs to help him, and it's up to her. It's her Christian duty to make sure no harm comes to him.

Joe has been nervous and anxious most of the day, more so this afternoon, and she suspects why: the person pressuring him to bring home information has asked him for more. Of course she still can't figure out why the folders would still be in

Joe's apartment and not in the possession of the man who attacked him, but she figures it must have something to do with timing. Perhaps Joe forgot to take the folders with him to a meeting and made the man angry. Perhaps those folders aren't at Joe's anymore, but with the man who is threatening him. The only way to know for sure is to keep an eye on Joe. The same way Joe seems to be keeping an eye on the woman who has come to talk to the detectives—which, if Sally is truthful, makes her feel a little jealous. It isn't only Joe keeping an eye on her—it's most of the men in the department.

Like everybody else, Sally has heard the rumors flying around the station. This woman has seen something that might bring the case to a close. Perhaps then Joe will be safe.

Watching Joe watching the woman was unnerving. His fascination was so obvious that at one point Sally was sure he must have known her. But of course he was just learning what he could, so he would have something to tell his tormentor to save him from another attack.

Standing outside, watching Joe from the corner where he can't see her, she cannot understand why he would have approached the woman, but she will keep on watching until she can finally help Joe out of whatever mess he has got into.

CHAPTER THIRTY-FIVE

The Avon is full of ducks, beer cans, and empty chip bags. Friday night's urine has drifted to wherever the hell urine drifts to. Patches of riverweed float among the litter. Somebody—the guy with the worst fucking job in the world—has come along and picked up all the used condoms. Strangely, the view is still pleasant. The dark water reflects the sunlight and plays with the shadows, though I'm not really a nature lover. You could pave the whole river in concrete and I wouldn't care.

As I approach her, Melissa stops watching me, as if I'm not even important enough for her to keep an eye on, and she doesn't look back up at me until I'm only a meter away. I become aware of how painful my crotch still is. Like the remaining testicle is feeling pangs of loss, and is now feeling fear being in the presence of the woman who took away its brother. She remains sitting. My heart is beating hard, in time with my throbbing testicle. I can't fathom why I'm suddenly so afraid.

"Take a seat, Joe." She keeps a tight hold of her smile.

I shake my head. "Next to you? You're kidding."

"You still upset with me? Come on, Joe. It's time to move on."

Move on? I heard that after Dad died. People hear it all the time. Calhoun probably heard it after his son hanged himself. Are we living in such a throwaway society that we're not even allowed to hang on to our hatred and remorse? I want to leap forward and show her that I'll move on once I've taken care of a few things. But I can't. Too many people around. Too many risks. Even if I could break her neck and get away, I have no idea where my gun is. I'm guessing it's with somebody who will send it to the police if something ever happens to her.

"Quite the job you have, Joe."

I shrug. I see where she's going with this, but force her to carry on.

"The cleaner at the police station. That must allow you access to some privileged information—evidence, reports, photographs. It must be fun seeing where the investigations are going. Tell me, did you ever want to become a cop? Did you try and fail? Or not try because you knew they'd realize what sick thoughts you harbored?"

"How about you, Melissa? Did you ever try?"

"Do you ever try to contaminate the evidence?"

If this is all she has to say, then I'm not in any trouble. "You're jealous."

"Of you?"

"Of me working among all those cops, all that information."

She raises her left hand to her lips and begins rubbing her finger slowly back and forth, the same way she did the other night. She moistens her finger and keeps rubbing. Then she quickly pulls it away, brushes it against her chest on the way down, and rests it in her lap.

"We're not that different, you and I, Joe."

"I doubt that."

"Do you notice the smell in there?"

"What smell?"

"Working there every day, you're probably used to it. But there's this smell in there. Smells slightly like sweat and damp blood, but it's power. Power and control."

"It's the air-conditioning."

"It was fun in there today, Joe. I got to see something you see every day. Seems like menial work for somebody like yourself."

"I do it for the love of the job."

"Does it pay well?"

"Does it need to?"

"You know what confuses me?" she asks.

"Several things?"

Her smile stretches. "How you can afford an expensive gun, nice clothes, a good watch, yet you live in a rat hole of an apartment."

I hate the fact that she's been in my apartment. I hate the fact that this is the woman who tidied up my messy wound. No way in hell am I going to thank her for that. "I have a good accountant."

"Being a cleaner pays well, huh?"

"It pays the bills."

"Lucky you earn cash from other areas."

"What's your point?"

"My point is you must have some money stored away."

"I have a couple of hundred dollars. Why?"

"Bullshit, Joe. How much you got?"

"I just told you."

"No you didn't. It's time you were honest with your partner, Joe."

"What?" I ask, and suddenly I know what game we're playing.

"You heard," she says.

"Obviously I didn't."

She rolls her head back and laughs. Hard. This really pisses me off. Nobody's laughed at me like that since those days at school when the laughter accompanied the words *Numb Nuts* everywhere I went. Other people are looking around. Nothing I can do but wait her out. Finally she finishes. "We're partners, Joe, whether you like it or not. Especially after what I've just done for you."

"And what's that?"

"Given the police a composite of what you look like."

I tighten my fists.

"Calm down, big guy. I gave them a description of somebody else."

"Why?" But I know the answer: it's because she wants money.

"Why not?"

"Stop being so damn evasive," I say.

"You don't like it? What do you like, Joe?"

"How about I tell you what I'd like to do?"

"I can imagine. You know," she says, "it was nice to go in there and talk to the detectives, to see for myself just how smart they really are, or, in this case, just how smart they aren't. They're easier to fool than I could ever have imagined. I always saw them differently, I guess. But they're just people, Joe. Real people, like you and me. I guess that's why you're so successful. It was disappointing, really. In a way."

"I'm not sure there's anybody like you and me," I say.

Slowly she nods. "I guess you're right."

"So why did you do it? Why go in there?"

"For the money."

"We're back to that, huh? You really ought to start listening. Let me explain it a little slower for you. I. Don't. Have. Any. Money."

"Come now, Joe, don't be so modest. I'm sure that if you don't have any money, a man of your abilities would be able to *get* money. A hundred grand should do."

"You've seen my place. How do you suggest I get that kind of money?"

"You seem to be full of questions, Joe, when you should only be full of answers. Yes and no. That's all I want to hear from you."

"Look, it just isn't possible to raise that kind of cash."

"You could always turn yourself in. That'd cover half."

Melissa is referring to the fifty-thousand-dollar government reward available to whoever provides the information that gets me caught. I can't believe it's so little, and surely it can't stay that way. If Melissa wanted that kind of cash, she would have turned me in already. Either it isn't about the money, or she's waiting for it to climb up in value before she turns me in. She'll just torment me and make some cash on the side first. I'm just an investment for her. It's like she's buying a piece of stock.

"I'm going to kill you. You do know that, don't you?" I tell her.

"You know, Joe, I'm going to enjoy working with you. You really are quite a laugh." She stands up, straightens her tailored outfit, sweeps her hair back. She's so beautiful it's heartbreaking. I wish she were dead. She hands me a box.

"What's this?"

"A cell phone. Keep it on you, because I'll be calling in a couple of days."

"When?"

"Five o'clock. Friday."

I look at the box. The phone is brand new. I wonder if she bought it with cash she stole from the dead hooker.

"You know, Joe, I think this is the beginning of a beautiful relationship. Isn't that what they say?"

It isn't what I say. So I tell her to go to hell.

"Obviously, it goes without saying that if anything should happen to me, the remaining evidence I have on you goes directly to the police, along with a detailed statement."

Sure. It isn't the only thing that goes without saying. Obviously I'm going to kill this woman at some point. I just need to do my homework first. That's something I'm good at. Life's all about homework. And I have until Friday at five o'clock to get my assignment done. She starts telling me the rules of her game. I'm to charge the phone when I get home because she'll be in touch. She reminds me that she still has my gun, which has my fingerprints on it. It can be used as a future murder weapon. She tells me she wiped my fingerprints off the knife before telling the police where they could find it, but it doesn't brighten this nightmare.

After she walks away, I stare at the water, drumming my fingers against the top of my briefcase while watching the birds. I tap some rhythm that I've never heard before. It seems my life is following that rhythm. Some of the ducks look back at me. Perhaps they want money too.

One hundred thousand dollars is an amount I can't fully comprehend, and I already know I'll never be able to raise it. Does Melissa know that too? Even if by some miracle I could get the money, nothing is stopping her from asking me for more in another year, or another month, or even another day.

The bus driver is some bored forty-year-old guy who wears a hearing aid and yells *Hello* at me as I get on, and *Have a nice day* when I leave, even though the day is winding down. When I get home the light on my answering machine is flashing. I push it, only to hear my mother's voice, insisting I go around there for dinner tonight. When she insists, it's best I go. She also tells me Walt Chadwick called and asked her out for dinner. She's accepted, and tells me of their entire phone call until my machine eagerly runs out of tape.

When I open the bathroom door the cat races out, and I feel bad because I'd actually forgotten about him. I take a shower, clean myself up, and dress in tidy clothes, hoping Mom won't be able to find anything in my appearance to complain about. I put the cat back into the bathroom when I finish, making him a promise that I'll pick up some food later on tonight.

I steal a car and park a block away from Mom's house. The sound of the beach brings a smile to my face. I imagine walking down there and going for a swim. I don't imagine hard enough to get wet.

I'm halfway to the door when Mom opens it and comes outside. She looks better than I've seen her in years. Before I can even say anything, she's hugging me. I hug her back—while subtly shielding my crotch—to stop her from clipping me over the ear.

"I'm so happy to see you, Joe."

"I'm happy to see you too, Mom."

She pulls away from me, but keeps her hands on my shoulders. "Walt's taking me out to lunch tomorrow. You know, I haven't seen Walt since the funeral, and your father's been gone six years now."

"Eight years, Mom."

"Time does fly," she says, then leads me inside.

It flies when you're having fun. I can't see how it could have flown for Mom, though. "So where are you going?" I ask.

"He hasn't told me. Said it's a surprise. He's picking me up around eleven o'clock."

"That's good."

"I'm going to go like this." She twirls around to show me her dress, an ugly thing with long sleeves that looks like it's been made from recycled sackcloth, then dipped in blood. "What do you think?"

"I can't remember the last time you looked so good, or so happy, Mom."

"You're saying I never look happy?"

"I'm not saying that at all."

She frowns. "So, you're saying I never look any good, then."

"I'm not saying that either."

"Then what are you saying, Joe?" she snaps. "That I don't deserve to be happy?"

"I'm not trying to say anything," I say, "other than you look really nice. I'm sure Walt will be thrilled."

I manage to say the right thing, because her face breaks out in a smile. "You think so?"

"He'd be crazy not to think so."

"You don't have a problem with it?"

"A problem? With what?"

"Your father has been gone six years now—"

"Eight."

"And I'm only going to lunch with Walt. I'm not marrying him. I'm not asking you to call him *Dad*."

"I know that."

She leans forward, and instead of hitting me, she hugs me again. "We have you to thank for this, Joe," she whispers. "If it wasn't for you, he would never have called."

She dishes dinner. Instead of meatloaf, she's cooked up one of the chickens she bought on special last week. It's too damn big for two people, but she'll throw half of it into the fridge as leftovers. Thankfully she's cooked the chicken to perfection. It's one thing my mother manages to get right. It's juicy and full of flavor, and chicken fat starts dripping down my fingers.

"I'll ring you tomorrow night, Joe, and tell you all about our lunch."

"Uh huh."

"Maybe this weekend the three of us can go out for dinner. Would you like that?"

"Sure. That'd be nice," I say, unable to think of anything worse. I clutch at a napkin Mom gave me. She's always saying I'm a sloppy eater.

She takes the empty plates and begins to clean up. I wrap some chicken into a napkin and put it into my briefcase for the cat. My hands are covered in chicken fat.

"I'm just going to wash my hands, okay, Mom?"

"Good boy, Joe."

I walk to the bathroom, eating a piece of chicken on the way. Stepping past the toilet brings images of her sitting in there with her nightgown hitched up around her waist, her glasses resting on the tip of her nose as she puts a few more pieces of her jigsaw puzzle into place. I crouch to my knees and hang my head, focus my eyes on the bath mat. The nausea starts to fade. When I turn on the bathroom light, my hand slips from the switch. I pull back the shower curtain. Mom has one of those combined shower baths, but she always uses the shower. I try to turn on the tap, but my hands keep slipping off it, so I crouch down and begin smearing the chicken fat at the end of the bath instead. I spend a minute spreading it out, covering a good-sized area. It comes off my fingers easily enough, and off my palms. It's clear too, so Mom won't notice the mess. The only way she'll see it is if the angle and light are just right. I eat the rest of the chicken. It's cold now. I grab the tap, and this time it turns easily enough. I wash my hands, then head back to the kitchen.

"Walt was so nice on the phone, Joe."

Walt. I'm regretting letting him go. "He seemed nice, Mom."

I sit at the dining table while she finishes off the dishes. I offer to dry them, but she says no. I keep watching her, wondering how this could be the woman who gave me life. How can she think I'm gay? What have I done to this woman to make her possibly think that? I'm her son, and she won't even give me the benefit of the doubt.

I'm not gay, Mom. I'm not gay.

She drones on about Walt for another hour or so before finally letting me leave. As I stand on the doorstep, surrounded by night and the sound of the beach and by the muggy air touching my damp skin, I glance up at the stars, all of them overlooking my mother. One day her spirit will be floating up there, finding Heaven and finding God. She'll be off to talk to Dad again.

I start grinning. Both God and Dad are going to be in for a hard time.

I give her a hug before I go. I'll miss her.

I park the same stolen car a block from home. Friday is quickly approaching and . . .

Jesus Christ!

I drop my briefcase and run over to the goldfish bowl. Some of the knives slip out of their restraints and they sound like drum cymbals being smashed. I put both hands onto the glass bowl. The water inside is murky. A few dozen scales are floating on the surface. I thrust my hand in and grope for either of my fish and, while I'm searching, I find them with my eyes. One is in front of my bed. The other near the kitchen. Each is covered in bloodless scratches. Melissa's message is obvious.

I make my way over to Pickle when the cat runs out from beneath the bed, hooks the dead fish in its claws, fires it across the room, chases it, gets it in its mouth, then runs back toward the bed. The fish falls from its mouth, but the cat keeps on running, either knowing it's been spotted and is about to be in a world of trouble, or still thinking it has the fish in its mouth. Either way, it's running as if its leg was never broken, and I realize that Melissa hasn't done this at all.

"Fucking cat," I yell, striding over to Pickle and kneeling down next to him. He looks dead. I pick him up—he's cold, but fish are cold anyway, right? I carry him over to the fishbowl and drop him in, hoping I have him back there in time. I pick up Jehovah, and carry her over and drop her in. Pickle is already floating on his side. A few seconds later, Jehovah joins him.

I swirl them around in the water, pushing them forward into a forced swim, and then I press on their little chests, and even though it seems none of this is of any use, I persist for another ten minutes before finally giving up. I whirl around and face the bed. This fucking expensive cat has killed my two best friends. I storm over, grip the edges of the bed, and lift it up on its side. A whole bunch of crap falls onto the floor. The mattress slides off and so do all the sheets. My groin is starting to hurt, but not as much as my heart. The cat looks up at me with shock, its head is tilted and its eyes wide open. When I lean down to pick it up, it backs away. Its ears are pricked back and it looks ready to kill me. I lean forward and try to stomp on its back, but it sees this and stops just before me, forcing me to stretch forward to correct my aim, and as I do, my groin screams out in pain. I stomp on the floor where the cat has just been, and the shooting pain in my phantom testicle drops me to my knees.

Puss stops in the center of the room and sits down. He looks at me silently. His ears are no longer pricked back. I loosely cup my remaining testicle. Okay. Time to change tactics.

"Here, kitty. Come on, fella. I just want to pet you." I start clicking my Goddamn fingers because it seems to be the sort of thing that cats like. I keep clicking them, and in my mind a movie plays with me in the leading role, wringing the stupid cat's neck. The cat must be watching the same movie, because it won't come near me. I make my way toward my briefcase. Both the cat and I look at the knife I pull out, and both of us know what it can do. It knows I'm about to test the adage and see just how many ways I can skin the little bastard. I can see the reflection of my eyes in the blade. For a few seconds I just keep looking at them, and all I can think of is how I have my father's eyes. Thinking of Dad makes me feel suddenly sadder at losing those I love, and then I get angry at the cat for making me feel sad.

"Good boy. Come on." I keep clicking my fingers. The cat meows.

Then I throw the knife. I'm quick. The knife is quick. The cat's even quicker. The blade digs into the floor exactly where he'd been sitting a split second earlier. Then he turns his back on me and slowly walks back over to the bed. I'm making my way to the knife when the phone rings. I don't want to answer it. All I want to do is kill this Goddamn cat. My testicle hurts like hell. The phone keeps ringing, and ringing.

I pick up the knife and throw it toward the cat, and the cat darts forward a second later without a knife protruding from him. He looks back up at me.

"I'm going to kill you, you little bastard."

The cat hisses at me.

The phone keeps ringing. It's giving me a headache. Ring, ring, fucking ring. Why isn't the machine picking it up?

I pick up another knife, then carefully make my way to my feet. The pain in my groin is going. I walk slowly over to the phone. It has stopped ringing and the answering machine is recording a message. The volume is turned down and I can't hear it. I interrupt the message.

"Hello?" I say, hoping that my goldfish are the only things I am losing today, but my gut instinct is that something has happened to Mom. That premonition is back, riding my inner thoughts. Why must life be so cruel to those I love? And why must those I love betray me? I took the cat in and gave it a home, and in return it has done this to me.

"Joe? Hi, this is Jennifer."

Jennifer? How does she know my mother? "What can I help you with, Jennifer?" I hear myself asking.

"You're not going to believe this, but we've just found the owner of the cat!"

She sounds excited. I look over to my bed. The cat is still sitting there. I take aim with the knife.

"Really." This means my mother is still alive and well. Thank God!

"Really! Isn't that exciting?"

"The cat isn't here anymore," I say, wondering how hard I need to throw the knife to pin him to the floor.

"What do you mean?"

"I gave him away to one of my neighbors."

"Can't you get him back?"

"Well, the thing is it kind of ran away." I'm still talking, but hardly listening to her or even to myself. My brain's on automatic. I can't take my eyes from the Goddamn cat, and all I can think about is Dad. Dad killing himself. Dad being found locked inside his car.

"You're kidding," Jennifer says, and for the first time she doesn't sound like she's desperate to see me naked. I look from the fishbowl to the cat.

"It gets worse," I say.

"Worse? Did you say worse? How?"

"Well, it didn't just run away. It ran out into traffic." No way in hell is she getting the cat back. It represents too much. Melissa betrayed me. Dad betrayed me. I won't be beaten by an animal with a brain a tenth the size of mine.

"Is this for real, Joe? Or are you trying to keep the cat?"

"If you don't believe me, you can come and dig the damn thing up out of the yard!"

"There's no need—"

"I hate meatloaf!" I scream, and she hangs up on me without another word. Guess I won't be seeing any more of Jennifer.

Rather than throwing the knife, I decide to take another crack at being nice to the cat in hopes of getting near it. I glance at my fishbowl. The murky water is dead still. This is what I get for trying to be a good person, a caring person.

"Come on, pussycat. Come and see Joe."

Slowly I lower myself to my knees. I am only a few yards from the thing now, and it has no idea what's about to happen. I continue to make my way forward. The knife's going to look good coming from the side of the cat's head.

"Come on. Come on. That's a good boy." I'm nearly there. I start to reach out with the knife. I'm going to teach it a lesson it will never forget. It moves into a standing position.

"Come on. It's okay."

Then the bastard runs. I bring the knife down hard and fast, but miss as it scoots around me. It heads toward the kitchen.

But then it sees the open door.

I throw the knife at the cat as it skids on the floor, changes direction, darts past my briefcase, and heads for freedom. This time the blade sails just over the cat's head and sticks into the door. He stops in the doorway, looks over at me, gives a meowing sound that makes me want to spend the next twelve hours stomping the life out of him, and then he's gone.

I get to my feet, race to the door, and look out into the corridor. If I had the ability, I would run after it, but my groin is throbbing and possibly bleeding. I close the door, slump onto the sofa, and stare at the goldfish bowl. Pickle and Jehovah are still floating on the surface. I can't tell who is who. And as I stare, my eyes mist over. I allow myself to cry. There's no shame in crying.

I will find that cat. I will find it and kill it. I swear.

I get up and move into the kitchenette. The night is young, and even though I'm suffering from setbacks, I need to push myself forward. My eyes are blurry from tears and sore from being rubbed. I'm shivering even though it has to be ninety degrees in here. I hang up the phone, pull the bed back onto its legs, and tidy up.

All I can do is move forward. Pickle and Jehovah would want me to.

I start to head down memory lane. Thoughts of buying my fish start flooding my mind. I bought them because I was sick of living alone. At first they only suited the purpose of giving my apartment a feeling of life, but within months there was a bond between us that I knew would one day be broken by death. But not this day. Not so soon.

I pour the murky water from the fishbowl down the sink. Dad keeps coming into my thoughts, and I wish he'd just leave me alone. I scoop my goldfish into a clear plastic bag, then tie it shut before heading downstairs. In the front lawn of this apartment complex—and the word *lawn* is being generous—I pull aside some of the weeds, then use my hands to dig a hole. I put the plastic bag inside, then scoop dirt back over it. I could easily have flushed Jehovah and Pickle away, but I did not want to insult their memories by having their bodies float around for eternity with pieces of shit. I pat the dirt down nice and tight before saying some words over the piece of ground where my friends lie. My eyes fill with tears. I swear revenge on their grave.

I look for the cat, and though I can't find it, I can feel its eyes on me. After digging the dirt out from beneath my nails, I manage to get into bed early, which is the only good thing to happen to me all night.

I dream of death, but of whose, I can't be sure.

CHAPTER THIRTY-SIX

Sally wouldn't mind living on a street like this. Every night she would leave her window open, listening as the ocean crashed against the shore. Every summer morning she could go for a swim before heading to work. She's sure the people living out here must be more laid back, more relaxed. Martin would have loved living out here, she thinks. He used to love the beach.

Yesterday afternoon, she stayed by the corner of the police station just out of sight watching while Joe talked to the woman. She fought with the idea of approaching Joe and asking him straight out what was going on; she was also regretting the chance she'd passed up to look through Joe's briefcase. If the opportunity arises again, she will take it.

Then she drove to the graveyard and, while standing above the grave of her dead brother, she concentrated less on grieving and more on Joe. She wanted to know, no, *needed* to know what was going on. She decided she couldn't wait. She apologized to Martin, promised him she would return the following day, and drove toward Joe's apartment. She was going to confront him. She had to, if she had any chance of helping him. Anyway, his stitches would need removing, and she had to give back the copy of his key she'd had made.

Only she didn't make it all the way there.

A few blocks from his apartment she saw him driving a car. And she is certain, absolutely certain, it was him.

She drives her car slowly down the street, checking every few mailboxes, watching the numbers climb. Most of the houses look as though they're only a coat of paint away from being charming character homes.

When the door she wants opens not long after she knocks, she knows immediately she has the right place. The resemblance is obvious.

"I'm sorry, but I'm not buying," the woman says, and starts to close the door.

"I'm not selling anything," Sally quickly says, but the door doesn't slow down. "My name's Sally. I work with Joe, and I was hoping—"

"Well, why didn't you say so," Joe's mother says, swinging the door open nice and wide. "I've never met any of Joe's friends. I'm Evelyn. Please, please, come inside. Would you like a drink? A Coke perhaps?"

"Sure. That'd be nice."

"Sally, Sally. That's a pretty name."

"Why . . . thank you," Sally says, and nobody has ever said that to her before.

Joe's mother leads her down the hallway and into the kitchen. The décor is around thirty years old, Sally thinks, and suspects Joe's mother has been living here that entire time. She sits down behind a Formica table, and Evelyn opens the fridge and a moment later joins her.

"So what time is Joe getting here?" Evelyn asks.

"Joe's coming here?"

"That's why you're here, isn't it? You're meeting Joe? It's a bit late for dinner, but I suppose I can still whip something up. Perhaps I'll call him and see if he's on his way."

"Actually Joe doesn't know I'm here."

Joe's mother pauses and the edges of her mouth turn downward. "I don't follow, dear."

"I came here because I wanted to talk to you about Joe."

Now the rest of Evelyn's features follow the direction of her mouth. "About Joe? Whatever for?"

From the moment Sally looked through Joe's personal file earlier in the day to get his parents' address, she knew the questions his mother was going to ask.

"I, well, there were a few things I wanted to talk to you about. I have some . . . concerns."

Evelyn starts nodding, slowly, as if she is suddenly saddened by Sally's possible concerns. "I know what you mean, dear."

"You do?"

"I have concerns of my own," she says, the downturned features of her face softening. "Tell me, do you like my son?"

"Of course I do. That's why I'm here."

Evelyn starts nodding. "I always thought more women would like him, but he doesn't seem to have any interest in them. He's . . . special, you know."

"I know. He reminds me of my brother."

"Oh? Your brother is that way?"

"He . . . is," she says, not saying *was*, because *was* has a finality about it that she doesn't want to think about right now.

"And you like Joe."

"I like Joe a lot," Sally says.

"That's good, dearie," Evelyn says, and she pops open the Coke she got for Sally and hands it over. "I like hearing that. It means there's still a chance for Joe."

"But these concerns, well, I don't really know where to start."

"We've already started, dearie."

"How long has Joe been able to drive?"

"What was that, dear?"

Sally takes a sip from the Coke. It's warmer than she thought it would be, either the fridge isn't set that cold or Evelyn only just put the can in there. "How long has Joe been driving?"

"I don't see how this relates to you liking him."

"Well, it doesn't, not exactly. But I saw him driving last night, and—"

"He was coming to see me. He's such a good boy."

"I know. It's obvious Joe has a big heart. He's really such a lovely guy. But I didn't know he could drive."

"You didn't know he could drive?" Evelyn asks, sounding surprised. "I thought you said you work with him."

"I do work with him."

"Then surely you must have seen him driving the cars around."

Does Joe tell her he drives the police cars around? It would be the sort of big-kid thing he'd do. She doesn't want to spoil the illusion for Evelyn. It's bad enough just being here, invading his privacy. Even now she's fraught with guilt, and scared about how Joe will react. By trying to help him, she'll likely end up hurting him, and he'll likely end up hating her.

"Sure. I was just curious as to how long he has been able to do it, that's all."

Evelyn gives the statement a dismissive shrug. "I don't know," she says. "Years, I imagine. But what I'm more interested in is you, Sally. I take it you're not married?"

Sally smiles. "No, no, not married," she says, and takes a mouthful of Coke.

"Do you have family? Any other brothers and sisters? And what do you do with Joe? Are you his receptionist? Do you clean the cars? Are you a cleaner?"

"I live with my parents," she says, wanting to get through this part quickly so she can get back to talking about Joe. "I don't clean the cars, and I don't think Joe does either."

"No, of course he doesn't. Why would he?"

Sally shrugs in reply. Why would a cleaner have a receptionist?

"What do you do then?" Evelyn asks. "At work, I mean."

"Well, I'm a maintenance worker. I kind of keep things in order."

"Oh, that sounds very interesting, Sally. You don't see many female mechanics. Do you want to sell cars one day?"

"Sell cars?"

"Yes. Do you want to sell them?"

Maybe selling cars is a dream of Joe's. "I guess I've never thought about it." She picks up her drink and takes another large swallow. Speaking to Joe's mother is turning out to be just as difficult as some of the conversations she has had with Joe. "The thing is, I came here to talk about something I think might be happening."

"Between you and Joe? Oh, that would be marvelous!"

Sally leans back, struggling not to sigh. Suddenly she can't go through with it. Joe has created a world for his mother to see him in, and no doubt it's taken a long, long time. She could destroy all of that with some careless words. No, she is best to end this. There are no answers here as to why Joe can drive. No answers as to who attacked him. She takes another mouthful of drink, trying to get through it quickly, wanting to get out of here.

"I knew Joe would find somebody."

"He really is something," Sally says, unsure of what else to say. She takes another mouthful. Only another mouthful to go.

"After his father died, well, I was unsure how that would affect him, you know what I mean? I thought it might mess him up a little. Make him a little odd."

Sally nods. She didn't know Joe's father had died.

"Joe became quiet. Withdrawn. Not long after, he moved out. Do you know, I've never been to his house? I worry about Joe. I suppose that's the job of a mother."

"I worry about him too." Sally finishes off her drink. "Well, I'd best be going."

"But you only just got here."

"I know. Next time I'll stay longer. I just wanted to come by and say hello."

"You really are a nice young girl." Evelyn walks her to the door and opens it. The night has cooled off in the fifteen minutes she has been here. She thinks it's going to start raining again. "Did Joe tell you about Walt?"

"Walt?"

Sally stands in the doorway with her arms wrapped around her body, listening as Evelyn recounts the story of Walt. When it's over, she thanks Joe's mother, then walks down the path to her car. She grips the steering wheel, but doesn't start the engine.

According to Evelyn, Joe is a car salesman. Joe was out test-driving a car when he ran into her old friend Walt.

She clutches the crucifix around her neck. Joe has created a fictional world to keep his mother happy. What else has he created? Joe is more than he seems and, in a way, that frightens her.

CHAPTER THIRTY-SEVEN

The next morning my internal alarm wakes me into what is another glorious Christchurch morning—according to some old guy giving the forecast on the radio. Looking out the window shows something different: gray skies and dark storm clouds on the horizon, which make me think the forecaster must be crazy or drunk. There is some condensation on the window and the floor is cold.

I stare at the coffee table before leaving for work. There is a tin of fish food on it and no dead cat. I leave my apartment and head downstairs and out into the first frost of the year. The lawn looks crunchy, and there are leaves filling the gutters. I'm shivering a little when I hand Mr. Stanley my bus ticket, and today he punches it. I wonder if this is an omen. I want to tell him about my goldfish, and I don't know why. I don't even know if he would care.

When he drops me off opposite my work, we exchange waves.

The day doesn't suggest that it's going to get much warmer.

I keep my hands buried in my pockets as I make my way across the road. Sally catches me by the elevator. We make inane conversation up to my floor, but mostly Sally seems preoccupied, and then she is gone.

I'm unable to gain access to the conference room, so I end up doing what I'm paid to do. I keep an eye on Detective Calhoun when he is around. I try to figure out just how he's feeling, but I don't know him well enough to see if he's going through a personal crisis. I also keep an eye out for Melissa, but she doesn't show. I vacuum and clean and wipe and do the general workday things that bring in the big janitorial bucks. Nobody treats me any differently. Nobody gives me the sort of look they'd reserve for a serial killer.

The station doesn't have the same buzz about it as yesterday, when everybody thought the case was about to bust wide open. Even the conference room is empty. I step inside and take a look around. The composite picture Melissa helped them with is on the wall. Dark, bushy hair; cheekbones that can't be seen, let alone felt; lots of stubble. A flat nose, big eyes, high forehead. The cold, calculating expression on his face looks mean, as though the person in this picture was born to be a criminal.

The picture in no way represents how I actually look. My hair is finer, swept back, and kept reasonably short. It's dark, which is the only similar thing, but I have high cheekbones with no flab, and my eyes are thinner too. And stubble? No way. I'm lucky if I need to shave once a month. I grin at the picture. It doesn't grin back. On the table with the folders is the knife. Shrouded inside a plastic bag, sitting inside a cardboard box, it has already been studied for fingerprints, blood, and DNA. If my fingerprints were found on it, I would know by now. All employees in this building have been fingerprinted. It's standard. Melissa wasn't lying. It isn't standard for all of us to have given DNA samples.

I grip the handle tightly, feel it beneath the thin plastic. This knife was stolen from me in circumstances I can never possibly forget. This knife was there the night I suffered my greatest indignity, my greatest pain, and experienced my greatest hatred. I quickly put it back down. It isn't mine anymore.

I take time to read the reports. The prostitute I left in the alleyway has been identified. Charlene Murphy. Twenty-two years old. I'd pegged her at being closer to thirty. Prostitution ages people fast. She was, however, a mother of one. That much I'd guessed. Her boyfriend isn't a suspect, since he was in jail at the time on unrelated charges. Her photograph is up on the wall keeping company with the other women.

The second whore who died, Candy number two, is still to be identified.

I don't need to take any information away with me, but I find myself collecting what I can anyway, more as mementos than anything else. I also take the tape from the recorder in the potted plant. I'm back in my office when Sally knocks at the door and comes in.

After the usual pleasantries, Sally stops talking, as if she's used up all the words she'd remembered for the day. She just stands there as if somebody has reached inside her and flicked the big *off* switch. About half a minute goes by, and then she just starts looking around.

"Sure is a cold day," she says, but the switch has been flicked to automatic now, so she doesn't really know what she is saying. She looks out the window. Looks at the ceiling. At the floor under the bench. Finally her eyes rest on my briefcase. "I forgot to make you lunch today. I'm sorry, Joe."

"Don't worry about it."

She keeps staring at my briefcase, and I guess she's figuring I'd like her more if she went out and bought the same one. She's trying to figure out whether I'd be impressed or devastated if she bought one that was better. The truth is she probably isn't thinking anything at all. She is frowning slightly, which suggests something is going on inside her mind, but the way her face is slightly scrunched up suggests the only thing happening in there is a whole lot of confusion. It's as if she wants to ask me a really big question, but has no idea what that question even is.

"Well, thanks for dropping by. I got a lot of work I ought to get started on."

This seems to snap her out of it. The switch inside of her doesn't go to *on*, because that isn't one of the positions. Other than *off* and *automatic*, she only has *barely functioning*, and she goes into that mode now.

"I'll see you later on, Joe."

"Oh. Okay then," I say, trying to singsong the three words.

She heads out of my office but doesn't close the door. I have to get up and do it myself.

I listen to the tape from the conference room. Lots of different theories, none of them right. The police are freaking out because they think I'm escalating. They think soon it'll be only a few days between my victims. Hell, maybe they're right. It's too early to tell.

The Everblue Motel is one of those dives you see in movies where bad things happen to unlucky people who just happen to be staying there the same night as some escaped mental patient. It's not far from town, but far enough for the land to be cheap, like those living nearby.

The motel is an L-shaped stretch of rooms with old paint and chipped windowsills, opposite brown grass and half-dead shrubs. The cracks in the sidewalk are full of rust-colored water. I count a dozen vehicles in the parking lot, ranging from the cheapest of the cheap to the most average, middle-class family sedan. Maybe it's discount Wednesday for the hookers. A few corroding shopping carts are lying on their sides, surrounded by weeds and cigarette butts. The neon sign is making a loud buzzing noise.

I park outside the office. Long ribbons of thick plastic cover the doorway, the type you'd find if you traveled back twenty years and entered a dairy. I brush them aside and make my way in. The room smells of latex and cigarette smoke. The walls and ceiling are stained. The carpet is patterned with cigarette burns.

The guy behind the counter must be in his forties. He's bald and overweight, and he stares directly at me as if he doesn't trust me. As if he thinks I'm going to grab his multicolored plastic ribbons from the doorway and take off. He is wearing a T-shirt that says *Racism is the New Black*.

I flash some police identification that isn't even mine—sometimes all you need is a policeman's business card with a name and no photo and it can open any door—and he shrugs and hardly glances at it. When I ask to look through the guest book, he spins it around and tells me to go ahead. His finger-nails, long and dirty, flick the pages open toward the date I indicate. Then he uses them to scratch at his barren scalp. He gets tiny pieces of skin stuck under them, and then he starts to pick them out. They drift onto the guest book, and he brushes them off with his hand.

We make miniature conversation as I look through the book. He has dealt with police before, so he says, and even rented a room once to a murderer. Of course, he didn't know the man was a murderer at the time. That hadn't come out until the guy was caught.

Fascinating. I tell him so.

I search through the dates, looking for the room Calhoun used. Of course, it won't be beneath his name, but I look nonetheless. My finger scrolls past lots of people called John Smith, and others with names like Ernest Hemingway and Albert Einstein. The Everblue seems a popular place for dead people, because even Abraham Lincoln has stayed here.

I turn the guest book back around so it faces Mr. Greasy. Slap the photograph of Detective Calhoun down on top of it. "You recognize this guy?"

"Should I?"

"Yeah, you should."

He takes a close look at it. "Yeah, I remember him. He came in a few months ago."

"Out of all the people who come in here, you remember this guy? Why's that?"

"I sure as hell remember the mess he made, and the noise he made while he was making it."

"You sure this guy did that?"

He shrugs again. "Does it matter?"

I guess it doesn't. I don't bother thanking him. Just nod, and leave.

My next stop is a direct contrast to the Everblue. The Five Seasons Hotel is closer to the center of town, among a handful of hotels, most around ten years old. Land isn't cheap here. It just looks it. I park the stolen car three blocks away and take my briefcase with me. The evening is getting darker and colder. There's going to be another frost.

The hotel is ugly. I don't know quite how to describe it as anything other than an artistic dream turned nightmare. Architects using braille to draw their plans. Painters using materials from the seventies. It looks like a lava lamp. It's fifteen stories high—not huge, but big enough when your major color is lime green. Spotlights around the foundation light it up at night. The hotel would look more in place in Disneyland as some scary ride. Amazingly, it's a five-star.

What's also amazing is that police personnel from out of town are put up here. It's taxpayers' money going to good use.

I already have a picture in my mind of what the interior will look like, but I quickly find I'm completely wrong. The walls are varnished wood, giving the foyer a strange type of antique look. A chandelier hangs from the ceiling with a million reflections of light. The carpet, a deep red color, is plush enough to sleep on and be comfortable. Where the carpet ends, checkered black-and-white linoleum takes over. The foyer is large enough to chase somebody around in for a good minute or so. The air is cool, and slightly scented. Could be jasmine, or lilac, or one of those other incense aromas that men all over the world have no idea how to distinguish from others.

I step up to the reception desk. It's a hell of a lot nicer than stepping up to the counter at the Everblue, plus the staff are doing a good job of keeping it warm in here. A young woman smiles at me—quite attractive: nice breasts, tight body, pretty face, blond hair pulled back, her makeup applied to perfection. Her uniform is dark green. The blouse is white, and it wouldn't take much to give it a splash of red. I wonder what she would say if I asked her to take it off.

I book and pay for a room with cash, then I sign my name in the guest book the same way it was on the cards. She asks me for a credit card she can swipe in case I make any extra purchases, and I tell her I'm a cash only kind of guy, and don't own one. She nods and smiles, and says that that's fine, then adds that they'll lock the minibar so I can't access it.

She puts me in room 712. I grab my key, which is actually an electronic card so could pose a problem. I thank her, wondering if I'll ever see her again. She thanks me, and no doubt has a similar thought.

A porter with barely enough personality to get by in life rides with me to the seventh floor. I have no luggage, but he comes along anyway. He seems depressed, and I figure it must be because he's over a hundred years old and is still a damn porter. My legs take me to the twelfth room. He takes the key off me, puts it into the lock, and the mechanism pops open with the same sound as a latch on a briefcase. He opens the door, then stands there like it's well within his Goddamn right to take a tip off me. Like he's just earned ten bucks for making this trip and providing no conversation. I give him five and he doesn't thank me. I close the door and head to the windows. My eyes take me out to the city beyond.

I decide to relax a bit. With my shoes off and my feet

breathing in the air-conditioned room, I struggle to believe, or perhaps don't want to believe, that outside this hotel I have a life that consists of mayhem and confusion and very little else.

The room is divine, the sort of place that gives me the motivation to become rich just so I can live here. You could stay at the Everblue for about a week and still pay less than you'd pay for this place for one night. The large window makes the view of Christchurch seem nicer than I've ever seen it, and combined with its height and the fact it's been raining, it even makes Christchurch look cleaner. The bed is so comfortable I'm afraid if I lie down I may never get up. I check out the minibar: one look at the prices and I think it's ironic that I'm the one being called a criminal. None of the items are accessible as the door to the minibar has been locked. The kitchen is filled with expensive appliances I have no idea how to use. The TV is a big screen with a remote control that has a hundred buttons.

I take the gamble and lie down on the bed. I end up spending forty minutes staring at the ceiling, allowing my mind to visit other places it hasn't been in weeks, catching up on old fantasies that include the woman from the vet, and thinking of new ones that include the receptionist downstairs, before finally using the phone to call home and check my answering machine. A moment later I'm listening to a man from the veterinary clinic, reminding me that I have a cat cage that doesn't belong to me. I don't need to wonder why Jennifer didn't call. I'll return the cage when all this is over.

The second caller identifies himself as Doctor Costello. He leaves a phone number where I can contact him. He says it's urgent. Says Mom's in the hospital. He leaves no other details. My hands are shaking and I struggle to hang up the phone. Has something happened to Mom? Of course it has. She wouldn't be in the hospital otherwise. Please God . . . Please let her be okay.

I punch in the number (I wrote it down on a complimentary Five Seasons pad with a shaky hand while listening to the message), and the phone starts ringing. I end up talking to a woman at a Chinese restaurant for about a minute, trying to ask how my mother is while being given the day's specials, until I realize I've dialed the wrong number. I slam the phone down and suck in a deep breath, but it doesn't calm my nerves. My hands are shaking violently, and I have to use both of them to dial. I close my eyes and begin to imagine a world without Mom, and as I imagine it, tears begin to well in my eyes.

CHAPTER THIRTY-EIGHT

A life without Mom. I refuse to think about it. She's the most important person in the world to me, and to think that something could be wrong . . . well . . . well, it hurts. More than having my testicle crushed into pulp and juiced. To imagine her gone . . .

I simply won't imagine it.

Simply can't imagine it.

A woman at Christchurch Hospital answers the phone and tells me I've just called Christchurch Hospital. I appreciate her insight. I ask for Costello and a long minute later he comes to the phone, bringing with him a deep, concerned voice.

"Ah, yes, Joe. Listen, it's about your mother."

"Please don't tell me anything's wrong with her."

"Well, actually, nothing is wrong with her," he says, and for some reason I can't explain I feel disappointment. "You can speak to her yourself. She's right here."

"But you're at a hospital," I say, as if I'm accusing him of something—perhaps of being a doctor.

"Yes, but your mother's fine."

"Then why didn't she call me?"

"Well, she's fine now, and since she's not going home tonight, this was the only way she could speak to you. She said the only way of getting hold of you was if I called. She's quite an insistent woman, your mother," he says, without any humor.

"What was wrong with her?"

"I'll let you talk to her."

The line goes quiet as the phone changes hands. A mumbling of voices and then, "Joe?"

"Mom?"

"This is your mother."

"What's wrong? Why are you in the hospital?"

"I chipped a tooth."

I sit there gripping the phone, pretty sure she's told me she just chipped a tooth, but knowing that's not what she said because . . . well . . . "A tooth? You chipped a tooth and you're at the hospital?" I shake my head, trying to make her words make sense. If she chipped a tooth, then wouldn't she be . . . "At the dentist. Why aren't you at a dentist?"

"I've been to the dentist, Joe."

She says nothing then. My mother, a woman who probably won't even stop talking when she's dead, offers me no explanation. A couple of weeks ago she was happy to tell me she was shitting water. So I have to ask. "Why are you at the hospital?"

"It's Walt."

"He's sick?" I ask, perhaps a little too hopefully.

"He broke his hip."

"Broke his hip? How?"

"He slipped in the shower."

"What?"

"He was having a shower, and he fell. Broke his hip. I had to call an ambulance. It was scary, Joe, yet exciting too, because

I've never been in an ambulance. The sirens were loud. Of course, Walt kept on crying. I felt so bad for him, but he was so strong. The ambulance driver had a mustache."

Uh huh. Uh huh. "You were at his house when he was showering?"

"Don't be silly, Joe. I was at home."

"Why did he call you?"

"He didn't need to call me. I was already at home. It was me who called the ambulance."

"Yeah, but why didn't Walt call?" I ask, somewhat confused—perhaps not as confused as I'd like to be, because there is a scenario being built here.

"Because he was in the shower," Mom says.

"Then how did he call you?"

"I was already there, Joe. What are you getting at?"

"I'm not sure," I answer, happy to let it go.

"We were getting ready to go out, so we decided . . ." She pauses, but I've already heard her mistake. "*He* decided to take a shower."

"He was at your house? You had a shower *with* him?"

"Don't be so rude, Joe. Of course I didn't."

Images start going through my mind. I squeeze my eyes shut. I'd tear them out if it'd help. The images don't budge. I'm sweating like a pig. I push my fingers at my closed eyes and thousands of colors appear—like in the chandelier downstairs—and I try to follow the colors with my eyes as they float across my mind. I'm happy to believe they didn't take a shower together. If she says so, then I'm happy to believe it. Happy to forget she said *we* instead of *he*. Happy to forget this entire conversation. She just has to tell me that . . .

"So, Mom, how did you chip your tooth?"

"It happened when Walt fell over."

"What?"

"It happened when—"

"I heard you, Mom," I say, trying to squeeze my eyes closed

even tighter. "But I thought you said you weren't taking a shower together."

"Well, Joe, we're adults. Just because we were taking a shower together doesn't mean anything of a sexual nature was happening. Just because in this day and age young people can't keep their hands off each other doesn't mean we were acting just as immorally. We're pensioners, Joe. We can't afford to leave hot water running all day. So we took a shower together. Now don't you go making a big deal out of nothing."

"So how did you chip your tooth? He knocked you over?"

I open my eyes, because if they're open, I see this lovely hotel room wall and not my mother taking a shower with some old guy. I don't want to question her. She has explained things in enough detail for me, yet the question has left my mouth before I could stop it. I didn't want to ask—God knows I didn't. Eyes open, I see a couple of chairs, some paintings, and I can see the hotel room door. Maybe I should run for it.

"No, no, he kicked me in the mouth. His foot slipped out from beneath him, and the heel of his foot kicked me in the mouth."

Don't ask, Joe. Just don't ask. "But how did his foot reach so high?"

"Oh, I wasn't standing. I was kneeling. I was . . . um . . . well, it just happened, Joe, okay? He kicked me in the mouth."

It just happened. What just happened? Oh God, please don't show me. . . .

Only my mind does show me. My entire shirt is wet. I become so scared that she might confirm exactly what she was doing that the moment she starts talking again I put the phone down and run to the bathroom, reaching the bowl only just in time.

A hiccup, a convulsion of my stomach, the taste of bile. Vomit explodes from me in a roar and splashes into the water, while drops of water and puke flick onto my face and roll down onto my chin. I keep coughing it up until I have no more to cough, but I keep coughing anyway, watching it form a yellow-ish soup in the bottom of the toilet. As my body shudders, all I can picture is my mother in the shower. My throat quickly becomes raw, and my stomach shrinks into a small ball of pain. I can taste blood as it drips off my lips and plinks into the syrup below. There is something floating in there that looks like one of my dead goldfish.

My mind is spinning and I feel light-headed. I reach out and slap the lever and the mess that surely couldn't have come out of me, but did anyway, is flushed away.

It hasn't stopped flushing before I kneel back over the bowl, trying to throw up once again. Now I'm only gagging. Blood clots land in the water and spread out into rose petal shapes. I flush, but the toilet hasn't regained pressure, so the petals don't disappear. They just swirl around the edges of the bowl. Strands of drool hang from my bottom lip. They stick to the rim of the bowl, and they stretch when I lean back, eventually breaking. The tops of the strands swing down onto the black linoleum. Thinking about the thousands of people who have sat here and pissed and shat is better than thinking about Mom and her broken tooth.

When I was in the faggot's house, I tried thinking of other things to take my mind away from what was going on, and in the process I thought about Dad and what he would say. Bending over the toilet, I start to remember something I saw. Something Dad was doing. I wasn't supposed to be home. I can't remember why, but what I can remember is coming home early and finding . . .

Oh God.

I start to gag, but I have nothing left to cough up except blood. I keep my eyes closed so I don't have to see the red water below, but behind my eyes the memory is playing. Im-ages of Mom and Walt in the shower fade in and out, replaced slowly with images of Dad in the shower. Only he's in there with somebody else. Who? And why in the hell did I walk into the bathroom when I heard the damn shower going in the first place?

That somebody else was another man.

Oh Christ. I open my eyes. My lungs hurt and my stomach is hot. My throat feels as though it's closed over. I try my best to shake the images away. Dad's trying to calm me as the naked guy dresses and leaves, and Mom isn't there to hear it because she is playing bridge at the local bingo hall. It was the last time she ever played.

I think back to the policeman and his boyfriend pounding the bedroom wall, and this helps to take away the memory, this false memory, because surely that never happened.

Of course! I'm remembering a dream. Dad wasn't gay. Of course he wasn't. And I never killed him. I loved him. Dad was as straight as they came, and why he decided to take his own life, I'll never know. And maybe I don't want to know.

I stand up, my legs like rubber. I wash my face and rinse out my mouth, but can't get rid of the taste. I pick up one of the complimentary soaps and take a bite. A white lather mixed with blood foams from my mouth.

Tastes like chicken.

Actually it's the vomit that tastes like chicken, and as I chew further into the soap, my mouth starts closing over and my throat starts to burn. My remaining testicle starts to throb, though more than anything it is itching. I wash the soap from my mouth and stumble back to the phone. Unbelievably, Mom is still talking.

"Okay, Mom, I'm glad you're okay," I interrupt. "And yes, I'll come and visit Walt while he's in the hospital, but my taxi's just arrived. I've got a meeting with a client. Got to go. Love you."

I glance at my watch as if she can see me, send a kiss down the phone, and have the phone halfway back on the hook when one of her words stops me from hanging up.

"What was that?" I ask, pressing the phone firmly against my ear.

"We had a nice talk. She really loves you, Joe."

"Who?"

"Your girlfriend. I'm never that good with names. There was an *s* in there somewhere. Maybe it started with one."

"You don't mean Melissa?"

"Melissa? Yes, that was it. I remember telling her she had a beautiful name."

"She came around?" I ask, deciding not to point out that Melissa has two *s*'s in her name.

"That's what I was saying. Joe, you really need to clean out your ears."

"She came around last night?"

"Joe. Do you ever listen to anything I say?"

I tighten my grip on the phone. I can hear my breathing getting out of control. "I listen, but Mom, this is important. What did she say?"

"Only that she was worried about you. And that she thought you were a really nice person. I liked her, Joe. I thought she was lovely."

Yeah, well, she wouldn't think Melissa was lovely if she knew what she was capable of. Why would she go and see my mother? Just to prove her control?

"I had no idea you had such a lovely woman in your life, Joe."

"I'm just lucky, I suppose."

"When will I see more of her?"

"I don't know. Look, Mom, I gotta go."

"Did you know her brother was gay?"

"What?"

"She told me."

"What?"

"That he was gay."

I have no idea what she's on about. It's as if she's picking up on another conversation somewhere, perhaps a faulty phone connection.

"Seriously, Mom, I really have to go. I'll talk to you soon."

I don't wait for a response. This time I hang up.

I walk to the window and look out at the city. I want to jump out and crash into the sidewalk below. My mind is churning with images of my mother and Walt, but they're only shadows now. The day is winding down. Daylight is being replaced by streetlights and headlights. Hardly anything happens on a Wednesday night. Garbage trucks are rolling up and down the streets, taking away the trash left by shop owners and businesses. I wipe at the tears running down my face with no idea why I'm even crying. Finally I start to focus on why I'm here. I turn on the hotel room light, then start to make myself familiar with my surroundings, doing what I can to forget about my mother. It's a distraction, but it works. I go back into the bathroom. I flush the toilet and spray some air freshener about the place. Only the distraction ends up pissing me off. It makes me think of what I have at home, or, more accurately, what I don't have. It's like being married, and then buying a swimsuit calendar. Thinking of my little apartment without the minibar and soft bed makes me want to start crying again.

I walk into the kitchen area—or *kitchenette*, as gays and hippies would call it. I rummage around in the drawers, searching for a knife that looks mean enough to do a rather mean job. I find one, walk to the bed with it, and study it beneath the bedside lamp. The blade isn't long; it's bigger than a fruit knife, but smaller than the standard issue given to horror movie directors. I sway my hand up and down, feeling the knife's weight and the balance, learning its specifications and limitations. It isn't something I'd pay for, and it's the first thing I've seen in this hotel that doesn't look horribly expensive. It will take either some serious amount of stabbing, or some serious accuracy.

I can do both.

I open my briefcase and take out a cleaning rag to remove my fingerprints from the knife. This isn't essential, but it's better to be safe than jailed. I slip on a pair of latex gloves, clean the knife once again, then slip it into a plastic bag from my briefcase.

I grab the list of phone numbers from my briefcase. Look up Detective Inspector Calhoun's and dial it from the cell phone Melissa bought me. Since it's a prepay, if the number shows up on Calhoun's caller ID display, it can't be traced back to me. Because of the latest break in the case, many of the detectives are putting in extra hours, and from what I can make out Calhoun is one of them. After six rings I'm beginning to doubt he's there. If he isn't at his desk the phone automatically switches through to his mobile, which these guys carry with them every moment of the day.

Finally he answers. "Detective Inspector Calhoun," he says, and I can picture him standing on a street somewhere with the phone pressed tightly against one ear and his finger jammed in the other.

"Evening, Detective."

"Evening, sir. How can I help you?"

"No, it's how I can help you."

"Who is this?"

"That's not really important, but what is important is what I know."

"I don't have time for any games," he says, and I picture him the same way as a few seconds ago, only now looking pissed off.

"This isn't a game. I know something."

"And what is that?"

I'm grinning, yet I'm also nervous. I can't remember the last time I had a reason to grin. I can remember the last time I was nervous, though. "I know that you're a killer."

Silence. Then, later than he should have replied, he says, "What the hell are you on?"

"I'm not on anything."

"Then what are you talking about?"

"Do you know who this is, Detective?"

"How the hell would I know?"

"I'm the person you're looking for."

"Look, if this is a joke, I'm not laughing."

I'm nodding down the phone line, like people do even though nobody can see them. At least I'm not waving my hands around. "You know I'm not joking."

"How did you get this number?"

"We're getting off track, Detective. Now, let's get to the point," I say, scratching at my testicle. The itch is getting worse.

"What point is that?"

I walk over to the window. Look out at the city. "Tonight's point, or moral, is that I know you have a sexual dysfunction that you attempt to put right by using prostitutes, and that that dysfunction has led to murder."

Rather than denying anything, or abusing or threatening me, he says nothing. We both stay that way for almost half a minute. I know he's still there: the sound of the open phone line hums loudly.

"This is bullshit," he eventually says, but doesn't hang up.

"That's not what Charlene Murphy thought when you took her to the Everblue. And I'm sure Daniela Walker would say differently too. Well, if you hadn't killed her."

He's silent for a few more seconds while he absorbs the fact that I know exactly what he's done. "What is it you want?" he finally manages to ask.

"Money."

"How much?"

"Ten grand."

"When?"

"Tonight."

"Where?"

"Cashel Mall."

"I can't risk being seen paying somebody off. How about somewhere more secluded?"

"Like where?" I ask, knowing he would ask this.

I can imagine exactly what he's thinking. His speedy answers are proof of that. He's suddenly inside that game he told me he didn't have time for. Like chess, he's setting me up, but again like chess, I can see it coming. I'm half a dozen steps ahead of the guy. Nobody's going to have ten thousand dollars on them, ready to make a payoff in thirty minutes, and nobody is going to want to make that payoff a few hundred meters from the police station in which they work. But he's seeing an ideal opportunity to eliminate me as a risk. Because I've sprung this on him pretty quickly, he hasn't had long enough to think it through properly. He thinks he's doing a pretty good job. Being clever. Being smarter than me. But I've been thinking through this all day. He's going to ask for somewhere way less public and much more secluded.

"You know where the Styx Bridge is?" he asks.

"Out Redwood way, right?" I ask. I went over it the other night to reach the highway when I took Walt for a drive.

"Meet me at ten o'clock underneath it. Don't try anything funny."

I'm no comedian. "I won't."

"How do I know ten grand buys your silence?"

Good question. I'm surprised he's asked this, considering he can't afford to fuel me with any suspicion that he's preparing to kill me. Again, I've been thinking about this all day knowing he had no choice but to ask it.

"For ten grand, I'll give you both the photographs and negatives of you at the Everblue. I'll give you the negatives and photographs of you leaving Daniela Walker's house on the night she died. And on top of that, if I wanted more money, I'd be asking for more. I just want enough to get out of the city before the cops close in on me."

"Ten o'clock then." He hangs up without waiting for a response. He's realized I'm cleverer than he first thought, I'm clever enough to have photos of him from the crime scene, and he'll wonder how this is even possible. It'll take him a while, but in the end he'll conclude that I'm lying. I look at my watch. I have more than three-quarters of an hour not to show up. Plenty of time not to do several things.

Plenty of time not to kill.

I reach down and scratch at my testicle through the padding, realizing it isn't my remaining testicle that has me in discomfort, but the missing one. The itch is where the skin is mending. Melissa left me some disinfectant and some talcum powder. I grab them from my briefcase and sit down on the edge of the bed. I remove the padding—it pulls at the hairs and I have to stifle a scream—then clean the area and sprinkle on the talcum powder. By the time I'm done, my testicle looks as though it's been dusted for fingerprints. I replace the padding and lie down on the bed and focus on not falling asleep. The problem is the bed is so comfortable I'm wondering if I can somehow steal it.

CHAPTER THIRTY-NINE

The graveyard is mostly deserted. It's late to be out here, but Sally wanted somewhere quiet to think. She parks next to a car that has a guy inside it slowly drinking from a bottle wrapped in a paper bag. He looks at her and she can see pain in his eyes and for a moment she wants to help him, to tell him that things will get better, but she isn't so sure it's true, not for this guy. She's seen him out here before, and she's seen him around the police station a few times too, talking mostly to Detective Schroder. She thinks he used to work there. She doesn't know his story, and doesn't want to ask.

She makes her way to her brother's grave. Long blades of grass, those close to the gravestones missed by the lawn mower, are bending under the weight of the dew. Other than going to church, she feels like the cemetery is the closest place to God.

Last night, rather than having some of her questions answered, Sally was only led further down the path of her confusion. No, further into the world of Joe's fiction. Just how much is he lying about? Did he attack himself?

She thinks about the blood on the stairs at his apartment building. If Joe attacked himself, he must have done it outside. It doesn't seem likely. As unlikely as Joe driving? She knows she needs to confront him. She was going to today at work, but she'd become scared. She didn't want to lose Joe. Though, really, that has probably already happened. Maybe his mother hasn't told him yet of her visit, but she soon will.

She wipes the back of her hand across her face, streaking the tears across her cheeks. Her breath is forming a mist in front of her face. She doesn't want to let Joe down.

The same way you let down your brother?

The tears start to come more freely. Nobody blames her for what happened to Martin, at least that's what they say, but she knows they do. She certainly does. Her parents must do. As for Martin and God, well, one day she'll find out. She pulls out a tissue from her pocket and dries her face. Across the graveyard, mist looks as though it's seeping out of the ground. Fog is hanging around the gravestones but doesn't have the strength to climb any higher. By the time she gets back to her car her legs feel damp.

She turns the heater on to full as she drives to Joe's apartment. The hot air dries her legs and her face. Sometimes on the way home from seeing her dead brother, she can't stop the tears.

She parks in the same spot she parked in the first time she came here. She grabs the first-aid kit from the backseat. She will help Joe by removing the stitches before she will help him by confronting him.

Nobody appears as she makes her way up to the top floor. The small splotches of blood are still on the stairs. Some of them have been smeared to the size of a watch face. She knocks, but nobody answers. A cat appears at the end of the hallway and walks down to her. It has a slight limp. She squats down next to it and starts petting it.

"Hey, little one, aren't you just the cutest?"

The cat meows as if to agree, then starts purring. She knocks on the door again, still hunched down next to the cat. Joe doesn't answer. Is it possible he has passed out again? Or been attacked? She knocks louder. Most likely he isn't home, but what if he is? What if he is lying on his bed, bleeding, the other testicle removed?

She reaches into her first-aid kit, where the copy of Joe's key has been since the day she had it cut. She stands up and inserts it into the lock. She realizes the chances are higher that she's looking for an excuse to enter rather than Joe being in trouble inside. This realization doesn't stop her from turning the handle and pushing the door open.

"Joe?"

Joe doesn't answer, because Joe isn't home. She closes the door behind her. The cat sits down on the table next to the goldfish bowl. The bowl is empty. Did Joe not feed them? Has he bought a cat to replace them? His clothes are scattered across the floor again, though this time there aren't any patches of blood on any of them. The pile of latex gloves she had made has become smaller. There are dishes in the sink, exposed food on the table. The bed is unmade, and has possibly been that way since the attack. Would Martin have lived like this?

Sally starts to walk around the apartment. This isn't right, being here, but whatever's happening to Joe isn't right either.

Happening to Joe?

She looks through the folders he has brought home from the police station—there are extra ones now. The photos are disgusting, and she can bear only to look at them for a few seconds. She replaces them. Why would Joe have these here?

Perhaps a more important question would be what he'd say if he came home and found her looking around his apartment. Yes, it's best that she goes. She is about to pick up the cat when it races under the bed.

"Come on, little one, come on. You can't stay under there."

But the cat thinks that it can. When she gets onto her hands and knees and looks under the bed, the cat is right in the middle. Next to it is a small piece of paper. Curious, Sally reaches under and grabs it.

It's a ticket from a parking building. The time and date printed across it are several months old. It doesn't make sense to still have the ticket, because the ticket gets handed back on the way out of the parking building so the guy in the booth knows how much to charge you. She reaches under the bed and puts the ticket back on the floor.

She clicks her fingers for the cat, which a moment later is purring in her arms. She carries it into the hallway, sets it down, then heads back outside.

CHAPTER FORTY

I try putting myself into Calhoun's head. He's seeing a chance not only to apprehend the Christchurch Carver, but also to eliminate the only person who knows about his secret life. I'm sure he's also weighing up the fact that he can't take any credit for it. He wants to be a hero, but if he takes me alive, he knows I'll talk. So he needs to catch me in a way in which he can have an excuse for killing me. It'll be difficult to do. Difficult to explain.

His easiest option is to kill me and hide my body. His glory will be lost, and the file I opened months ago with my first victim will remain open. Nothing will be added to it, but it will never close. There will be no glory to be had. The Christchurch Carver will vanish. While everybody is investigating the case, he can be off somewhere playing golf.

I slip my jacket on, adjust my gloves, and leave my room. I keep my hands thrust in my pockets, but it doesn't matter, since I don't pass anybody. I make my way to the top floor and head along to Calhoun's room. The number was in his file. Problem is, the only way I can get in is with a key card.

I get in the elevator. Just as the doors are closing, a maid comes out from a nearby room, almost like fate intended it. I slap at the open door button on the inside panel, and step back into the hallway. The maid smiles at me as we cross paths. She looks in her fifties, has the worn-out look of a mother who has maybe six kids and has to clean up after hundreds of adults forty hours a week. Her black hair is dyed, and she looks so thin that if I picked her up and threw her into the wall, she would land in a thousand pieces. I smile and nod back, then turn and watch as she comes to a stop a few doors down.

I wait for her to go inside, then, looking around to make sure we are still alone, I go in after her, knowing there has to be something I can say to convince her to give me the key card I need.

I reach my arm over her shoulder before she even knows I'm there, and pull it tightly across her throat, using my other hand to support the back of her head. I tighten both arms slightly to slow down her breathing. She, of course, is starting to struggle, but quickly stops when I suggest it isn't in her best interest. She stops fighting, and I'm wondering if she's gone through this before. Maybe that's why she's got six kids.

I don't want to do anything to her. Not sexually, anyway, because she's old enough to be my mother. Here she is, just doing her job—a low-paying, demeaning job like my own—and suddenly it could cost her her life. Well, I'm going to give her a chance to hang on to it. For now.

I tell her to shut up or she's going to die. Then I tell her to keep facing ahead, that if she turns, if she tries to see me, she will die. From my voice she knows I'm not bluffing.

I ask for her key card. She lowers her hand to her waist and unclips it from her waist, and hands it to me. She knows it isn't worth dying for. She's thinking I can steal all the towels and free soap I want from any room I want. With my arm still

around her throat, I tuck the key card into my pocket, lead
her forward, and push her onto the bed. When I straddle her
back, she doesn't complain, doesn't cry out. She's a quick
learner. Then again, I also threatened to kill her husband and
her kids.

I use a sheet to bind her arms and legs, another to cover
her eyes.

I tell her to keep still for twenty minutes, because I'm going
to be back. Perhaps even sooner. If she's gone, I'll find her and
kill her. If she's still here, I'll let her go. I don't want to create
a crime scene. I can't afford any attention coming this way.
Satisfied she isn't going anywhere in a hurry, I head into the
corridor, wheel the cart into the bedroom so nobody will see
it, then close the door.

I put the key card into the lock of Detective Robert Calhoun's room. He'll be waiting for me, probably getting pretty
impatient by now. I figure he'll give me maybe another ten
minutes. Even if he's leaving now, he still has to drive into
town. I've plenty of time to go through his room.

I close the door behind me, shutting myself into complete
darkness, then reach into my pocket and pull out the small
flashlight I've brought along, then realize there's no point in
sneaking around, and turn on the lights. The kitchen's bigger
than mine, and Calhoun has a larger range of utensils, pots,
and cutlery. I see he made himself a sandwich before leaving
for work.

In order for the police to get cheap rates, they need to do
their own housecleaning, which includes dishes. Calhoun is a
man in his fifties away from his wife, which means the dishes
at the moment are stacked high and haven't been washed in
about a week. He'll probably live off junk food for a few days
before he'll wash them.

I pull out my knife and set it on the bench next to its twin,
making sure they're indeed identical. Satisfied, I wrap them
into separate plastic bags, careful not to smudge Calhoun's

fingerprints. I slide the bags into my pockets—mine in the left, Calhoun's in the right.

Perfect.

I look through his drawers, his suitcases. Even though he's been here more than a month, he's hardly unpacked. I find a collection of pornographic magazines, a pair of handcuffs (standard issue—though not for police), and a leather gag with a rubber ball in the center to keep people quiet. I consider taking it with me, but it's probably not wise. Anyway, I'm happy with my own technique. There are other sex toys, many of which I've never seen. The man's a real deviant, and I begin to admire him.

The door automatically locks behind me when I leave.

It looks like the maid has struggled to escape from her bindings, but has failed. Pretty much what I expected. I move into the kitchen and find a third identical knife, which I put into a different plastic bag.

Back in the bedroom, I tell the maid to shut up and to keep facing away from me. Then I untie the sheets, put my arm over her shoulder, and hand her a thousand dollars. This will definitely buy her silence, and I still consider myself up a grand after not paying Becky the other night. Plus it's good not to make another crime scene. I feel her eyes scanning over the money, her mind already spending it. I can see her thinking what she has to do to earn more. I tell her to stay where she is for another five minutes. If she understands, she's to nod. She nods vigorously while still looking at the money. I toss her key card onto the bed (a hard decision because I could have a fun time going from room to room), turn my back, and walk away, closing the door behind me. She's probably thinking that unless there's a report of a crime, there's no reason for her to tell anybody what happened. The knife from Calhoun's room feels heavier than the one I took there, even though it's identical. His fingerprints are weighing it down.

Sometimes it's embarrassing to be so competent. Back in

my room, I put my knife back in the kitchen, then clean the one I got from the room with the maid, slipping it back into a bag.

There is still plenty to do. Life would be easier if I could go back to the car I parked with the dead woman in the back. Sure, I could throw the murder weapon in the trunk, then call the police, but I never actually stabbed her, and by stabbing her now, well, any pathologist with enough knowledge to identify an arm from a leg will realize the wounds are post-mortem. Especially after all this time. No, I need somebody new. Somebody fresh.

I'll go out tonight and do some window-shopping. There won't be any homework involved, because I can't base spontaneity on homework.

Tonight should be fun.

Tonight should bring a smile to my face.

After all, I haven't been shopping in ages.

CHAPTER FORTY-ONE

The biggest crime in Christchurch—apart from fashion and Old English architecture, glue-sniffing, too much greenery, bad driving, bad parking, lack of parking, wandering pedestrians, expensive shops, the winter smog, the summer smog, kids riding skateboards on sidewalks, kids riding bikes on sidewalks, old guys yelling Bible passages at anybody passing by, stupid policemen, stupid laws, too many drunks, too few shops, barking dogs, loud music, puddles of urine in shop doorways in the morning, puddles of vomit in the gutters, and the gray décor—is burglary. Burglaries occur every few minutes. Mostly thanks to teenagers who will grow up to become armed offenders who shoot people to get enough money to buy their daily prescription of drugs. Up there with burglary is car theft. Cars are stolen almost as often as homes are broken into. Therefore, you'd think more people would have car alarms. But they don't. They prefer to spend their money on expensive car stereos, which end up in cheap pawnshops. Therefore, stealing another car is not difficult.

Not when you know how. Not when you're as good at it as I am.

I'm driving around the outskirts of town in my new car, a Ford something or other, browsing for merchandise, looking for somebody who'll take my liking, or perhaps a house that looks reasonably unsecured, when it comes to me. An idea. As I know from experience, spontaneous ones are sometimes the best. I have to remind myself that sometimes they're not.

My briefcase sits on the passenger seat, loaded with knives, scissors, and a pair of pliers. The briefcase is the toolbox for the modern serial killer.

I head toward one of the nearby movie-theater complexes, which seem to be springing up all over the city at the rate of about one a year. I park this car among the many others. Here I wait, idly scratching at my crotch, flicking the window wipers every thirty seconds or so to clear the view. The flow of people is interrupted by the sessions starting and stopping and by the slow, the gossiping, and the disabled taking the longest to make their way to their cars. Finally, I spot the perfect victim. In her thirties, I guess. Long blond hair, high cheekbones, shiny wheelchair. I figure a person like this has nothing to lose, so killing her won't really be a crime—hell, she won't even feel half the things I'm planning to do to her.

I watch as the breathing corpse courageously makes her way into her car, using her arms to transfer her weight from the chair to the driver's seat. Then, with a skill only cripples can acquire, she swings the chair onto the roof of her car and clips it down. Amazing. It will be the last time she ever does it.

I follow her home. The Ford is a late model and handles nicely. I turn on the air-conditioning and listen to the stereo. Quite the relaxing drive. I pull up outside a house a few down from hers, and give her twenty minutes to get inside and get herself settled. I'm guessing she lives alone. First, she's a cripple and nobody would want to love her; second, if she has a partner, then he would have been with her at the movies.

Until now I never considered there was a use for the disabled, the retarded, and the crippled.

The house has a single story—can't expect more for somebody in her condition. The garden is poorly looked after. The wheelchair ramp leading to the front door has a welcome mat at the bottom of it. I walk up just after eleven o'clock. Fumble with the lock. For somebody who lives inside a wheelchair, she has poor security. Life's like that. Those most prone to being attacked—the old, the weak, the beautiful—generally have maybe a chain across their door and a safety lock. Not much. Not much at all to somebody like me.

The first port of call is the kitchen, where the appliances are all at waist level. I open her fridge and examine the contents. I do this not because I'm hungry, or thirsty, but because I've done it at many of the other victims' houses. The fridge offers nothing exciting to choose from. It appears she's a vegetarian. I don't get vegetarians.

I select a carton of milk, drink directly from it, and set it down in the middle of the table. I wipe my arm across my mouth to get rid of the milk mustache, then make my way down the wide, uncarpeted hallway to her bedroom.

No time for mucking around. Don't want to risk having her scream. So it'll have to be straight in there, and straight into it.

I'm in her room and subduing her before she's even aware of what's happening. I stop hitting her when a sudden searing pain appears in my hand. It feels like my little finger has been broken. I pray it hasn't, figuring that since God didn't help me out with my testicle, He owes me one. I just hope He's in a good mood.

I won't need to worry about binding the woman's legs. No point. Just her hands. I use the cord from her phone next to the bed. She isn't going to be needing it. When I have her secure, I start massaging my finger. Feeling begins to seep back into it, and I breathe a sigh of relief. God loves me after all.

The padding on my testicle will stop me from doing what I'd normally do, but at least I can do us both a favor and save us some time. Careful not to get my hands too bloody, I use the knife I cleaned last night and, when I'm done, I pack it away and take out the one with Calhoun's fingerprints on it. The risk of smudging the prints now that the victim is dead is minimal. Even so, I'm careful when I slip the blade into one of the already open wounds.

When I'm finished, I go through her cupboards and drawers, and end up borrowing some gear that she won't be needing anymore. I'm about to leave when I hear a humming coming from her living room. It's a fish tank. I stand silently and watch perhaps two dozen fish moving back and forth in the blue light. Immediately I think of Pickle and Jehovah. Immediately I wish I had picked another woman to have killed and not a fellow fish lover. The temptation to select two fish from this tank to keep is powerful, but I know I can never replace the two I've lost. No. The emptiness in my life must remain—at least until I've had the chance to mourn. The joy of having two new fish will only taste like ashes.

I stay feeling pretty bad for killing Little Miss Cripple as I'm leaving her house. She loved fish, and I loved fish. We lived alone with them. They were our friends. We were their gods. Before she was just a person I didn't know, but now she's somebody I can relate to. In another life, maybe we could have been friends. Or even more. I leave the front door open, figuring her body will be found quicker that way by a concerned neighbor or late-night burglar. The best I can do for her now is to hope she has a nice funeral. Before walking to my car, I check if I've got any blood on me. A few dark spots have flicked onto me, but they're close to impossible to see on my dark overalls.

I drive directly to the hotel, make sure no policemen are around, then go to my room. Safely inside, I clean down the actual murder weapon, soak it in some bleach for ten minutes that I took from work, then roll it back into the plastic bag.

Ideally I'd like to put it back where I got it, but this isn't an ideal world. I'll dump it elsewhere.

I remove the pad from my testicle, knowing that I'll have to replace it soon. I sit on the edge of the bed first and examine my genitals in the mirror. I'm expecting to see this black, infected thing that will probably see me either in the hospital or in a morgue. What I see is wrinkled skin covered in dry blood and talcum powder, and as I dab it away with a damp corner of the towel, I see that Melissa's work has been effective. The area is inflamed from all the scratching, and on closer examination, I see why it has been so itchy. The stitches are overdue for removal.

I don't want Melissa making another visit to help me out, so I head into the bathroom and grab the small sewing kit that's wrapped up in a matchbook-size box next to the soaps. With a towel beneath me on the bed, ever so slowly I use the needle to tug at the stitches, loosening them enough to then use one of my smaller knives to cut them. My whole groin, the base of my stomach, and the tops of my thighs start to hurt, but the pain is tolerable—the hardest part is knowing what will happen if I slip. But I don't slip, and each thread vibrates through my body as I draw it through and away from the skin. I wonder if this wouldn't be a better procedure if I were drunk, but decide that it probably wouldn't be—not at the prices I'd have to pay to access the minibar. My sac begins to bleed, but only lightly.

I clean up and take a long shower. The nozzle is directional and I can control the pressure of the spray. It's wonderful. My groin feels better, and I wonder why I didn't become a surgeon instead of a cleaner. After half an hour, I climb out and towel myself down. All the blood is gone—both the cripple's and mine. The throbbing has gone too and, better still, so has the itching. I'm recovering. I will never be the same, but I'm recovering nonetheless. I collapse between the cool sheets and close my eyes.

CHAPTER FORTY-TWO

The next day is work as usual. The old guy giving the forecast earns his pay by getting things right. I guess he's looking out the window at the frost rather than reading off the report in his hand. My biggest concern is running into Detective Calhoun. I use the stairs rather than the elevator, scratching at my crotch the entire way down. In the foyer a bunch of tourists is being given directions by the doorman in English, which they are having trouble understanding. A few taxi drivers carrying luggage to and from taxis. People checking in. People checking out. No Calhoun. I look outside. The storm clouds last night weren't bluffing. Every surface I can see is wet.

I check out of the hotel. I keep looking around so often that the hotel clerk must think I'm paranoid. There aren't any extra charges. The clerk asks me if I've had a pleasant stay, and I tell him I have. He asks me where I'm from, and I realize I can't say Christchurch, because then I'd look like an idiot. Who the hell spends a few nights in a five-star hotel in their own city? I tell him I'm from up north. He asks me exactly where, and I suddenly understand why he is asking all these questions—he is hitting on me. I tell him Auckland, and he tells me he is from Auckland too. He tells me it's a small world. I tell him it's not small enough, and he has to think about this for a few seconds until he realizes that in my small world he wouldn't even exist. I can actually see his thought process as his smile slowly disappears.

I walk to work. It's one of those nothing kind of days, where it could end up being sunny or could end up raining but you just don't know and don't really care. I'm feeling good about a whole lot of different things, among them that my testicle isn't itching this morning. Sally is on my floor when I get to work. She looks me up and down. She seems distracted.

"Do anything exciting last night?" she asks.

Here we go again, back to people's fascinations about what other people do with their time. "Not much. Just stayed at home and watched TV."

"Sounds nice," she says, then walks off.

I begin my day with cleaning the toilets on the first floor. The body of the crippled woman is found. Tragic, apparently. Inhumane too, people are saying. A disgraceful country we must be living in, according to the news. *Where will it end?* people keep asking, but nobody asks me. In my office, I use a felt marker to darken the spots of blood on my overalls and make them look like ink stains.

While the stressed-out detectives look for the killer, I sit in my office and make a call with the cell phone. I sit with my chair against the door just in case Sally comes along and tries to come in.

Detective Calhoun answers. I apologize for not meeting him two nights ago. He tells me exactly what he thinks of me. We exchange a few more pleasantries before agreeing to meet once again, this time at six o'clock tonight, at the Walker house. Reluctantly, he agrees. Without thanking me, he hangs up.

After lunch, I listen closely to find out if the detectives are plotting to stake out the Walker place. Nobody makes any reference to it. Calhoun has kept the information to himself. That means he's sticking with his game plan of killing me. Then suddenly everything around the station gets even busier. I don't get the details, but enough to know another body has been found this morning—this one nothing to do with me. Some guy has gotten himself killed in a pretty nasty way at a church somewhere here in town. So the workload is doubled because now they have the dead woman in the wheelchair, and the dead guy at the church, and what they really need is twice as many cops.

Every half hour or so I run into Sally, but she doesn't seem in the mood for talking. She'll look at me from the end of a corridor or stairway, and she'll stare at me with this look on her face that suggests she is lost, but not once does she come up to me and make the sort of inane conversation that makes me want to scream. I must admit I miss the lunches she makes, and I make a mental note to suggest my hunger to her so it may inspire her to start making them again.

Four thirty rolls along, and with it, the chance to enjoy my day. Back in my office I make another cell phone call, this one also to the police station. I ask to speak to somebody in homicide. When I say I may have some information, I'm transferred directly to Carl Schroder's phone.

I skip the part where I'm supposed to give him my name, telling him I know how these things work, and although I'm willing to help, I'm not prepared to testify in court for reasons I don't want to discuss, but which mostly involve my own safety. He disagrees with my fears, but doesn't push it, probably because ninety-five percent of calls he gets are from crackpots. Regardless, he sounds desperate to know what I know. I tell him it isn't what I know, but what I've found. I give him directions to the trash dumpster three blocks away from last night's crime scene. When asked how I found it there, I answer by telling him I saw a man dropping it off, and once I learned of the murder today, I decided to call them.

A brief description of the man?

Sure. Why not? I give a brief description of Calhoun before hanging up on more questions. It's nothing like the picture of "me" hanging in the conference room.

When I get home, I take about three steps before sensing something is different, but I can't figure out what. It's as if somebody has come through here and shifted everything a few degrees out of whack. I stand in one spot, turning a complete circle, but in the end I can't come up with any tangible reason why I should feel something is out of place. It's just a feeling. Maybe Melissa has been back here. Maybe she hasn't.

I slip on a pair of latex gloves and put my hands under the mattress, searching for the parking ticket I kept as a memento months ago. Only I can't find it. I bury my arms in until I'm up to my shoulders, swirling them around, searching, searching . . . but it's gone.

Melissa?

Why would she even look here?

But I already know why. People hide things under their mattresses all the time. It was stupid of me to hide the ticket there.

But then I remember flipping the bed when trying to get hold of that stupid cat. I get down on my hands and knees and look under it, and sure enough, there's the ticket. I put it in my briefcase, then take off my gloves.

After walking a few blocks, I use the usual mode of illegal transport to make my way to the house where I'm meeting Calhoun. Each of us is intending to kill the other, though, supposedly, neither of us knows that. By the time I get there it is five forty. I'm sure I've beaten Calhoun because he has a long day dealing with the dead.

I park several blocks away and walk. The night is as cold as the morning, and I fear winter may end up being just as long as summer. When I reach the house, I suddenly have this fear that maybe the residents have moved back in and family life is under way again. I suck in a few deep breaths. No, if anybody was living here, I'd have heard about it by now.

I use my skills to unlock the front door and use my foot to close it behind me. I stand still in the hallway and listen for sounds of life. No one here. The bedroom seems the place to be, since it has the most history now, so I head there first. I open my briefcase and, regretting the lack of a firearm that could end this whole drama quickly, I pull out a hammer. Under the circumstances it's the best I can do. But looking at it, the hammer seems the wrong way to go—too easy to end up putting a hole in his skull and killing him. I head to the kitchen to look for something better. I return to the bedroom, now the proud owner of a large frying pan. It's nonstick.

I sit on the bed and watch the hands on my watch tick around, waiting for Detective Calhoun to arrive.

CHAPTER FORTY-THREE

She's sick of not knowing. Sick of the questions. Sick of being sick.

At four fifteen, Sally leaves work. She doesn't need to justify leaving early. Others here know her father is in bad shape and that she wants to spend time helping him. Not that anybody would notice—it's been a very active day in the world of a homicide detective. She's always hated days like this, and hates that they come around so often.

At four twenty, when she reaches the parking building, Henry isn't here. She isn't sure whether she ought to be disappointed or flattered that he must only show up at four thirty for her. She doesn't know whether to feel used or wanted.

She drives past the police station, does a U-turn, and finds a parking spot on the opposite side of the road. Four thirty arrives, but Joe fails to. She can never remember him not leaving exactly at four thirty. Has he left already?

She waits another five minutes. Still no Joe.

*Just what are you doing? Planning on following him around?
Still trying to help him?*

Exactly. She wants to see if he's meeting anybody. Perhaps
the woman he spoke to earlier in the week, the witness from
the police station. Five minutes later, she starts the car and,
disappointed, pulls away. She wasn't comfortable about waiting anyway.

She's at a red light when she sees Joe in the rearview mirror on the sidewalk. The lights turn green. She doesn't know
what to do. A car behind her starts tooting. By the time she
turns around, Joe's already disappeared. He's probably already
on the bus.

She starts driving to the graveyard, but a few minutes later
she finds she's not actually going in that direction, but back
toward Joe's apartment. She needs to talk to him away from
the station. She hopes talking doesn't turn into confronting.
She parks down the street and decides to wait twenty minutes
at the most. He arrives in half that time.

She waits in the car imagining the outcome of their talk
and trying to figure out whether she should go and knock on
his door, or just drive away. Plus sits waiting to see if anybody
else is coming to see him, and all that waiting takes the decision to talk to him out of her hands because Joe is only in
his apartment for a few minutes before coming back out. He
starts walking away from her. She begins to follow him. By
the time she rounds the corner, he's turning left down another street. She slows down a little. She has never followed
anybody before, and she suddenly realizes she isn't very good
at it. She inches her car closer to the corner, and is about to
go around it when Joe appears from the left, driving through
the intersection.

In a different car from the one she saw him in last time.

She keeps pace with him, trying to keep a car between
them, until he slows down in an upper-class area and pulls
over to the curb. Sally keeps on driving, watching him in the

rearview mirror. He climbs out and walks to the end of the block, his briefcase swinging slightly back and forth with his momentum.

She follows him to a two-story house, where he heads up the path and disappears from sight within the alcove of the front door. Something about the house is familiar, but she can't figure out what. And if it were something as innocent as meeting a friend, why would Joe park a short distance away? Why not just up the driveway? People who park a few blocks away are normally people who are having affairs, she thinks. Parking a few blocks away is definitely an affair kind of thing to do, but Joe isn't an affair kind of guy. He's not a . . . a what? Well, he's not a sexual kind of guy. He's Joe. He's like her brother. Only Joe can drive and sneak around and can steal and lie.

She drums her fingers against the steering wheel. She wishes she had the confidence to go and knock on the door and ask Joe what is happening, but if he is in danger, she may only cause him more grief.

Ten minutes pass. Twenty. After a while, Sally starts to realize she's whispering a prayer. She wants Joe to reappear and carry on; she wants him to be okay. Maybe something bad is happening to him, and all she's doing is sitting out here and waiting, letting the bad things happen to Joe the same way she let the bad things happen to Martin five years ago.

"Stupid, stupid, stupid," she mutters, hitting the palm of her hand against her forehead.

Then, a few minutes later, a car pulls into the driveway and a man climbs out. She's slightly too far away to recognize him, but, like the house, something about the man is familiar. He moves quickly to the front door and steps inside.

CHAPTER FORTY-FOUR

Calhoun starts to turn as I make my way from behind the bedroom door. He raises his arm to protect himself from the swinging frying pan. He's able to get his elbow in the way; the pan cracks into it, then deflects into his chest. He staggers backward, and I stumble forward, crashing into him. We both drop to the ground, and then he's reaching into his jacket for his gun. My mind's racing so fast that I have time to comprehend that I'm failing, time to ask why he never had his gun in his hand in the first place, time to speculate that he wanted me to trust him first so that he could learn what I knew. I make my way to my knees as he leans upward, and I can see the surprise in his face because he knows who I am, but that knowledge doesn't make him any less desperate to kill me.

I crash my head forward, connecting with his forehead and hurting myself as much as him, but at least his hand falls away from the gun. Lights flare behind my eyes—a hundred, no, a thousand of them—all at once and all in the same shade of white, but then the reds start to filter through, but compared to the pain I've known lately, this is nothing, and I'm quickly able to recover. I wobble back and the room spins only a little. I know Calhoun must be feeling the same way, just as I know I can't give him a second chance. I'm still holding the frying pan, and I quickly decide to use it.

When I look at him, there are two Detective Calhouns, two bedroom doors, two of everything. I shake my head and the room keeps spinning, but the images begin to form into one. I roll my body, raise my heavy arms, and swing the pan against the side of his head. It connects with his cheekbone and jaw, possibly breaking the former and maybe dislocating the latter. He falls back to the ground and doesn't move. Exhausted, I let the pan fall to the floor.

I roll him onto his front and bind his hands behind him, then tie his legs. When I try to open his mouth, I discover I've dislocated his jaw. Since I need to make conversation with him later, I grip hold of his mouth and try to move it back. Nothing happens. I tap it with the hammer—softly at first, then harder—and after a few blows it clicks back into place. I open his mouth and place the egg inside, then change my mind. I won't risk the egg slipping to the back of his throat while he's unconscious and killing him. I use a pair of the husband's underwear to gag him instead.

By the time Calhoun wakes up I have him sitting in a chair I've brought up from the dining room. I've used rope to secure him to it and, because the chair has metal legs, even if he can somehow tip it over it won't break. I wrap duct tape around his legs and reinforce them to the chair, and run more tape around his arms. Unless he's Harry Houdini, he won't be going anywhere.

I crouch in front of him. He's staring at me, as if the face he saw before being knocked out couldn't possibly be the one he's seeing now. How is it possible that Joe—Joe the cleaner, Joe the fucked-up retard—is doing this to him? Can it be that the man they've been looking for has been working for them all this time?

I nod, confirming that yes, it is not only possible, but better than possible.

He grunts, either to confirm his surprise, or to ask me why, or perhaps to test the gag in his mouth. Whatever the reason, he can't sustain much of a noise. The pain in his jaw must be killing him. Blood hangs off his bottom lip. I want to tell him it's nothing compared to having a testicle torn off, but I don't want anybody else knowing about that.

"You killed her, didn't you?"

"Uh-uh." He shakes his head. "I didn't ki' any'ody."

"Yes, you did."

This time, shaking his head, he repeats himself. Almost. "No. No, I didn't, you cwasy fasdid."

I think he has just called me a crazy bastard. Perhaps I am. Perhaps that's my problem. I test his theory by standing up and punching him in the stomach.

Will you look at that? He was right. Only I'm a bastard who needs to make a deal.

"I'm going to take off your gag," I say, leaning forward once more. "You know the drill. If you don't, then assume it. Any sound," I say, raising the knife to his mouth, "has an unpleasant ending for you. Nod if you understand."

I'm still being a bastard, because I'm holding the tip of the blade directly beneath his chin, so as he nods, he keeps pricking himself. I ensure this by raising the knife higher every time his head rises. In the end, he nods with his eyes. I use the knife to cut his gag. It falls away and hangs around his neck like a collar.

"Better?"

He nods. In fact, his whole body is nearly nodding.

"You can talk, you know. That's the point of removing the gag."

"Listen, Joe, do you know who I am?"

It's a stupid question, but I answer it anyway. "Of course I do."

"Now, do you understand that it's bad to do this? It's bad to tie people up. Especially policemen."

"I'm not a moron."

"No. No of course you're not. I understand life is difficult for . . . for, well, for special people like yourself. I understand . . ."

I hold my hand up. "Listen, Bob, let me stop you right there. Just because I'm a cleaner doesn't mean I'm a Goddamn moron, okay? You need to start realizing I'm not the same idiot you've seen every day since you've been in this city."

He tilts his head slightly as he takes this information in, and slowly he starts to do the realizing he needs to do. He comes to the conclusion that I'm not Slow Joe, but Angry Joe. I'm Superintelligent Joe.

"Look, Joe, I didn't mean to offend you. It's just that, well, it was one hell of an act. You can't blame me for being fooled," he says, which sounds like an attempt at flattery.

"No, I can't blame you, but you can stop sucking up, Bob."

"You haven't crossed the line here yet. If you let me go, I can forget this ever happened. We can both carry on with our normal lives. Once you do something, though, once you hurt me, there's nothing I can do to help you out. You understand that, right? If I'm dead, I'm useless, right? Okay? You're obviously an intelligent guy, I'm sure you understand. And I'm sure you know a useless dead cop means trouble for you, Joe, and neither of us wants any trouble, right?" he says, which is his way of assuming that neither of us wants a dead cop. "We both know that. It's just too much hassle. So how about you untie me, huh? Untie me and we can discuss any concerns you have. We can talk about what you want."

"Don't you want to know what we're going to be talking about?"

"Sure I do, Joe, sure I do, but you've got to untie me first, okay? Untie me and give me back my gun, and we'll go downstairs, or wherever you want to go because it's up to you, I promise. This is your ball game and you're calling all the shots here, so we'll go where you want to go and we can discuss whatever it is you have in mind, no matter how long it takes."

"No guesses as to who I am? Other than Joe the Janitor?"

"You're just the cleaner. Joe the cleaner. Nobody else. I don't care if you're anybody else, and if you are, then it's none of my business. You can be anybody for all I care. But to me you're just the cleaner. Just Joe. Joe who hasn't committed any crimes other than making us all think you were slow. How about it, Joe? How about you untie me?"

He's sweating so much I'm starting to worry that he might be able to slip out of the knots and that the duct tape will just run off him in long, silver streaks.

"Do you know who I am?"

He shakes his head. "No."

"Come on, you do know. I'm the Carver."

"I don't know who you are, and after you've let me go, I won't even think about it. Okay, Joe?"

This, of course, is all bullshit. Bullshit that is taught to these guys when they become cops. He's trying to negotiate with me, but he has nothing to bargain with. He knows that, but what else can he do? He keeps using my name, trying to relate to me, trying to make me see him as a real person.

"Let's make a few assumptions. First of all, let's assume I'm telling the truth. Secondly, let's assume I'm not about to let you go. Thirdly, let's assume you don't cooperate with what I want. Do you know what happens then?"

He nods. Assumptions are something that cops aren't supposed to make. They're supposed to use facts, not maybes. However, Calhoun has been to some of the crime scenes. He can safely assume what will happen to him without needing any further evidence. All he has to do is swap, inside his mind, his own body for that of one of the women.

"Yeah, I know."

"Good. Then let's get a few of the ground rules out of the way. First of all, you're all alone. Help isn't coming, and you have no way to escape. However, don't let this get you down. You've probably figured out that if I wanted you dead, you'd be dead already, right?"

He nods. He probably knew that from the moment he came to.

"Because if you agree to what I want, which is most likely, you'll not only get out of here with your own life, but you'll get paid an income for surviving."

At this, he slowly starts nodding—at the word *income*, not *life*. Suddenly he not only survives, he becomes richer. This is sounding like a pretty good deal to him. He's already paying for more hookers and he doesn't even know yet how much he's earning.

"The second thing is that I ask the questions, and you answer them truthfully. Failure to do so will jeopardize both aspects of the first ground rule. Any questions?"

He opens his mouth, but nothing comes out. Yes, he understands. Perfectly.

"I suppose you want to know how much money and what you need to do for it?"

"Please."

"Twenty thousand dollars, and it's simple to earn. You don't need to kill anybody for it, because you'll be leaving that to me."

He nods at this. Thinks twenty grand isn't a lot of money to get tied up for, but it's better than getting tied up and shot. Twenty grand is a lot of money to earn for doing nothing. This is the part of the plan he likes. The part of the plan I knew he would like.

CHAPTER FORTY-FIVE

"I don't want anybody to die," Bob starts, as if he really means it, and as if I'd really care even if he did. People dying isn't a relevant factor for him, or for me. Under other circumstances—better circumstances, he'll be thinking—we could have laughed at his joke.

What is relevant is Daniela Walker.

I lean back on my elbow. If I smoked, now would be the time to casually light up an expensive cigarette. If I were an evil mastermind, now would be the time I started petting my white Persian cat. But I'm just a cleaner with no goldfish to feed. An average, everyday Joe. If I had my mop, then maybe I would stroke it. If I had my metal bucket, I could beat out a rhythm. All I can do is turn the knife over and over in my hands, watching him watching the blade.

"Come now, Bob, you've killed before. I don't see how you can feel bad about somebody else dying."

"I haven't killed anybody."

I shake my finger back and forth. "No, no, no. I said no

lying. Do you remember what I said would happen if you lied?"

He nods. He remembers.

"Good. I know of a couple of ways we can do this," I say, reaching into my briefcase and rummaging around. "I can start by using these," I pull out a pair of sharpened gardening shears, "on your fingers. For every answer I don't want to hear, I'll remove one finger."

Actually, I won't. I'm not going to remove any of them, but as long as he believes I'm going to, that's all that really counts. This is where his assumptions are going to lead him astray. I watch his face as he studies the gardening shears. It takes no effort to imagine how they can wrap around any one of his fingers, how the blades can sink through his flesh, and how with a little bit of extra effort I can get them to snap through the bone. His imagination already has all his digits scattered across the floor behind his chair.

I'm capable of this. Melissa would be too. And so is he.

The three of us have all killed.

"You did kill her, didn't you?"

He nods.

"Can you tell me why?"

He shrugs. "I'm still not sure."

Not a detailed answer, but I believe it to be the truth—at least as far as he understands it.

"Would you like me to help you understand why?"

He does the wise thing and nods.

"It's because you can," I start. "The ability is inside you. You've always wanted to feel the power. What would it be like to kill somebody? Imagine the control! You imagined it, but of course it's only a fantasy. You couldn't admit to yourself that it's something you'd actually like to try. In your mind you think about the outcomes, of how you could escape the blame, of how to make yourself look like the innocent party. Plenty of ways of doing it, but why explore them? After all, you're only thinking about it, you're not exactly considering it. Then one day the fantasy is no longer enough. Not the fantasy of killing, but of sex. Violent sex. So you hire a whore, but it isn't the same, because she isn't a real victim. You want to kill her, because that's ideally where the violent sex leads, but you know there's no point in killing a whore because they're already dead. They're zombies tanked up on bad luck and bad breeding. You needed to kill a better class of person, and then along came Daniela Walker. A victim of domestic abuse who refuses to follow through with laying charges against her husband."

He says nothing. I think about the indications in the pathology report that said Daniela had previous injuries. If she'd left her husband, she'd still be alive. And somebody else wouldn't be. Calhoun surely would have found somebody else.

"She threatens him, she even goes to the police, but at the end of the day her fear of him and her love for him prevent her from acting. This woman is a loser. You can't understand how she could even have married a guy like that, let alone have his children. But you forget he'd been charming when she met him, the same way you were charming when you met your wife."

I look at him. My speech hasn't made any impact. If it's true, and I believe most of it is, then he isn't going to let me know. This annoys me, but not enough to jump up and cut his throat. I sit and wait.

"You're new in the city," I continue, "so the opportunity to act out is irresistible. You know her address and learn the pattern of her movements. Her husband's at work, her children are away at camp, so what could be better? Before you attack her, you decide to frame the husband, because what possible candidate could look any more attractive as her killer? Then you answer the question. One person fits the bill perfectly, and that person is me. So what do you do? You frame me for a murder I didn't commit, and to be honest, Bob, I never really appreciated it. But you're lucky, because you're being given the chance to change the way I feel about you. You can either leave this house a richer man, in terms of both money and character, or you can leave inside a body bag on your way straight down to hell. Of course, needless to say, punishment down there will be eternal, and eternity, Bob, is a very long time."

I start wondering what I'm talking about. Hell? Who gives a damn about Satan? The limp-wristed, red-skinned moth-erfucker is a figment of the Christian imagination, designed solely as a deterrent for killers, thieves, rapists, liars, hypo-crites, and mime artists—yet a lot of bloody good that's done.

"Whether you rot in hell or not isn't my concern. What is my concern is what you did to poor Daniela Walker. From what I've learned, and from being here," I spread my arms out to encompass the room, "I've come to some expert and insightful conclusions."

"Good for you."

I smile. "You broke into her house during the late after-noon, climbed upstairs while she was showering, and waited for her in the bedroom. In this bedroom."

It's a familiar scenario.

"She had no chance. After all, you had the element of surprise on your side, as well as being bigger and stronger. Her fear, her imagination, made her react, but not quickly enough to escape you. You struggled with her, managed to force her onto the bed, and she managed to reach to the bedside table and clutch at the only weapon she could find." I point to the table for effect. "She fought with you and managed to stab you with the pen she'd been using to fill in her crossword puzzles. The wound wasn't deep, but it was enough to piss you off. You tossed it away, then got back to business. Except the pen was your mistake, Bob, but you know that, don't you? At the time, after you killed her, nothing else mattered. The pain was gone, as was any concern of being caught. The pen was the fur-thermost thing from your mind. Until you came back. Then it became the biggest thing on your mind, and it was only a matter of good luck that you were able to swap it unnoticed. At least unnoticed by everybody except me."

"What is it you want?"

I shake my head. "Bob, Bob, Bob. I thought we had an understanding. You know you're not allowed to ask the questions."

"Just tell me what you want."

"That's another question."

"No, it isn't. It's a request."

"And that's a lie." I hold up the gardening shears. "You're just asking for it, aren't you?"

He shakes his head. "No. I swear."

"What about Daniela? Was she asking for it?"

Bob's face is wet and he's looking down into his lap. We're both sweating. It's not warm outside, but somehow this house is still retaining the heat from the summer. The windows have been closed for three months now, so the air is stale and tastes like bad meat. I move over to the window. Open it slightly. Suck at the air outside. The smell, the thick air, the pressure on my skin—it is similar to my apartment the week I spent in bed with a bleeding ball and a bucket full of piss. I'd got used to the feeling, but it is a great relief to be rid of it now.

I sit down, remove my jacket, and clutch at my damp shirt. Thoughts of going to the beach are hammering the front of my mind. I can feel the pull of the sea and the sand, even though I'm five or six miles from the nearest drop and grain, even though a trip to the beach tonight would be a pretty miserable experience.

"Answer the Goddamn question, Bob."

He tilts his head to look at me. He looks sorry, but he's sorry to have been caught, not sorry for killing Daniela Walker.

"I didn't mean to kill her."

The air seems to be getting stickier by the minute. I don't reply to his answer. I just sit still, silently reasserting my dominance over this man. The room is cooling. Somewhere, Melissa is dreaming about her money. Somewhere nearby a dog is barking. Some place further away the police are coming closer, if they've not done so already, to discovering a match for the fingerprints on the murder weapon they found in the dumpster.

Bob is now a condemned man. He's effectively on death row. It's just that nobody has told him. His family, especially his wife, will have to live with the stench of blame. How can she justify not knowing what a monster her husband really is? Or how does she explain that she knew and never did anything about it?

I've been wondering whether Bob has an alibi for several of the killings. He was in Auckland for the first few. However, because of the seriousness of this horrific series of murders, the police will work their way around any small inconsistencies, and when nobody else shows up dead, they will be satisfied with labeling Calhoun the Christchurch Carver. I've learned enough from cleaning their hallways to know that they're so hard-pressed for a suspect, they'll keep their mouths shut, never mention all the DNA evidence that never quite matched up, and if a few more bodies show up every now and again they'll use a copycat defense. It'll keep them happy, and the media, and the country. It'll even keep me happy.

"Okay, Bob, explain how killing her was an accident."

He looks up. Stares into my eyes. He shrugs, then he looks down at the floor, then he shrugs again. He seems really unsure. "I followed her home, to talk to her, right?" he says, still looking down. "I wanted her to charge her husband with assault, 'cause the guy's a real asshole, right? Shit, you probably saw him. Stuck-up, arrogant bastard. So full of himself, sure that he's above the law, that it's his right to beat the crap out of his wife. So I follow her home to tell her she's making a mistake, and when I get here, I find that she's home alone."

"It wasn't your job, Bob. You were here to work on my case alone."

He sighs. "I know. I know that, but, well, it just happened."

"Did you know she was going to be home alone?"

"Not really."

"That sounds like a *yes* to me, Bob."

"I suspected."

"Which is why you followed her, right? Because you could only talk to her while she was alone. Having her husband in the same room wasn't going to make for a useful conversation."

"I guess so."

"You guess so. Okay, then what happened?"

"I sat outside for a few minutes, considering what to do."

"Considering whether to kill her or not?"

He shakes his head. "Nothing like that."

"What then?"

"I don't know. I just sat there, watching the house, thinking about the best way to convince her of what she needed to do. Finally, when I went to the door and knocked, there was no answer. I was going to leave . . ." he says, but doesn't finish the sentence.

"But you stayed," I tell him.

"I stayed," he says. "For some reason I couldn't tell you, I stayed."

"Because you saw an opportunity."

"No," he says. "It wasn't like that. I was worried. What if she wasn't answering because her husband was home beating her up for not having dinner on the table or for not cleaning his shoes or whatever excuse the piece of shit needed? Anyway, I checked the door and it was locked, but I had some keys on me designed for picking most house locks, so I used them."

I know the keys well. I also know that domestic abuse isn't about a man who is in love with his wife too much; it's about a man who is in love with the ability to control her.

"I checked around the kitchen, the living room, looking for her."

"Did you call her name?"

"No."

"Is that because you didn't want her to know you were there?"

He shakes his head. "That wasn't it at all. I didn't want to let the husband know I was there, in case he was home and hitting her. I wanted to catch him in the act."

"That's pretty lame, Bob."

"No it's not. This is a big house. I couldn't be sure what was happening, and where."

"So then what?"

"She was upstairs sitting on the bed. Sobbing."

"Which is why she didn't answer the door, I suppose?"

"That was my thought. When she saw me, she started to freak out. I quickly explained who I was, but she was recognizing me anyway."

"She must have been relieved you were a cop and not a homicidal maniac," I say.

If he sees the irony, he doesn't let it show.

"She sat down again, and we began to talk about her husband, but mostly about her. You see, the issue was her, not him. He was always going to be a wife beater. There was no way of stopping him. What people don't understand is that these guys can't be rehabilitated. I mean, what the hell are you going to rehabilitate them to? All he's ever known is violence. I tried talking to her, calmly and reasonably, and that was okay, at first."

He pauses and looks at me. His eyes look damp. I wonder if crying is beyond this madman's ability to act. I prompt him to continue with a slight repositioning of the gardening shears. I'm eager to hear his thoughts.

"Pretty soon she couldn't see my way of thinking, my way of understanding."

"The correct way, you mean?"

"Yeah. Do you know what it's like, Joe, to know you're absolutely right about something—I mean, beyond any doubt—but you can't get somebody else to agree with you? It's not that they don't understand, or that they don't want to. They've become so used to doing the wrong thing that there couldn't possibly be another way."

"Get back to the point, Bob."

"We ended up disagreeing, pretty quickly actually, and then we were arguing. In the end she started screaming at me to leave. I asked her to calm down, but she wouldn't. Then she tried to call the police, so I had to stop her. She slapped me, so then I hit her back. Next thing I knew she was dead and I was standing over her naked body."

He stops talking. We both listen to the silent room. Peaceful, but still warmer than I'd like. I believe most of his story, but he's left something out.

"Next thing you knew," I repeat.

"I didn't mean for it to happen."

"A touching story, Bob," I say, reaching to my eyes with an imitation hanky, wiping away pretend tears. "It seems you've gone for a classic defense strategy. Do they teach you that at training college, or did you pick it up being a cop? See, Bob, what you've done here is extremely common. You've shifted all the blame onto the victim. She's the one who disagreed, she's the one being unreasonable, and she's the one who hit you. If she'd refrained from doing any of those things, then she'd still be alive today. Am I right?"

No answer.

"Am I right, Bob?"

Again the shrug. "I don't know."

"Come on, Bob, you do know. It's the whole domestic abuse scenario over again. She deserved to be punished, didn't she, because she stepped out of line. If she'd done what she was told, if she'd simply obeyed, then she'd be living the contented and happy life. But she didn't, so you killed her—not that you remember doing so. That's the second common phase here, Bob. How many killers have you put away who've told you they don't remember anything? How many have told you that if it weren't for the crazy way this or that particular female acted, then none of this or that would have happened? Now tell me what really happened."

"That is what happened."

"Yeah, most of it probably did, but I'd bet my life on it . . ." I pause, create dramatic effect, then change my mind. "No, I'd bet *your* life on it that you do remember killing her, and were aware of every second of it."

"I can't remember."

He sounds like a whining child. "There's no such word as *can't*, Bob." I lift the gardening shears to prove my point.

He says nothing until I start to rise.

"Okay, okay." He'd have his hands out in a defensive gesture if he could, waving them in the air like a maniac. "I do remember."

"Oh? And what do you remember?" I don't need to know this for my plan to work. I'm just interested, as a fellow participant in this game of life and death.

"We argued, like I told you, and she picked up the phone and threatened to call the police. So I hit her, and once I did that, I knew there'd be no way to shut her up."

"Come now, Bob. She's a domestic-abuse victim. She's used to keeping her trap shut when a man hits her."

"Not this time. She told me I was going to lose my job for what I'd done, and she was right too, so I hit her again, this time harder. Then I shoved her onto the bed and . . ." He stops, either to think of what to say next, or to invent it. "Well, I needed to make it look like she was one of your victims, Joe."

"And you knew just how to do it. You screwed that prostitute I killed the other night. You did to her what your wife won't let you even think about. And you take that experience from Becky the Whore to Little Miss Domestic Abuse."

"I had to make it look real," he says, and he says it in a defeated tone, not the kind of tone somebody who stands by their work would use.

"Is that all, Bob? Or did you want to enjoy yourself as well? Come on, you can tell me. I'm not here to judge you. I just want to hear how you're no better than me." He stares right at me. His face, tight with rage, spits the answer at me. "Sure, I enjoyed it. Like, I mean, what wasn't to enjoy? Pure power."

"Pure power. Isn't that the answer, Bob? Isn't that what we all look for?"

"What do you want from me?"

"That's a question, Bob."

"I don't give a shit, Joe. Just tell me what you want, or fuck off. You're wasting my time, you little asshole." I'm not shocked at his sudden outburst. Over the last hour, I've touched several nerves. Before all of this is over, a knife is going to touch several more.

"The requirement is simple. All you need to do is listen."

"That simple, huh?"

"That's right."

"Bullshit," he says. "What do I have to listen to?"

"A confession."

"Yours?"

"Funnily enough, no. But it's your job to be my security, my insurance if you like. You knew from the moment you saw my face I was either going to kill you or make a deal. Well, here's the deal, Bob. I will give you twenty thousand dollars, in cash, tomorrow night, to listen to a confession. That's all you have to do. Just sit and listen and remember. Do you think you can handle that?"

"Then what? You let me go, is that it?"

"That's it."

"And what's in it for you?"

"My freedom. Yours too."

"And if I refuse?"

"I'll kill you. Right now."

"I want half the money now."

"You're not really in a situation to ask for anything, Bob." I stand and walk over to him.

"What are you doing?" I tilt the chair back and start dragging it across the carpet. It's damn heavy, and my testicle starts to throb.

"Joe? What the hell are you up to?"

"Shut up, Bob." I continue pulling on the chair, and it makes scuff marks across the carpet, but finally I manage to get Calhoun into the bathroom. "I'm afraid you'll have to spend the night here."

"Why?"

"Safer that way."

"For who?"

"For me."

I pull out some duct tape. "Anything else before I seal you up for the night?"

"You're a real psycho, Joe, do you know that?"

"I know lots of things, Detective Inspector."

I run the tape across his mouth. Then I head back into the bedroom and take the parking ticket from my briefcase. I squat down behind Bob, grab the skin on the back of his hand, and start twisting until he unclenches it, then I push his fingertips against the ticket.

"No going anywhere, Bob. Oh, and the toilet's there if you need it." I grin at him, then walk back into the bedroom, closing the door behind me. I put the ticket into an evidence bag, then into my briefcase.

I lock the house before leaving. It's dark when I get outside. I feel like I'm suffering from heat exhaustion, but after a minute in the cool air that problem disappears. The streetlights throw a pale glow into the black night. I drive Calhoun's car into town and grab the ticket from the machine at the entrance to the parking building. I head up the ramps—the number of cars getting fewer the higher I drive—until I reach the very top, where there is only one. I don't turn the car sharply enough, and end up scraping the corner of the front bumper all along the side of the other car, leaving a deep graze and a line of small dents. I notice that the tires on the other car have half deflated over time. I climb out. The smell coming from the trunk of the abandoned car is barely noticeable.

With nothing else to do, I head toward home and toward the end of another long night.

Another phase completed.

CHAPTER FORTY-SIX

She doesn't know this is where she is driving to until she pulls up the long, twisting driveway lined with beautiful trees, which is ironic because she wanted to come here earlier and found herself driving in a different direction. She can't park in her usual spot because the church has become a crime scene, so she parks out on the street and uses a smaller entrance to walk through.

Sally makes her way to her brother's grave and crouches down next to it, not over it. She's always careful about that. She has a whirlwind of scenarios racing through her head, but she can't comprehend any of them, and the ones she can almost grasp keep floating away from her.

Joe and the second man had been inside for at least an hour. She had been relieved when Joe came out okay, and tempted to follow him, but she was more curious about who the second man was. She'd waited another half hour, but he hadn't shown up. Most likely he lived there.

She starts brushing her hands back and forth through the

grass, letting the soft textures tickle her palms. The grass is wet. She had written down the address before leaving. What she would do with that information she wasn't sure. Probably just leave it scrawled across the notepad in her front seat for the next few weeks before balling it up and tossing it out.

Joe driving different cars. Joe with files at his house. Joe with a missing testicle. Joe secretly meeting people.

Well, okay, Joe went to somebody's house, the same way she's gone to other people's houses. Gone there and had coffee, played some cards, killed some time, ate some dinner. What is so suspicious about that?

Nothing. Except Joe parked two blocks away and left in a different car. Plus the house—somehow she knows that house.

"So what do I do, Martin?"

If her brother could reach out from his grave and offer her some advice, it wouldn't be *Do nothing*. It was her doing nothing that had got Martin killed five years ago. It has been her lack of responsibility, her laziness, her unawareness. She was doing nothing five years ago when she should have been doing something. She should have been doing anything to stop Martin from being hit at forty miles an hour in a thirty-mile zone. It wasn't the school's fault. It wasn't even really the driver's fault. It was her fault. She knows some people would blame God, and she suspects her parents split the blame between her and Him.

That's why her mother flinches when she puts an arm around her. That's why her parents didn't try to convince her to stay at nursing school, and allowed her to give up her career to help them pay the bills.

It was difficult not to hate God. It was His fault for making Martin intellectually handicapped. It was easy to lay blame with her, though. It was her fault that Martin had run out into traffic. Her fault for forgetting how excitable he could be when she finished her studies early and got the chance to pick him up from school. She'd rung home to say she could pick

Martin up. Her mother had told her not to worry, but Sally had gone ahead and worried. She loved the look on Martin's face when he stepped out of school and saw her waiting there for him.

The rules were always simple. Her parents had told Martin a thousand times. He was never to cross the road. And she knew the rules too. She was never to park across the road and wait for him there; she either parked on his side of the road, or she walked over. Her parents reminded her time and time again, but the problem when people remind you so often is that you start to ignore it. The words go in, but they don't settle anywhere. The other problem was she was late. Only by two minutes. How many times has she remembered the route she took to his school that day? A red light there that could have been green. A person towing a trailer ahead of her at twenty-five instead of thirty miles an hour. A pedestrian crossing with people taking their time to cross it. It all added up, and in the end it came to two minutes. It all added up the same way all the ages in the graveyard add up and divide to get an average of sixty-two. Just simple mathematics combining to end a life.

She'd pulled up outside the school two minutes later than she should have. She'd opened her car door two minutes after she should have opened it. And Martin had seen her from across the road. It all came down to mathematics, basic physics, and human dynamics. Martin getting excited. Martin running over the road to meet her while she was getting out of her car. Martin getting in the way of an object moving much faster than he was, weighing much more than he did. She'd run to him and knelt by his side. He was alive, but that had changed two days later. She'd let her brother down when he'd needed her most.

She won't let Joe down. He needs her. He needs somebody to look out for him, to protect him from whatever madness he's got himself involved in.

CHAPTER FORTY-SEVEN

The walk home takes me through streets that smell like wet dog. My clothes stick to me, my underwear keeps on bunching up into my ass. When I get home, I bury the murder weapon and the gloves in the yard. I make my way upstairs, pulling my keys from my pocket to . . .

For fuck's sake!

On the floor directly outside my apartment door is Pickle. Or Jehovah. It's too damn difficult to tell. I spin around, looking for the fluffy bastard that did this, but it's gone. I crouch down, and touch my dead fish with my finger. It feels rubbery.

I find an evidence bag in the kitchen. I'm bending over the fish when I hear the meowing. I look up, and at the end of the hall is the Goddamn cat. On the floor ahead of it is the other goldfish. Slowly the cat reaches forward with its paw, pushes the fish a few inches toward me, then pulls its paw back. He tilts his head, then meows at me. I take a knife from my briefcase, which is still by the door. Keeping his eyes on me, the cat reaches forward and pushes the fish even further toward me. Then it sits. What the hell is it trying to do? I get hold of the biggest knife I can find.

"Come on, pussycat. Come on."

It starts toward me, covers half the distance, stops, turns back toward the fish, stops, then turns back toward me. It meows. I tighten my grip on the knife. Then it moves slowly back to the fish, picks it up softly between its teeth, and carries it toward me. It stops a few feet away, lowers the fish to the floor, then takes a few steps back. Once again it meows. I get on my hands and knees so I can slowly crawl forward. I keep the blade of the knife ahead of me.

And then I understand what it's doing. It's offering my fish back to me. It meows again, but this time it is more of a whispering whine.

"There's a good boy," I say in my friendly voice, happy to lull it into believing I no longer have any urge to see it skinned.

"Come on, fella. I'm not going to kill you, boy. I'm not going to break your neck."

It meows and comes another few steps closer. I keep moving toward it. Closer now. Less than an arm's length away. Closer still . . .

We reach each other, and it pushes its head down and head-butts my fist.

Then the bastard starts purring.

And me? What do I do?

I start petting the damn thing. I'm tickling it beneath its chin as if it's just the greatest little cat in the world.

I look to the floor where my two dead goldfish are. I'm going to have to bury them again. I tighten the grip on my knife, then use the tip of it to start scratching the top of the cat's head. It tilts its face sideways to get a better scratching position for itself.

All I have to do is thrust down, and this little cat that I saved will . . .

Saved. Now that's the key word. I saved this thing, I spent money on it, I brought it into my home, it repaid me by killing my goldfish, and after all of this I'm saving it again. Saving it by not killing it. I put the knife away.

Under the observing eyes of the cat, I put the two goldfish into an evidence bag. I will bury them later.

Back inside I sit down on the sofa. The cat jumps onto my knee and I keep petting it. After a few minutes it falls asleep.

Before I go to bed, I stare at the coffee table and wonder if I will buy any more fish. Maybe when all of this is over. Without them, I feel like a piece of my life is missing. I feel empty. Though not as empty as I felt yesterday.

When I wake the next morning, I'm sweating and the cat's on the end of my bed. I've had another dream. I can remember Melissa. We were together somewhere, I think a beach or an island, and I realized I'd formed a misconception about our violent relationship. Rather than killing her, I was lying with her, both of us enjoying the sand, the sound of the sea, and the sun. It was as though we were having a good time.

A nightmare.

The smell of the sea comes with me from the dream and lingers in the room for a few minutes. I get away from it by climbing into the shower. I wash away the night, the tackiness, and the dregs of the dream. When I come out, the cat's sitting on the kitchen floor cleaning itself. I find something in the fridge that looks like meat and the cat seems happy enough to believe it.

Before leaving for work, and after making myself some toast, I check through the briefcase and study my assortment of tools. More importantly I check to make sure the Glock I took from Calhoun is fully loaded. It is. All fifteen rounds ready to react to the tip of my finger pulling in the mechanical trigger. The first cartridge ready to be introduced to the chamber, ready to be struck by the firing pin, the powder inside ready to be ignited. The gas, the pressure, the explosion.

The power.

It takes less than a quarter of a second for the trigger finger to obey the command of the shooter. Milliseconds later, the firing pin is hitting. For the whole cycle to progress from nerve impulse to firing of the cartridge, I'm looking at a third of a second. The bullet travels at nearly a thousand feet per second. The target can be dead in less than a second.

I place the gun back in the briefcase. Let the cat out of my apartment. Go to work.

The place is a madhouse.

I step into a flurry of detectives and officers. The buzz is much bigger than any of the previous days. The men have their sleeves rolled up, their ties loosened. Conversations are spilling from every corner, every cubicle, every office. Excitement hangs in the air like a half-deflated balloon. I don't hear any full conversations as I make my way through the clusters of people to my office, but I pick up on several snippets.

"How long have you known him?"

"I heard his son killed himself."

"Has anybody checked his hotel?"

"Where else can he be staying?"

"How many do you think he's killed?"

"And you knew him."

"And you had dinner with him."

"And you were working with him."

They're looking for Calhoun. Hunting him. I close the door to my office. I'm only alone for ten seconds before Schroder knocks and walks in.

"Morning, Joe."

"Morning, Detective Schroder."

"Have you heard?"

I shake my head. "Heard what, Detective Schroder?"

"When was the last time you saw Detective Inspector Calhoun?"

I think about it. "Yesterday at work," I tell him. "Didn't

you see him, Detective Schroder? He's the guy with the gray hair."

"Did he say anything to you yesterday at all? Anything out of character?" I think about our conversation, his description of killing Daniela Walker. "Not that I can think of."

"You sure?"

"Umm . . ." I give my thought process around ten seconds, which is a long time when someone's staring at you. I'm going for that dramatic effect thing, and then finally I repeat my original answer. "No, Detective Schroder. When was the last time you saw him?" I ask.

"Let me know if you think of anything," Schroder says, ignoring my question.

Without waiting for an answer, he turns and hurries off, as if he needs to be everywhere else at the same time. He doesn't tell me why they're looking for Calhoun.

I start my working day by cleaning the toilets, which is one of those jobs that makes anybody reflect on the decisions they've made in life. By the time I finish, over half the people on the crowded fourth floor have gone. The rest are paying no attention to me. Are any of them checking the house where I left him? Apparently not. Why would they? Because he left two victims there?

With plenty of officers out there searching, with plenty of detectives thinking of places for them to go, it's possible they'll stumble across him. And if they do, what will Calhoun tell them? Can he risk telling them about me? No, he can't, because then I'll tell on him. I take some small relief that the police are thinking he's in hiding, probably planning on leaving the country, not reminiscing about his crimes by hovering around old scenes.

I lug the vacuum cleaner into the conference room. The room is a mess. Folders, photographs, statements. Cigarette butts squashed into full ashtrays, food wrappers balled on the table, empty take-out containers stuffed into the trash. Files litter the floor, and among them—lying in the center of the huge table—are two murder weapons. The first is mine, which Melissa used. The second is from Calhoun's hotel room. Both are covered in a thin, white powder.

I look up at the composite drawing Melissa detailed for them a few mornings earlier. Pinned up next to it is the photograph of Calhoun. It's a stretch to find any real similarity between the two, but that doesn't matter, because they have fingerprints now, and that's as good as a confession at this stage in the game. His absence today only helps make him look guiltier. He knew the murder weapon had been found, knew he had to get the hell out of Dodge.

I sit at the table, pick up each of the plastic bags in turn, and study the knives. I don't take them out, rather just admire them through the bags. Actually, *admire* is the wrong word. What I do is remember. Mine has a history. Calhoun's has a story. Short story, perhaps, but oh so important.

After cleaning the room then grabbing my cassette recorder (not just the tape), I go back to my office and have lunch. The rest of the day is hectic for everybody but me. For me, it's only stressful. I watch every person as though they're watching me, ready to put me under arrest because they've found Calhoun tied and taped to a chair in Daniela Walker's house.

At four thirty, making sure nobody is looking, I hide the parking ticket with Calhoun's fresh fingerprints on it behind his desk. I can't just put it in one of the drawers—the desk will have been searched already. This way it could have been overlooked, and when they search his cubicle again, they'll find it. If not, I'll find it when I vacuum and hand it to Schroder. I let it slip out of the evidence bag without touching it.

I'm twenty-five minutes into my stroll to the Walker house, on what is becoming a lovely Friday evening, when my cell phone rings. It plays a small tune that makes me cringe. I slip it from my pocket and flip it open.

"Hello, Melissa."

"Hello, Joe. Having a nice evening are you?"

"I was."

"Oh, come now, Joe, that's not very nice. I've been think-ing about you, you know. Thinking I'd like to take you back to the park once more and show you the other half of a good time."

"What do you want?"

"My money. Have you got it?"

"Not all of it."

"No? Well, that's not really good enough, Joe, is it? I said a hundred grand. Anything less is wasting my time."

"I've got eighty, and I can get the remaining twenty next week," I lie, knowing it sounds far more realistic. She goes silent for a minute. That's okay, she's paying for the call.

"Eighty grand will do for the weekend, Joe, but since you've let me down, it's going to cost you another forty next week."

"I can't get forty."

"That's what you said about the hundred, and look how well you've done."

"Fine."

"Where do you want to meet?" she asks.

"You're leaving it up to me?"

"Of course not. I just wanted to give you some hope. That's all."

"I'm not leaving it up to you. If you want the money, then it's on my terms."

"If you don't want to go to jail, Joe, then the terms are mine."

"Fuck you."

"Fuck you too, Joe."

Look at that. Just like a married couple.

"Listen, you've got my gun," I tell her. "You shouldn't be too concerned with where we meet."

"I don't trust you, Joe."

"It's a house where I killed somebody."

"They still there?" Her voice picks up an octave. I shake my head, even though I'm on the phone.

"Previous victim. The place smells like death, though. I can even give you a guided tour."

"Is this the place you took the whore to the other night?"

"That's the one," I say, knowing she followed me there and killed the hooker I had in the trunk of the car while I was inside.

She seems to like this idea. "I'll meet you there at six o'clock, Joe. Don't make me wait."

She hangs up. Damn it, that doesn't give me long. I catch the bus. Don't want to steal a car. Of all the times to be caught, today would be it. I can sense it. The day is warming up, as if summer is making one last stand and it's doing it this evening. Christchurch weather. Schizophrenic heat and all that.

I reach the house and enter my final evening as the Christchurch Carver.

CHAPTER FORTY-EIGHT

I decide to pass the house and keep walking. It's five forty-five. I walk to the end of the block, then come back. I don't spot any odd-looking vehicles. No signs of a stakeout. No Melissa. It's suburbia at the height of normalcy.

Walking the front path to the doorstep feels like coming home. I've been here so many times over the last few weeks it's becoming a regular part of my life. The husband of the dead woman will probably start charging me rent. At least this will be my final time here. I take the sights in without any feelings of nostalgia. No tears to be shed.

The house is still warm. Seems it will stay that way until winter kills off every green thing in sight. If the police have been here today, now will be the time they burst in to apprehend me. Not that they will, of course. They're not here. I'm sure of it. However . . .

I close my eyes. Wait. Count off a slow minute in which I listen to every sound in the house and in the street. A lawn mower, some woman shouting to her son to hurry up, a car moving by. Inside all I can hear is my own breathing. If the cops are here, I'll tell them that I thought it was part of my job to clean this place. That I thought it was an extension of police headquarters since dozens of detectives have been here a few times now. I'll mispronounce *extension* and pause for a few seconds looking for a replacement.

I open my eyes. Nothing. I'm still alone.

When I reach the bedroom I move straight through to the bathroom and smile at the man bound to the chair inside. At some point during the night, or perhaps today, he has pissed himself. The room stinks and he's a mess, the whole scene is somewhat sad and pathetic.

I meet his eyes and see the hatred I saw last night. They're red and puffy as though he has been rubbing them, but I know he hasn't. He looks like he hasn't slept since I saw him yesterday. His shirt is hanging out, and the collar is stained with blood. His arms are red from trying to break the tape and rope. Even his short hair looks ruffled. Flecks of blood have dried on the surface of the duct tape. The right side of his jaw has turned a dark gray. A large bump has risen on the front of his forehead. He must know they're there, since he can get a good view of himself in the mirror.

"No, no, don't get up," I say, putting out my hand. He doesn't laugh, or for that matter, even attempt to make conversation.

"Okay, Detective Inspector, here's the deal. Twenty grand buys your ears and your mind, okay? Just don't forget I have the gun, and I also have a tape of last night's conversation." I show him the tape recorder that's been living inside a potted plant for months. "You try anything, or anything happens to me, that tape goes to your colleagues. Nod if you understand."

He understands.

"Here's the thing. In another," I glance at my watch, "five minutes, we're going to have a visitor. She's going to be coming up here, and she's going to be blackmailing me. However, like you, she's also a murderer. I imagine you'll recognize her. It's your job to remain quiet here in the bathroom. Once she's confessed, I'll open up the door, she'll see you, and she'll be just as incriminated as you and I are. What we'll have then is a three-way stalemate. Agreed?"

He grunts.

"I'll take that as a *yes*."

Another grunt. He shakes his head, perhaps seeing a problem with the plan, but it doesn't matter. I close the door, then wait on the edge of the bed with my briefcase and without the eighty thousand dollars.

Ten minutes later I hear the front door downstairs open. I stay where I am. She'll find me without too much difficulty.

This is it. This is where my phases and plans have led me.

I hear Melissa walk into the kitchen. The fridge door opens. Then it closes. Are we really that alike? I hope not.

A minute later she comes up the stairs.

"Damn hot up here, Joe."

I shrug. "No air-conditioning."

"I'm surprised there's still any power to this place. That the money?" she asks, nodding toward the briefcase.

"Uh huh."

I keep staring at her. She's more beautiful than the night we met. More beautiful than the day she blackmailed me. Her black miniskirt is showing long, tanned legs. She's wearing a dark purple jacket, which matches her purple shoes. Her blouse is silky black. She is going for some type of power dressing look, and succeeding. She steals a look at her expensive-looking watch. Once again I wonder what she actually does, and how she gets her money. Maybe she really is an architect.

"Got a date?" I ask.

She laughs. "You can always make me smile, Joe."

"I try."

"Actually I was just seeing how long it was going to take you to cut the crap and give me my money."

I lean back on the bed. "I still have some concerns."

"Oh, is that so. Well, poor little Joe, tell Melissa all about it."

"Once I give you the money, what's stopping you from going to the police anyway?"

"I'm a lovely person, Joe. I'd never lie."

Yeah. Damn lovely. "You lied to me."

"You're lie-worthy."

"You haven't answered my question."

"Come now, Joe. What you're buying here is trust. What kind of world is this if we can't all trust one another? Once I have the money, everything I have on you, Joe, goes in a safe place so if something should happen to me," she waves her hand around in the air, "oh I don't know—maybe something along the lines of having my throat cut—then what I have on you goes to the cops. And only then."

"And how do I know you won't keep coming back for more?"

She shrugs. "I guess you don't." She lets her words hang in the air. She's thinking she'll be back for more money at some point.

"So how does it feel to be up here," I ask, "in the presence of death?"

"There's nothing dead up here."

"There was."

"Where did you kill them?"

I stand up and walk to the opposite corner, so now I'm standing along the same wall as the bathroom door, but at the other end. "I killed each of them on the bed," I say, taking the credit for Daniela Walker's death.

"This bed?"

It's unmade, the blankets and sheets wrinkled from use. You can still see dried drops of blood. "That's the one."

She makes her way toward it. I can clearly see the Glock in her hand. My Glock. Even as she studies the bed she keeps the weapon pointed at me. Steadily.

"How did it feel?" she asks.

"You ought to know."

She turns to me and smiles. "That's true, Joe. You know, sometimes I feel as though we have something special between us."

"Blackmail?"

"No."

"We're both killers?"

She shakes her head. "No, not that either."

"What then?"

"I think it's our love of life."

"Poetic."

"If you insist."

I haven't insisted on anything. "So how did it feel for you, Melissa?"

"How did what feel?"

"Killing."

"I've done it before."

"You're kidding me."

"Only a couple of times. Nothing as fun as the other night, though."

I have to agree. "They are kind of fun, aren't they?"

"See? We're sharing. We aren't so unalike, Joe." She begins rubbing her free hand over the bed, as if she's trying to feel the death that took place here, trying to soak it up into the pores of her skin.

"I think we're more similar than you really know."

Hand still on the bed, she turns to face me. The gun is still pointed in my direction. "And how's that?"

"Because I also find you lie-worthy."

She straightens up, glances at the briefcase.

I nod toward it. "Go on, open it."

Keeping the gun on me, she reaches over and snaps the left clip, then the right. Looking back to me, she opens the lid, then turns to look inside.

"What the hell are you up to, Joe? Where's my money?"

"You're not getting any money, Melissa." She looks genuinely surprised. It seems she never thought I wouldn't actually pay her. "If that's the way you want to play it, then I'm going directly to the police."

"Oh? And how are you going to explain your involvement?"

"I won't need to."

"Think again, bitch." I nod toward the bathroom.

"You got a video camera set up, Joe? Come on, don't be so childish. I'll just take the tape with me now. Then I'm going to shoot you in the balls. Oh, what I mean is *ball*."

"What I have is even better than a video camera. Why don't you check it out?"

She moves toward the bathroom door, keeping the gun pointing ahead of her. When she reaches it, she opens it slowly. She peers inside, then laughs. Maybe she thinks I've bought her the ultimate gift.

"A cop? You're going to kill a cop?" she asks.

"I'm not going to kill him. He's too valuable for that."

Behind her, I can see Calhoun's eyes wide open in surprise at seeing Melissa. He recognizes her from the station. His eyes dart from left to right, deciding which of us is more dangerous. This is the woman who gave him a description of the killer. This is the woman who has me at gunpoint, yet I'm the man who knocked him out and tied him up. What in the hell, he's wondering, is going on? And when will he be getting his money?

I can also see the thoughts going through Melissa's mind. She likes collecting police things, and she's wondering if she can collect this guy. She's measuring him up to see if she has room for him in her house. Perhaps the corner of the living room, or next to the fridge.

"I don't understand what you're playing at, Joe," she says.

"He's my witness to what you really are."

"Oh? And what do you have on him?"

"Enough."

She looks around the room. It's obvious that she hates losing. Slowly she begins shaking her head. I can hear her teeth grinding. She looks angry. "You're forgetting one thing, Joe."

"And what's that?"

"I don't need him."

Before I can react, she grabs a knife from my briefcase and runs into the bathroom. She stands behind Calhoun and his eyes widen in fear because he knows as well as I do what's about to happen. The chair jerks beneath him as he tries to pull away, but it's no good. She holds the knife to his throat and watches my eyes. I look from the eyes of the detective, who has just become as still as stone, to the eyes of the woman behind him. Hers reflect amusement, a sense of enjoyment. Not for what she's about to do to the cop, but what she's about to do to my witness. I've hardly taken a step, but now I don't dare move any closer.

"Think about this, Melissa," I say, my words almost flustered. I put my hands ahead of me, palms outward. "Think about what you're doing."

Calhoun is pleading with his eyes, and as Melissa takes the knife away from his throat, his pleading moves to relief—then to horror as he sees the knife plunge back into sight on the way toward his chest. His eyes sparkle with fear, then all the sparkle evaporates in an instant as the knife punches into his body.

A sound, which is both gurgle and grunt, comes from him at the same time, and he struggles harder against the rope, as if the metal blade that has punctured his chest isn't a knife, but a high-voltage battery from which he's drawing power. Even so, it's not enough to give him the strength to break the rope and tape that bind him. The chair dances back and forth as his body weight waltzes it across the floor. Blood squirts up from his chest. It pools around the blade of the knife and quickly blossoms over his shirt. Melissa leaves the knife in him, then steps away to watch. Blood has splashed onto the mirror, and even the ceiling. He begins trying to cough more of it up, but because of the tape across his mouth it becomes impossible. He begins choking, his face turns red, and I'm not sure if he's choking or bleeding to death. The front of the duct-tape gag turns red. His face turns from red to purple, the same purple the sky was when I viewed it from the park with my testicle turned to pulp. The chair waltzes faster over the linoleum floor, the legs tap-dancing to some dying rhythm. His eyes are as wide as they can be, and in them I can see all sorts of fear and knowledge. Fear of dying. Knowledge that his last few seconds in this world are happening right now.

He looks at me and I think he wants me to help, but I can't be sure. I stand motionless, unable to do a thing to save him. His throat begins to swell and his mouth is full of blood. It's a race to see which will kill him—the stab wound or the choking—and when he stops moving, his head slumped forward and his ragged breathing eerily silent, I can only guess.

I stand with my mouth open and my tongue nearly hanging out, sweat dripping down my forehead. "You stupid bitch," I manage to whisper. "How could you do such a thing?"

She reaches over to him and pulls away the duct tape. Blood gushes from between Calhoun's lips and spills over his shirt. "I'm surprised that you thought I wouldn't. I told you no tricks, Joe."

"No, you didn't."

"Well, you should have assumed it. I still want my money."

"I don't have it."

"Get it."

I look back at the body. "Maybe he's still alive," I whisper. I'm about to move forward to check when she interrupts me.

"Maybe," she agrees, and she grabs hold of the knife and pulls it away.

"Don't . . ." I say, letting my voice trail off.

She leans in close and listens for a pulse. Whether she hears one or not, I can't know. What she does do is drag the knife across his throat. Then she steps back. Dips a finger into the wound and puts that same finger into her mouth. She sucks on the blood.

"If he wasn't dead, he sure as hell is now. And unless you want the police busting your ass on Monday, I suggest you give me my money."

"Give me four hours."

Melissa looks down at her jacket and sees a few splotches of blood. She takes it off. Her nipples are standing out as if she's got small coins tucked in the front of her bra. She drags the knife over the dead man's throat once more, making a squelching sound that reminds me of walking in wet shoes. Then she steps around behind him to cut the ropes and tape. After she drops the knife to the floor, she raises one of Calhoun's arms and places his hand on her right breast. Softly she moans.

When she looks over at me, she is smiling. "You want to try it?"

"You promise not to slap me?"

"No, you idiot. Do you want to see how he feels?"

"He feels dead."

"If you can get the money that quickly, Joe, we've still got a deal."

"Where and when?"

She drops the arm and takes a look at her watch, mentally studying her schedule. "Ten o'clock. Our park. Don't be late."

Our park. Sure, I won't be late. "I'll be there."

"No tricks, Joe."

"No tricks."

With that, she turns to leave and I'm left alone with a useless corpse.

CHAPTER FORTY-NINE

Be prepared. That's the Boy Scout motto. It applies to anything in life. It's like doing your homework. I simply can't stress enough how important that is.

I stand at the window for a few more minutes watching in case Melissa comes back. It's a clear evening, a few stars are out already, a faded moon growing in strength. Melissa disappears between streetlights and reappears at the following one until she reappears no more. When I'm satisfied she's gone, I point the remote control at the wardrobe. With the push of one button I turn off the video camera that's running in there. The crippled chick's video camera.

I rewind the tape, then sit on the edge of the bed to watch tonight's footage through the small viewfinder. I hadn't started the unit recording until I moved over into the corner of the bedroom. The lens was zoomed out to capture most of the room, which included the bed. I continue watching the tape. I can see Melissa stroking the covers, then, soon after, opening the bathroom door and murdering the policeman.

Because of the angle of the lens I've managed to stay out of the footage. If I was in it, I would have edited it out. Seems I don't need to.

I take the dead detective's gun out of the waistband of my pants and set it on the bed for easy access. The gun's ready to fire, has been the entire night. It was my protection against Melissa in case anything went wrong.

As it turned out, everything went perfectly.

Melissa didn't cut all the bindings away from the policeman, so I grab a knife and finish the job. He smells of piss and death as I drag his heavy corpse into the bedroom, careful not to get any blood on me. When I dump him on the bed, he bounces once before becoming still.

I look around the room for something I can use to wrap the body. The blood will just soak through the sheets, so I go back into the bathroom and rip down the shower curtain, scattering the plastic rings to all four corners. I roll it around him. The end result is an odd-looking cocoon, which looks ready to hatch a being from some 1950s B-grade sci-fi movie. His blood smears across the inside of it, painted on the curtain of this womb. I use duct tape and his shoelaces to secure the curtain. Back in the bathroom I wash down the knife Melissa used to kill him, dry it, and put it back into my briefcase.

I drag the cocoon downstairs by the feet, its head thudding on every step, then across the floor and into the adjoining garage. He leaks from the shower curtain where I haven't done the best of wrapping jobs (men can't wrap—simple fact) and stains the carpet. I dump him on the garage floor, turn on a light, and look around. The tools of my trade are here. I pick up a plastic can of gas from next to the lawn mower and shake it. Seems mostly full. Perhaps around three gallons. I carry it back into the house.

The idea is simple. Fire isn't a foolproof way of destroying all evidence, but it sure is a hell of a lot better than cleaning the house from top to bottom. Even then, if anything was suspected, chemicals can be used to show washed-away blood, and from there a link to Calhoun could easily be made. Fire is a far greater guarantee that nothing will be found.

Naturally, burning the corpse here isn't such a good idea. It takes extreme heat to burn through bone, and depending on how quickly the neighbors contact the fire department, the chances of the body burning into dust before they arrive or of the house burning down completely are about as great as my testicle growing back. The pathologist will study the body, the damage to the severed throat, the bruised jaw. He may even find tape residue on the face and rope burn on the ankles and hands. Even if it's burned to a skeleton he'll find serrated edges in the sternum from the knife. They'll know Calhoun was murdered and framed.

I take the lid from the gas can and begin splashing it across the carpet and bed. The smell of gas quickly fills my nostrils. At first, maybe for a few seconds, I like it, but then it quickly becomes nauseating and I want to throw up. When the room's wet enough to burn quickly, I make my way through the other upstairs rooms, leaving a trail of gas as I go. Downstairs I do the same, leaving a trail on the stairs. I save some for the trip.

I grab my briefcase and head outside. I suck in a few deep breaths of air to clear my lungs, then spit the taste of gas from my mouth.

I go for a walk. The car I stole yesterday after work is still where I left it a few blocks away. I drive it to the house, back it into the garage, close the door, then stuff the body in the trunk. I didn't want to risk driving a stolen car tonight, but now I can't risk not to. Carrying a limp body draped in a shower curtain over my shoulder and walking through town with it would look suspicious, even for this city.

I look for a match and can't find one. Again the cigarette lighter from the car comes in handy. Thirty seconds later it's glowing red. I hold it onto a rag in the garage, then throw the burning rag into the house. Fire spreads across the floor and climbs the walls, racing quickly up the stairs. Born from nowhere and now it's alive everywhere. Alive and hungry. I don't need to supervise it. The rest should be child's play.

I open the garage door and drive out into the street. I glance back at the house through the mirrors but can't see any signs of fire. I don't bother to wait around. It'll happen.

As I drive away from the city, I turn the stereo on to hear the same song that was playing in Angela's bedroom the day I killed her. It seems so long ago. It must be an omen, and I take it to be a good one. I can't help but sing along as I head north. My spirits are high, the evening is warm, and things are going well. Life is good.

Tonight I'm looking for an ideal place to dump a body. I can't afford for this one to be found. I drive through the plains that make up Canterbury, searching for one of those crazy dirt roads that take you approximately nowhere. After an hour, I find one. A wire fence closes it off from the public. I fumble with the lock.

When I've eventually driven far enough, I stop the car, open the trunk, and drag the cocoon through the trees. I spend half an hour digging a pit knee-deep with a shovel I borrowed from the garage. I am still wearing gloves. My fingers are wet-rubber damp again. When the hole's deep enough, I kick the side of the corpse and it rolls into the grave with a thud.

This is option country. If I leave the pit open, the body will rot quickly beneath the sun, and the small animals that live out here will make sure any evidence is quickly gnawed away. However, this is risky. Should some hick farmer wander by, he'll be making the most exciting discovery of his life. Plus there probably won't be a lot of sun over the following days and weeks.

I climb into the pit and, using a knife, I slice the cocoon

open. With the gardening shears, some pliers, and the hammer, I start removing his teeth and his fingertips. A grisly job, but I whistle as I work and the mess isn't as bad as I would have thought. I keep things pointed away from me to lessen the chances of getting blood on myself, but I still fail. After a while I get into the swing of things and the time goes quickly.

I dump the teeth and fingers into a separate plastic bag, along with his wallet and identification. Then I douse the rest of the corpse with the last of the gas, use the car lighter again to light another rag, then toss it in with the corpse. It smells like a barbecue. After fifteen minutes most of him has burned away and I'm feeling hungry. Whistling again, I fill the hole in, stamp it flat, then drag some leaves and dead grass over it. I walk back to the car and toss Daniela Walker's spade into the trunk.

I stop a half mile or so from home, soak the car in gas, and set it on fire. In this part of town nobody will care enough to call the fire department. I walk the rest of the way to my apartment, carrying the video camera and the plastic bag.

It's nine thirty. I still have half an hour.

I make two copies of the videotape, though I need only one. I store one in my apartment. The second I put in my briefcase to store later in a safe place. I strip the detective's wallet of cash and fold it into my pocket, then toss the wallet into the plastic bag. The fingers I'll grind up later and feed to the neighborhood dogs. The teeth I'll take a hammer to.

At nine fifty, I walk to the park. It's still a warm night and the moon is out in full and the stars unusually bright, but maybe I'm just seeing things clearer now. What's definitely clear is that it's a perfect evening for romance and death. In the waistband of my pants is the dead man's firearm, which I've no intention of using. Also tucked into a sheath in the back of my pants is my small knife with the two-inch blade.

The park is completely empty when I get there. I step onto the grass and walk to the place where I lost my testicle. It feels colder here. The trees stand out in the moonlight and point at me with dark fingers, covering most of the stars. I stand by the patch of grass where my life changed forever. I wonder if it's still stained with my blood, but it's too dark to tell.

At ten o'clock, a lone figure walks toward me.

CHAPTER FIFTY

She's in bed when they come for her. In bed thinking about Joe. Wondering where he was tonight when she went to his apartment and knocked on the door. She hadn't gone inside. Hadn't driven to his mother's in case he was there. Hadn't driven to the house where she saw him last night, even though she supposed she should've.

The last time the police came to her house was five years ago. They came two days after Martin had died. Back then it had been one police car. They had come to take statements in the most gentle way they could. This time several of them are parked right outside. They have their lights flashing, but their sirens are muted. The banging on the door, however, is not. The lights send red and blue patterns racing left and right across her wallpaper through thin gaps around the curtains. There is nothing gentle about this.

She hears her mother and father asking what's going on, then her name. She climbs out of bed and puts on a robe just as the door opens. Detective Schroder is there, looking stressed and tired and pissed off. He's looking at her as if she's guilty of something.

"What's going on?"

"You're going to have to come with us, Sally," he says, and she's never heard him sound like this.

"What?"

"Come on, Sally."

"Can I change?"

He stalls, obviously wanting to say no, but then calls for a female officer, who comes into the room. "Make it quick," he says, then closes the door behind him.

The officer doesn't talk to her as she changes into a pair of jeans and a T-shirt. She recognizes the woman, has seen her around at the station and even spoken on occasion, but right now this woman is acting like a stranger. She tugs on a jacket, some socks, and her shoes.

"Let's go," the woman says, and opens the door.

Half a dozen policemen stand in the hallway. They're asking her parents questions and not answering the questions her parents are asking them. She tries to tell them everything's okay, but she doesn't know if that's true. They don't handcuff her, but they put her in the back of a squad car and rush her away. She notices that over half of the police cars stay at her house. If they're searching her room, she hopes they'll tidy it up afterward. Almost all her neighbors are standing on their front lawns watching. She doesn't know what's going on. She's scared and confused. Has she done something wrong at work? Do they think she's stolen something? Have they decided, five years later, to charge her for her brother's death?

The drive to the police station is the quickest she's ever had. The urgency to get her there seems undermined when they take her into an interrogation room, leave her alone, close the door, and disappear for half an hour. She paces the room, sits down, then paces it again. Her heart's racing, her hands are shaking slightly, and she's becoming more frightened with every passing minute She's never been in here before. The room is cold and she's thankful for her jacket. The chairs are uncomfortable. The table is marked with the passages of other people's time. Fingernails, keys, coins, anything they could find to scrape messages into the wood.

She doesn't know the man who comes into the room at the thirty-minute mark. Just an average-looking guy with average features, but he frightens her. He asks her to hold out her hands and she does. He takes swabs of her skin and when she asks why, he doesn't tell her. Then he leaves.

It's another ten minutes before Detective Schroder comes into the room, by which point she's crying. He sits down opposite her and places a folder on the desk. He doesn't open it.

"Sorry for all the drama, Sally, but this is important," he says, and smiles at her as he slides a coffee across the table toward her. It's as if he's suddenly become her best friend. But there isn't any trace of warmth in that smile.

"What's going on?"

"How well do you know Detective Calhoun?"

The detective who went missing? What has that got to do with her? "Not well. Why?"

"Do you ever socialize with him?"

"Socialize with him?" She shakes her head. "Never."

"Never been for a drink with him? Never run into him at a restaurant? At a shopping mall?"

She glances at the coffee, but doesn't touch it. "I already told you never," she says, annoyed that Schroder thinks she's lying.

"Ever been in his car?"

"What?"

"His car, Sally. Ever been for a ride with him?"

"No. I've never seen him outside of this building. I've never had dinner with him, never had a drink with him," she says, her voice growing a little stronger now, but inside she's just about ready to break down.

"Seen him today at all?"

"You asked me that this morning."

"I'm asking you again."

"Why don't you believe me?" she asks.

"Answer the question, Sally."

"No. I don't know the last time I saw him. Yesterday, maybe."

"Maybe?"

"I see everybody here all the time. I don't even know if I saw you yesterday but I'm sure I probably did."

He nods, accepting her answer. "Do you like fire, Sally?"

"Fire?" As confused as she was a moment ago, this question makes even less sense. "I don't understand."

"Fire. There was a fire tonight. That's why your hands were swabbed. We were looking for signs of any accelerants."

"But you didn't find any, did you," she says, not as a question but as a statement.

"You could have worn gloves."

"But I didn't set fire to anything!" she says, her voice raising.

"It was a house."

Suddenly everything she's seen on TV, all the cop shows and all the movies she's watched with her dad, it all comes in handy, because right then she knows exactly what to say next. "I want a lawyer."

Schroder leans back and sighs. "Come on, Sally. Just be honest and you won't need one," he says, which is something else the cops say on TV too. "How long have we known each other?"

She thinks about it. She doesn't see the harm in answering this one without a lawyer present. "Six months."

"You trust me?"

"Until tonight I would have, but no, not now. Not at the moment."

He grunts, then leans forward again. "The place that burned

down, it was a crime scene. It's where Daniela Walker was killed. It was also where Lisa Houston was murdered."

She recognizes the names: both victims of the Christchurch Carver.

"I didn't burn the place down."

"And you've never been in Detective Calhoun's car."

"No."

"And we have your word for that."

"Yes."

"Okay. Then you've got nothing to worry about. No need for a lawyer."

She knows it doesn't work that way. "Then why do I feel so worried?"

He smiles at her, but she can't find any warmth in it.

"Let me show you two things," he says. He opens up the folder, revealing a plastic ziplock evidence bag sitting on top of a photograph. It has a parking ticket in it. She can't get a clear look at the picture beneath it.

"We found this today behind Detective Calhoun's desk. It's quite interesting really, what we learned from it. It has his fingerprints on it. We know that, because everybody who works here has their fingerprints on file. Everybody. Even people who aren't police. The cleaners, for example. Even Joe. Even you."

She doesn't know what to say, so she says nothing. She tightens her grip on her crucifix. She's been hanging on to it since the moment she arrived here.

"The second set of fingerprints on the ticket belongs to you."

"What does that mean?"

"In itself? Not much. It means you and Detective Calhoun each held this ticket at one point. You know, we went to the parking building this belongs to. The date on it is five months old."

"Five months?"

"That's right."

Five months? A small bell starts ringing in the back of her mind. Something familiar, but what?

"We went to the parking building and we drove up each level. We weren't sure what we were looking for. It was probably just a false lead. Only on the top we found Detective Calhoun's car. The ticket wasn't for that, though, because his car could only have been there for a day at the most. When he parked it there, he hit the car next to him. Left a huge scrape all the way along the side of it. We'd found his car, that was good, but it meant we had to deal with the owner of the second car. Insurance companies were going to have to get involved. No doubt the owner would be pissed off. Any idea what happened then?"

She shakes her head, too scared to speak.

"We ran the plate. Turned out the car was reported stolen five months ago. Reported one day after the time code on the parking ticket. That means the car was stolen at night, parked there, and the following day the owner went to drive to work and found out he couldn't. So we opened up the car. Want to guess what we found in there?"

She shakes her head.

"We found a body in there."

She gasps and tightens her grip. The corners of her crucifix puncture her skin.

"It was wrapped in plastic, and surrounded by ninety pounds of cat litter."

"Cat litter?"

"It absorbs the smell."

"I had nothing to do with it."

"It seemed odd that Detective Calhoun would dump his car next to a car with a body hidden in it. Odd that we would find the ticket for that car after we'd already searched his desk. It was as though it were placed there for us to find. Odd that your fingerprints are on it. Any idea why he would park there? Any idea how this ticket showed up?"

"No," she says, but that's not strictly true. She does have an idea, and she doesn't like it. Not at all.

He lifts the plastic bag away. The photograph beneath it is of the car she saw parked up the driveway of the house yesterday. The same car Joe left in.

"This is his car. You're telling me you've never seen it?"

"I . . . I don't know," she says, remembering seeing somebody walk into that house, somebody she recognized from a distance but couldn't place.

He lifts the photograph away, and beneath it is another evidence bag. Inside it is the small pad she wrote on yesterday. It's the address of the house where Joe went.

"Why did you write down this address?"

"Is that . . . is that the house that burned down?" she asks.

"Yes, it is," he says. "You had the address written down on a pad in your car."

"Oh Lord," she says—not to Detective Schroder, but to herself. She knows why the house looked familiar to her. She saw a photograph of it in the folders at Joe's house when she flicked through them. The same day she picked up the parking ticket from beneath his bed.

"Joe," she whispers.

"What?"

She starts to sob. It's all starting to make sense. The folders. The wound. Joe driving the detective's car.

"I . . . I had nothing." She chokes on a sob, can't catch her breath, and feels like she's going to pass out. She shakes her head, grits her teeth, and inhales loudly. Then, surrounded by more tears, she finishes her sentence. "I had nothing to do with this. Please, you must. Must believe me."

"Then tell me, Sally. Tell me how I've added all of this up wrong. Tell me where I should be looking."

So she does. She starts by telling him about the smile Joe gave her that day in the elevator two weeks ago, she tells him what a sweet guy Joe is, then starts to tell him the rest.

CHAPTER FIFTY-ONE

The homework has been completed. The work carried out. Now it comes down to the sales pitch.

Melissa walks slowly across the grass toward me. My gun in her hand. She trusts me enough to meet me in a dark park at night, but not enough to come unarmed. No surprise there. Nor is there any surprise for her when I produce Detective Calhoun's gun and point it at her.

I stand my ground and wait patiently. She stops a few feet away. She's not smiling. Perhaps she sees no humor in the situation. Nor does she show any fear.

"Seems you can't get enough of me," I say, looking her up and down. She looks good.

"Does seem that way, doesn't it? You got the money?"

I shake the plastic bag I'm carrying. "I've got something better than money."

She lifts the gun to my face. "Oh?"

I hand her the plastic bag. Both of us are keeping our guns trained on the other. She quickly glances into it.

"A video camera."

"That's right."

"What's this for?"

"You may want to watch the tape."

"You bastard."

"Why?"

She flings the camera back at me. "You fucking bastard."

I start to laugh. From her abuse it's obvious she's figured things out.

"I've got copies of that tape, Melissa, and if anything should happen to me along the lines of, oh, I don't know, anything at all, then a copy of that tape will find its way into the hands of the police."

"You played me," she says.

"Wasn't difficult."

She grunts. "You're on that tape too, Joe."

"Actually, I'm not. Not that it matters. If you kill me, what are the police going to do? Dig me up and arrest me?"

She stares at me silently for a few more seconds, then sighs. "It's a stalemate then. Just as if anything happens to me, Joe— to use your phrase, *oh, I don't know, anything at all*—copies of everything I know about you will make their way to those same people."

"Sounds like a pretty good deal," I say, and this is the best result I can hope for. It's the result I've aimed for. Sure, I still want to feed her through a branch chipper, but with self-preservation in mind, it's not the sort of thing I can do. Maybe one day if I can get my hands on the evidence she has against me, or if I ever discover I have cancer and only weeks to live.

She nods and slips the gun back into her handbag. "Well, I can't say it's been fun, Joe."

"Nor can I." I too put my gun away.

"What did you do with the cop?"

I shrug. "The usual stuff."

Neither of us turns away. The conversation is over. The rules have been stated and we both understand them. Yet here we are, a few feet apart, neither of us able to turn our back on what's happened. We've gone through so much, and for us to walk away empty-handed would be heartbreaking. It's anticlimactic. It would be like waking up on Christmas morning and finding out everybody you know has given you the same style of socks.

The moonlight strikes her face and makes her skin look pale. Again I'm struck by how beautiful she is. If it wasn't for the fact I wanted to take a knife and . . . We both step forward into an embrace and start kissing. She's stuffing her tongue into my throat as if the Holy Grail is down there somewhere, and I'm trying to stuff mine into hers. Our bodies grind into each other. My hands are roaming behind her back. Hers are behind mine and she's not trying to get my gun.

I can't understand it, and for a moment I think of Calhoun's original description of killing Daniela Walker. One second he'd been talking to her, the next she was dead. It's happening to me right now and I'm hardly aware of it because my body's on automatic. Ten seconds ago I was staring at her, and now I've got my hands digging into her back and squashing her perfect breasts against my chest. After a few seconds we pull back and look at each other, neither of us sure what to say, neither of us sure what the hell is going on. I think she's in as much shock as I am.

I can see hatred in her eyes, and I'm sure there must be anger in mine . . . and then we're kissing again, harder this time.

We pull back. I can't tell if the hatred and the anger are fading away or increasing. She opens her mouth to say something, I do the same, but all we end up doing is grabbing hold of each other. We lock in a passionate embrace, our lips mashing and our tongues darting. Nothing else matters anymore, and I have no doubt that all across the world people are finding love at this exact moment. I've no idea what I'm finding, but I like it.

Like the week I spent in bed with my ball sac in tatters, time seems to come and go, as though I am in a place where time doesn't really matter at all, but only events. The moon is still out and we are walking beneath it, trying to hold each other while stumbling . . . where?

She takes me back to her place. She drives us there. We keep looking at each other, and every intersection, every traffic light, I keep waiting for the spell to break, but it doesn't. Then we're in her bedroom, and if I could think I'd be thinking she's going to kill me. Only we're not killing each other, instead we're both naked and she's lying on top of me with my testicle pressing against her, and I have no idea how much time has passed since we first kissed. I expect to feel the damp grass on my back, even though I can see her ceiling.

Is this really happening? I look up at her, and she's got this grin on her face. It's a similar grin to when she ripped apart my left nut, but I can't see any pliers nearby. The hatred has gone.

Yeah, this is happening.

Time becomes muddled again as we play beneath the sheets for what feels like forever, then we're lying side by side and staring at the ceiling. Finally I fall asleep. Saturday rolls around and starts with us being all over each other. We take a lunch break. It's pouring with rain outside, it lands heavily on the roof and I never understood until now how the sound of rain can be romantic. It's just like all those books I read said it'd be like. We eat cheese on toast and we don't really talk about much, if anything really, yet there is nothing awkward about the long patches of silence, just as there is nothing awkward about the fact I'm down to one testicle because of her. She doesn't apologize for it and I don't tell her how annoyed I am by it. We spent the afternoon in her bed and the room gets darker as the evening sets in. The rain keeps getting heavier. The house is comfortably warm. We soak in the bathtub for an hour and now we finally do talk beyond things like *are you hungry* and *do you like how this feels*. We talk movies and books and music.

Saturday becomes Sunday and the rain eases but doesn't disappear. I wake up and stare at Melissa and I can honestly say I feel no desire to kill her. I watch her sleep, but I'm thinking about how it would feel to tear her apart, to dig my fingers and a knife into her flesh, and deconstruct her as painfully as I can. . . . And I could too . . . and it would be fun—but I would never hurt her.

I know what this feeling is. Watching her, knowing I could kill her at any second, I know that eventually—if not today, if not tomorrow—I am going to need to sort out my life. She wakes and smiles and wishes me good morning.

"So, Melissa, apparently you kill people," I say, after wishing a good morning back to her.

"Apparently."

"You any good at it?"

"Exceptionally."

"You want to meet my mother?"

She laughs, and we end up making love. Afterward, I think back to that moment when I stood in the crippled woman's house, looking at her fish. At the time I didn't take any because I knew they would not fill the emptiness I felt. Did I know then what I know now? That I was in love with Melissa?

All the killings, the fantasies, and now they've ended and what I've found is love. It seems as though my life has followed the pages of a typical romance novel. I feel like a regular Romeo, and Melissa the beautiful Juliet.

I get up, get dressed, make conversation, and suddenly I am on the street, walking to my apartment, cars and pedestrians moving around me, and life is still a blur. Every now and then I'll realize I've crossed a street or gone around a corner without being aware of it. The city looks pretty good on a Sunday morning. I get wet as I walk, but it doesn't bother me. I think of my future, which is something I never really think too much about. I know that I'll never be caught. I'm far too clever for that. In contrast to what everybody learns, in contrast to what they believe, sometimes the bad guy will get away with it. That's just life. Live and learn.

A happy ending to a happy life. That's what it comes down to. I was happy as Joe the Christchurch Carver, but now I'm even happier as Joe the Romeo. This crazy mixed-up world has taken it upon itself to find me true love, to find me companionship. I'll leave my job and find something far less menial. With a cat, and with a wife-to-be, the possibilities for my future are endless. I've lost two fish, but I have gained something even better.

I'm at the steps to my apartment building when a car screeches to a halt right next to me. I start to go for my gun, but then I see that it's Sally driving. That's why the car screeched—people like her are crap drivers. I can't even imagine how somebody with her condition can have got a license, but figure it must be in the same tradition that they are given jobs—that whole forcing her kind into trolley-pushing positions. She opens the door and races around the car toward me, leaving it running. She's puffing, as if the twenty-feet jog has taken it out of her. I have a can of cat food in my hand that I can't even remember buying. My briefcase is God knows where. The sun is out, the breeze is warm, and for once it isn't too hot. It's just perfect. One moment I am alone, the next Sally is here. And she is crying.

Sighing, I put a hand on her shoulder and ask her to tell me what's wrong.

CHAPTER FIFTY-TWO

I'm worried that my neighbors will walk by and stare at me. I'm worried they might think this woman is my girlfriend. I can do much better than Sally. In fact, I already have.

"Sally? What's wrong? Why are you here?"

"Because you live here," she says, trying to catch her breath. I wonder where she got my address from.

"Okay. What do you want?"

She looks up and down the street, but for what I don't know. There are only two parked cars. One's empty. The other has two people in the front seat facing each other and talking animatedly. I figure the passenger is a hooker, and the driver a man short on cash.

"To talk. To ask you something."

I suck in a mouthful of air and swallow it down. She's going to cry even more when she asks her question and I have to reject her. One woman in my life is enough. Given the speed at which she pulled up, I figure she's been busting for a while to get her feelings for me off her chest.

"Okay. What is it you want to ask?"

"I don't want you lying to me anymore, Joe," she says, her voice suddenly getting louder.

"What?"

"No more lies," she says, and she adds anger to her increasing volume.

I've no idea where any of this is coming from, and I'm not sure what to say. I can't figure out what she means by my lies. I didn't even know people like her were aware when they were being lied to.

"Okay, Sally, just take a deep breath," I say, and then, just to prove I'm just like her, I add, "Oxygen comes from trees."

She takes in a deep breath and her face seems to settle, but only a little. I figure she's preparing herself to ask the big question, but she probably isn't preparing herself to receive the big rejection. I will have to tell her that it's not that I'm not interested in having a relationship with her, it's that I'm not interested in having a relationship with anybody. It's times like this that I see that having women like me this much can be a curse.

It's best to get this over with. "Okay, Sally, Joe can't listen long. I'm on my way out."

"But you're just arriving!" she shouts, the frustration back on her face within seconds. "I saw you! I've been waiting since Friday night! I had to keep coming back, and back. I wanted to wait inside your apartment, but I couldn't. I chose different corners to wait around. Sometimes I'd fall asleep. Sometimes I'd go home and rest a few hours. Sometimes I'd drive around the block, looking for you. I didn't think I'd get a chance. I wouldn't have, not on Friday night. Not yesterday either. But they don't think you're coming back. That's why hardly anyone is left."

Her face is red and puffy. It looks like she's spent much of her waiting in tears. "They? Left? What are you talking about, Sally?" I ask, but of course she probably doesn't know.

She never does. Her world is full of kittens and puppies and good-natured, God-loving, extra-smiley people. She doesn't have the ability to really understand anything at all. It's probably a nice innocent life to be living if you aren't aware of it.

She wipes a palm across her cheeks, smearing the tears.

"You have to tell me, Joe."

"Look, Sally, take a deep breath and tell me what's so important."

"I want to know about your scars."

Her comment throws me off balance. "What?"

"I was thinking about them. They didn't look old enough to be from your childhood."

I remember coming home Friday and feeling that things in my apartment were slightly out of whack by a few degrees. I'm getting that same feeling now. Only it isn't my apartment, but the entire street. The entire world. I tighten my grip on the can of cat food. I take my hand off Sally's shoulder and rest it next to my pocket. The one with the gun in it. The people in the car parked up the road are looking at us. The passenger door has opened slightly. The driver is talking on a cell phone, probably organizing another date. The hooker is getting ready to leave.

"Have I ever told you about Martin?" she asks, changing the subject. She obviously doesn't care about the scars anymore. She's probably even forgotten that she asked. She lifts a hand up to her face and takes another wipe at the tears.

"That's your brother, right?"

"You used to remind me of him. But not anymore."

"Okay . . ."

"Are you really retarded, Joe?"

"What?"

"It was the parking ticket. That's why I'm here. The address in your file at work is your mother's address. The police had no idea where you live. But I . . ."

"The police?" I ask, my stomach suddenly tightening and taking a sudden lurch downward. "What about the police?"

"The police don't think you're coming back. They waited, but you never showed. I told them where you lived because I've been here. I helped you, Joe. At work. In life. I helped heal you when you were attacked. It's my fault more people have died since then."

"You didn't help me, Melissa did," I snap, but of course she doesn't know what I'm talking about. "Look, Sally," I say, trying to sound calm, but the problem is I'm not calm. My voice is wavering; I feel like the world is crashing down on me. "What do you mean about the police?"

"You phoned me. I came around. I helped you, Joe."

I look up and down the street. Cars are pulling into it from both ends. Vans too. Both doors on the parked car are open now. Neither of the occupants is a hooker. Both of them start toward us. The guy is tucking his cell phone into his pocket and reaching into his jacket for something else. Sally looks around at the noise of the sudden traffic. She looks surprised to see so many vehicles in such a crappy street. Her mention of the parking ticket and the police not knowing my address is setting off a lot of warning bells. It's shifting the world off its axis. I unzip my jacket pocket and slip my hand inside. I look at the approaching cars and vans. I look at the couple walking toward us.

"I thought you were special," she says, and she sounds disappointed.

"I . . . I am special."

"I can't believe you killed them."

I take a step back. Slow Sally has figured out something the police haven't been able to.

"What are you talking about?" I ask, looking over her shoulder.

"You're him. You're the Christchurch Carver."

I tighten my grip on the gun. I can't use it out here because it's too loud. But I can use it to force Sally up to my apartment, where I have other tools. Or to go for a drive in her car. Maybe somewhere scenic, like a trip into the bush. Anything. I just need to get the hell off this street.

"You're wrong, and you can't go around saying things like that. Look, come upstairs and . . ."

"I gave them your address. I had to. What choice did I have? The house you went to on Friday, why did you burn it down?"

She glances over her shoulder in the direction I'm looking. Suddenly all the traffic comes to the same kind of screeching halt that Sally's car came to a minute ago. The two people walking toward me start to run. The warning bells get louder. The world shifts even further, things are spiraling out of control.

"Jesus, what are you talking about?" I ask, watching the doors on the vans and cars opening. People in black clothing are starting to emerge. They start toward me. A wall of people wearing body armor. I recognize most of them.

"I'm sorry, Joe."

"What have you done? What have you done?"

"Step away from him, Sally," somebody yells. It's Detective Schroder's voice. No, this is impossible.

"Impossible."

Sally shakes her head. She's probably wondering how she could have got things so wrong over the last few months. I'm thinking the same thing. I drop the cat food, pull the gun from my pocket, and pull Sally toward me, my fingers looping over her crucifix and shirt. I point the gun at the side of her head. She cries out, but says nothing.

"You've got the wrong man," I say, talking in my Slow Joe accent.

I push the weapon hard against Sally's skull. Somebody screams at me to put it down, to put it down, but they're still too far away to stop me. Unless they shoot. And they won't shoot, will they? I'm Joe. Everybody likes Joe. And I figure some of them probably like Sally too. I tighten my grip. I can't face spending the rest of my life in prison. I can't face that at all. Because that's what'll happen. They'll see the gun I'm holding belonged to Calhoun. They'll search my apartment. They'll find my knives. They'll find the videotape I made with Melissa. There's no way I can Slow Joe my way out of that one. No way at all.

"Put the gun down," Schroder says. I've never seen him look so mad. So . . . cheated.

"You put your guns down," I respond. "Or I'm going to shoot her."

"We're not putting them down. You know that, Joe," he says, trying to sound calm, but being betrayed by the slight tremor in his voice. "You know we can't risk letting you go. Just put the gun down and nobody here has to be hurt."

Schroder's a moron if he thinks I'm going to put the gun down. I wish Melissa were here. She would know what to do. Or Mom.

"I'm Slow Joe," I say, but nobody answers. "I'm Joe!" I shout. *They can't do this to Joe. I'm one of them.*

But they are doing it. They're in control here, and that's the last thing I want. Why are they so confident I'm their man? The answer suddenly hits me. My fear of what they'll find if they search my apartment has already come true. Sally said they were here on Friday night. They've already found the tape. Found the knives. Found the folders and the audio tapes.

There's nothing I can do here. No way for me to gain the upper hand, unless . . .

The idea doesn't jump out of nowhere, because it's always been there, a plan B always hiding in the depths, just waiting for the opportunity to jump out and kick me in the ass. Jesus, it's still possible to regain control, but it's the worst fucking way imaginable. Still, it's either that or spend the rest of my life in prison. It's a decision I need more time to consider, but

I don't have more time. I don't have anything. Other than a gun.

The men are only a few yards away now, all their guns pointing at me. I decide to take away their control. I decide to make this all about Joe. I shift the gun from Sally's head to my own. I dig it under my chin so the barrel points upward. Sally gasps when she sees what I'm doing. Nobody else does. I think of Melissa. I'm going to miss her. I would have thought having control would make me feel stronger for these few seconds, but it doesn't.

"Put down the gun," somebody else screams, but I don't.

"Please, Joe. Please, we can help you," Sally says, but if she had any clue at all she would know that nobody can help me now.

I'm Joe. Slow Joe. I'm the Christchurch Carver. I'm the one who calls the shots. I'm the one in control. I'm the one who decides who lives and dies.

My legs feel weak. I feel like I want to be sick.

Well, live and learn.

I suck in a deep breath, close my eyes, and squeeze all the way on the trigger.

EPILOGUE

Police Confirm "Melissa" Link to New Murder

Police have confirmed that the officer found dead in a central city park four days ago is a likely victim of Christchurch's Uniform Killer.

"We have evidence to believe that this new murder, of Officer William Sikes, is related to the three others that are already linked with the woman calling herself 'Melissa,'" said Detective Inspector Carl Schroder, who is leading the investigation.

In all four cases, the victims were law-enforcement figures. Two of them were security guards whose bodies were naked when discovered by members of the public, and their uniforms were missing from the scene. The body of Melissa's first alleged victim, Detective Inspector Robert Calhoun, has never been found, but a video of a woman killing him was found at the home of cleaner Joe Middleton, whose trial for the Christchurch Carver murders is set for next month.

The trial date depends on Middleton's continuing recovery from wounds sustained during his arrest. Witnesses told the Christchurch press that he was holding a gun to his head when an unnamed woman knocked it and he fired into his face, resulting in injuries that were serious but not life threatening.

Police have interviewed Middleton, but gained few leads in their hunt for Melissa, whose name is believed to be a pseudonym. The woman had been helping with their investigation days before Middleton's arrest for the Christchurch Carver killings. Detective Inspector Schroder will not comment further, other than to say that she was a key witness.

ACKNOWLEDGMENTS

Here's a bit of number crunching for you. *The Cleaner* is my fourth book to be released in the United States, but it's actually the first book I had published in my part of the world (New Zealand), and the second book I ever wrote. I wrote it back in 1999, it got signed in 2005, it's 2012 now, and my biggest thought is, where did those years (and my hairline) go? I remember the excitement of getting the publishing contract, and the fear there was a mistake somewhere and the contract would be taken away from me. I remember learning the publishing date would be fifteen months later and how that time was never going to pass.

In the original acknowledgments for *The Cleaner*, I started out by saying that writing is a lonely thing, and yet so many people are involved in the process. It's not as lonely these days. Since *The Cleaner* was first published I've met some truly wonderful people, made a lot of friends, been to a bunch of countries I never thought I'd see (have thrown my Frisbee in 22 of them), and have hung out with authors I truly admire.

Between 1999 and 2005, *The Cleaner* was read by many of my friends who, between them, offered enough support and encouragement to keep me going. Paul and Tina Waterhouse, who would return the manuscript with hundreds of corrected errors. Daniel Williams read the manuscript with enthusiasm and then left the country. Aaron Fowler, Philip Hughes, David Mee, Kim McCarthy, Nathan and Samantha Cook— all of you really helped. And David Batterbury—in late 2004, I confessed to Dave that I was a writer, and he asked to see something. Just when I was thinking being a writer wasn't going to work out for me, he read *The Cleaner* and loved it. We'd fire up the Xbox on Friday nights, him and Paul Waterhouse and me, and we'd talk about the book. They made me promise to keep on submitting it. Which I did. And the rest is history.

Revisiting the novel to create this longer and improved edition for the U.S. market has been a lot of fun. Which brings me to Sarah Branham, my editor and friend at Atria who has done nothing but amazing things to the books over the last few years—and who will do amazing things to future ones too. Judith Curr, Lisa Keim, Mellony Torres, Emily Bestler, Janice Fryer, and the rest of the Atria team—thank you so much for bringing this book to another part of the world.

And of course no acknowledgment can be complete without mentioning Jane Gregory—the world's greatest agent— Linden Sherriff and Claire Morris, who work with the world's greatest agent, and Stephanie Glencross, Jane's in-house editor who, if I had to sum up in one word, I would go with . . . well, it can't be done in one. So I'll go with two words—super brilliant. Though she would find some really clever way of editing that down.

I also just want to wander back down the time line a bit here. Harriet Allan, my first publisher here in New Zealand at Random House, read this manuscript way back in 2005 and saw it had a future. Nerrilee Weir, the rights manager at Random House Australia, got the book into the hands of foreign publishers. Germany was the first. Germany is where *The Cleaner* became a bestseller, and that's really where the ball started rolling. And for that I can thank two of the coolest people in the world—Markus and Kirsten Naegele.

Before I go, I would again like to thank you, the reader. Thank you for the kind emails, for coming to say hi at book festivals, for saying nice things on Facebook. Bad things may happen in the books, but it's your kind words that encourage me to continue making those bad things happen. See you next time!

Paul Cleave, Christchurch, September 2012